LOCAL CALL

In the envoy ship's telescope, a tiny cylinder lay silhouetted against the black of space just above the edge of the light sail.

"Why are there no lights?" Kit wondered aloud. The alien ship was completely dark, dimly illuminated by distant Sol and the glow from the light sail.

"Maybe the ship is a derelict after all."

Their concentration on the viewscreen was suddenly broken by a muted tone. Four sets of eyes were drawn as one to the small viewscreen symbol signaling the arrival of a message on the short-range, ship-to-ship communications band. And there was but one other ship within six hundred light-hours of them . . .

By Michael McCollum
Published by Ballantine Books:

ANTARES DAWN
ANTARES PASSAGE
A GREATER INFINITY
LIFE PROBE
PROCYON'S PROMISE
THUNDER STRIKE!
THE CLOUDS OF SATURN
THE SAILS OF TAU CETI

THE SAILS OF TAU CETI

Michael McCollum

A Del Rey Book

BALLANTINE BOOKS • NEW YORK

A Del Rey Book
Published by Ballantine Books

Copyright © 1992 by Michael McCollum

Library of Congress Catalog Card Number: 92-90143

ISBN 0-345-37108-9

Manufactured in the United States of America

First Edition: August 1992

For Catherine

PROLOGUE

FASLORN OF THE PHELAN STOOD ON THE BRIDGE OF the starship *Far Horizons* and watched as thick bundles of gossamer thread poured forth from their storage holds. The shroud lines had been streaming aft through half a dozen changes of the watch. Now the first phase of the star brake's deployment was nearing its end.

Faslorn let his eyes roam the ship's instruments as the last few *kel* of bundled lines leaped free. His attention returned to the screens as the star brake's million-*kel*-long mass stretched to its full length and suddenly grew taut.

"Sound the alarm," Faslorn ordered. "Rebound coming."

The warning echoed through every corridor of the giant starship, and thousands of crew members stopped what they were doing and anchored themselves. Faslorn wrapped a six-fingered hand around a nearby stanchion and held on tight. Far out along the star brake, he could see the reflection wave racing toward *Far Horizons*.

The rebound wave struck the ship and caused the deck to jump beneath his feet. He barely noticed the rolling motion as stresses redistributed themselves throughout the starship. All of his attention was taken up by the screens. His twin hearts beat a little faster as he scanned the giant construct on which depended his own fate and that of one hundred thousand crewmates.

"No damage to brake or ship," one of the deployment technicians reported.

Faslorn made the Phelan equivalent of a sigh. "Very well. Cut the restraining straps."

All along the folded brake, tiny glittering lights illuminated the eternal night of space as the straps that kept the brake furled were cut. With the restraints gone, centrifugal force took over. There was a vast rippling as the gossamer fabric of the brake began to unfurl.

1

It was difficult to observe the progress of the deployment. The furled brake had been a long line that twisted and turned on its way to the vanishing point, but as the mass unfolded, it revealed the reflective film that made up the bulk of its surface area. There is nothing in space more difficult to see than a one-hundred-percent-reflective surface. It reflects the blackness of space while distorting the reflected images of stars. To an observer, it seems as though the universe has been wrenched into convolutions by some giant, unseen claw.

Far behind the starship a giant flower opened its petals to space, marking the end of a voyage that had lasted more than three Phelan lifetimes. It was a voyage that had begun in fire and would end by grazing the photosphere of the small yellow sun that was their destination, which at the moment was merely the brightest point of light in the sky.

Faslorn's would likely be the last generation of Phelan to live their lives between the stars. Within a few dozen *tarn*, they would encounter the thinking beings of the yellow sun. It was Faslorn's task, and that of his shipmates, to win a home among the strange bipedal creatures who styled themselves *Homo sapiens*. If he was successful, the next generation of Phelan would be born with solid ground rather than steel deck beneath their feet. If not, Faslorn's line would likely end with him.

"Look how it fills the sky," his assistant said. Overhead the star brake had expanded until it blotted out the cold point of light that had once been home.

Faslorn's gesture was the Phelan equivalent of a smile. "That it does, Paldar. It won't be long now before they notice us."

As the commander of *Far Horizons* watched the continuing dance of deployment, he thought of the difficult task before him. It was somehow symbolic that the stars behind were slowly being blotted out by reflections of the stars ahead.

Far Horizons was committed. There would be no turning back. The fate of two intelligent species would be decided by what happened next.

1 STARHOPPER

1

THE RUDDY ORB OF MARS COVERED ONE FULL QUADRANT of star-flecked sky and flooded the transparent dome with ruby light. But as beautiful as the sight was, Victoria Bronson had eyes only for the pyramid-shaped collection of fuel tanks and piping silhouetted against the planet. After twenty years of planning and three years of construction, *Starhopper* was nearly ready. Soon tankers would pump a hundred thousand tons of liquid hydrogen into the craft's capacious fuel tanks. Ten days later, assuming no glitches were found during the complex countdown, humanity's first visitor to another star would be hurled outbound on its long journey into the deep black.

People had dreamed of travel to the stars for almost as long as they had known the tiny points of light were distant suns. While poets wrote paeans to starflight, engineers bemoaned the prodigious energies involved. Writers of escapist fiction dreamed up fantastic schemes for flitting between stellar systems, while physicists attacked the problem with no less imagination. Scientists speculated that wormholes, extraspatial dimensions, or warped space-time might prove to be chinks in the armor of the Einstein barrier. Unfortunately, the efforts of the scientists proved no more effective than those of the poets and writers. Despite everything, the stars remained uncomfortably beyond the outstretched grasp of humanity.

That is, until the year 2217. In that year, a young Martian physicist named Dardan Pierce suggested that the time had come to begin exploration of the nearer stars. In a paper published in the *System Journal for Astrophysics*, Pierce laid out the parameters for a successful interstellar crossing. Pierce's starship was no fanciful faster-than-light speedster, but rather a craft requiring most of a human lifetime to make the journey. At the end of his paper, he exhorted his colleagues to build an instrumented probe as a demonstration project, and to send that device to explore the worlds known to circle Alpha Centauri, Sol's closest neighbor in the firmament.

The engines that would drive humanity's first interstellar probe would be powered by antimatter, a technology first developed in the middle of the twenty-first century. The earliest antimatter-powered spacecraft had used micrograms of the volatile stuff to heat hydrogen, which was then expelled through conventional rocket nozzles. Modern craft consumed kilograms of antiprotons, converting hydrogen to relativistic plasma before channeling it rearward through a series of magnetic nozzles.

The *Starhopper* booster would accelerate its instrument package to one-tenth light speed. As each tank was drained of reaction mass, it would be jettisoned. At the end of the boost phase, the giant engines would grow cold and *Starhopper* would coast outbound toward Alpha Centauri, having left a trail of debris extending all the way back to Mars in its wake. Nearly half a century after launch, the instrument package would command the booster to turn end for end and begin decelerating. Again, fuel tanks and their supporting structure would be jettisoned as they were emptied. Even the engines would be discarded once they had finished their task of slowing the instrument package to intrasystem velocity.

The *Starhopper* that entered the Centauri system would bear little resemblance to the one that left Mars. The instrument package represented only 0.1 percent of the original vehicle mass, but even so, at 110 tons, it was as large as a small spaceship. The instrument section contained maneuvering engines, antimatter, reaction mass, a power reactor, communications gear, and instruments able to wrest the secrets from the half-dozen alien worlds known to orbit the Centauri suns.

Tory Bronson lay on her back on the carpeted deck of a Phobos surface dome and gazed up to where the interstellar booster maintained a station on the larger of the two Martian moons. She thought of all the problems and crises that had been bested since the program's conception. At times, Dard Pierce had often told her, it had seemed as though the probe would never be built. Even now, the coalition of governments, universities, and corporations that supported *Starhopper* were grudging in their largesse.

Tory had been three years old when Pierce published his original paper. By the time he had gathered enough backers to begin planning in earnest, Tory had entered the University of Olympus, on Mars. It had been her intention to become a lawyer. She first heard about the project at one of Pierce's lectures, which she attended because she needed the extra credit for a science class. That might have been her only exposure to *Starhopper*, had not her career plans changed at the beginning of her sophomore year, when she was fitted with her first computer implant.

Like antimatter propulsion, the implants were an old technology that had been steadily improved over a century of use. The first implants had been simple aural devices, little more than fancy hearing aids that allowed the user to subvocalize a command, then receive the computer's response directly to the inner ear. In those days, implants had been little more than status symbols for the rich—subminiature cellular phones for conducting business while pretending to do something else. Not until a method for directly stimulating the brain was developed did the modern computer implant become possible. The heart of a modern implant was its molecular computer and direct stimulus/response microcircuit. Once implanted behind the left ear, or the right ear for left-handed people, it sensed the complex electrical rhythm of the brain and translated conscious thoughts into electrical impulses that were then transmitted to a remote computer. The computer's response was then translated back into brain waves and the required patterns induced in the sensory centers of the brain.

There were limitations, of course. The wearer had to learn to think in a manner that the implant interpreted as a command, and not as the background noise that was normal thought. It was a little like learning to wiggle one's ears; no one could precisely describe how to accomplish it, but once the skill was mastered, it was never forgotten. Also, the implants did nothing to make the wearer more intelligent. What they did do was provide phenomenal memory, to the point where wearers could "remember" things they had never known.

There were other practical limitations on implant use. Most people quickly reached a point at which additional data merely confused them. The problem, long known to students, was called "avalanche effect" because it felt as though one were being buried under an avalanche of data. The symptoms were that anyone who tried to delve too far into a subject ended up disoriented and muddled.

Curiously, there were a few people who seemed immune to the problem. No matter how complex the task, these rare minds were able to keep the goal in view without becoming mired down in detail. Such clearheadedness was an inborn talent. It could not be taught or learned. Those so blessed found themselves in demand as managers, organizers of complex projects, and, most especially, as high-level computer synergists.

A synergist was not a computer programmer, since the computers had long ago been given the ability to program themselves. Rather, synergists watched over the flow of the automated software-generating programs and nudged them in the proper direction. For, like the vast majority of human beings, computers, too, tended to become bogged down in the details.

Upon learning that she was immune to avalanche effect, Tory Bronson switched from the College of Law to Synergistic Science. There she met Ben Tallen, another Synergism candidate. After dating for most of their sophomore year, they agreed to move in together. As time went on, they began to talk about landing high-paying jobs with some Earth-based megacorp, and though the subject rarely arose, Tory, at least, had visions of marriage.

A month before graduation, Tory was accessing the list of companies who would be interviewing at the university placement center and discovered the Starhopper Project. Remembering the lecture she had attended years earlier, she decided to check it out. What she wasn't prepared for was Ben's reaction when she told him about it that night at dinner.

"What the hell are you interviewing with them for?" he asked around a crust of pizza.

"I've got a free period and it sounds interesting."

"Don't be a frump!"

"Who are you calling a frump, skinker?"

"You, if you interview with that damned black-sky project. You know who's behind it, don't you? Old Centauri Pierce over in Astrophysics! It's his hobby. He's gotten a bit of funding from the local yokels and now he's trying to scam Earth into lofting the rest."

"So where's the harm in listening?"

"The harm, my dear demented love, is the damage you may do to your chances of getting on with an EarthCorp. If they hear you've been talking to nuts, they might decide you aren't the proper material for them."

Ben's crack about "local yokels" irritated her. Like most Martians, Tory had a deep inferiority complex when it came to anything concerning Earth. She was especially aware that the University of Olympus was considered by some to be a cow college. Ben, on the other hand, was a terrestrial exchange student who never tired of telling everyone he could have gone to New Yale or Harvard. When asked why he hadn't, he always said that he'd wanted to improve the curve at Olympus U. instead.

Tory still remembered the hot flash of anger that had surged through her at Ben's crack. "Well I'm *going* to interview with them and if the high-and-mighty corporations from Earth don't like it, tough!"

She would have forgotten all about it if Ben hadn't decided to taunt her one final time.

"Don't say I didn't warn you!"

To her surprise, Tory found herself attracted to the idea of being part of humanity's first attempt to reach the stars. The more she thought about it, the more attracted she became. Her interest, coupled with Ben's clumsy attempts to dissuade her, drove her to accept the offer—at less than half the going pay scale for newly minted synergists. She told Ben of her decision a week before graduation. The resulting argument led to their breakup.

Two weeks later, they had sat together in the lounge of Olympus Spaceport, waiting for the ferry that would take Ben up to the interplanetary liner docked at Deimos. They made small talk and promised to write every week, though both knew the promises were empty. Tory remembered how awkward it had been to kiss Ben good-bye, and the feeling of relief as his lanky form disappeared into the embarkation tube.

That had been three years ago. Since then, Tory had held a variety of jobs with the Starhopper Project. Her latest made her responsible for the software that would fly the interstellar probe on its decades-long journey. Since software was at the heart of any modern system, her position placed her in de facto command of construction on Phobos. There were others more senior, but no one with a clearer picture of the state of the project at any given moment.

She was startled out of her contemplative mood by a voice that suddenly emanated from her computer implant.

"Are you awake up there?"

The voice belonged to Vance Newburgh, who, like Tory, was a synergist hired directly out of college. His speech was marked by a strong Australasian accent, a hint of which made it through the implant.

"I'm awake," she thought. *"What's up?"*

Her custom of coming up to the surface once each week to

view *Starhopper*'s progress was well known. It was, she told the curious, her way of keeping one foot planted firmly in reality. An occupational hazard for those who dealt with direct computer-to-mind interfaces was that they sometimes became unsure of what constituted reality. More than one had fallen to his death because he'd forgotten that there was nothing theoretical about the concept of gravity.

"Message from the university. Professor Pierce requests your presence at an emergency meeting of the governing board."

"When?"

"Tonight. Oh-eight-hundred hours, Conference Room 100, Lowell Hall."

"I'll attend via screen."

"Negative. The message says 'in person.' "

"But that's silly. Doesn't he know how much work we've got to do before next month's launch?"

"I presume he's been reading our progress reports."

"Then he should know that software certification is a week behind schedule and still slipping."

"No argument there, partner."

Tory let her anger cool a moment. *"Does he say what this meeting is about?"*

"No. Shall I tell him you can't make it?"

Tory shook her head. The habit of a lifetime was hard to break even though Vance was a kilometer distant and the conversation was taking place inside her skull. *"Negative. You know how fragile the coalition is. How long before the afternoon shuttle leaves for Olympus?"*

"Twenty-seven minutes."

"Get me a seat. Tell them to hold until I get there."

The ground steward who helped passengers aboard the Phobos-to-Olympus shuttle let his gaze linger on Tory Bronson as she made her way up the embarkation tube. He saw an attractive woman of some twenty-five standard years. Like many Martians she was tall and lithe, her alabaster skin unmarked by the sun. Her green eyes possessed a barely discernible slant, and her hair was so black that it shone with a blue luster. She wore it in a hairnet to keep it out of her face in Phobos's minuscule gravity field. He noted her pert nose set above a wide mouth, the lines of which fell most naturally into a smile. But she wasn't smiling now. She had that absentminded look common to people deep in thought or those actively accessing a computer implant.

Tory swarmed through the embarkation tube by pulling herself hand over hand, ignoring the small moon's two-tenths-percent of a standard g. She found an empty seat near a port and strapped down, failing to notice the stares of the other passengers as the steward went immediately into his prelaunch briefing. She stared at her own dull reflection in the viewport and considered what could possibly have triggered an emergency meeting of the project governing board. Whatever had happened, one thing was certain. It couldn't be good news.

Almost as complex as the design of *Starhopper* were the politics that sustained it. The University of Olympus managed the project for a consortium of institutions of higher learning, while funding was provided by several private foundations and the governments of Mars, Lagrange Three and Four, and several asteroid colonies. Several Earth megacorps had contributed to the project in the hope of being chosen to provide materials and services. Some had, some hadn't.

It was an arrangement guaranteed to spark arguments. The prime function of the governing board was to arbitrate disputes and to apportion costs equitably. It also delved too much into decisions that, in Tory's opinion, at least, should be left to the engineers.

Tory had hoped she could divine the reason for the unexpected summons by reviewing the minutes of the last several board meetings, so she had hurriedly begun to run through them all the way to the spaceport. Her haste was necessitated by the fact that her implant would not work once the ferry departed Phobos; the broadband communications link would lose synchronization once the ferry passed beyond effective transmitter range. Tory had gone through loss-of-sync once in training. It was an experience she didn't care to repeat.

She had often tried to describe what it was like to wear an implant to people who lacked the experience. It was like trying to explain sex to a six-year-old. Besides an eidetic memory, implants gave their users an extra set of eyes with which to see. When Tory gazed at the *Starhopper* booster she saw more than its physical form. In her mind she could visualize the vehicle's complex plumbing as it snaked through the first-stage booster. She could visualize the temperature variations that would play across the vehicle during launch. To her, *Starhopper* was less a machine than a living creature straining to enter its natural environment, the cold black of interstellar space.

Tory was none the wiser when she finished her review of the meeting minutes. Satisfied that there was nothing she herself had done, or failed to do, to trigger a crisis, she willed her implant into silence, leaned back, and resolved to enjoy the flight.

The shuttle lifted away from Phobosport with a burst of attitude-control jets. Once clear of Phobos's inner traffic zone, the pilot turned the ship until its nose pointed back along the orbit it shared with the moon. Seconds later, the engines came alight and Tory felt a gentle hand pressing against her. When the initial burst of retrofire was finished, the pilot turned the ship to give his passengers a panoramic view of Mars.

Despite being only half Earth's diameter, the red planet was huge. Phobos had once been a free-flying asteroid. Following its capture by Mars—an event the astronomers still argued about—the small moon had stabilized in an orbit six thousand kilometers above the rust-colored sands.

It had been nearly two centuries since the first humans had set foot on Mars and died there, a century and a half since the establishment of the first Martian colony. Humankind still had a considerable way to go before the planet would begin to grow crowded. For despite its diminutive size, the lack of an ocean gave Mars a land area nearly as great as Earth's. The red planet supported 250 million souls, compared to the ten billion who inhabited Earth.

Twenty minutes after leaving Phobos, Tory noticed a circular shadow detach itself from the sunrise terminator and strike out across the Tharsis highlands. She frowned. Phobos was close enough to cast a shadow on Mars, but in the wrong position. Deimos, on the other hand, was too small and distant to have any hope of shading the Martian landscape.

Having eliminated the only two possibilities, Tory felt the thrill that comes from a suddenly recognized mystery. She watched the shadow for several seconds before a spark of reflected sunlight caught her attention. Understanding burst upon her like the static discharges that illuminated the Martian sky during summer dust storms. The reflection had come from sunlight bouncing off a light sail in a lower orbit than the ferry. It had been the sail's shadow that she had been watching cross the Martian desert.

Light sails used the pressure of reflected sunlight to propel their nonperishable cargos across the Solar system. They were slow, but less expensive than even a ship in a Hohmann transfer orbit. This sail was probably towing a load of ice from Saturn's rings and using Mars's gravity to shape its approach to the inner moon. The Phobos distillery was the main reason they were building *Starhopper* there. The hydrogen-cracking facility was to be the source of the interstellar probe's reaction mass.

As the shuttle dropped, the light sail grew larger beyond the viewport. The sail, Tory knew, was a large circular sheet of metallized plastic only a few angstroms thick. It and its brethren were the largest constructs ever built by man, and the flimsiest. The largest sail ever constructed measured a full hundred kilometers across, yet massed only a few hundred tons.

Tory searched for the cargo pod, but couldn't see it. Within a few minutes the giant apparition floated across her field of view and was gone. She noted with approval that the shuttle's pilot was giving the sail a wide berth. While the monomolecular "sailcloth" was as light as the scientists could make it, it could do serious damage to even a warship if encountered at velocity differentials of several kilometers per second.

The shuttle dropped lower. Minutes later their destination came into view over the sharply defined horizon line. Olympus Mons was the largest volcano in the Solar system, so large that it could be seen as a speck in Earth's telescopes. It was one of the dots that Percival Lowell's subconscious had strung together to produce the most famous optical illusion in the history of science, the famous canals of Mars.

Most Earth dwellers were surprised to learn that the capital of Mars was located in the caldera of a volcano. Olympus had been a spectacular volcano in its day, but luckily its day was several billion years in the past. The modern Olympus Mons spewed forth nothing more lethal than water vapor saturated with carbon dioxide. These milder eruptions were the reason the Olympus colony had been founded in the first place, for nothing was more precious on dry Mars than water. Olympus Mons was a primary source of it.

The ferry dropped precipitously toward the spaceport tail first, oblivious to the tug of the rarefied atmosphere against its non-aerodynamic shape. A thousand meters above the spaceport, the ferry's engines came alive. Seconds later, it grounded on a tail of plasma fire without a bump.

2

TORY EMERGED FROM THE AIRLOCK INTO A TRANSPAR-
ent debarkation tube that ran a hundred meters across the fused
sand of Olympus Spaceport. Beyond the tube, the Martian night
was lit by million-candlepower polyarcs. Another ferry lay near
the Phobos craft, passengers and luggage streaming through its
connecting tube into the subterranean passage that led to the
main terminal. Tory grimaced at the sight. It meant that the
weekly liner from Earth was in orbit and that the spaceport
would be more than its usual madhouse.

As she entered the terminal, Tory willed her implant to synchronize with the Olympus city computer. Once she received
the connect signal, she sent a call to Dardan Pierce.

"Hello, Tory," came back the immediate answer. *"Where
are you?"*

"Spaceport."

*"Good, get over here as soon as you can. The others will
have gathered by the time you arrive."*

"What's up, Dard?"

"You'll have to ask Hunsacker," came the curt answer. *"He
called the meeting."*

"But he's on Earth."

*"Not since noon, he isn't. He showed up in my office and
asked me to gather up everyone within reach."*

"All right, I'm on my way."

"One more thing," Pierce's silent voice said. *"Hunsacker
brought some people with him."*

"Who?"

*"Praesert Sadibayan, an underminister for science in the
Hoffenzoller administration, and his assistant. I want everyone
to be on their best behavior. Pierce out."*

"Bronson out," Tory replied absentmindedly.

A tube car deposited her at University Station half an hour
later. Like most Martian structures, the University of Olympus

14

was mostly underground. It was topped at ground level by a large surface dome anchored by cables woven from the monomolecular filaments used in the construction of light sails. The most direct route from the tube station to Pierce's office was through a series of underground corridors, but after nearly a year on Phobos, Tory decided to take a few minutes longer and stroll through the dome.

The dome was home to University Park, a complex of pathways, flower beds, and terrestrial shrubbery grown tall in Mars's gravitational field. During the day the park was crowded with students hurrying between classes. It was no less crowded at night, though less obviously so. After sundown, the surface dome was lit in soft multicolored hues and suffused with herbal fragrance. That made it a favored place for couples to seek solitude together. At the park's center bubbled one of the few water fountains on Mars. The low gravity produced a spectacular display while providing the growing plants with the humidity they required.

As Tory reached the stairwell leading down into the astrophysics department, she inhaled the fragrant air one last time. Classes had ended hours earlier, leaving the corridors below deserted. Her Phobos boots made lonely clicking sounds on the fused rock floor as she walked. The clicks echoed the length of the empty halls. Turning in to a side corridor, she noted light spilling through a translucent office door at the far end.

"Tory, thank God!" Pierce said when she knocked on his door. He was a balding man with intense eyes and a manner to match. In his early fifties, the astrophysicist was still a vibrant man. His enthusiasm was contagious, especially where the Starhopper Project was concerned.

The office was as she remembered it. Printouts and record cubes were stacked everywhere. One wall was filled with holograms showing Pierce and various companions posed in front of well-known Earth landmarks—souvenirs of his long hunt for money to fund the project.

"What's going on, Dard?"

"What do you mean?"

"Don't give me that innocent look. You wouldn't have interrupted software validation for anything less than a first-rate emergency. You especially wouldn't have interrupted the work at Hunsacker's request unless you knew what was going on."

"Guilty as charged," he said. "You're here to give a progress report."

"We file daily progress reports, weekly progress reports, and monthly overviews! Would the board like hourly reports, too?"

"They're more interested in your personal perspective on the project. In your position, you have a better feel for how things are going than anyone."

"Can't you even give me a hint?" As she asked the question, Tory was struck by Pierce's expression. It was hard to imagine bad news coming from anyone with that gleam in his eye. It was the look of a child on Christmas morning.

"Nope. Just so I won't be unpleasantly surprised, how *are* preparations going?"

"You've read the reports."

"Humor me."

"All right." Tory gave him a quick rundown on what they had accomplished in the last week or so. Most of the work involved software checkout, which couldn't be hurried.

"Sounds like you're about to get back on schedule."

"I would if I weren't interrupted so often. Give me another month and I'll deliver you a ship ready for space."

Pierce didn't respond immediately, and Tory noted the same look of anticipation he'd worn a few minutes earlier. When he finally did speak, it was to suggest that they go to the conference room.

Conference Room 100 was large enough for a dozen participants to gather around an oval table. The room was crowded as the two of them arrived, with the project's governing board and staff standing around in small groups chatting with one another. The scene resembled a faculty tea.

"Tory, I'd like to introduce Boris Hunsacker, project coordinator on Earth," Pierce said after steering her to one of the groups. "Boris, this is Tory Bronson, of whom you've heard so much."

"Good to meet you at last, Boris." Hunsacker was smaller than Tory had imagined from Pierce's stories. She reached out and shook his hand.

"The same, Tory." He converted the handshake to a kiss on her hand. "I must confess that I envy you. The rest of us are politicians and bean counters. You actually work on humankind's first interstellar probe."

Tory laughed. "You sound like an engineer, Boris."

She received a smile in return. "I'm afraid that I haven't been a practicing engineer for many years. I still haven't lost the urge to stroke the hardware, I'm afraid.''

"I'd be pleased to show you around if you make it up to Phobos this trip.''

"Is that a general invitation?'' a familiar voice asked from behind her. Simultaneously, her implant came alive. *"How you doing, frump!"*

Tory turned around and gasped. Ben Tallen stood directly behind her with a grin on his face.

"Ben! What are you doing here?'' *"And why didn't you tell me you were coming, skinker?"*

"The subminister brought me. I'm his assistant.'' *"Perhaps we can go out for a drink after this is over?"*

"I'd like that." "When did that happen? I thought you worked for Tramton Industries?''

"Not for the past year or so. I find the legislative arena a lot more interesting.''

"I take it you two know each other,'' Pierce said as he watched the two.

"We're old friends, Professor,'' Tallen replied. As he spoke, he caught a gesture from a small dark man across the room. "You'll have to excuse me. The boss wants something. Would you like to meet him, Tory?''

"Certainly.''

The two of them threaded their way to the opposite end of the room. "Tory, may I present my boss, Praesert Sadibayan, underminister for science. Sir, Miss Victoria Bronson. I think I may have mentioned her on occasion.''

"Oh, just a hundred times or so,'' Sadibayan replied with a grin. "You broke this young man's heart, Miss Bronson.''

"I doubt that, Mr. Subminister.''

"It's true! He did nothing on the trip out but worry whether he would have time to see you.''

She turned to Ben. "Really?''

He nodded. "If you hadn't been here tonight, I was going to hop the first Phobos shuttle.''

"I'm flattered.''

Sadibayan turned to face his assistant. "See how easy it is if you're honest with women, Ben?''

"I only wish I had your skill, sir,'' Tallen replied with mock humility.

The buzz of conversation around them was interrupted by the chime that announced the start of a new class period. Dard asked everyone to take their seats. He gestured for Tory to take the chair next to his own.

Pierce began by introducing everyone. Besides Boris Hunsacker and the two terrestrial government representatives, Tory was surprised to learn of the presence of a representative of the Martian parliament.

Pierce said, "Your show, Boris."

"Thank you, Professor Pierce," the project's terrestrial representative said. He nervously shuffled a series of printouts before continuing. "I'm sure all of you are wondering what the hell this is all about, so I won't keep you in suspense any longer than I must. However, I need to give you some background information, so please bear with me. Lights off, cube on!"

This last was addressed to the room monitor, which dutifully dimmed the lights and activated the holocube perched at the center of the table. The cube showed an old-fashioned two-dimensional photograph. It was a picture of a starfield, with a yellow point of light at the center. There were a few other stars scattered across the field of view.

"This, gentlemen and ladies, is a photograph of Tau Ceti taken late in the twentieth century. In those days, Tau Ceti was a type K0 yellow-orange dwarf star, quite unremarkable save for its proximity to the sun. It is just twelve light-years from here, practically next door."

The scene changed. Again, the view in the cube was two-dimensional. It was obviously the same starfield since the scattering of stars was largely the same. Only the central point of light had changed. It was now a brilliant burst of white.

"This was taken on August 25, 2001. That was the day that Tau Ceti went nova. The event created quite a stir among astronomers. Like the sun, Tau Ceti was still on the main sequence when it exploded, and main-sequence stars aren't supposed to do that sort of thing. Even today we have no theory that explains how a star like Tau Ceti could possibly have exploded. The fact that it did, however, suggests that our theories on the subject need some revision."

"Wasn't there another anomaly associated with the nova?" Roger Aaron asked. Aaron was a member of the faculty of the University of Olympus, and the governing board's recording secretary.

"There was. Initial recordings of the nova suggested a deficiency of a few percent in the nova's light output. Those readings may have been in error, however, since later observations showed the light curve to be well within tolerance for a Type Two nova.''

"All very interesting, Boris," one of the board members said. "But what has all of this to do with us?"

Hunsacker's response was to touch the cube control. The nova burst faded from the screen, to be replaced by a modern holographic image. Again the view was centered on the same starfield, but Tau Ceti was no longer a brilliant flame. The central star had subsided to the yellow spark that had preceded the nova. That spark was surrounded by a milk-white ring of light, marking the outermost expansion of the gas cloud that had been ejected by the explosion two centuries past. There was a new point of light in the hologram. Another yellow spark had appeared just beyond the gas shell.

"What's that?" Sharon Milos asked, pointing to the point.

"*That*," Hunsacker replied in triumph, "is the reason for this meeting. This holo was taken two weeks ago by the observatory on Luna. The spectrum is that of Sol, with a slight Doppler shift toward the blue end of the spectrum." Hunsacker paused to let the import of what he had just said sink in. All around the table there were looks of perplexity that slowly turned to looks of wonder.

"A light sail!" Tory exclaimed, remembering the glint of sunlight she'd seen out the viewport of the Phobos ferry.

"A light sail," Hunsacker agreed. "We've managed to triangulate it using the telescope on Europa. It is two light-months out, and moving in at five percent of the speed of light. Its origin is almost certainly the Tau Ceti nova.

"Ladies and gentlemen, it would seem that we are about to receive our first visitor from another star!"

There was a stunned silence in the conference room for nearly a minute before anyone spoke. When someone did, it was Carse Groschenko, the project comptroller and a retired astronomer.

"None of this has been on the news!"

"That is the doing of my boss," Sadibayan replied. "Minister de Pasqual requested that the Lunarians not announce their discovery until after I spoke with you people."

"And they listened to him?"

Sadibayan shrugged. "A considerable portion of Luna Observatory's operating budget is handled through my department. That made them amenable to the idea. I must impress on each of you that this is a Lunarian discovery, and that it is only right that they have the honor of announcing. What you learn here must not go beyond this room. Agreed?''

A mutter of assent ran around the table. There was a tradition in science that those who made great discoveries controlled the timing and method by which their findings were made public. It was a tradition that had grown out of some notable public-relations disasters in the past.

''You're saying we are about to have *alien visitors*?'' Tory asked.

Sadibayan shook his head. ''Not precisely. The vehicle won't be manned, except possibly by corpses—not after two hundred and fifty years in space. It may be a derelict cargo pod blown away from Tau Ceti by the nova, or a message from the sentient species that died in the nova!''

''The urge to be remembered must be a powerful one in any thinking being,'' Pierce muttered.

The revelations were coming too quickly. First the shock of learning that humanity was not alone in the universe, followed immediately by the realization that the beings who built the light sail were dead. Tory had a sudden vision of doomed sapients working desperately to get their ark away before Tau Ceti exploded. The vision was so vivid that she almost missed Hunsacker's question.

''How quickly can *Starhopper* be made ready for launch?''

Tory stared at him, not comprehending for long seconds. Then, suddenly, the reason for this emergency meeting of the governing board made perfect sense.

''You're planning to send *Starhopper* out to meet the alien?''

''Of course.''

''But you can't!''

''Why not?''

''*Starhopper* is the only interstellar probe we've got. We can't waste it. No telling when we'll be able to scrape together the resources to build another. Send another ship to look over the light sail. Leave *Starhopper* for the job it was designed to do.''

''I'm afraid that is impossible,'' Hunsacker said. He touched the cube control. The starfield vanished, to be replaced by a graph in which two brightly colored lines were suspended in a three-dimensional gridwork. One line sloped sharply upward, while a second followed a curve with much gentler slope.

''The red line plots the increase in the observed strength of the Tau Ceti nova over the first two weeks after the explosion. Five days after the initial explosion, Tau Ceti's output had increased by one hundred thousand times. The blue line shows the calculated velocity of a hypothetical light sail caught in such an explosion.''

''Proving what?'' Tory asked as she eyed the holocube.

''That the light sail's velocity is the result of its having been ejected by the nova. Had it launched while Tau Ceti was a normal star, its velocity would be less than one percent that of light. What that means is that the light pressure from the sun is insufficient to slow it much. It will arrive in the inner system in forty months' time, zip from one side of the system to the other within a few days, then head back out into interstellar space. If we are to have any opportunity of examining it, we must meet it as far out as possible. *Starhopper* is the only vessel in the system with the delta-velocity capability to make rendezvous.''

Tory thought about it for a moment and was forced to concede his point. A spacecraft's performance is measured by its ability to change velocity, its delta V capability. The alien light sail was falling toward the sun at fifteen thousand kilometers per second. In theory, a vessel able to accelerate to that speed could rendezvous with it. In practice, things weren't nearly that simple.

A human spacecraft would have to race away from the sun to intercept the light sail before it entered the system. Once well beyond the orbit of Pluto, the explorer craft would turn over and begin decelerating. It would shed all of its outbound velocity and then begin accelerating back toward the Sun with the light sail in pursuit. If the maneuver was properly done, the probe would match velocities with the light sail just as the alien derelict overtook it. Humanity would then be able to use the *Starhopper* probe's instruments to learn what they could about the alien intruder.

All of this maneuvering required a prodigious velocity change. 'To match orbits with the light sail in time to do any good was the equivalent of accelerating to fifteen percent of light speed. And as Hunsacker had said, only *Starhopper* came anywhere close to having the necessary delta V capability.

''All right, *Starhopper* is the only spacecraft in the Solar system that can catch this light sail. That doesn't mean we *have* to send it out. How do we know we'll learn anything worthwhile?''

''Damn it, we're talking about a vessel built by alien sapients,'' an exasperated Hunsacker muttered. ''How can we *not* learn from it?''

''No sense getting upset, Boris,'' Pierce said calmly. ''Tory's questions deserve an answer. What do we know about this light sail?''

Hunsacker put up the hologram showing Tau Ceti, its light ring, and the sail just beyond the ring's milky boundary. "From its infrared spectrum, we estimate the sail temperature to be fifty degrees Kelvin. That is a bit high for that distance from Sol, but not excessively so. We can also estimate its size.''

"Surely it isn't close enough to show a disk,'' Groschenko said.

Hunsacker laughed. "No, not anywhere near close enough. We can put an upper bound on its size from the fact that we didn't detect it before now. To have escaped our notice, the sail cannot be larger than a thousand kilometers in diameter. It may be smaller.''

Pierce looked at his comely assistant. "They've got the proxies of every one of our sponsors on Earth. Even if we wanted to stop them, we couldn't. How long before we can launch?''

Tory activated her implant and quickly reviewed the project's status. "A month, Dard. We'll need to accelerate the certification process. That shouldn't be a problem now that the mission has been shortened. There's a big difference between a voyage lasting a few years and one lasting half a century.''

"What about fuel loading?''

"We'll need to get priority at the Phobos refinery.''

"I will take care of it, Miss Bronson,'' Jorge Contreras, the Mars government representative, said from across the table. He scrawled a note on his electronic notepad.

Pierce nodded. "Then we launch one month from today. Let's talk about what *Starhopper* is going to do when it gets there. Boris, you've had the most time to think about it. What say we begin with you?''

3

VICTORIA BRONSON SAT AT THE BAR AND NURSED A DOUble Scotch, her second. Ben Tallen regarded her with curious eyes.

"What's the matter with you?" she asked petulantly after intercepting his third sidelong glance in as many minutes.

He sipped from his beer before answering. "Of all people, I would expect you to be the most ecstatic about this discovery."

"I am . . . sort of."

"Then why the long face?"

"It's hard to explain."

"I'm listening."

"I've spent the last three years of my life working on that damned probe."

"So?"

"So, we built it to go to the stars, not to take pictures of a bit of space flotsam."

"It's damned important flotsam."

"Why? Just spotting it tells us that we aren't alone in the universe. What else can we learn from it?"

"We'll learn how aliens build light sails, for one thing. If an anthropologist can reconstruct the whole history of a prehistoric people from a few pottery shards, just think what they'll be able to do with a light sail to study. And you people are going to make it happen! There isn't a ship in the system with one-tenth of *Starhopper*'s speed. Without it, we'd have to watch in frustration as the sail zipped right past us."

"Then what you are saying, my ex-love, is that I made the right decision when I went for that interview?"

She had meant the comment as a jibe. To her surprise, the expected witty rejoinder did not materialize. Both of them sat without speaking for a long time.

For her part, Tory tried to analyze why she had reacted the way she had. Ben was right; normally she *would* have been

23

ecstatic at the prospect of examining an alien artifact. Her negative reaction had possibly been an unconscious response to the unfairness of it all.

What a cruel joke for God to play on those poor unknowns who had died with their exploding sun. They must have known that another intelligent race inhabited Sol, a mere twelve light-years off. Yet, with both species on the verge of a technology that would have made contact a certainty, Tau Ceti had exploded, snuffing out billions of intelligent minds in a single instant. What if it had been the Sun that had gone nova rather than Tau Ceti? Would some alien be sitting in a bar on his distant world at this very moment, contemplating the lost bipeds of Sol III?

What *were* the chances of two races at nearly equal technology levels springing up so close together, and at the same moment in history? For a long moment Tory toyed with the idea of overriding her implant's safety interlocks and posing the question to the Olympus city computer. She resisted the urge. Compared with operating an implant, driving a groundcar under the influence of alcohol was an exercise in caution.

"There you are!"

Tory and Ben Tallen both turned around at the shouted accusation to find Dardan Pierce striding purposefully in their direction. If anything, his look was even stranger than the one he'd worn in his office earlier in the evening.

"Hello, Dard. Drink?"

"We've been looking all over for you two. Why aren't you on the net? Never mind, I see why."

"Ben and I wanted to talk. We've a lot of catching up before I head back to Phobos tomorrow."

"Not tomorrow and probably not for the rest of the week."

"What's happened?"

"Sadibayan received an emergency flash from Earth. Two hours ago the light sail lit up like a Christmas tree."

"Lit up?"

"Began emitting blue-white light with a black-body radiation curve equivalent to five thousand Kelvin. It is also emitting charged protons at relativistic velocity."

"Huh?"

"So far as we can tell," Pierce continued, "someone is ionizing hydrogen atoms and then using a very strong electrical charge to repel them away from the sail."

"Why would they want to do that?"

"To slow down, of course. They're sweeping up the interstellar gas in their path and using it to retard their velocity. They've turned the sail into an electrostatic brake!"

"They?" Ben asked.

Pierce didn't appear to hear the question. "We were wrong about the size, too. The sail is a hell of a lot bigger than one thousand kilometers. It was probably furled until quite recently."

"Furled?"

"Folded up! A fully deployed light sail would produce a strong parasitic drag on a two-hundred-and-fifty-year-long voyage. Better to stow it until you need it to decelerate. Less of a problem with wear and tear, too."

"You speak as though there's a crew aboard," Tory said. Despite the warm fog the Scotch had laid over her mind, the implications of Pierce's statements were beginning to sink in.

"We think there is. Come on, let's get you a sober pill. We've got plans to make. This changes everything."

There were only three people left in the conference room when Pierce returned with Tory and Ben Tallen. Tory walked with a rolling gait as she sought her place at the table. It had been nearly a century since the invention of Quiksober, yet the spatial disorientation that was the wonder drug's primary side effect had never been completely tamed.

She switched on her implant and let it run through its self-test sequence. When she was certain it was operational, she asked, "All right, what do we know?"

Tory's intention had been to request the file reference for the new data so that she could access it. Boris Hunsacker misunderstood her request, or possibly the data had yet to be input into the computer. He called for the lights to be dimmed and the holocube to be activated.

The familiar starfield was much as it had been. Tau Ceti blazed bright from within its shell of gas, but the light sail, which had formerly reflected an anemic version of Sol's spectrum, now blazed forth like a new nova. The former dim yellow spot was now the blue-white hue of a mercury-vapor lamp.

"Brightened some, hasn't it?"

"An understatement, Miss Bronson," Sadibayan replied dryly. "When it first happened, Luna thought it had exploded."

"Did it blaze up all at once?"

Hunsacker nodded. "The time from onset to maximum was

only three milliseconds. That's the primary reason we suspect an electrostatic braking device. If friction were the cause, the temperature wouldn't have shot up so precipitously. We also wouldn't be seeing relativistic protons.''

"Friction?"

"One of the Luna astronomers postulated that the sail had run into a gas bubble surrounding a comet nucleus out in the Oort cloud," Hunsacker explained.

The subminister shook his head. "Anything dense enough to make it glow like that would have ripped it apart."

"Can we detect any deceleration yet?"

"No way to tell, damn it. We could judge its speed well enough when it was reflecting sunlight. It's a simple matter to measure Doppler shift from a known spectrum. Now that it's emitting light on its own, we've lost even that clue."

"So we don't know how fast it is slowing?"

"Not directly. If they intend to stop inside the Solar system, they have to decelerate at something around one-thousandth of a standard gravity."

"That isn't very much."

"More than enough to halt short of the sun. Remember, they've got one hell of a long distance to fall."

"If they're slowing, they won't arrive as quickly."

"True. We now estimate that the sail will reach us in five years rather than three and a half. A precise figure will have to await a better estimate of their deceleration constant."

Tory had been reviewing the technology of electrostatic brakes ever since activating her implant. The idea had a surprisingly long history. An electrostatic brake was essentially a device for sweeping up hydrogen across a vast region of space and funneling it into a spacecraft's path. In effect, the spacecraft would plow through an artificially enhanced Solar wind. Every impact on the craft robbed it of momentum, causing it to slow.

The literature contained dozens of proposals on how to accomplish the trick. All relied on the fact that there were some hundred thousand hydrogen atoms per cubic meter even in deep interstellar space. Most methods used a tuned laser to ionize the hydrogen over a large region in front of the ship, then attracted the ions with a powerful negative electrical charge. The electrical field acted as a giant invisible funnel that concentrated the interstellar gas onto a collecting device such as a light sail. If the surface of the sail was then positively charged, the ions could be reflected back the way they had come before impact.

Reflecting the ions allowed twice the momentum transfer of merely bombarding the sail, while protecting the sail's surface from erosion at the same time.

"Electrostatic brakes work well enough when a ship is moving at high speed," Tory said, quoting from an encyclopedia article she had just scanned, "but their efficiency drops off drastically with reduced velocity."

"Once close to the Sun, they'll transition to light-pressure braking," Hunsacker replied.

"I think not," Pierce responded. He, too, had been busy with his implant. "Tory's right. Electrostatic braking efficiency falls off rapidly as you slow. Even with optimistic assumptions for both electrostatic and light pressure, they'd still be going too fast to stop by the time they reached the Sun. They must be planning an aerobraking maneuver near the sun to finish the job. That's a ticklish thing. If they hit that soup too fast, the passengers will be turned to red mush."

"How do we know the mush would be red?" Ben asked. The question sounded like a joke and drew him a baleful look from Sadibayan. In truth, he had been completely serious.

Tory felt a small shiver run up her spine. The aliens were using their light sail like a giant parachute. If they were to go into Solar orbit, they would practically have to dive into the Sun. Whoever had thought up this scheme must have been truly desperate. After a moment's thought, however, she chuckled quietly to herself.

Sadibayan turned his disapproving look from his aide to Tory. "What's so funny?"

"We are," she replied. "Here we're worried that they will fly too close to the Sun and end up like Icarus. Yet, they launched from out of the heart of an exploding nova. I doubt they will be frightened by the prospect of diving headlong into our little star!"

"All right," Pierce said after the technical discussion had gone on for nearly an hour, "now that we have all reviewed the new information, what do we do about it?"

"Luna makes their announcement!"

"I'm sorry, Miss Bronson," Sadibayan said, "but that is not going to happen. My orders from Earth are that no mention will be made of this discovery for the time being."

"Why the hell not?" Pierce demanded.

"We need time to study the implications of the situation. We don't know how people will react."

"But that's censorship!"

"Nevertheless, that is the way things are going to be. Anyone who divulges a word about the light sail beyond this room will not be allowed to participate in the investigation. Is that clear?"

The three scientists in the room nodded grudgingly.

"Perhaps we should look to our defenses," Contreras said.

"Don't be paranoid!" Hunsacker snapped. "Surely you don't think they crossed twelve light-years of space to attack us!"

"Who knows what they intend?"

"How many soldiers do you think one ship can carry, for God's sake?"

"How many men did Cortés have?" Contreras replied dryly. "Some of my ancestors thought they could handle him. History proved them wrong."

"Not the same situation at all."

"Isn't it? These are refugees from an exploded star. What are they going to do when they discover their chosen refuge already inhabited?"

"But they must have known this system was occupied before Tau Ceti exploded," Tory said. "By the late twentieth century, Earth was the center of a bubble of radio noise that stretched more than seventy light-years in all directions."

"Would an alien have found comfort in twentieth-century news broadcasts?" Contreras mused.

"I tend to agree with Boris," Pierce said. "This ship has been in space two hundred and fifty years. They are fleeing the destruction of their star, looking to start over. If we were to abandon Mars, would we fill our vessel with weapons or seed corn?"

Contreras's jaw set stubbornly. "Depends on how many potential slaves there were where we were going."

"Do we know they *are* refugees?" Ben asked.

"That," Pierce replied, pointing toward the light ring that surrounded the image of Tau Ceti, "is a very persuasive argument. Rather than preparing for conflict with these aliens, I think we should make plans how we can help them. After so much time in space, no telling what shape their ship is in."

"Perhaps their life-support system has already failed," Hunsacker responded. "They may all be dead and we are arguing about nothing."

"Then who unfurled the sail?"

"An automatic sequence triggered when the ship closed to within a predetermined distance."

"We are speculating in a vacuum," Praesert Sadibayan said. "What we need is information, as quickly as we can get it. Obviously, we can no longer send the *Starhopper* probe out to rendezvous with them. They might mistake it for a weapon."

"What other option have we?"

"I propose that we send a diplomatic mission instead."

"You said yourself that *Starhopper* is the only spacecraft in the Solar system with the ability to rendezvous with the aliens," Tory pointed out. "How are you going to deliver your diplomats?"

"The probe masses one hundred tons, I believe. We will replace it on the booster with a manned spacecraft of equal mass."

Tory nodded pensively. "That might work. Since the aliens won't be here for five years, we'd have time to make the switch."

"How long?" Sadibayan asked.

"Two years."

"You're joking!"

Tory shook her head. "Look, *Starhopper* isn't just any spacecraft. It's a highly integrated system designed to survive half a century in space and then perform a series of complex, autonomous investigations. You can't just dismount the instrument package and put a manned ship in its place. There are literally thousands of interfaces to be redone. The main computers are in the instrument package, for God's sake. Dismounting the upper stage from the booster is equivalent to performing a lobotomy on a human being."

"The computers can be transferred to the manned craft."

"Sure they can. What about the thousands of distributed processing units that go with them? You also have to remount those and then cobble together the proper interconnections. Then all you have to worry about is the software, which must be completely rewritten."

"Surely what you have can be modified."

"Not on your life! We have to strip the various modules down to their fundamentals, modify them to account for the differences between ship and probe, then reassemble, debug, and recertify. It's taken three years to get *Starhopper*'s control codes to the point where we think they ought to be. Changing them will take eighteen months, minimum!"

"There has to be a faster way."

"There isn't . . ." Tory froze while she consulted her implant. It took fifteen seconds for the idea to gel.

"What is it?" Sadibayan asked.

"I suppose the software could be rewritten en route. You'd need a large team on the ground for the actual reprogramming, then someone aboard ship who was intimately familiar with every aspect of *Starhopper*."

"Could you do it?"

Tory blinked. So far she had been solving a purely intellectual problem in software management. It hadn't occurred to her that the solution might affect her personally. "I suppose so. That is, if it can be done at all."

"Who else?"

"Vance Newburgh and possibly a few others on the project staff."

"What would you need?" Sadibayan's matter-of-fact tone sent a chill up Tory's spine.

"My implant, of course. The probe's computers. An interface linking the two, and a lot of people backing me up."

"You'd have them. Are you interested in the job?"

Tory swallowed hard. She'd signed with Project Starhopper to do something important with her life, but this was more than she had bargained for.

"May I have time to consider my answer?"

"Of course. We will want to consider all potential candidates in any event. Still, I'd like to know whether you are interested in the position."

"Interested, yes. Brave enough to go through with it, I'm not so sure."

"Good enough for the time being. Now, then. Where are we going to find a ship that masses less than a hundred tons?"

4 MINISTER FOR SCIENCE JESUS DE PASQUAL GAZED AT THE blue-white spark just beyond the Tau Ceti nova and wondered whether he should feel blessed or cursed. It had been two weeks since Farside Observatory had first detected the dim, Doppler-shifted reflection of Sol that betrayed the presence of the alien light sail.

The news had initially thrilled him. Often during his days as a university professor he'd told his students that the universe was too large a place to be inhabited by a single sentience, and it was pleasant to obtain confirmation of what had always been an article of faith. The Doppler shift readings were a disappointment, of course. With the derelict inbound at fifteen thousand kilometers per second, no ship in the Solar system could possibly catch it . . . no ship, that is, but one!

De Pasqual had been startled when he realized that the *Starhopper* probe had more than sufficient legs to rendezvous with the alien light sail. Unfortunately, it was damnably awkward for him to ask for it to be diverted to that use. Though he was personally in favor of exploring the Centauri worlds, practical politics had caused him to oppose the project on the two occasions when it had sought science grants from the current administration.

The problem was that there was no constituency currently in favor of interstellar exploration. After two hundred years of hugely expensive space initiatives, Earth's multitudes were asking what they had gotten for their money. So, to save the rest of his department's budget from a meat cleaver, de Pasqual had gone before the science committee and testified, "Mr. Chairman, there is no scientifically valid reason for exploring the Centauri suns at this time! It is widely held that the Centauri worlds cannot support life, and should we desire to examine lifeless worlds, we have eight of our own to keep us busy."

It had seemed a wise move at the time. After all, he'd traded

31

nothing for something. With an alien light sail in the sky, however, that bargain might begin to appear more than a little short-sighted to his patrons on the system council. Nor would the man in the street remember how much he had complained about the cost of science when faced with the prospect of a shipload of bug-eyed monsters on his doorstep. He would first demand that the military do something about it, then go looking for scapegoats to blame for humanity's lack of preparation. The one thing working with the public had taught de Pasqual over the years was that they never held themselves to blame for anything.

Luckily, de Pasqual had done something even before he'd known there were aliens aboard the light sail. It had been his original intent that the ministry for science be seen leading the effort to examine the derelict light sail. With the derelict suddenly blossoming into a full-blown starship, the ministry—and by extension, de Pasqual—looked better than ever.

He thanked the patron saint of thieves and bureaucrats that he'd wasted no time in dispatching a message to Luna Observatory asking that they delay any announcement of the discovery. Then, after a quick survey of the computer records, he'd placed several calls to terrestrial sponsors of the Starhopper Project. Since most of these were high on the ministry's grant list, obtaining their proxies had been a relatively easy matter. Once he'd obtained their proxies, he'd dispatched Praesert Sadibayan to Mars to negotiate for the probe.

As he congratulated himself on the foresight he'd shown, de Pasqual considered how best to proceed now that the light sail turned out to be manned. It seemed obvious that if the ministry for science was to maintain control of the discovery, he would have to insure that the alien starship remained a secret. Otherwise, powerful men on the system council would contrive to take the glory of discovery for themselves. After passing the new data on to Sadibayan, along with orders to maintain strict security, de Pasqual sat back to consider who else to let in on the secret.

First Minister Hoffenzoller would have to be told, of course. He was de Pasqual's chief patron and a man who never forgot a snub. There were a few others in the administration whose cooperation he needed, but was unlikely to get unless he let them know what was going on. And, despite de Pasqual's distaste for all things military, someone from the admiralty would have to be coopted to obtain a ship with which to meet the aliens. Knowing the military, they would undoubtedly insist on one of their own to command the expedition. By and large, however, the council and the bureaucracy would have to be kept in the dark, at least until after the survey craft was safely on its way.

Luckily, a previous minister for science had had the foresight to convene a conference regarding first contact with aliens. De Pasqual turned to his workstation and spent ten minutes reviewing the results of that long-ago gathering. He finished with a grin. It was almost as though someone had foreseen the precise situation in which he now found himself. The regulations were written loosely enough so that they could be bent to his own personal needs.

Captain First Rank Garth Van Zandt, Terrestrial Space Navy, frowned as he plodded down the ramp from the landing boat at Olympus Spaceport. Seventy-two hours earlier he had been aboard his ship in Earth orbit, preparing to go on leave. But instead of immersing himself in the Hawaiian surf, he'd spent the last three days strapped to an acceleration couch aboard a navy speeder. Antiacceleration drugs had burned his eyes, dried out his nasal passages, and kept him from more than a few hours of fitful sleep. The journey's discomfort was the primary cause of his current irritation. His mood was not helped by the fact that he had been given no clue why he'd been summoned to Mars.

A lanky, blond-haired man with a self-important air waited just beyond the security gate that separated customs from the main spaceport concourse.

"Captain Van Zandt?"

"Yes, sir."

"I'm Benjamin Tallen, Subminister Sadibayan's assistant."

"Pleased to meet you."

"Good flight?"

Van Zandt laughed for the first time in three days. "Obviously, Mr. Tallen, you've never experienced the many luxuries to be found aboard a navy speeder. They consist primarily of relief tubes fore and aft, rations that taste like cardboard soaked in dog urine, and a sensation like having two people sit on your chest. I enjoyed the trip about as much as the time I spent in traction when I broke my leg."

"Sorry to hear that. It might not have harmed anything to allow you to travel on the Earth liner, but things are beginning to boil here. The subminister thought it important for you to be in on planning from the very beginning."

"Planning for what, sir?"

"You'll learn that from the subminister himself. Do you need to collect any luggage?"

Van Zandt held out the small kit bag he carried. "This is all I had time to pack."

"We'll authorize a drawing account for you at the Bank of Mars. Take time tomorrow to properly outfit yourself."

Van Zandt chuckled. "I've heard about discretionary expense accounts, but I never expected the use of one myself."

"The stories are grossly exaggerated, and the expense is trivial when you consider the good it will do. Remember, you represent Earth. The people you will be dealing with have little cause to love us, Captain. It is important that you make a good impression."

The younger man led the way to a car that sent them arching high above Olympus Mons before the guide tube descended into one of the kilometer-high pressure domes in the new section of the city. The car deposited them inside the lobby of a luxury hotel. Like all structures beneath the dome, the lobby lacked a roof.

"I trust this establishment meets with your approval," Tallen said.

"It almost makes up for the journey," Van Zandt replied, gazing across an opulent space where polished fused silica glittered everywhere. The lobby was almost as large as a spatball field.

"Good. Let's get you registered and down to the lower levels."

The ritual of hotel registration had not changed appreciably in half a thousand years. With one thing and another, it took fifteen minutes before Tallen ushered Van Zandt into the subminister's suite of rooms. Praesert Sadibayan had been working at his computer workstation. He strode to greet his visitors.

"Captain Van Zandt? Subminister Sadibayan of the Ministry for Science. Good of you to come so quickly."

"My admiral said that it was urgent."

"It is indeed!"

Sadibayan returned to his desk and palmed a scanner plate. There was a muted click from somewhere inside the desk as a drawer popped open. Sadibayan retrieved a sealed folder marked with various security sigils. He thumbed the spot that would deactivate the self-destruct mechanism and removed several computer printouts.

The subminister opened the dossier and began to read. "Garth Martin Van Zandt. Age: thirty-six. Born: January 9, 2204, in New Aberdeen, South Wales, Australasian Confederation. Graduated Terrestrial Space Academy, 2226. You ranked in the top one-third of your class. You've held the usual progression of shore and space jobs, and have served aboard ships of both the Messenger and Corvette class. You were promoted to command the destroyer *Currant* fourteen months ago. You are unmarried, physically healthy, and overdue for leave. Correct?"

"On all counts, Mr. Subminister."

Sadibayan let his brown eyes focus on Van Zandt. "You may be interested in the fact that Admiral Carnevon speaks very highly of you. He says that you are one of his brightest officers, resourceful and flexible in your response to new situations. 'An original thinker' was the way he described you."

"I'll have to thank the admiral the next time I see him."

Sadibayan continued reading. "You have also served a tour as military attaché in our Lagrange embassy, so you are at least aware of diplomacy."

"Yes, sir."

"One thing puzzles me, Captain. Why did you spend so much time in corvettes?"

Van Zandt shrugged. "I made the mistake of embarrassing one of my superiors during my first tour as a ship commander. It was during an exercise against the fleet flagship. *Minotaur* was in a high elliptical orbit around Luna, with a low perilune. I put my corvette down practically on the mountaintops, popped up while *Minotaur* was making its close approach to the surface, and put two simulated missiles into her. The flagship's commander was Aaron Dalgren. He filed a formal protest alleging that I had endangered both ships and crews. The protest was not upheld by the referees.

"Unfortunately, Captain Dalgren was promoted to admiral shortly afterward, and given command of all fleet corvettes. He made it clear that he was very irritated with me. I only recently worked my way out of purgatory and managed to get promoted to destroyers."

"You made quite a name for yourself considering the fact that you were in official disfavor. You won the Rickover Award, I believe."

"I had a good crew, and I was lucky."

Sadibayan leaned back. He placed his elbows on the arms of

the chair and steepled his fingers in front of him. "How would you like to go back to corvettes, Captain?"

"Sir?"

"Your superiors have given me the power to offer you command of a corvette. Interested?"

"Is that what this is all about?"

Sadibayan nodded.

"I'm sorry to disappoint you, Subminister, but my career plans do not include backsliding."

"Is that what you would consider it?"

"Yes, sir. You have to understand how it is in the space navy. An officer works his way up through the fleet, commanding ever larger and more important ships. There aren't that many of them. If you miss your turn, you become stuck in grade. If I give up *Currant*, I've lost my opportunity to prove myself in destroyers. That means I will never advance to cruisers."

Sadibayan's look was one that Van Zandt couldn't quite decipher. "Captain, we would like you to command the corvette *Austria*. She was decommissioned two years ago and sold to the Martians as a customs craft. They just finished overhauling her. As we speak she is being modified to mate with the *Starhopper* booster. The mission is to take her out beyond Pluto, and once there, to intercept an inbound starship."

Van Zandt regarded the small chocolate-colored man for half a minute without speaking. He couldn't decide whether the subminister was serious, or merely possessed a defective sense of humor. When the silence had stretched uncomfortably long, he cleared his throat and said, "You can forget what I said about not leaving *Currant*, sir. I accept the command!"

Sadibayan grinned. "I thought you would."

"How long will we be out?"

"Three years, more or less," the subminister replied in an offhand manner. "Depends on the aliens on board the ship, of course."

At the mention of aliens, Van Zandt's mouth popped open.

Sadibayan went on to review the data Luna Observatory had gathered on the light sail. Van Zandt listened with intense concentration. It became obvious that Admiral Carnevon had not been told why the ministry for science needed a naval officer. He didn't particularly like that, or the political approach that was being taken. On the other hand, it wasn't his job to like it. He had been offered command of the expedition, which was more than sufficient for one career. He pushed the misgivings from his mind and concentrated on what Sadibayan was telling him.

Austria had been one of the oldest ships in Earth's fleet before it had been sold to the Martians. The extreme delta V necessary for rendezvous required that the corvette be stripped of all non-essential systems, and the weapons had been the first things dismounted from the ship. Not only were they excess mass, no one wanted to send the wrong message by dispatching a functioning warship to intercept an alien starship. Out beyond Pluto, it seemed, diplomacy would be its own reward.

With the weapons had gone the targeting computers, both magazines, and the crew bunks. Coldsleep tanks were being installed in what had been the bunk-room. *Austria*'s new crew would spend much of the outbound flight in suspended animation, both to extend their limited supply of consumables and to make the voyage go by more quickly. The ship's life-support system would sustain them for a minimum of five years, but they had only sufficient food stocks to keep eating for two.

"How many crew?" Van Zandt asked after Sadibayan told him about the coldsleep tanks.

"That is still under study. A minimum of four. If the engineers can squeeze a bit more margin out of their calculations, we may send six. For now, the crew consists of yourself, a ship's engineer, a linguist, and a combination biologist/medical doctor."

"Do I get to pick the engineer?"

"Sorry, no. By Hobson's choice, the ship's engineer will be a young lady by the name of Victoria Bronson. She is the only one who can make the necessary software modifications on the fly."

"Surely a naval officer could learn what he needs to know."

"Believe me, Captain. We have looked into this matter extensively. So far as this expedition goes, Miss Bronson is more necessary than you are."

"What about the other crew members?"

"The ship's doctor and exobiologist has tentatively been chosen, as well."

"Who?"

"Actually, I believe she is Dardan Pierce's personal physician."

"Damn it, Subminister, cronyism is no way to staff a ship."

"Actually, Captain, I'm told that she is quite competent. You will be given the opportunity to meet her, of course, and if you find you can't work with her, then I suppose we can bring the matter up.''

"What are this doctor's qualifications?" Van Zandt asked. He was becoming less enchanted with his new command by the second.

"The problem is political. Pierce demanded that he be allowed to choose a member of the crew other than Miss Bronson. That was his price for allowing us to take over the *Starhopper*."

"I'm surprised he didn't demand to go himself."

Sadibayan smiled, as though he'd just thought of a joke. "Please, Captain, don't give him any ideas."

"What about the fourth crewman?"

"That would be the linguist. We are searching for a qualified individual right now. Any suggestions?"

"I'd like the opportunity to review the candidates before any offers are made."

"Of course, Captain."

"What about someone to negotiate with the aliens once we get there?"

"Unless we're allocated another berth, I'm afraid that job will fall to you, Captain Van Zandt. Think you can handle it?"

"I can try. What other modifications are they making to the corvette?"

Sadibayan listed several systems that were being upgraded for the long journey. Among these were *Starhopper*'s twin computers, which were being installed in the corvette's number-one hold. Also, a large microwave communications antenna was being anchored to the ship's hull.

"Why microwave?" Van Zandt asked. "A comm laser is a lot more efficient across that sort of distance."

"A comm laser looks too much like a weapon. One powerful enough to punch a message from beyond Pluto also would be good at carving on the alien ship."

"It doesn't really matter, I suppose," Van Zandt mused. "We'll be too far out for two-way communications anyway."

"It isn't for conversations. We want a continuous broadcast of your approach to the alien."

"In case they destroy us, you mean?"

Sadibayan nodded. "That would be most unfortunate."

"I would call it a major tragedy."

The subminister was unsmiling as he shook his head. "It will only be a major tragedy, Captain, if they destroy you and we don't learn how it was done."

5

MOSCOW HAD ITS ST. BASIL'S CATHEDRAL, PARIS THE EIFfel Tower, and San Francisco the Golden Gate Bridge. Every great city possessed its signature monument or architectural masterpiece, a symbol by which it was known. Olympus, Mars was no exception. The structure that symbolized the Martian capital rose two full kilometers above the northernmost rim of the volcano's caldera. Its builders had dubbed it the Adverse Weather Communications Facility. Everyone else called it the Aerie.

Communications between the surface and the orbital relay satellites were via comm laser. No other transmission medium had the bandwidth to handle the necessary volume of information. In the early days of the colony, dust storms had blotted out the visible-light lasers for weeks and even months at a time. The colony had been forced to fall back on radio circuits, which were themselves none too reliable in the spring and fall when the Martian dust was blowing.

Because the rim of Olympus Mons was already some twentyfive kilometers above the arbitrary "zero elevation" line that substituted for sea level on Mars, the Olympus city fathers built a communications tower to finish the job of getting above the worst of the obscuring dust. The comm lasers atop the tower were maintained in continuous standby mode, ready to take over should their ground-based counterparts become obscured. The glass sphere that housed them also included a restaurant, a bar, and a small banquet facility. These made the Aerie a favorite dining spot for both Earth tourists and the Martian upper crust.

Shortly after its completion, Victoria Bronson's third-grade class had visited the Aerie. They'd ridden the lift two kilometers up the side of the tower to stand with noses pressed against the curved glass wall as they oohed and aahed at the panoramic view. Now Tory found herself staring out again across the lighted domes of Olympus. This time she was deep in thought concerning the voyage on which she was about to embark. She didn't hear Praesert Sadibayan come up behind her until he spoke.

"Ah, Miss Bronson, there you are! May I present Captain Garth Van Zandt, Terrestrial Space Navy? He will command *Austria* on the expedition."

Tory let her eyes focus on the man with Sadibayan. He was of medium height, with sandy hair and a light complexion. His features were nondescript save for his eyes, which were blue and commanding. His figure was terrestrial muscular. After a few seconds, she realized that he was examining her with equal intensity. She blushed as their eyes met.

"Captain Van Zandt," she said, holding out her hand, "I'm pleased to meet you."

"The name is Garth."

"I'm Tory to my friends."

"Very well, Tory. May I buy you a drink?"

"Of course."

Van Zandt turned to Sadibayan and bowed. "Thank you, Mr. Subminister. If you will excuse us . . ."

"By all means," Sadibayan replied. He quickly turned on his heel and made his way back to the main reception.

There was an awkward silence as they both stood looking out across the lighted city. It was broken finally when Tory said, "I didn't expect you so soon. Mr. Sadibayan said that he would have to send to Earth for a naval officer. That was . . . five days ago."

Van Zandt laughed. "Sounds about right. My orders read 'by the fastest available transportation.' The subminister saw to it that I followed those orders to the letter. I'll be days recovering. I take it that you people are in a hurry."

Tory nodded and explained the desire to meet the alien ship as far out as possible. Van Zandt listened intently. He had his own suspicions about why everyone was so rushed. As a student of military history, he knew full well the advantages that flow from being one of the few privy to a closely held secret.

When she finished, he said, "I'd like to hear more. Let's get that drink and find someplace quiet where we can talk."

An hour later, Tory found herself laughing at a long, improbable story about how Van Zandt had arranged to have a case of caviar destined for fleet headquarters rerouted to his ship's mess.

"Didn't the admiral ever figure it out?" she asked.

"Never. My exec is now known around the fleet as the Great Stone Face."

All of the awkwardness was gone as she laughed again. They were supposed to be reviewing the details of the mission. However, their discussions left plenty of room for war stories.

"I have to say, Garth, that you aren't what I expected."

He arched his left eyebrow.

"When they sent for an Earth naval officer to command, I guess I expected some hard-driving martinet."

"A cross between Horatio Hornblower, Captain Bligh, and Captain Kirk, perhaps?" he asked.

"Something like that."

"There's a kernel of truth in the popular misconception that commanding officers are sons-a-bitches and martinets," Garth admitted, "but only a kernel. Commanding a spaceship is far more complicated than the challenges those old sea and wind sailors ever faced. The equipment requires a higher level of training, the medium is far more deadly than the ocean ever was, and space crews expect to be treated like the professionals they are. A captain who resorts to the cat-o'-nine-tails may find his cabin suddenly vented to space some night. No, people work best when you interfere with them least. Not that situations don't arise that call for a steady hand on the tiller, you understand. On the few occasions I do pull rank, I expect to be obeyed instantly."

Tory nodded. "I can live with that. Just remember, I never learned how to salute properly."

He laughed. "Another old wives' tale. Have you ever tried to salute in microgravity?"

She shook her head.

"As the arm comes up, torque causes the body to rotate in the opposite direction. Then, if you snap your hand down smartly, you go into a wobbly spinning motion. If your head happens to contact something solid, you can knock yourself out. Any other preconceptions that I can lay to rest for you?"

Tory gnawed on her lip. There was one subject that had been on her mind since she'd agreed to go on the expedition. She weighed the consequences of bringing it up now versus waiting, and decided it was best to get everything on the table as quickly as possible. "Is it true what they say about spacers?"

"Depends on what they say."

"The word is that things get pretty friendly aboard ship on long patrols."

Van Zandt stared at her for long seconds. His mouth curled

up slightly at the edges as Tory's ears began to burn. "I presume you're asking about sexual liaisons aboard ship?"

She nodded, surprised at her own awkwardness. After all, if she was to be cooped up in a vacuum-sealed can with this man for three years, she had every right to know what "duties" he expected her to perform.

He sighed and leaned back. "It is true that space crews on long patrols often form close bonds, and sometimes those bonds involve sexual liaisons. People get together for companionship, or just to have a warm body next to them at night. Such relationships can last a day, a week, a patrol, or a lifetime. There is but a single rule and it is inviolate. Whatever happens, it must be agreed to by both parties. There can be no coercion involved. Does that set your mind at ease?"

"What happens when the spacers have wives at home?"

He shrugged. "Some are faithful, some aren't. The same goes for the wives. I know of several arrangements where one woman is married to two spacers. It makes for a comfortable relationship unless both ships are in orbit at the same time. Or was your question a subtle way of asking whether I'm married?"

She felt her complexion grow even redder. "It wasn't. Are you?"

"Divorced," Van Zandt said. "My wife didn't like the long separations that go with patrol duty. We ended our contract amicably and are still good friends. You?"

"No."

"Boyfriend?"

"No one steady since I graduated from college." Tory averted her gaze. "You must think me old-fashioned."

"Not at all. I am aware that Martian mores are different from those of Earth. No need to apologize for them." He looked down at his glass, which was empty. "I need a refill. How about you?"

"Yes, please."

She watched him as he made his way through the crowd toward the bar. After three years on Phobos, her thoughts were of more than the mission.

Tory Bronson stared bleary-eyed at her workscreen and wondered what it was that she had been about to do. She had returned to Phobos ten days earlier to a nearly insurmountable problem. In theory, dismounting the *Starhopper* instrument package from the stack and adding a fleet corvette in its place was little more than a recalculation of vehicle mass and balance. In practice, it meant a major overhaul to the vehicle's control software.

Nor was there anyone else to do the work. Once she decided what was to be done with each of about ten thousand different subroutines, the small army of programmers she'd been promised would guide the computers in their work, but determining what had to be done in the first place was a job that required a single brain and a single vision. At the moment that brain ached from overload.

The biggest headaches were the subroutines that checked the instrument package's health from millisecond to millisecond. All were carefully designed to keep the interstellar probe functioning for the half century of unattended flight required to get to Alpha Centauri. Every subroutine would interpret the removal of the instrument package as a major system failure, and would attempt to route around the failed component. When that failed, God only knew what they would do. Most of the health-monitoring routines could simply be deactivated, of course. Most, but not all. Some were vital to the proper operation of the booster. Figuring out which category each routine belonged in was the difficult part of the job.

Since her return to Phobos, Tory had been at her workstation from breakfast until long after the corridor lights went blue. She never really caught up, but the extra hours kept her from falling farther behind. She had forgotten what it was like not to feel tired. Fatigue caused her work to suffer, which made her less productive, which required longer hours, which increased her fatigue. She had no difficulty in recognizing the vicious cycle for what it was. Recognizing it and being able to do something about it were two different things.

Her only respite from the tyranny of the computer came during meals hurriedly gulped down at her workstation and the two hours each day she spent answering Garth Van Zandt's questions. He, too, was working long hours as he struggled to learn everything he could about his new command. She didn't envy him his task. Even after three years of watching *Starhopper* go together beam by beam, she was still trying to master the tiniest details of the booster's construction. Van Zandt had less than six weeks to cram three years of knowledge into his brain, and was handicapped by not even having a simple computer implant. Nor did he have time to learn to use an implant even if he decided that he needed one.

Tory rubbed her eyes and turned her attention back to the workscreen. A schematic diagram of the *Starhopper* booster was displayed in its three-dimensional depth. To the untutored the diagram appeared a hopeless clutter of multicolored lines. To Tory, this was the least complex schematic that would allow her to follow the simulation she was running. It helped that the project computer was keeping track of the thousands of parameters affected by the modification she had just made to the control software. Even for one certified immune to avalanche effect, it was enough to give a person a headache.

After fifteen minutes of following a millisecond-by-millisecond projection of plasma flow in the booster's energy converter, she became aware that someone was standing behind her. She glanced over her shoulder to discover Ben Tallen's lanky form.

"Ben!" she cried with a start. "Make some noise the next time so you don't scare me out of ten years' growth."

"Sorry," he said. "You were into it pretty deeply there. I didn't want to interrupt something important."

"When did you get in?"

"I arrived on the evening ferry and came right over. Have you eaten?"

She shook her head, suddenly aware of the emptiness in her stomach.

"How about showing me where one can get fed around here."

She rubbed her tired eyes and said, "I really shouldn't. I've got four computer alarms to check this evening before I call it a night."

"You've got to eat sometime."

"All right. Give me ten minutes to see if anything else is going to pop up on this run."

"What are you doing?" he asked, gesturing at the diagram on the screen.

"I'm changing the bus timing on the booster control feeds to accommodate *Austria*'s data links. I have to check to see if I messed anything up when I made the changes."

"And did you?"

"Hundreds of things," she replied. "That's the problem with this damned software. Everything affects everything else."

"Aren't the modifications going well?"

"They're not going badly. You just have to be damned careful about introducing problems, especially in the fuel-feed system. Think of it as messing with your own genetic code."

He nodded and studied the schematic drawing she had displayed on the screen. It was obvious that he had no idea what he was looking at.

"*Starhopper*'s fuel-feed circuits and controls," she explained, "plus a bit of the engine control circuitry."

"What's it do?"

"It aligns the antimatter before injecting it into the reaction chamber where the proton-antiproton annihilation reaction takes place."

"I'll take your word for it," he said with a laugh.

Tory cleared her screen and accessed another schematic diagram—one used for briefing visiting politicians and university presidents. It showed generic drawings of the interstellar probe's antimatter torus, reaction mass tanks, and the various engine circuits. She spent the ten minutes explaining the operation of the booster to him, after which she guided him to the deserted project cafeteria.

"How much of that explanation did you understand?" she asked after gulping down half a sandwich.

"About a tenth," he said.

"Before getting this job, I thought plasma physics was difficult, too. Now I find I speak this strange language that people can't understand."

Ben put down a drinking bulb of coffee and nodded. "I know what you mean. I never understood politics before I signed on with the science ministry. Now it's all so clear to me."

She shrugged. "You can have it. Politics involve people, and people ain't logical."

He laughed. "You want to know who I feel sorry for?"

"Who?"

"Those poor bastards riding that light sail. If we have trouble figuring ourselves out, just think of the trouble they'll have understanding us."

"Or we will have understanding them," Tory said.

"All personnel! Final warning. Stand clear of the landing area. Monitors, report status."

Katherine Claridge, M.D., stood in her vacsuit on a small hillock at one end of Phobos and listened to the ground controller issue final instructions for the landing of the *Starhopper* booster. She wasn't alone. Around her were Garth Van Zandt, Tory Bronson, and most of the project personnel on Phobos who could be spared from their other duties.

Kit Claridge was a short blond woman who had to work to keep her weight down. Despite this, she was in exceptional shape for her age, fifty standard years. She was assistant chairman of the medical school at the University of Olympus, and the occupant of the Steinmetz Chair for Exobiology. She was also Dardan Pierce's personal physician.

Pierce had broken the news of the alien light sail to her two weeks earlier. She had been doubly dumbfounded by the news. First, she had thought him incapable of keeping a secret of that magnitude for longer than thirty seconds. Secondly, she had been struck speechless when he offered her a berth on the ship that would go out to meet the aliens.

"Are you sure you want me, Dard?" she'd asked after regaining use of her lower jaw muscles.

"Why not?"

"Shouldn't there be some sort of selection process? There are other exobiologists who are far more renowned than I am."

"They aren't M.D.s. I've checked. You are filling two berths for the price of one. Efficiency in all things, I always say."

"But damn it, you don't hand your doctor the biggest scientific plum in history without consulting someone. My God, they'll hang you in effigy at the next meeting of the System Society for the Advancement of Science. You have to at least appear to play the game."

"Look, Kit. I don't know all of those other biologists, but I do know you. I don't care what Sadibayan thinks, or de Pasqual, or even the first minister. I want you."

"But why, for heaven's sake?"

"Because you won't panic when you meet the aliens, no matter how slimy they may look. You'll look at them with that same Olympian detachment you use with me every time you tell me I'm too fat. This is the first opportunity human beings will have to make a good impression on another species. I know you'll represent us well. What's the matter, don't you want to go?"

"Want to go? I'll kill to go! I just don't want you to get in trouble."

"Look, if they want *Starhopper*, they have to let me fill a billet. The one I've chosen is the biologist slot. That's you, unless you don't want it."

She'd shut up at that point lest he change his mind. She'd spent the next two weeks in a daze, still unable to believe her good luck. Hell, after this expedition, she just might become the most famous exobiologist who ever lived.

Exobiology had been a science in search of a subject for nearly three centuries. Generations of practitioners had written millions of scientific papers on what alien life-forms ought to be like, all without having even a single nonterrestrial specimen to study. Yet, dangling from that blue-white light in the sky was a ship, and in that ship were living, breathing, *thinking* beings from another star. At the least, they would bring with them the Tau Cetian equivalent of body lice, intestinal bacteria, perhaps even shipboard cockroaches. To Kit Claridge, that was a veritable alien ecology!

Finally, all of her patients had been referred to other doctors, her classes reassigned, and her administrative duties finished. She packed a single kit bag and caught the morning ferry to Phobos, arriving the day before they planned to bring the booster down to dismount the instrument package. She'd spent much of her first day becoming acquainted with Garth Van Zandt and Tory Bronson.

She shaded her faceplate with a gloved hand as Phobos's rotation brought the sun above the local horizon. The ground in front of her was unnaturally flat. It had been leveled off as a landing field next to the Phobos distillation facility. This was where small mountains of ice covered in reflective foil were landed after being towed into position by light sails. Once landed, they were carved up and carted off to the refinery. It was also from the landing field that tankers delivered their cargoes of slush hydrogen to the Earth liners and other vessels in orbit about Mars.

Kit listened as the safety monitors reported the field clear of all personnel. When they finished, the general comm circuit resounded with the noise of a radio-borne siren. The clumps of vacsuited figures arrayed behind safety barriers suddenly ceased their chatter.

"All right, *Starhopper*. You are free to descend," the chief controller radioed.

"Thank you, Control," came the voice of Phobos's most experienced approach pilot. "Beginning the descent now!"

There were a series of sparks low on the western horizon, where the pyramid-shaped interstellar booster hovered. For a long time nothing seemed to happen. Slowly, the gap between booster and horizon began to grow. Over the next ten minutes, *Starhopper* climbed the sky. The sparks came again as the booster was silhouetted against the ruddy orb of Mars. Attitude-control jets fired from a dozen places around the body of the main booster, giving the impression of a set of anticollision lights flashing in unison, and the two-hundred-meter-wide truncated pyramid rotated about its yaw axis in response.

Kit had a momentary case of the jitters as she found herself gazing directly into the gaping maw of the booster's powerful engines. Should those light off, everyone within line of sight would be instantly vaporized. Kit shook off the morbid thought. Tory Bronson knew all there was to know about the booster and she was standing calmly not ten meters away.

The small reaction jets flared again and *Starhopper* began its descent. With the red planet as a backdrop, the booster was enormous.

Starhopper continued its slow descent. The port pilot was taking no chances with the only vessel in the Solar system able to catch the alien starship. Three times he fired the reaction jets to slow the pyramid's fall. Then, two meters above the field, he fired them for a few seconds. Blue-white exhausts splashed down onto Phobos's rocky surface. Then the jets were silent and *Starhopper* began to fall.

It took all of five minutes for the booster's landing feet to contact the field. As it grounded, a slight shiver went through the structure. Throughout the landing, the general comm circuit had been unnaturally quiet. The silence was suddenly broken as dozens of spectators exhaled heavily and resumed breathing.

"All monitors. Secure the booster," the chief controller ordered. "Let's get it tied down now!"

Atop the instrument package, a single vacsuited figure unstrapped and began to clamber down the structure like a child moving across a jungle gym. This was the port pilot. He carried with him the control box that had allowed him to manually operate the booster's attitude jets. He ignored the vacuum monkeys who were busily tying down the craft.

"All secure," came the report from the chief monitor after cables were slipped through pad eyes inset into the rocky plain and made taut. A moment after the announcement, other figures went to work unbolting the small instrument package from the two massive booster stages below it.

6 PROFESSOR ELIAS GUTTIERIZ HAD FINISHED TEACHING for the day. It had been difficult to concentrate on ancient Phoenician dialects and their effect on the speech patterns of North Africa when he had so much else on his mind. Still, Guttieriz had only lost his place once while wading through the prepared lecture. He considered that an accomplishment. He was halfway to his office when he was overtaken by an excited student aide from administration.

"Sir, the chancellor wants to see you in his office right away!" the breathless student exclaimed.

Guttieriz, who had been expecting the summons, merely nodded. He gestured for the student to lead the way, and both of them moved off in the gliding motion that is the most efficient means of locomotion on Luna. Guttieriz was a small man with black hair, a neatly trimmed mustache, and an incipient paunch. He knew his looks were far from impressive. It was enough that several influential papers on the fundamental structure of human language had earned him his reputation as the Solar system's preeminent linguist.

"Ah, Eli!" the chancellor exclaimed as Guttieriz entered his office. "Come in and sit. Drink?"

Guttieriz moved to the chancellor's couch. "Whiskey if you've got it, Hal."

The chancellor poured amber liquid into two long-stemmed, low-gravity glasses and handed one to Guttieriz. He then sat on the opposite end of the couch.

"Have you made your decision yet?"

"Not yet."

"Time is getting short."

"How can I make a decision when I haven't even been tendered a formal invitation?"

"You've been asked if you would consent."

"That isn't the same as actually being invited."

The chancellor removed a message flimsy from his pocket. "You'll have your invitation this afternoon. I just received this from Jorgensen. He says that the board has reviewed the qualifications of several eminent linguists and has decided that you are most qualified to go out to meet these aliens."

"I could have told them that."

"What will be your answer?"

Elias shrugged. The hunching of the shoulders imitated the motion by which one climbs out of a moonsuit. To a Lunarian, that particular gesture represented a desire to escape the suffocating feeling that comes from a dilemma with no easy solution.

"To tell you the truth, Hal, I dislike being the subject of this . . . this . . . cattle show! If they want me, why didn't they just ask me. I will not present myself like some prize pig down in the farm tunnels. Frankly, I have half a mind to turn them down."

"You mustn't!"

"Why not? Because the president won't like it?"

"Precisely."

"Then the president can step out the nearest airlock without a suit."

The chancellor sighed. Not for nothing did Eli Guttieriz have a reputation for being difficult. Still, the man was a genius in his field. "Look here, Eli. This alien business is important for the whole human race. These beings have crossed twelve light-years of space. Think of what they know that we do not."

"I have thought about it."

"Have you really? What industries will their knowledge make obsolete? Who will gain power from their arrival, who will lose it? What will be the effect on those of us here in Luna?"

"What the hell do I care? I'm a scholar."

"Let us not be coy, Eli. We both know that you have a soft spot in your heart for your adopted world."

"A soft spot in my head, you mean. I like it here because the people aren't quite as rude as at home in Liverpool. Although I do miss the English rains."

"The Martians have already snapped up two berths, and the terrestrials have a man in command of the expedition. You're Luna's last hope. If you turn it down, then the offer goes to Hayward Wilson."

Guttieriz, who had been enjoying his position of power, was suddenly scandalized. "That poor excuse for a scholar? You can't be serious, Hal!"

The chancellor shrugged. "He scored rather highly on the board's health evaluation."

"Especially the muscle between his ears, I imagine."

The chancellor's expression clouded. "I need your answer, Professor Guttieriz. Will you accept or reject the offer?"

"You are asking me to ignore the humiliation to which I have been subjected and do it for good old Luna?"

"Screw the humiliation! Think of what this will do for your reputation. It won't harm the reputation of this university, either."

Guttieriz drained his whiskey and set the glass down on the end table. "If the invitation comes this afternoon, I will communicate my acceptance by early evening."

"Excellent," the chancellor said. "I'll get to work arranging transportation. Thank you, Eli. I was afraid we were going to have to draft you into the navy and order you to go."

Eli laughed. He could just see himself sent out to do battle armed with a copy of *Hamad's Encyclopedia of Phonemes*.

"So what did you think of our ship?" Van Zandt asked Kit Claridge. He, Kit, and Tory were seated in Phobos's premier—and only—drinking establishment. The work crews had finished mounting the corvette atop the *Starhopper* booster that afternoon and the three of them had toured their future home.

"Impressive," the doctor replied.

"What about you, Tory? Just another day at the office?"

"Any day that gets me away from my terminal is a good day." Tory sat sideways in a booth while her two shipmates shared the opposite side. She'd put in a particularly long shift the day before and was feeling lethargic. She had been yawning throughout the tour of the ship.

"What word on our fourth?" Kit asked.

"The board finally stopped frittering. They selected Elias Guttieriz to join our little band."

"Has he accepted?"

Garth nodded. "He should be here late next week. We'll start full crew training the day after."

"Is it certain they aren't going to add a fifth slot?" Tory asked.

"I convinced them that it wasn't wise. I know the calculations say we can get away with another crew member, but damn it, you don't go out on something like this without a margin of safety. I'd hate to run out of food a month before we return."

"Oh, I don't know," Kit said lazily. "That never bothered the Donner party."

"Who?"

"Never mind. It was a bad joke."

Tory, who had let her eyes fall to half staff while listening to the byplay, idly keyed the reference into her implant. That brought a history of the Colorado Administrative District of the North American Directorate, and the history of Donner Pass. Kit was right; it was a *very* bad joke. She sat up and drained her drinking bulb with a quiet slurping noise. "Well, see you!"

"Where are you going?" Garth asked.

"Back to work. Lots to do!"

"Like what?"

Tory listed the subroutines she was debugging.

"I thought Vance Newburgh had already checked those out."

"He did. I'm running an independent analysis."

"Do you have reason to suspect the quality of his work?" Garth asked, his manner suddenly serious.

"No, of course not. Vance is one of the best we've got."

"Have you found any errors?"

"Not so far."

"Then why double-check Newburgh's results?"

"Because I'm the one getting in that ship, not Vance."

Garth gestured for her to sit. "Let's talk. You listen to this, too, Kit. We need to get a few things straight."

Tory sat. She felt as if she was a little girl again, about to be lectured by her father. This was evidently one of those times when Van Zandt felt the need to play captain.

"Look, people, we've all been working hard to get ready for launch. That's good. But it isn't good if we wear ourselves out doing it. Tory, how much sleep did you get last night?"

Tory told him.

He swore softly. "You will not go back to the office tonight. I want you to go home and get eight hours of uninterrupted sleep. Doc, can you give her something?"

Kit reached into her medical pouch and withdrew a small white pill. "Here, take this when you get home. It will relax you."

Tory pouched it, but not before giving Van Zandt a dirty look.

He continued without pause. If he saw the look, he chose to ignore it. "Let's say you find a mistake in Newburgh's work and fix it. What is the probability that you have taken a perfectly good piece of software and ruined it?"

"I don't know."

"Eighty percent, according to the studies on fatigue we've done in the navy. That's why I want you fresh when you're working. It could mean the difference between a successful mission and blowing up."

"All right, I'll get a good night's sleep."

"You'll do more than that. When was the last time you saw your family?"

"I don't know. Last year sometime."

"Anyone who is about to embark on a three-year mission has to have time to get their life in order. If you don't, you will be worried about things at home and not concentrating on your job. I want you headed down to Mars within the next seventy-two hours. I don't care what you do, but you are to avoid thinking about that damned booster and its software. Report back here on the twenty-second. That's the day Guttieriz arrives. I want you bright-eyed and alert, and ready to work your butt off."

"What about all the things I have backed up on my desk?"

"Turn over your duties to Newburgh and the programmers, then forget us."

"But . . ."

"That's an order, Chief Engineer."

"Aye, aye, Captain."

"Good. Now sit still while I order another drink. We're here to celebrate getting *Austria* mounted. Kit, ready for another?"

"Aye, aye, sir," the older woman mimicked.

Soon the three of them were chuckling at one of Van Zandt's stories and already Tory could feel the weight begin to lift from her shoulders. Maybe the Old Man—did they really call the captain the Old Man anymore?—knew what he was doing.

Tory felt her pulse pounding in her ears as she trudged up the side of the mountain. Besides her own ragged breathing, the whir of a ventilation fan set on high was loud in her ears. Pea-sized globules of perspiration beaded on her forehead before breaking loose to run down into her eyebrows, only to be captured by the headband of her helmet. Without that necessary accessory, she would be blind.

She trudged the last few meters to the flat spot she had been aiming at for more than an hour. As she reached it, she turned to look downslope to where Ben Tallen was towing the equipment sledge behind him. Her eyes followed the snakelike track of their ascent in the ocher dust to the vanishing point, and then beyond to the rented Mars rover they'd left parked at the base of the mountain. The big vehicle looked like a child's toy from her vantage point.

"How's this, skinker?"

"High enough for me, frump!" came back the gasping reply.

She waited for Ben to climb to her level before taking the tow rope from him and hauling the sledge onto the flat area that had been carved by the thin Martian wind. By silent consent, the two plopped down on the large bundle secured atop the sledge to catch their breath. Tory gazed out across the spectacular panorama as she rested.

Due east, its base invisible below the steeply curved horizon, was Olympus Mons. The upper third of the volcano's shield was in view, silhouetted against the nearly black sky. The mountain on which Tory sat was a small volcano at the edge of the Plain of Amazons. They were some twenty kilometers lower than Olympus's peak, making it impossible to see the caldera, but by squinting hard, it was just possible to make out the threadlike vertical form of the Aerie.

Below and all around them was the red surface of the high Martian desert. It was local summer, which meant that winds were light and blowing dust was at a minimum. Visibility in the thin atmosphere was nearly as good as on Luna, with only a minute softening of detail with distance, and none of the blueing that is characteristic of Earth's atmosphere.

"We'd best move if we don't want our legs to cramp up," Ben said after they had rested for five minutes.

"Right," she replied without enthusiasm. As her joints creaked inside her suit, she reminded herself that this trek into the wilderness had been her idea.

They worked as a team to drag the pressure tent off the sledge and unfold it. After several attempts, they got it spread out so that there were no folds in the heavy underlining. Working in opposite directions, Tory and Ben anchored the tent every twenty degrees around its circumference, driving stakes deep into the crumbly ground. Finally, Ben hooked up the environmental unit and pressed a control. The tent began to slowly inflate.

Ten minutes later, it was a silver igloo straining at its moorings. Ben set up the reinforcing rods that maintained the shape of the small tubular airlock while Tory unloaded the case of food and other supplies from the sledge. She piled the boxes inside the airlock, crawled in after, then sealed the outer flap behind her before cracking the valve that let air in from the main section of the tent. She pushed the supplies inside and crawled in after.

Once inside, Tory struggled out of her suit, pushing it to one side when she finished with it. She resealed the inner airlock flap and signaled Ben that he could enter. He retrieved the chemical toilet from the sledge and repeated Tory's performance with the airlock. She unsealed the inner flap and pulled the toilet inside, moving it to its place behind the privacy curtain. She then turned to help Ben off with his suit. It was hard work with the two of them and all their supplies in the tent. It took another twenty minutes to arrange things so that most of the clutter was out of the way. Ben busied himself unrolling the electrically heated sleeping bags while Tory plugged two prepackaged dinners into their power unit.

"Well, was it worth the climb?" Ben asked ten minutes later as he munched on pressed chicken loaf covered in something that was advertised to be brown gravy.

"Don't you think so? Where else can you find a view this spectacular?" she asked as she gestured toward where the sun was setting. She had dialed the tent to full transparency so they could see out. Because of the dust in the air, Martian sunsets were always spectacular.

He smiled. "Too much red if you ask me."

"I suppose I would think the same about blue and green if I ever went to Earth."

"Care to make a bet on that?" he asked. It was an argument they'd had before. Ben maintained that love of trees and water was embedded in humanity's genes, while Tory thought it an acquired taste. "How was your visit home?"

"Not what I'd hoped for," Tory said. Her parents had been happy enough to see her, but it hadn't been twenty minutes before her father was grilling her about where she was going for three long years. She had given him the cover story that she had accepted a three-year contract from an asteroid mining company, to begin immediately after *Starhopper* launched. Her father had called her inconsiderate for not telling them earlier, while her mother and sister had made a fuss over her.

She'd stayed with her parents for three days, then called Ben and asked him if he wanted to go camping. It had taken two more days to arrange transportation and rent the equipment. "Camping" on Mars bore only the faintest resemblance to the same activity on Earth.

The two of them lay propped on their elbows, facing one another after dinner. Ben regarded her with serious eyes.

"What?" she asked when she noticed him looking at her.

"You're beautiful when you're red."

She laughed, glancing down at herself. Martian dust was the same consistency as talcum powder. It covered the suits and the interior of the tent with a fine ocher layer, and despite their best efforts, had covered both of them from head to toe as well.

"Do you think so?" she asked.

"I do. Also, I've been noticing how much you've changed since college."

"How so?" she asked, wondering what he was getting at.

"You're more mature. You seem to care less about what other people think than you did."

"Hah!" she said. "I'm still crushed whenever anyone makes even the tiniest critical comment about my work."

"Well, you show it less. I remember a time when you had to dress precisely right and go to all of the functions everyone else was going to."

"You should talk," she said. "Who was it that had to have that new pocket computer because Bill Ames had bought one?"

"Not the same thing," he said with a grin. "That was simple envy on my part. I didn't care what Ames thought about me, I just didn't want him to have a better computer."

"I stand corrected."

Although spectacular, sunsets in the thin Martian atmosphere were over quickly. When it was nearly too dark to see one another, Ben got to his knees and activated the overhead glow-lamp. At the same time, Tory dialed the surface back to silver. They had to be careful about heat loss at night. In their scrambling, they met in the middle of the tent, where Ben folded her into his arms and kissed her.

"Who's Gloria?" Tory asked when their lips parted.

Tallen blinked and was quiet for a long moment. "Where did you hear about her?"

"Do you remember Hideki Sato from school?"

Ben nodded.

"The project hired him as a programmer last week. We were talking about the software changes when I mentioned that you were back on Mars. He told me to say hi for him and then asked me how you were getting along with Gloria. Who's Gloria?"

"Someone I met on Earth. Her father is on the board of directors of Tramton Industries."

"Oh, she's rich!"

He shrugged. "She isn't hurting for credit."

"Is it serious between you two?"

"We've talked marriage, but haven't agreed to anything yet. Lately, I've been wondering if that would be such a good idea."

"Oh?" Tory asked.

"I've recently come to realize that I may still be in love with someone else."

"How recently?"

"Very," he said as he leaned forward to kiss her again.

She pulled back this time. "Are you suggesting that we take up where we left off?"

"Why not?"

"Because I'm about to ship a zillion kilometers out into space."

"That's a problem, but not an insurmountable one. Truly, I didn't realize how much I miss you."

"Are you sure you aren't just suffering from proximity syndrome? I'm here and Gloria isn't."

He sighed and released her. "So young to be so cynical."

"You still haven't told me how we are going to carry on a romance while I'm out at the light sail and you're back on Earth."

"We could write each other long love letters."

"Who's going to deliver them?"

"They'll go out as official comm traffic. You may be interested to know that Underminister Sadibayan has assigned me to be liaison to the project technical staff."

"Really? I suppose congratulations are in order."

"They are indeed. It's my job to assemble the threat team. That's one reason I'm still here. I'm going to ask Vance Newburgh to join once he finishes modifying the software for launch."

"Threat team?"

"A poor title. It's more an adverse-impact evaluation group. Each datum you people send back will be analyzed for adverse effects on our military capability, economy, and social institutions. There will be another team to evaluate positive impacts, and several groups of specialists to study any alien technology you tell us about."

"It's nice to know we'll be able to get our questions answered when we call home."

"You're more likely to get a long list of questions that need answering,'' he replied. ''But don't change the subject, which if I remember correctly was you and me.''

She regarded him for long seconds before answering. ''You're serious, aren't you?''

''Damned serious.''

''What about Gloria?''

''That's something I need to work out.''

Tory nodded. ''I need to work some things out as well. Can we talk about this later?''

''Sure. How about we get this dust cleaned off and get some sleep? I'll use the electrostat on you if you use it on me.''

''That sounds like a come-on, Mr. Tallen.''

Somehow his look of innocence didn't ring true as he reached for the dust attractor and Tory wriggled out of her undersuit.

7

PHOBOSPORT, WHERE THE MARS FERRIES LANDED, WAS ON the opposite end of the moon from the field where *Starhopper* was being modified. Despite this, Tory was able to catch a glimpse of the big booster during final approach. *Starhopper* looked like one of the pyramids of Egypt transplanted to the Martian moon.

The ferry landed and a tired Tory Bronson pulled herself hand over hand through the embarkation tube. It was a pleasant tired, nothing like the fatigue that had sapped her strength before she went on leave. As she exited the surface lock into the main terminal, Tory was surprised to discover Kit Claridge standing among those waiting for the disembarking passengers.

"Kit! What are you doing here? Something wrong?"

"Nothing wrong," the doctor assured her. "I heard you were scheduled in and wanted to see how the prescription took."

"Prescription?"

"How was your leave?"

Tory smiled. "Great. Ben and I had a marvelous time. It was almost like our college days."

"What did the two of you do?"

"Believe it or not, we went camping! We spent two days in environment suits trudging the Olympus foothills. We watched the sunset from the top of Sutter's Peak, then snuggled together all night in a pressure tent."

"To each their own. Personally, I would have preferred the diversions of civilization."

Tory laughed. "We didn't rough it the *whole* time. Ben took me to the theater and the opera."

"That's more like it. What opera?"

"The Barber of Seville."

"With Standish Barnes in the lead?"

"The one and only."

Kit sighed. "I saw him in *Carmen* ten years ago. Is he as handsome as ever?"

"Hard to tell under all that makeup."

They walked as they talked. "How do things stand between you and Ben?" Kit asked as they entered the main Phobosport terminal area. Suddenly, she sounded very like a doctor diagnosing a patient.

Tory shrugged. "He wants to get back together. I told him we'd have to wait until after my return. Then, if we're both still interested, we'll see what happens."

"A wise move. A lot can happen during a three-year separation."

"How go launch preparations?"

Kit sighed. "I never realized there was so much to getting a ship ready for space. We're on schedule . . . barely. All supplies have been loaded except the antimatter fuel and hydrogen reaction mass. Garth has a full week of onboard simulations planned, by the way. They begin at oh-eight-hundred hours tomorrow. If he's happy with the results, we fuel in ten days and launch in twelve."

"And software certification?"

"Going smoothly so far as I know. Garth has been meeting daily with Vance Newburgh. If there's been any screaming, they did it behind closed doors."

Tory made a mental note to check with Vance via implant as soon as she was alone. "What about Guttieriz? Did he ever show up?"

Kit nodded. "He was able to get an earlier ship and arrived the day before yesterday."

"How is he?"

"A bit of a stuffed shirt at first, but he's loosened up some in just two days. I think he'll do all right."

"He'd better. It will be difficult getting a replacement out beyond Pluto."

"There's always the airlock solution."

Tory shivered. "On that cheery thought, I think I'll head for home."

"Need any help with your luggage?"

"No, I don't really have that much."

"All right," Kit said. "I'll see you at the ship at oh-eight-hundred tomorrow. By the way, the captain has asked me to tell you to get a full night's sleep. He says that you're going to need it."

"Tell him that I intend to do just that."

Tory collected her luggage, then sailed the kilometer to her apartment in long dives down tunnels bored straight through the moon's interior. She didn't even bother to unpack upon arrival. She merely flung her kit bag into a corner, spent ten minutes in the bathroom preparing for bed, then lay down on the rock shelf that was all that was needed in Phobos's gravity field. She lightly fastened her restraining straps, lay back and closed her eyes. Despite her best efforts, however, she found she couldn't sleep. She was too excited.

The four of them stood in their vacuum suits at the base of *Starhopper* and gazed up at their new home. *Austria* looked like an afterthought perched atop the booster. The fleet corvette was composed of three spherical modules connected by an external gridwork of braces. Across its surface was the usual panoply of ungainly mechanisms that make most ships of deep space look as though they were assembled in a junkyard. A dozen thruster clusters were mounted to the sides of the corvette, while large heat rejection "wings" were in their stowed position for launch. A long boom jutted at right angles from the middle sphere. At the end of it was the stowed parabolic antenna that would be their primary communications link with Earth.

The corvette had been anchored to the booster by a series of high-strength cables, and a forest of fiber optics ran from the corvette's aft airlock to the body of the interstellar booster. Inside *Austria*'s number-one hold were both of *Starhopper*'s main computers. Though much of *Austria*'s original equipment had been stripped to lighten the ship, the corvette's engines had been retained. The naval craft had the capability to separate from the booster and maneuver on its own if the delta V requirement wasn't too large.

Garth turned to the three members of his crew and announced that he would go first. He stepped forward and inserted his right gauntlet through a strap that hung down from the sloping cable running from the corvette's midships airlock to an anchor point behind them. The strap was attached to a powered cable tow. As soon as Garth touched the tow, he was jerked off his feet and lifted skyward as the unit climbed the cable.

He reminded Tory of a circus performer as he hung there by one arm, swinging in a slow pendulum motion. The cable tow halted as Garth cleared the landing stage outside the airlock. He dropped off the hanging strap, sending the tow unit back for the next rider. A few seconds later, he disappeared through the airlock.

Tory was next to ride the tow into the black sky. She, too, sent the unit back before palming the airlock control. The outer door opened, she stepped over the raised coaming, and closed the door behind her. A few seconds later, she was buffeted by a brisk wind as air refilled the lock. A green light illuminated overhead, signifying that it was now safe to open the inner door.

She found Garth in the airlock anteroom. He was already half out of his suit. He waited until she removed her helmet and let it drop to the length of its safety lanyard.

"Ready to go to work?"

"Ready."

"As soon as you've stowed your suit, get up to the control room and start the diagnostic routines. I want continuous health monitoring on all systems from now to launch. If anything is going to go wrong, I'd rather have it happen while we're still tied to this big rock."

"Right."

She stripped off her suit and slipped into the shipsuit that would be standard apparel for the next three years. To her surprise, Garth made no attempt to watch her. For ten long seconds, both of them rubbed shoulder blades in their underwear as they studiously ignored one another.

Tory finished dressing just as the third member of their party entered from the airlock. She waited until he, too, had removed his helmet.

"You must be Professor Guttieriz. I'm Victoria Bronson, chief engineer."

"Hello, Miss Bronson," he said as he shook hands with her. "Since we're going to be together for quite some time, perhaps you should call me Eli."

"I'm Tory. Sorry I wasn't here to greet you when you got in."

"No problem. I understand you were on Mars."

She nodded. "A little rest and relaxation prior to heading out."

He laughed. "It's been a lifelong ambition of mine to see Mars. Here I am and I won't have the opportunity. Oh well, another time."

"Kit still has to cycle through," Garth warned. The suiting chamber was the size of a comm booth and one more person would cause it to overflow.

"On my way, Captain. I'll see you later, Eli." As she moved

through the middle sphere's circumferential passageway, she willed her implant to connect with the *Starhopper* computer just beyond the steel bulkhead. She immediately received the connect tone signifying that the link between herself and the computers was operating properly.

Tory pulled herself hand over hand to the axis passageway, and from there up into the topmost of the ship's three spherical modules. It was from the upper sphere that *Austria* was controlled. Besides the control room, it contained a wardroom, the converted bunk room, and four tiny crew cabins. Each spherical module had an independent life-support system able to sustain life for long periods in an emergency. The control module, however, had the amenities that would make the voyage bearable.

Tory noted that her meager luggage had been delivered and secured in her cabin. She swarmed through the axis passageway to the control room, where she maneuvered herself into one of two acceleration couches and drew a safety belt across her midsection to loosely restrain herself. She then swung the engineer's console over the couch and activated it.

The console lit up with a satisfying "no anomalies" message as she began turning on the health-monitoring subroutines. She watched the progress of the self-test software in her mind as it began exercising each system. It took the better part of an hour for the health monitors to run completely through a single cycle. She was hard at work on the third such when Kit Claridge poked her chubby features through the hatch.

"Lunch!"

Tory blinked. As was normal while under the influence of her implant, she had lost track of the time. That was a difficult concept for non–implant wearers to understand, since the implant time signal was accurate to the microsecond. Yet knowing the time isn't the same as being aware that time has passed. For that Tory consulted her stomach, which agreed that lunch was overdue.

Twelve days later, Tory was again strapped into her acceleration couch. This time she was using all of the available restraints, including the ankle loops that kept her legs from flopping around. *Starhopper* was no longer tied to Phobos. All cables and other ground connections had been removed following fueling of the booster.

"Launch status check, Engineer!" Garth ordered from the couch next to Tory's. All trace of the friendly banter he had cultivated over the past six weeks was gone. He was now a ship's captain facing the most critical moment in any flight—lift-off!

"We're ready, Captain," Tory responded as she finished checking the booster's status via her implant. She had also scanned the readouts on the main viewscreen.

"Very well," Van Zandt replied. "Pass control to the ship's computer. Let's see what the brain can do. Monitor and be prepared to override."

"Aye, sir."

Down in *Austria*'s hold, the twin electronic brains came fully awake and began their own prelaunch checks. They polled the health of thousands of mechanisms, then compared notes. The booster's twenty-four massive reaction-mass tanks were filled with slush hydrogen as ten kilograms of antiprotons orbited in the booster's four magnetic confinement tori. *Starhopper*'s mass had increased by more than one hundred thousand tons over the past forty-eight hours, and the additional inertia would make the booster/corvette combination's response to commands sluggish. The additional inertia of all that reaction mass made it especially critical that everything work properly on lift-off.

The automatic checkout continued for nearly ten seconds. At the end of that time, the computers reported their readiness for launch.

"Ready, Captain. All systems check out nominal."

"Stand by," Van Zandt ordered. "Professor Guttieriz!"

The small linguist was strapped down in his cabin aft.

"As ready as I'll ever be," came the reply.

"Professor Claridge?"

Kit, too, was strapped down in her cabin. "Ready to launch, Captain."

"Chief Engineer Bronson?"

"Ready, Captain."

"Very well. Control, this is *Starhopper*. We are ready to lift."

"Your trajectory is clear of traffic, *Starhopper*. You are cleared out of the inner zone."

"All right, Engineer, you may release the jinn from its bottle."

Tory sent the impulse that transferred final control to the computer. The effect was immediate. Somewhere aft, a dozen small reaction jets came alight. Nothing happened for a second or two; then the radar altimeter began to register a slow climb. When the velocity indicator registered one hundred meters per second, the reaction jets fell silent.

Starhopper continued to drift slowly skyward. It had escaped the small moon's gravitational hold and was now in orbit about Mars.

"We're safely away, Captain," Tory reported unnecessarily.

"Very well, Engineer. Begin final checks of the antimatter system and electromagnetic nozzle. We head into the deep black as soon as we clear the inner traffic zone."

Faslorn of the Phelan stared at the image of Sol and its planets and marveled at the sight. His ancestors had studied this yellow star from the moment they'd discovered it to be the source of artificially generated electromagnetic radiation. Following the destruction of Tau Ceti, his predecessors had studied Sol to glean as much information as possible. For much of the long voyage from the home system, however, Sol's nine children had remained invisible to Phelan telescopes. All the knowledge they had of the system came from human broadcasts.

It had not been until the cycle of Faslorn's birth that the ship's telescopes had first picked out the faint sparks of Sol's attendant worlds. Jupiter had been first, of course, followed by Saturn, Venus, and Earth. Over the revolutions, all of the Solar planets had been observed save two. The innermost, Mercury, was lost in the glare of the star, even when advanced obscuration techniques were attempted. The outermost, Pluto, was too far out and badly positioned for observation. Neither failure was of much interest to the Phelan. Their vision remained firmly fixed on the third of Sol's children.

For all the time they could see them, Phelan telescopes had watched the changing pattern of sunlight on the Solar worlds. Each planet showed as a nearly full circle when on the far side of the sun and as a tiny sliver of light when near. As they watched, Faslorn and his crewmates saw a system very like home. Two worlds in the home system had been twins of Jupiter, while hot, cloud-shrouded Milsa had been Venus's counterpart. Earth . . . Earth resembled lost Phela as closely as one world can resemble another. Even the oversize Luna had its counterpart in Phela's largest moon.

Faslorn's interest, however, was in none of the worlds of Sol. His attention was fixed on a patch of violet-white fog that would have been invisible had the computers not noted its presence.

"The astronomers are certain that this is a ship coming to meet us?" Faslorn asked his chief adviser.

"There can be no doubt," Rosswin replied. "They have been

observing the cloud for twenty watches. At first they thought it the exhaust of an interplanetary liner en route from Mars to an outer world. They became suspicious when the cloud did not move like a ship in the main planetary plane. When it did not fade away at the proper time, they began taking Doppler measurements. There can be no doubt. It is moving directly toward us.''

''How fast?''

''At the beginning of this watch, at zero-point-zero-four-one-three fraction of luminal velocity.''

''What is the delay in the light reaching us?''

''One-quarter cycle.''

''Then if the vehicle continued boosting, it could actually be moving much faster by now. Could it be a weapon?''

''Our human psychologists put the probability at less than two dozen parts in a gross,'' Rosswin replied. ''They think it more likely that the humans have modified the interstellar probe they were building and are using it to send a ship out to meet us.''

Faslorn's posture showed his concern. ''A development we had not foreseen.''

''What are your orders?'' the adviser asked. His lower two arms hung at his sides, much as a human's would, while the upper set was clasped across the barrel of his chest. The position was that of respect, a subordinate awaiting instructions.

Faslorn's ears flicked as he considered this new factor in their plans. ''Perhaps this is not the problem we had feared. It will give us the opportunity to fine-tune the masquerade before we have to face the human multitudes.''

''Is that wise?''

''What choice have we? You will issue orders to all human specialists. I want to be advised of their preliminary assessments as soon as possible.''

''It will be done.''

8

TORY BRONSON WOKE TO A BITTER, BITING COLD. SHE lay there and wondered what had gone wrong with the power to her sleeping bag. Surely Ben hadn't gotten up during the night and dialed the tent back to transparency so that he could look at the stars. He'd been on Mars long enough to know better than that, hadn't he?

She found that willing her eyelids open was the hardest work she had ever done. When she could finally see again, the tent on Sutter's Peak was nowhere to be found, and in its place was a translucent barrier only a few centimeters in front of her nose. She watched without understanding as the glass alternately fogged and then cleared in time with her breathing. Then an ice cube melted somewhere inside her brain and her memories came flooding back.

They had spent six weeks climbing the mountain of velocity after leaving Phobos. Each day the Sun shrank a little as the thrum of the engines continued without letup. Those long weeks had been punctuated by periodic engine shutdowns as empty reaction-mass tanks were jettisoned—Tory envisioned a long string of white spheres extending all the way back to Mars like a string of pearls. They had passed the orbit of Jupiter at the end of the first week, that of Uranus during week two, and Pluto only three days later. Once out of the Solar system, they had continued accelerating until they were moving as quickly outbound as the light sail was falling inward. By the end of the sixth week, *Austria* was two dozen times Pluto's distance from Sol.

For much of the journey, Tory had been too busy to think about the enormous gulf of space between herself and home. The first week she'd done nothing but watch the operation of the booster. Her only breaks had been for meals, quick trips to the head, and catnaps. She'd used her implant to monitor the flow of plasma, the interplay of magnetic fields, and a thousand other parameters. The booster had become a living, breathing entity to her; the steady flow of antiprotons and hydrogen into the reaction chamber were its lifeblood, the network of fiber-optic cables its ganglia.

At the end of a long week Tory had retired to her cabin to sleep the clock around. After that, she'd joined the others in standing the regular watches that Garth insisted on while the engines were operating. When not on watch, Tory repaired software glitches uncovered by the health monitors. The worst of these she shipped to the programmers on Mars and Earth, and the minor problems she repaired herself. Besides watches and software maintenance, she took her turn cooking, cleaning, and performing light maintenance.

None of which explained how it was that she was freezing with her nose pressed up against a piece of frosted glass. Her situation reminded her of a joke she'd once heard: "You know it's going to be a bad day when you wake up lying facedown in the gutter and can't remember how you got there!" Then, as though the thought had been a catalyst, her sluggish brain gave up another memory.

She was in her coldsleep tank in *Austria*'s converted bunk room! She was still puzzling over that fact when a flesh-colored blur entered her field of view. There was a quiet clicking noise from somewhere far off, and her vision suddenly cleared as the glass cover retracted into its recess. Several moisture globules were dislodged by the sudden motion. They floated up and away, confirming what Tory's body had been telling her for the past several minutes: the thrum of the engines was absent and the ship was in zero gravity. She had no opportunity to wonder whether that was good or bad before a haggard Kit Claridge leaned over her.

"How are you feeling?" the doctor asked.

Tory let the words trickle down through her brain as she pondered their meaning. It was only after her strangely lethargic mental processes converted the sounds into words that she thought to wonder the same thing. How *was* she feeling?

There was the cold, of course; but that was an external stimulus, and so it didn't really count. As she tried to swallow, she became aware that her throat and mouth were as dry as Martian dust, and her stomach was tied into a small, hard knot. She became aware of a dull ache that suffused her muscles, and sharper pains coming from the various places where the medical cuffs encircled her limbs. The soles of her feet burned, too. She could think of no reason why that should be.

She took a long rasping breath. "I'm cold," she croaked out.

The doctor's look of concern was transformed into a quick smile. "Hell, who isn't? Here, let me help you out of the tank!"

Kit did something out of Tory's line of sight, and the long cylindrical lid moved up and out of the way. The doctor helped free her arms and feet from the cuffs, then leaned over and lifted her bodily.

"Where's Garth?"

"Up in control catching up on the mail. You're third to be awakened. Eli's last." Kit maneuvered her weightless form to the sanitary compartment as she spoke.

Tory nodded her understanding. The movement caused the liquid in her inner ear to slosh unpleasantly. She wondered whether she should activate her implant, then put it off when another question occurred to her.

"How long?" she whispered. With her throat, a whisper was the best she could manage.

"Five hundred and twelve days," Kit said. "Right on schedule."

"And the alien?"

"A hell of a lot closer than it was, but still nothing to brag about."

"Then we made it!"

The doctor nodded. "We begin decelerating one week from today." She maneuvered Tory's body to the ship's zero-g shower. When they reached it, she anchored herself to a stanchion and pushed Tory inside the closed cubicle. "I've programmed it for a quick warm-up," she explained as she activated the watertight door.

Tory grabbed the railings inside the stall just as a stream of tepid liquid sprayed out of the overhead. The water warmed swiftly as it flowed down her flanks in rivulets and then into the gridwork built into the shower base. A stream of swiftly moving air carried the liquid away.

Tory lifted her head to face the oncoming stream. She opened her mouth and stuck out her tongue, slaking her thirst. Then she went limp and held on to the railings as the life-giving flow chased the cold from her body.

When she finally exited the shower, she found Kit ready with a large, fluffy towel. She wrapped herself in it. After the warm embrace of the water, it was a shock to return to the cold air of the cabin.

"What do you remember?" the doctor asked as she handed Tory a fistful of pills to swallow.

"I remember launching, and the outbound flight."

"Do you remember going into the tank?"

Tory concentrated. It seemed to her that she did remember it, but hazily. She'd been frightened—she remembered that well enough. In her opinion the coldsleep tank looked entirely too much like a coffin. There had been something else, too . . .

When she had arrived in the bunk room, one tank had already been occupied and its top frosted over. As the oldest person on board, Eli Guttieriz had the honor of being first into the tanks and last out.

She remembered Kit ordering her out of her clothes and giving her a fistful of medications to swallow as she floated naked next to her open tank. They had reached cruising speed two days earlier and had shut down the engines. Tory remembered pulling herself down against the soft interior lining as she slipped her feet into the restraints at the base. Kit had helped snap restraints onto her arms. Shortly after that, Tory had felt the sudden prick of a needle, after which she had lost feeling from her neck down. She remembered Kit's explanation that the anesthetic was to allow her to be intubated without discomfort.

"Well, then," Kit had said, smiling down at her patient. "Ready for dreamland?"

"I guess so."

"All right, I'm starting the cycle. You'll find yourself getting sleepy in a minute or so. Meanwhile, try to think of something else."

"Like what?" Tory felt her inhibitions slowly drain away as drugs began to course through her veins.

"Anything at all. Eli took his mind off things by asking if I would share his cabin with him."

"What did you say?"

"I told him that we would talk about it when we woke up."

"And will you do it?"

Kit shone a light in each of Tory's eyes. "I might. It gets lonely out here."

"That it does."

"You could ask the captain, you know."

"Could I?" Her voice had slurred the words as her eyelids grew heavier. How was that possible in zero g?

"It would make things less awkward."

Tory remembered being puzzled as the doctor's voice faded into silence.

The present-day Kit thumped on Tory's bare knee, making her foot jump. "I said, do you remember going into the tank?" She wore a worried expression as she waited for Tory's response. There were those who came out of the tank substantially less intelligent than they'd gone in.

"I remember. We were talking about my asking the captain if he wanted to . . ."

"Wanted to what?" Garth's voice boomed from across the cabin.

Tory found it impossible to be embarrassed with all of the chemicals coursing through her veins. Still, she realized that she ought to be. The doctor covered for her. "Just girl talk, Garth. Nothing to bother command authority."

"How's the patient?"

"She seems to be coming around. It will be a few hours yet before she feels human."

Garth looked at Tory and grinned. "When you feel better, come up to the control room and look at the light sail. It's a hundred times brighter than the last time you saw it."

Tory awoke again and this time knew immediately where she was. She was clipped to the bulkhead in her own cabin, having just slept an indeterminate time. She felt better than she had, which meant that she merely felt lousy. She carefully unclipped and pulled herself to the wash station. There she got her first good look in a mirror.

She grimaced. Her face bore the same haggard look that both Kit's and Garth's had. The gauntness, she knew, was a side effect of coldsleep. A few days of proper diet would fill out her cheeks, but how long would it take to overcome the lingering lethargy?

She unclipped her hairbrush and ran it through her locks. Her hair was just enough longer to confirm that she had been a year and a half in hibernation. As she brushed it forward, she noted that she could now see the ends of her bangs. Making a sour face, she broke out an ugly zero-g hairnet and slipped it on. Then she rummaged in a drawer for her makeup kit and spent another couple of minutes putting on a proper face. She checked her image in the mirror one last time and decided that it would have to do.

She opened the hatch and floated out into the passageway. As she moved, she remembered Garth's arrival in the bunk room while she had been clad in a towel and looking like death warmed over. She also remembered what she and Kit had been talking about, and blushed in retrospect. The memory also got her to thinking about the social arrangements aboard ship.

So far as she knew, everyone had kept to their own cabins for the six weeks they had accelerated into the great black. One reason had been the watch schedule, which had been as effective a chaperon as any teacher at a high school dance. With each of them on duty a quarter of each day, not to mention performing all their other duties, there had been little enough time for a couple to spend time in private. And if Kit had gone to bed with either of the men, she had been extraordinarily discreet about it.

Kit had confirmed that she would be moving in with Eli Guttieriz as soon as he recovered from coldsleep, making the social equation considerably more complicated. She had been right to suggest that it would be less awkward if Tory formed a sexual liaison with the captain. Tory wondered if that was what she wanted.

She prodded her psyche and found no overwhelming objections. There was Ben to consider, of course. A liaison with Garth would lead to awkward questions when she returned home. Still, she'd made no promises, nor had she asked for any. Besides, the chance Ben would remain faithful to her for three long years was nearly infinitesimal.

What about her feelings for Garth? He was certainly an attractive man, and she respected him for the skill he had shown molding four disparate individuals into a team. But that wasn't love. No, any arrangement they made would be one of convenience only. She remembered their conversation in the Aerie, about relationships being based on nothing more than having a warm body to snuggle up to at night. She had to admit that particular reason was a lot more compelling than it had once been. There was something about the immensity of space that drove people to seek reassurance wherever they could.

The only problem lay in how to let Garth know of her interest. After all, she had grown up in a society where forwardness was frowned upon in young ladies. It made no difference that the attitude was a holdover from the days when Mars had been a barren frontier. It was the way Tory had been brought up.

She felt a flash of irritation at herself. She would be a fool to let her inhibitions rule her life for the next three years. They were a long way from home on a dangerous mission, and no one knew what tomorrow would bring. Why shouldn't she seek the companionship of a virile, considerate man? All she really needed was to screw up her courage and make Garth the offer. The worst he could do would be to turn her down.

That, she realized, was what frightened her most. What if she asked and he said no? Was it possible to die of mortification, and if not, was that good? It was a very hesitant Tory Bronson who made her way to the control room.

Garth was strapped into his acceleration couch, reading something on his screen as she drifted up through the open hatch. He caught movement out of the corner of his eye and twisted around to look at her.

"Feel better?"

"Much," she replied. "How long did I sleep?"

"Twelve hours."

She let out a low whistle. "That long?"

"About the same as Kit and I did when we first came out of the tank."

"What about Eli?"

"He was decanted eight hours ago. He's in his cabin, recuperating. I predict that he'll need at least a couple of days to bounce back because of his age."

"And Kit?"

"She's in the infirmary, cleaning things up. Care to hear what's been going on at home since you went to sleep?"

"Sure."

"Well, it seems some enterprising reporter wondered why we launched in secrecy and hired an amateur astronomer to get photos of the probe on its way to Alpha Centauri. When he couldn't find it there, he talked his editor into paying for a sky search. When they found that we were headed toward Tau Ceti, they also found the light sail."

"What happened?"

"The shit hit the ventilator when the news broke. The system council went into emergency session and demanded to know why the vast majority of the councilors hadn't been told. Our friend Minister de Pasqual came close to losing his job. The storm blew over, and for the past year, they've been building an impressive organization to evaluate data as we transmit it. By the way, your friend Ben Tallen has been promoted. He's now the administrator in charge of alien investigations."

"Good for him! Is he still on Mars?"

"Not according to the return address on the dozen or so private messages on file for you in the computer. They were all transmitted from Earth."

"Oh."

"Want to see the light sail?"

"I'd love to."

Garth did something to the controls, and the screen cleared to show a bright spark of blue-white near the now familiar ring of the Tau Ceti nova. Garth was right—it was a lot brighter than it had been. Even so, it was still only a dimensionless point of light, an electric spark silhouetted against a background of black velvet.

Tory stared at it for a long time while she worked up the courage to broach the subject she had come to talk about. Finally, she took a deep breath and plunged ahead.

"Uh, Garth, do you remember what we talked about that night in the Aerie?"

"We talked about many things."

"You were telling me about relationships aboard ship . . ."

"What about them?"

"Are you aware that Kit and Eli are moving in together?"

"I'd be a poor captain if I weren't."

"And you approve?"

"It's none of my business. It will only become my business if they can't get along and it affects their . . . work."

"Well, Kit suggested that things would be less awkward if . . . you know."

He sat up in his acceleration couch and stared at her, unwilling to help her by acknowledging what must be blatantly obvious. She swallowed to regain control of her traitorous voice and tried again.

"What I mean is, would you like me to move in with you?"

To her surprise, he didn't answer immediately. When he finally did, he shook his head slowly. "I don't think it would work."

A sudden flame engulfed her face and ears. She was so surprised that she blurted out, "Why not?"

"Dr. Claridge and Professor Guttieriz may look upon sex as light exercise, but a pair of romantics such as ourselves need something more. I suggest that we fall in love with one another first."

"You can't just fall in love the way you order a new air bottle!"

"Sure you can. The human psyche is a wonderful instrument. Provide the proper stimulus and you always get the proper response."

"What about after the mission?"

"Then we fall *out* of love with each other, if that is what we want. I start slurping my morning coffee, you start leaving your underwear hanging in the sanitary cubicle. Inside a week, we won't remember what the attraction was."

"You're serious, aren't you?"

"Of course," he said. "Take a survey of old married people and see how many of them were in love when they first wed. I think you'll be surprised."

"How do we go about falling in love?"

"Dinner in my cabin with the lights turned low, for starters. I've a bottle of wine that I was saving for when we get our first good look at the alien starship. We'll crack it open and drink to romance. Afterward, we'll sit close together, watch a holo, and you can pretend to laugh at my jokes."

"I'm game if you are."

He bowed as low as he was able from his sitting position. "May I call on milady for drinks this evening?"

She grinned. "I doubt I will be very good company. I have to do a complete software scan."

"Good point. I expect to be somewhat busy myself. What do you say to tomorrow night?"

"It's a date."

"And to seal the bargain?"

She floated toward him and pressed her lips lightly to his. Despite their best efforts, the kiss lacked ardor. When they parted, Van Zandt sighed.

" 'The spirit is willing, but the flesh is weak.' We'll try again later when we're both more rested from the coldsleep."

"You're the captain," Tory replied as she moved to the other acceleration couch. She was both disappointed and exhilarated. It was a decidedly odd frame of mind.

9

"BRING THE TELESCOPE TO FULL MAGNIFICATION," KIT Claridge ordered.

Beside her, Tory moved to comply. The two of them were running an observation program ordered by the scientists on Earth, photographing the region around the light sail in the ultraviolet wavelengths to map the river of plasma that flowed toward the alien craft. There ought to be visible effects where the inbound and outbound plasma streams interpenetrated. With luck, the scientists might be able to estimate how far in front of the light sail the starship was suspended.

"Full mag," Tory reported. "No problems encountered."

"All right. Begin the observation cycle."

It had taken six weeks for *Starhopper* to climb to four percent of light speed, and twice that long to back down again. First they had to halt their outbound flight, then accelerate back toward the Sun as the light sail overtook them. The craft had reached its maximum retreat from Sol at 1034 hours on May 1, 2242, when it achieved an "altitude" of 650.378 light hours. Garth celebrated the occasion by sending a message to Earth claiming the system record for a manned spacecraft. It was indicative of the distances involved that the message would require twenty-seven days to reach Earth.

The two women sat back in their acceleration couches and regarded the starfield in the middle of the screen. The task of mapping the energetic hydrogen was made more difficult by the softly glowing fog that hugged the screen's lower edge. This was spillover from *Starhopper*'s own plasma drive. It would continue to degrade their long-range sensors until they pulled alongside the alien.

A week earlier, Kit had attempted to perform the same experiment. The sail had just begun to show a disk, and the research teams on Earth had asked that they map the plasma flow to get a better idea of the power the aliens were pumping into

77

the interstellar medium. Midway through the hour-long observation, something had gone wrong with the telescope. An unexplained glitch had overloaded the delicate sensors, ruining the data. After reviewing the recordings of that session, Kit had requested that Tory monitor the telescope with her implant to insure that the instrument was working properly.

"Scanners are recording normally," Tory reported.

Kit shrugged. "I can't figure it out then. Maybe I flubbed a switch setting."

"I'll watch for a bit more before going back to my other duties."

"Thanks. I can use the company. I hardly have time to go to the head, let alone engage in some good old-fashioned human interaction."

"I know what you mean."

With the light sail so close, the relatively relaxed work schedule of the initial approach had suddenly gone by the boards. Demands for observations were rising asymptotically. It seemed as though every analyst on Earth had suddenly decided that he must have new data soonest, and the communications delay didn't help. With nearly two months between request and response, they were likely to get a dozen follow-up requests for the same experiment.

"What was that?"

"What was what?" Tory asked. She'd been concentrating on following the software routines and had not been looking at the screen.

"I saw a flash."

"Where?"

"The light sail."

"Are you sure?"

Kit nodded. "It was like a beacon. The image brightened for an instant, and then was gone."

Tory watched for a dozen seconds but saw nothing. She was about to put it down to overwork on Kit's part when it happened again. The flash was too quick to properly register on the human retina, but it seemed to orginate from the center of the light sail.

They watched intently until the flash reappeared thirty seconds later. Tory noted that the telescope was set to study the middle ultraviolet, which meant that whatever was causing the flash was invisible to the unaided human eye.

They watched the phenomenon for several more cycles. It

appeared and disappeared at random. The shortest interval between flashes was ten seconds, the longest a minute and a half.

"What do you think? Are they trying to communicate with
us?"

"Comm laser?" Tory responded. "It's possible. They may
have trouble locking on to us at this range. They must know
we're here. They've been staring directly up our drive flare for
eleven weeks now."

"Weapon?"

That, too, was a possibility. Tory remembered how paranoid
it had seemed when they'd insisted on not including a comm
laser on *Austria* because it would look too much like a weapon.
Suddenly, it didn't seem paranoid at all. "Of course!"

"What?"

Tory indicated the telescope controls with a sweeping gesture.
"What is it we are attempting to do here?"

"We're mapping the ionized hydrogen cloud . . . Oh!"

"Correct. We're coming into range of the laser that's doing
the ionizing! Every time it scans across us, we see a flash. I'll
bet the wavelength is precisely the one that is most efficient at
ionizing interstellar hydrogen."

"No bet. You'd better notify the captain."

Garth Van Zandt stared at the recording of the light sail and
waited for the flash. They had slowed the image down a hundred
times. Even then, it was amazing how quickly the sudden bright-
ness came and went. It was a testimonial to the acuity of the
ship's telescope and the human eye that the two women had seen
it at all.

"Spectrum?"

"Pure monochromatic light," Kit replied, reading off the
wavelength.

The captain grunted his assent. "You nailed it, Tory. It's definitely their ionization laser. We'd best get this news off to
Earth."

"I've already done that. I'm collecting data on power now."

He nodded. "That ought to tell us how close we can approach
without getting fried."

Tory frowned. "I hadn't thought of that. Do you really think
it could be dangerous?"

"Depends on how tightly the aliens have it focused. If we
knew the scan rate, we could use the duration of the flash to
compute the beam spread. In any event, if they're harvesting

hydrogen from across as large a volume of space as we think, they aren't using a flashlight.''

"Why are the flashes so erratic?" Kit asked.

"The beam probably misses us on most passes," Van Zandt responded. "We only see the flash when it scans directly over us.''

"Doesn't that give us the information we need to compute the width of the beam?''

"Does it?''

"Sure," Tory said. "We take the minimum interval between flashes and assume that is the result of our seeing two successive scans. Then we take the maximum interval and compute how many scans we missed. If we assume they scan the beam so that it completely fills the space in front of them, that tells us the maximum size of the beam at our distance from the alien. We then use that data to compute the beam spread.''

"Might work," Garth agreed after several seconds. "I doubt it's quite that easy, however. What if your min or max intervals between flashes change?''

"Then we recompute with the new data. Eventually we'll converge on the real value.''

"All right, set it up.''

"Right!" Tory suddenly got that faraway look that told the others she had activated her implant. To all outward appearances, she had left the room.

"How are we going to approach the alien if the laser turns out to be dangerous?" Kit asked.

Garth stroked his chin. "That could be a problem. Still, I doubt they are scanning all of circumambient space. That would be inefficient. If I were designing their system, I would limit the laser to the volume from which I could sweep up hydrogen. No sense in wasting power on hydrogen they can't harvest.''

"What does that mean?''

"No matter how strong a field they're using to attract the charged ions with, there's a limit to how far they can pull them in at their current speed. The laser is probably confined to a narrow cone directly along their line of flight. If we move to the side, we should be able to get out of their focus. Once Tory tells us the scan rate and the width of the beam, we'll be able to compute the size of the cone they are using . . . I hope.''

"And all we need do is steer clear?''

"That's the idea.''

"What if they can point the laser like a weapon?''

Garth's shrug was Gallic in its expressiveness. "That's what we're here to find out, isn't it?"

No longer was the light sail a distant point of light against the black velvet of the firmament. Over the last several days the alien construct had grown from a tiny disk, to a lighted moon, to an entire world that seemed to hover just beyond the reach of *Starhopper*'s drive flare. Tory estimated the light sail's diameter at 19,987 kilometers from edge to edge—three times the diameter of Mars and two-thirds larger than Earth. As for the sail's overall mass, she could only guess. The true scale of the alien artifact was just beginning to register on her.

"Give me a reading on the plasma density," Van Zandt ordered.

"No change in the last hour."

Austria was submerged in the river of ionized hydrogen that was flowing out of space and onto the surface of the light sail. The plasma density was high enough to affect the focus of the magnetic field in their nozzle assembly. Of late, glowing coronas had begun to appear at various points along the booster. Worst of all, the ion fog had dramatically increased the glare produced by *Starhopper*'s own fountain of plasma, and the suffused radiance of their drive flare had effectively blinded many of their most sensitive instruments.

"Keep monitoring. Advise me the instant there is any change plus or minus."

"Aye, Captain."

Except for hurried breaks for personal hygiene, neither Garth nor Tory had left their stations for the past three days. They ate and slept in rotation, with one of them always awake and manning the controls. Nor were there any of the soft touches or words of endearment they shared off duty; when on the bridge, the captain and his chief engineer were all business. Kit Claridge and Eli Guttieriz were likewise unable to pursue their personal relationship. They were kept busy fulfilling the insatiable demands of the Earthside scientists for observations during the approach. For the first time in the voyage, the communications delay worked in their favor. Had the scientists on Earth been able to observe the approach in real time, their demands would have quickly escalated to the point of overload. As it was, they had to attempt to get all of the observations programmed on Earth a month earlier.

Tory let her attention turn back to the light sail. They were fifty thousand kilometers in front of it, with a closing rate that was little more than an interplanetary walk. They were seven minutes from engine shutdown and had begun a search for the starship that must be somewhere in front of the sail. At this range, however, looking for the manned craft was very much like looking for the proverbial needle in a haystack.

The pattern of light and dark that had been discernible for weeks now stood out in stark contrast on the viewscreen. The sail billowed out as though filled with an invisible wind—as indeed it was. Some parts reflected the blackness of space, while others concentrated the ion glow. The two effects combined to produce moving spokes of light as the sail rotated slowly. If God were ever to build a kaleidoscope for His own use, then it would surely resemble the light sail.

By concentrating, it was possible to make out the points where individual shroud lines attached to the main body of the sail. The attach points were arranged in twelve concentric rings, with shroud lines numbering over a thousand. The lines themselves were invisible, but their arrangement revealed a great deal about the sail's construction. Whatever material made up the sail, its overall strength was little better than tissue paper. This result surprised Tory until she remembered that tissue paper was many thousands of times thicker than even a human light sail. No matter what reasonable thickness she assumed for the sail, the material's strength-to-weight ratio was far beyond anything known to human science.

Of the ionization laser there was no sign. It had been four days since *Austria* had last seen the ultraviolet flash. As Garth had surmised, the laser scanned a narrow cone lying directly along the light sail's flight path; the aliens weren't wasting their precious energy on those portions of the interstellar medium beyond the reach of their electrostatic particle scoop. Once *Austria* left its scan cone, the laser had appeared to go dark.

"Thirty seconds to engine shutdown," Tory reported.

"Make sure the others know that," Garth ordered.

Tory made the announcement, then turned back to the screen. The plan called for them to shut down their engine and drift, allowing the sail to overtake them. The specialists on Earth thought an unpowered craft would appear less threatening than one that rushed directly at the aliens, spewing a fountain of charged particles before it. Tory hoped they were right.

The chronometer in the corner of the viewscreen counted off the seconds. Suddenly, the thrum of power was gone. So, too, was the pull of acceleration. Tory rebounded into her straps. Her stomach did a quick flip-flop, then steadied. On the viewscreen, the luminescent fog from the drive flare began to slowly dissipate, reminding Tory of the slow clearing that follows a Martian dust storm.

"Stand by for a radar pulse."

"Standing by."

The ship's radar had been one instrument blinded by the interaction between the light sail's ion river and *Starhopper*'s drive flare. Garth waited several seconds to allow the fog to clear. When "seeing" conditions had improved sufficiently, he ordered, "Pulse!"

The overhead lights dimmed as Tory funneled maximum power into the forward antenna. The disruption lasted but a moment, and it took less than half a second for a glowing apparition to begin forming on the viewscreen. The object resembled an ancient parachute, except the "canopy" had far less depth to it than any parachute. Perhaps a more apt image, Tory thought, was that of a dinner plate suspended from a spiderweb. The shallow convex shape of the sail was due to its rate of spin, with centrifugal force maintaining its shape. Tory quickly calculated the amount of rotational energy stored in the sail and wondered if that was the aliens' power source.

The shroud lines, invisible at this distance to both eye and telescope, stood out starkly in the wavelength the radar used. They formed a fuzzy conical shape on the screen, the point of which converged ten thousand kilometers in front of the light sail. A tiny dot of light at the cone's apex hinted at a solid object there.

"Magnify!"

The screen was slow to paint this time. Eventually they found themselves staring at the very tip of the shadowy cone. Around the apex was a shape so indistinct that they could tell little beyond the fact that it possessed dimension.

"That's it!" Garth exclaimed.

It was all Tory could do to nod agreement as large globular tears came unbidden to her eyes. The surge of feeling was all the more intense for the speed of its onset. Here were the people who had crossed twelve light-years of emptiness to meet their human counterparts. The alien starship was in sight and all of the speculation was about to end!

* * *

The control room was crowded for the final approach. Garth and Tory continued to work strapped into their couches, while Kit and Eli floated behind them. The two observers had anchored themselves to handy stanchions in an attempt to keep out of the way.

"See anything?" Kit asked.

"Not yet," Tory answered over her shoulder. She had the telescope slowly scanning the point in space where the starship was located. They were closing with the alien craft at a few hundred kilometers per hour, and from a direction well removed from the ionization laser's cone of operation.

"There!" Eli shouted.

"Where?" Garth snapped.

"Lower right-hand quadrant. Just above the edge of the sail."

Tory looked to where he directed. Sure enough, something glinted where there had been no star a few seconds earlier. Coming in from the flank as they were, the sail showed a limb like a planet. Despite their proximity, however, the shroud lines remained invisible to all but the sensors.

"Magnify!"

"Can't. We're at maximum already."

"All right. Keep the scope trained on that spot."

The object on the screen began to take shape slowly. The bright point was transformed over several minutes into a bullet shape with the rounded end pointed directly at the sail. A minute later, the bullet became two shapes—a large cylinder and a smaller sphere.

Garth gave the order to paint the starship. The scanning radar was far less powerful than the single pulse they had used earlier, but more discerning of surface detail. Everyone held their breath and hoped the starship's crew would not interpret the new signal as an unfriendly act.

"How is the microwave link?" Garth asked Eli.

The linguist glanced down at a hand-held monitor. "Going out strong, Captain! Earth will be watching this same scene in another six hundred and thirty hours."

"My God, how large a ship is it?" Kit asked when the radar began to paint the alien vessel's image on the screen. Dimensional information appeared unbidden to answer the question. The central cylinder was slightly more than four kilometers long, with a diameter of one kilometer. Its shape was highly reminiscent of a human Lagrange colony—hardly surprising since both were designed to simulate planetary conditions in space. The shroud lines terminated in the spherical structure at the aft end of the cylinder. Doppler measurements showed cylinder and sphere to be rotating at different speeds. The sphere's movement was synchronized with the twice-an-hour rotation of the light sail, while the cylinder rotated about its axis once each forty-eight seconds.

"How much centripetal force at the periphery?"

"I make it eighty-seven percent of Earth standard," Tory reported.

"That proves they're from an Earthlike world, at least in terms of gravity."

"Not necessarily, Captain," Kit said. "Remember, Saturn's gravitational field isn't much stronger than Earth's. They may be from a gas giant."

"Let's get a surface temperature reading from the hull."

"Infrared radiation peaks at twenty C."

"Still sounds like Earth to me. Still, Kit has a good point. Let's not jump to conclusions."

Just then, the screen switched from radar display back to the view from the ship's telescope. A tiny cylinder lay silhouetted against the black of space just above the limb of the light sail. The resemblance to a Lagrange colony was uncanny. Complex machinery could plainly be seen covering the starship's hull. Some of the machines would be heat-rejection mechanisms, Tory knew; rejecting waste heat to the vacuum of space was a much larger problem than most people realized. Other bits were undoubtedly sensors, while still others might be weapons. Distance and lack of familiarity with Tau Cetian technology made it impossible to be certain of anything.

"Why are there no lights?" Kit wondered aloud.

Until then Tory hadn't realized that the alien cylinder was completely dark. It was dimly illuminated by distant Sol and the glow emanating from the light sail.

"Maybe the ship is a derelict after all."

"Why should there be lights?" Guttieriz asked. "Who is going to see them out here?"

"Whatever the reason," Garth replied, "let's make sure that we're getting pictures of everything."

"Scanning," Tory reported. Through her implant she was aware that a dozen different data streams were wending their way back toward Earth. Each passing second gained humanity several million bytes of additional data concerning the alien craft.

Their concentration on the viewscreen was suddenly broken

by a muted tone. The noise was so ordinary that it took a few seconds to register. Then four sets of eyes were drawn as one to the small symbol that had suddenly appeared in the lower corner of the viewscreen. The icon was that of an old-style telephone, signaling the arrival of a message on the short-range, ship-to-ship communications band. The only problem was that there was but one other ship within six hundred light hours of them . . .

Garth looked sharply at Tory. ''You aren't playing a joke with your implant, are you?''

The look on her face convinced him of her innocence. ''What do we do?'' she asked.

He took a deep breath and reached for the communications control on his instrument panel. ''We answer it.''

2 THE PHELAN

10

THE VIEWSCREEN BROKE UP INTO MULTICOLORED static, then cleared. It took a moment for Tory's eyes to focus on the being who stared out at them.

The alien was covered in dense white fur. Its mouth was buried in a short black muzzle, above which were two large eyes. The eyes showed horizontal slits in place of round pupils. Atop the cranium was a pair of motile ears from which tufts emanated. The ears were carried erect, like a Great Dane's.

Before anyone could respond, the alien opened its mouth and words began to stream forth from an overhead speaker. The words were in accentless Standard. "Ladies and gentlemen, welcome to the Phelan starship *Far Horizons*. We have watched your progress with much excitement. Do you wish to come aboard?"

There was a long silence while Garth regained his composure. "Yes, please," he finally said.

"Very well," said the being in the screen. "Recorders on, and we will transmit approach instructions."

"Recorders on!" Tory announced.

There was a sudden high-pitched keening noise over the comm circuit. It lasted less than a second but signified that considerable information had been received.

"The recording will give you an approach corridor and velocity profile, Captain. We will monitor your progress and guide you back on path should you stray."

"Stray?"

"You must be aware of the laser with which we ionize interstellar hydrogen. It is very powerful. You do not want to encounter it during your approach. The control lines with which we attach our ship to our propulsion device are also a potential hazard. You could severely damage us if you collide with one. It would not do you any good either."

"I can imagine . . ."

"Not to worry, Captain. If you follow our instructions, you will remain quite safe."

"Acknowledged."

The alien turned slightly. The movement, which was vaguely reminiscent of a human being moving to break contact, brought a strangling noise from behind Tory.

"Wait!" Eli Guttieriz shouted.

The being's ears cocked in the direction of the screen. "Is something wrong?"

"We have questions to ask."

"We also, Professor Guttieriz. However, would it not be better to wait until you are safely aboard our ship? Satisfying your curiosity is undoubtedly a matter of many hours."

"How do you know my name? You can't see me!"

Tory glanced at the small repeater screen that showed them what was going out over the commlink. Sure enough, the pickup was still tightly focused on Garth. How *had* the alien known it was Eli who had spoken?

The barely seen white shoulders performed an elaborate shrug. While recognizable, the movement was obviously unsuited to the alien's physique.

"You four have been profiled in broadcasts from Earth, Professor. Since I saw that it was not Captain Van Zandt who had spoken, I assumed that it must be the only other human male aboard your ship."

"Who am I?" Kit asked.

After a moment's hesitation, the alien replied, "Katherine Claridge, Ph.D. and M.D."

"How can you possibly know that?"

"We have a recording of a lecture you gave a few years ago on Mars," the alien replied. "We matched your voice pattern to that in storage."

"Who the hell are you people?"

"My personal name is Faslorn, Doctor. My people are the Phelan. As your scientists have already surmised, we are refugees from the Tau Ceti nova. The ship you see before you is named *Far Horizons*. It is the ark that carried us to safety when our star exploded."

"What is your purpose in coming here?" Garth asked. The question was inane, he thought, but he wanted to get the answer on the official record being transmitted back to Earth.

"That should be obvious, Captain. We come seeking a home to replace the one we lost. We hope that you will allow us to settle near the warmth of your star. We are not beggars; we are prepared to pay for your assistance.''

''In what medium of exchange?''

''There is only one currency that holds its value over interstellar distances. That is knowledge. Aboard this ship we carry the accumulated knowledge of our species. We are prepared to share all we know with humanity if you will allow us to establish a colony in your system. Our requirements in terms of land are quite modest. We need a few thousand hectares on which to grow food and to settle our people, and will be pleased to take land humans consider worthless. I hope you will advise your superiors of what I have told you.''

''How did you know to come here to Sol in the first place?''

The alien made a gesture the significance of which was lost on the humans. ''My ancestors picked up your radio signals some fifty years before they learned that our star was unstable. When it became obvious that our world was doomed, we built this ship and three others. We sent the others to the stars you know as Epsilon Eridani, Epsilon Indi, and Alpha Centauri. *Far Horizons* was assigned Sol. There weren't very many other choices.''

''Only four ships?'' Tory asked. ''Were you so few, then?''

''On the contrary,'' Faslorn replied. ''The population of Phela was twenty percent greater than the current population of your Earth. All but those few on the ships perished in the nova.''

Tory shivered. To think of all those lives snuffed out in a single instant.

''How did you learn to speak our language?'' Eli asked.

Faslorn emitted a sound that was reminiscent of a chuckle. ''We have monitored your communications for most of the time we have been in transit, Professor. Aboard this ship we use the human tongue more than our own. I'm afraid that you will find little use for your specialty here.''

''One thing else—'' Eli said.

The alien interrupted him. ''Please, we will have several weeks in which to learn all about one another. Our immediate problem is to get you safely aboard our ship. Please play the audiovisual and set up for your approach, Captain Van Zandt, and notify us when you are ready to begin the procedure.''

''All right.''

''Faslorn out.''

''*Austria* out,'' Garth replied as the screen went blank.

No one spoke for nearly a minute. Except for the recording

symbol that had replaced the telephone icon on the screen, it would have been easy to convince Tory that what had just transpired was a case of mass hypnosis.

When he had regained control of his thinking, Garth punched for the audiovisual the aliens had sent them. It was a diagram showing the light sail with its two conical zones of danger—one forward and one aft—an hourglass shape into which they must not stray. As they watched, a stylized booster-corvette combination moved slowly toward the cylindrical starship. Glowing alphanumerics showed position and velocity vectors for every moment of the approach. A broad three-dimensional highway of glowing light marked the approach lane. The symbology the aliens were using was right out of the *Space Pilot's Handbook*.

Garth froze the display on the screen. "Can we feed this into the autopilot?"

Tory consulted the raw data in the computer. "No problem. They've followed standard data-base format precisely."

"Then set it up." Garth keyed the display back to life.

The cylindrical starship continued to grow on the screen. At ten kilometers the icon representing the human spacecraft halted and split in two. An alien voice announced that it would be necessary to separate their propulsion and crew modules at that point, leaving *Starhopper* in station-keeping mode until it could be taken under tow. The unseen alien was apologetic, but explained that the big booster would not fit through *Far Horizons*'s ship lock. It also represented too great a safety hazard to be taken aboard the starship.

"Anyone have a problem with separating from the booster?" Garth asked after the short announcement concluded.

"It will take half an hour to unplug everything. The engineers made it possible to separate, but not easy."

"If anything goes wrong, we'll be helpless in there," Eli muttered.

"We're helpless right now," Tory reminded him. "All they need do is shine that laser in our direction."

"Kit?"

"I agree with Tory," the doctor replied. "We came here to learn all we can. Let's get on with it."

The display continued. After separation, the truncated cartoon spaceship moved along a gentle curve toward the forward end of the alien cylinder. There it halted while a rectangular hatch on the front face of the cylinder opened wide and the icon moved inside. The audiovisual ended as the hatch closed again.

Kit was the first to speak. "Does it strike anyone that these people know us entirely too well?"

"What do you mean?"

"They speak our language with absolute precision, they are conversant with our conventions for computer graphics and data storage formats, they imitate both our facial expressions and involuntary gestures. They even have a recording of me lecturing several years ago. Where did they get that, and for God's sake, why did they save it?"

Eli shrugged. "As refugees, it benefits them to know everything they can about us."

"But is it to *our* benefit for them to know so much?"

Tory and Garth were alone in the control room again. Garth had shooed the two others back to their cabins and made them strap down as a precaution. The accelerations they were using during the approach were moderate, but he didn't know when he might have to throw the ship into a violent maneuver.

Where most objects in space show a sharp demarcation between sunlight and shadow, the cylindrical craft glowed all over, as though from some inner light. The effect was due to one side being illuminated by a wan Sol while the other reflected the electric-blue sheen emanating from the light sail. The ship was sheathed in glowing plasma. Streamers of Saint Elmo's fire hundreds of kilometers long danced up and down the shroud lines. The effect was surrealistic as the humans slowly drifted toward their rendezvous point.

As the cylinder rotated about its long axis, they were treated to an ever changing panorama. The hull had the cluttered look of a junkyard. As Tory watched each new bit of alien technology come into view, she was reminded of a trip to the Olympus Museum of Science and Technology when she was sixteen.

The museum had featured a retrospective on humanity's conquest of the air, and the centerpiece of the exhibit had been an ancient bomber borrowed from the Smithsonian in New Washington. As Tory walked beneath the huge wing of the old aircraft, she'd been struck by the number and variety of objects protruding into the airstream. Having just finished a class in high-school physics, she was aware of the need for streamlining. Whatever function these bumps and protrusions had served must have been important, or else the designers wouldn't have compromised their creation so. Yet she could think of no function they might serve.

So it was with the Phelan starship. Each mechanism on the outer hull obviously had a purpose of some kind. Precisely *what* purpose, no one could say. In spots the alien cylinder looked as though it had been infested with a plague of piping. Other regions were swept as clean as a Martian plain after a dust storm. What function did those interlocking crosses of black and silver serve? Or the oversize metal Christmas tree? Or the small glass spheres jutting outward on thin stalks? There were many hatchlike openings in the hull. Were these access ports used during the ship's construction, or sally ports ready to spew forth fighter craft to do battle with humanity's small space navy?

"Impressive, isn't it?" Garth asked. Tory turned her head to find him watching her.

" 'Daunting' is more like it."

"Oh, I don't know. We probably could do as well if we had to."

"Are you suggesting that we could build *that*?" She gestured at the screen.

"Why not? If we knew decades in advance that the Sun was going to nova, who knows what we might build?"

"I admire your optimism."

"They aren't that far ahead of us. If they were, we wouldn't be able to recognize their machinery at all. As it is, our two species are at surprisingly comparable levels of development."

Tory laughed. "So just because the damned thing is a kilometer in diameter and four kilometers long doesn't hide the fact that it's only a Starship Mark I?"

He reached across the divide between the acceleration couches to caress her arm. "Precisely, love. Don't let them overawe you. Remember, the eyes of a skeptic see more than those of an acolyte. They put their pants on one leg at a time."

She tried to visualize a Phelan putting on a pair of pants and realized that she didn't know enough about their anatomy to make an informed judgment. She had no idea what a Phelan looked like from the neck down. Still, Garth's point was well taken. She was a professional observer on this trip. It was necessary that they all keep an open mind and a slightly jaundiced eye if their information was to be of use to the people at home.

"Range and velocity check!" Garth said, signifying that the time for philosophical discussions had passed.

"Five kilometers distance, down to fifty kilometers per hour approach speed," Tory answered after consulting three separate instruments. It would be a tragedy for the starship to cross twelve light-years of emptiness only to end in a traffic accident this close to the Sun.

As they closed to three kilometers and made directly for the front end of the cylinder, Tory noticed something that hadn't been visible before. Suspended nearly a kilometer in front of the cylinder was a much smaller sphere than the one behind. The new sphere was a dull ebon that matched the blackness of space. Nor did it provide much of a radar return. Extending forward from the sphere was a thin conductor with a highly negative electrical charge. This, then, was the device that swept up ionized hydrogen after the laser excited it. Tory reported her discovery to Garth.

"That sphere must be where they house the laser," he said. "It has to be vibration-isolated from the rest of the ship if they're going to have any kind of pointing accuracy. What better place to put it than suspended from a cable held taut by the ship's deceleration?"

To confirm Van Zandt's guess, Tory checked the surface temperature of the sphere. Sure enough, it was radiating considerable heat to space. The black coating gave the radiation signature a pure "black body" distribution, and made it likely that the sphere was the heat-rejection device for the ionization laser.

"Velocity?" Garth asked as *Far Horizons* swelled to fill the screen. No longer were they approaching another vessel. The starship was now a planet-sized object hanging above them, poised to crash down on the unwary.

Tory announced their velocity and the attitude-control jets hissed twice to further slow the ship. She held her breath as they crossed in front of the starship. The forward face of the great cylinder was as cluttered as its flanks.

"There's the ship lock."

In front of them was the opening in the starship's hull. The port looked just as it had in the aliens' audiovisual. What hadn't been obvious was the proximity of the ship lock to the cable from which the laser sphere was suspended.

"Tight fit," Tory muttered.

Garth agreed and wondered aloud at the level of energy being fed to the ionization laser.

"Brush that cable and we're liable to find out . . ."

Of necessity, the lock had been placed close to the giant ship's axis of rotation. To do otherwise would have made it nearly impossible to dock with the rotating cylinder. *Austria*'s screens went momentarily blank as the hatch opened to reveal a brightly lit interior. They regained their sight as the light-amplification circuits adjusted for the sudden brilliance, but there was little to see of the starship's interior save for the brightly lit, cavernous compartment beyond.

"Eli!"

"Yes, Garth."

"Tell Earth that they're about to lose contact."

"I already have. I don't know whether they heard me. The plasma density is wreaking havoc with my signal-to-noise ratio."

"Tell them again," the captain ordered, "and keep telling them until we're aboard the alien ship."

"Aye, sir."

Garth halted *Austria* with two quick bursts from the attitude-control jets, then waited for the open port to rotate into line with their prow. Thirty seconds later, with the rectangular port sweeping ponderously toward them and the axis cable but a few tens of meters over their heads, Van Zandt twisted his control stick again. This time a long burst from the jets sent them drifting forward. *Austria*'s nose turned white as it drifted across the threshold and into the lighted interior. Soon, the whole corvette had passed through the open port.

"Damn!"

"What's the matter?"

"There's not enough room in here to rotate the ship. I'm just going to have to let her flop down onto the deck."

"There can't be much spin gravity this close to the axis."

"We're still liable to bend something. Can't be helped, I guess."

With that, he fired another burst to kill their forward velocity. A gentle hand seemed to grip *Austria*, pulling it toward the bright blue deck that made up one side of the compartment. The landing was more sensed than felt. Only when she found herself floating into her straps did Tory realize that they had grounded against the starship's curved deck.

She switched the aft view onto the main viewscreen just in time to see the oversize hatch swing ponderously into place. The black firmament became a ribbon, then a string, then non-existent. Things that happened in vacuum did so in total silence. Even so, Tory wondered if the sound she heard in her mind was that of a cell door slamming shut.

* * *

Faslorn watched the strange craft float through the open hatch and then settle down. He had to admit that the humans seemed to know their business; the approach had been as smooth as anything a Phelan pilot could accomplish. He wondered if the computer had been allowed to control the ship, or whether Van Zandt had been flying it himself. He suspected the latter. The human psychologists aboard had spent generations refining their picture of the human psyche. Soon the accuracy of their deductions would be put to the test.

With the human ship safely aboard, Faslorn ordered the hatch closed. The order was passed on just as the technician analyzing the communications signal the humans were broadcasting made her report. Their signal was in the millimeter band, with a respectable bandwidth. Faslorn wondered why they didn't use the much more capable laser links that had given his eavesdroppers so many problems over the years. He resolved to ask them when he had the chance.

"Rosswin."

"Yes, Faslorn," his second-in-command responded over the ship intercom.

"Announce to all members of the crew that the humans are aboard. The masquerade begins now. Make that a Prime Message and demand acknowledgments from all sector heads."

"That message has already gone out. Acknowledgments are coming in now."

"What about our preparations to receive the humans?"

"Complete. I just finished checking them myself."

"You are certain?"

The return gesture was a human affirmative rather than the flexed-arm stance that served the same purpose among Phelan. "We have profiles on each of the crew and predictions of how they will react to any predictable stimulus, both singularly and in groups. They will be under full observation while they are aboard, and we will update our behavior predictions in real time."

"What about our special need?"

"It's far too early to make a recommendation, of course. I suggest that we concentrate on the two females for the time being. The biologists think they may be inclined to be more sympathetic to our cause than the males."

Faslorn signed off and then moved to the high-speed lift that would take him up three levels to the axis transport system.

From there he would move to the forward end of the ship and the hangar where the humans had landed.

Excitement coursed through his two hearts as he hurried to the waiting lift. This was what he had trained for all of his life. He would soon know if all that training had been in vain.

11

NEITHER TORY NOR GARTH MOVED FOR A LONG minute after *Austria* came to rest. The reality of being inside the alien starship was too overpowering. Months of mental preparation hadn't prepared them for the storm of feelings that accompanied their canted view of the surrounding white walls and blue deck.

Garth was the first to recover. He used his armrest controls to cycle through the views from the various hull cameras. They showed *Austria* surrounded by a compartment shaped like a wedge of cheese. At the apex ran a complex structure of tubes and beams akin to the climbing gyms popular with Martian children. Opposite the maze lay the spongy blue covering where *Austria* had come to rest. In several views it was possible to see places where their ship had sunk a meter deep into the covering.

"What do you suppose *that* is?" Tory asked, pointing to the complex framework running along the starship's spin axis.

"Probably the keel. Trace it far enough back and you'll find the light sail anchored to it."

With *Austria* lying on her side, their acceleration couches seemed attached to the aft wall of the control room. Van Zandt unstrapped and floated to a formerly vertical bulkhead that was now a deck listing at an angle twenty degrees from horizontal. Tory followed Garth's example and soon the two of them were balanced on the balls of their feet, flexing their leg muscles to get the kinks of long inactivity out.

"Five percent standard," Garth estimated the pull of local spin gravity.

Tory consulted the ship's computer and shook her head. "You're high. Two-point-three percent."

A shiver suddenly ran through the ship. A moment later, the faint sound of rushing air could be heard beyond the hull. Within seconds, expansion fog began to swirl across the view from the outside dorsal camera. *Austria*, accustomed to the vacuum of space, creaked and groaned as pressure built up around her.

"Atmosphere check," Garth said as the hurricane noises died away.

"Pressure: one-point-oh-two standard. Temperature: minus one hundred degrees and warming. Composition: nitrogen seventy-four percent, oxygen twenty-four percent, helium one percent, carbon dioxide point-oh-five percent. The rest are trace gases. It's too cold for water vapor to register, of course."

"Not precisely what we're used to, but close enough for government work," he replied. "All right. Safe all propulsion systems."

"Safed."

"All radars off."

"Off."

"Computer power to internal . . ." The safing procedure took a few more minutes. "Shall we go find Eli and the doctor?" Garth asked when it was over.

"After you," Tory responded.

The two of them clambered aft through the axis passageway. Spin gravity, though minuscule, was strong enough to disorient them as they moved through passageways made strange by the starboard list.

They found Kit and Eli in the wardroom. Garth reported Tory's analysis of the surrounding air. Kit concurred, having just run her own evaluation.

"So breathing won't be a problem?"

"Not due to chemical composition, anyway. I can't say the same about microbes, unfortunately. I'm afraid we don't have many tools to evaluate that threat."

"*Is* there a threat? I thought current theory didn't allow for the possibility of extrasolar microbes living off human beings."

"It doesn't. Care to bet your life on the theory being right?"

"I see your point. What can you do?"

"I suppose I can culture skin grafts from each of us, expose them to the local air and water, then check for allergic reactions and other problems. It's crude, but might be effective in identifying hazards."

"How long to run tests?"

"A week, maybe two."

"You can't do it any faster?"

"Not if I'm going to prove Tau Cetian biochemistry is safe. The skin tests would only be preliminary anyway. To do it right, one of us should live outside for a few weeks while the rest of us stay bottled up in here. If our human guinea pig doesn't die in thirty days, maybe it's safe out there . . . maybe not.''

"And that's your medical recommendation?''

"Actually, no,'' Kit said. "I recommend that we don't worry about microbes.''

"Why not?'' Eli said. From the pinched expression he wore, he didn't relish the tack the conversation had taken.

"Because cross-species infection works both ways. We're as big a threat to the Phelan as they are to us. Bigger, in fact. We're merely risking our individual lives. They are risking a large fraction of what is left of their whole species. Obviously, if they thought there was danger, they wouldn't have let us aboard at all.''

"You hope.''

Kit nodded. "I hope.''

"All right. Tory, log my decision, please. Eli, what is our communications status?''

"We're off the air, Captain. I shut down as soon as we came aboard. All I was getting back were reflections. Even if we were penetrating the hull, we lost our lock the moment we lost the guide stars.''

"Right,'' Garth responded. "We'll have to see about getting back on the air.''

"Do you think the Phelan will help us?''

"All we can do is ask. Any movement out there yet?'' Garth gestured toward the wardroom viewscreen.

"Nothing.''

"Temperature?''

"Minus forty and still warming,'' Tory reported.

"Shall we call our hosts and see what they have planned?''

Guttieriz manipulated the intercom. He had to stretch to reach the controls. All it took was one depression of the attention key to receive an immediate response.

"Yes?'' a Phelan said from the depths of the screen. Tory wasn't sure, but she thought it was Faslorn.

"Dr. Claridge has expressed some concern about the possibility of disease.''

"You may rest easy, Captain. Our biochemistries are sufficiently different to preclude any contagion.''

"You're sure?''

"Quite sure.''

Kit Claridge gave the rest of them an "I told you so" look, but said nothing.

"Then we're ready to leave the ship."

"Excellent. Please wait a few more minutes, Captain. We need more time to heat the air in the hangar."

"When shall we venture out?"

"We will meet outside your ship in ten minutes. I will then guide you to our administration center—what you would call our 'city hall.' "

"We are honored. I'm sure you must have many other duties aboard this ship."

"I have waited my entire life for this moment. It is you humans who do me the honor."

With *Austria* lying on her side, the only airlock not obstructed was a small one normally used for maintenance. After ten minutes that seemed like ten hours, the four of them made their way through canted corridors to the port side of the ship. Garth opened the circular hatch manually and levered himself into the maintenance tunnel beyond. The other three watched as he worked himself up the long sloping tunnel like a mountain climber negotiating a rock chimney. It took a few seconds for him to wrestle the outer door open. Tory's ears popped as he did so, and she was suddenly engulfed by a blast of frigid air. They crowded around the tunnel as Garth climbed out into the pure white light from the hangar bay, then disappeared.

"Who wants to go next?"

"I will," Tory said with more courage than she felt. She slipped into the tunnel and reached the open outer door fifteen seconds later. Once there, she gingerly clambered out onto the perch formed by the open hatch. She was a full five meters above the blue-covered deck. Foreshortened, Garth Van Zandt squatted below her, gazing intently beneath *Austria*.

"What's the matter?" she yelled.

He glanced up at the sound of her voice. "Nothing. Just checking for damage."

"Find any?"

"Nope. This stuff seems to have cushioned us nicely."

She glanced around for handholds and found none. "How do I get down from here?"

He grinned up at her. "Jump!"

She felt chagrined at being reminded that a five-meter drop in a two-percent gravity field was nothing to fear—and after she'd lived all those years on Phobos! Even on Mars such a drop was the equivalent of jumping off a single-story house on Earth. This close to *Far Horizons*'s axis of rotation, they were nearly in microgravity. It was a measure of Tory's mental state that none of these rationalizations did anything to calm her nerves.

She dangled her feet over the edge, sought purchase with her hands, and pushed off. She hung for long seconds in the air before landing feet first on the cushioned deck with flexed knees. The precaution proved unnecessary. The blue covering proved to be thick and yielding, and she barely noticed the impact.

"Some sort of low-density foam," Garth responded to her unvoiced question at finding herself standing ankle deep in the stuff. He returned to peering beneath *Austria*.

"What are you doing?"

"Wondering if the four of us can right her in this gravity field."

"Don't think so. Even at two percent, we're talking a couple of tons of weight and a full hundred tons of inertia."

"Perhaps we could roll her over," he said, "at least far enough to clear the midship's airlock."

"Maybe," she said, her tone doubtful.

Just then Kit Claridge appeared in the open hatchway above them. She stood precariously on the ledge before stepping off. Like Tory, she seemed to hang forever in midair. She landed on her rounded posterior and quickly bounced up again, grinning.

"Not very dignified," Tory commented.

"But fun. Where are our hosts?"

"They haven't shown up yet. Maybe they're waiting for all of us to get here."

Less than a minute later, Eli Guttieriz joined them. As he picked himself up, a hatch opened in the far bulkhead. Tory could have sworn it hadn't been there a moment earlier.

The being who entered moved toward them with the scuttling motion of an Earth crab. It was, Tory realized, the motion any quadruped would take moving in low gravity. Except the Phelan wasn't a quadruped. Or rather, he was one only in that he used four of his limbs to move. There were two other limbs, however, for a total of six. It made him look like one of the many-armed Hindu or Shinto gods.

Like a human, the Phelan was axially bisymmetric, with a torso from which various appendages sprouted. The triangular head was mounted on a long, flexible neck that gave every impression of allowing him to look directly behind. The motile

ears were constantly moving, as though scanning their surroundings. The thin torso was topped by a wide set of shoulders
atop a second, somewhat narrower set. Two small, nimble arms
were suspended from the upper shoulders, while the second set
of shoulders was situated about where the bottom of a human's
rib cage would be. The lower pair of arms was long and heavily
muscled. Faslorn used these intermediate limbs along with his
stumpy legs to move in a knuckle walk like an ape or a chim-
panzee.

Faslorn quietly spread all four of his hands with his palms up
in a gesture of welcome. In so doing, he displayed his various
sets of fingers. There were six fingers on each hand, with two
opposable thumbs outboard of four long fingers. The gesture
also displayed the fact that the upper Phelan arms had two elbow
joints and a wrist joint. One of the elbows operated backward.
The arrangement allowed Faslorn to extend his arms in a motion
reminiscent of a scissor jack.

The Phelan's body was covered with a soft white down that
wasn't feathers, but wasn't fur, either. Tory filed a mental request to ask to inspect that marvelous pelt when she knew the
aliens better. Black patches were arrayed across Faslorn's body,
seemingly at random. His clothing consisted of a pair of shorts
and an equipment harness, to which was pinned the gold comet
of a spaceship captain. The insignia was identical to the one on
Garth's collar, making Tory wonder whether the costume was
native to the Phelan or merely an attempt to conform to human
ideas of dress.

For a long minute, humans and Phelan regarded each other.
The gulf between them was far larger than the three meters of
cold air that separated them. It consisted of all the developments
that had taken place during six billion cumulative years of separate evolution. Not for the first time, Tory wondered if there
was a universal principle that allowed for two races so alike
physically, a mere twelve light-years apart, at practically the
same moment in history. It seemed too big a coincidence to
shrug off. Perhaps, she thought, it merely seemed a coincidence, like the seeming coincidence that lunar eclipses on Earth
only happen when the Moon is full. Whatever the underlying
phenomenon that had resulted in Phelan and human living
so close to one another, she looked forward to learning all
about it.

No one spoke. It was as though they had each silently agreed
to savor the moment. In a way, both species were losing their

virginity. Never again would either meet an alien intelligence for the first time. Tory felt a hot, stinging sensation as tears began to form. Nor was she alone. A quiet sniff from Eli Guttieriz proclaimed that he, too, was having difficulty controlling himself.

Faslorn was the first to speak. "I do not know whether you appreciate how much your presence means to us aboard this ship. We have studied you humans for all of our lives. To actually meet you at last . . ." The too perfect voice subsided into inaudibility.

"We feel much the same way," Garth said.

"Do you truly?"

"To meet other intelligent beings has been a dream with us for half a thousand years."

"It has been one much longer with us," Faslorn replied. "In fact, our ancestors were contemplating ways to contact you humans even before Tau Ceti went nova."

"Were they?"

"I must admit," the alien said with the closest his physiology would allow for a smile, "that they hadn't contemplated making the journey in person. Before we enter the habitat proper, is there anything I can do for you?"

"Our ship." Garth said. "Can it be righted?"

"Righted?"

"Set erect on its landing jacks."

"Of course," Faslorn said. "I will have the orders issued. Also, you will be interested to know that we are preparing to take your power module in tow."

"How?"

"You may find the operation interesting. I have arranged for you to observe it when it takes place tomorrow. Is there anything else?"

"Communications. We're currently off the air. Earth will be getting worried."

"Our technicians are working on the problem. The difficulty lay in our not knowing how you were communicating with your base. We weren't able to arrange a substitute in advance."

"We use a beam of coherent microwaves—" Eli began.

"Yes, we became aware of that as you came aboard. We are setting up a maser with the same frequency distribution. You should be back in contact within the hour."

"Excellent."

"Also, we will be sending our own messages of friendship now that you are aboard."

"Why didn't you do that months ago?" Eli asked.

"We thought it best to wait for your arrival, Professor Gutieriz. Come, let us go where there is more heat and gravity."

Faslorn led them toward the hatch in the bulkhead. The humans trailed him in a small, compact knot. Once outside the hangar bay, he directed them to a small lift. It was a tight fit, but they all managed to crowd inside. The door closed and the lift began to move. Their weight started to increase almost immediately.

The first thing Tory noticed after the lift door closed was Faslorn's smell. The odor wasn't unpleasant, just different. It reminded her of a combination of cinnamon and paint thinner, and she was surprised that she hadn't noticed it before. Perhaps the air in the hangar deck had been too cold; or else, coming from storage tanks, it had been purged of telltale traces of the starship's builders.

The next thing she noticed was that her implant had lost touch with the computer in *Austria*'s hold. The loss-of-signal warning sounded silently in her skull the moment the door closed. Garth noticed her pained expression and asked what was wrong.

"My implant. It just went off line."

Faslorn, who had taken up position in front of Tory, demonstrated the flexibility of Phelan vertebrae by turning his head completely around. She found herself looking into two dark eyes.

"The hangar walls are impervious to radio signals, Miss Bronson. Is this a problem?"

"It causes me to lose contact with *Austria*'s computer," she explained.

"I confess we have nothing like your implants and do not, yet, understand how the device functions."

"No secret there," she replied. "An implant is just a particularly wideband radio transceiver with a direct mind interface."

Faslorn emitted a sound unlike any they had previously heard. Whether it signified humor, distress, or something else, Tory had no idea. "An unavoidable pitfall of studying your race from afar is that our information comes from entertainment programs. We are forced to infer a great deal from very little solid information. We have seen your actors simulate implant use, of course, but have been frustrated by the lack of hard data."

Eli Guttieriz frowned. "I shudder at the impression you must have of us if holovision is your primary source of information."

"You would be surprised how much usable information is buried in such a broadcast, Professor. Unfortunately, very little is of the hard, technical variety. Miss Bronson, would you consider it forward of me to ask questions concerning your implant?"

"Go ahead."

"This loss of signal. Did you suffer mental anguish? Disorientation?"

"Not at all. It was more like walking from a noisy room into a silent one. A minor nuisance, no more."

"Yet disorientation can occur."

"Sure, but only when transmission delay causes an implant to fall out of sync with its base computer. Usually if you stay within a hundred kilometers of your source, there's no problem."

Faslorn's head bobbed up and down in a good imitation of a human nod. "Then implant transmissions are never placed on the satellite feeds?"

"Of course not. The time delay involved in getting the signal out into space and then down again would cause a user's eyes to cross."

"Would you be willing to explain the human-computer interface to our scientists? Perhaps they can duplicate the signal so that we can place you back into contact with your ship."

"I'll do better than that," she replied. "I'll have *Austria*'s computer print out the interface specs later."

"That would be most kind of you."

Faslorn turned to face front just as the lift came to a halt. The ride had taken the better part of a minute, yet spin gravity still hadn't risen to the level they had calculated for the starship's outermost deck. As the lift doors retracted, they found themselves facing a large compartment with more than a hundred aliens arrayed in two groups in front of the lift doors. The smell of cinnamon and paint thinner was suddenly overpowering, and there were other smells as well. Besides the machinery odor common to spacecraft, there were less identifiable fragrances—thousands of aromatics that had developed on a world far from Earth, the by-product of an entire alien biosphere.

Tory paid not the slightest attention to the impending olfactory overload. Beyond the waiting aliens was a transparent wall, and beyond, an artificial world.

As every member of the crew had commented at one time or another, *Far Horizons* bore an uncanny resemblance to a human Lagrange colony. Like the big colonies that orbited in the gravitationally stable points in the Earth-Luna system, the starship was a vast hollow cylinder that had been spun on its axis to produce an artificial gravity field. The ends of the cylinder had then been sealed and a tiny replica of the Phelan home world built inside it.

The compartment in which they found themselves was high up in the forward end cap of the great cylinder—the end farthest from the light sail. Their vantage point gave them a panoramic view of a tubular green-gold world. Overhead at the cylinder's axis of rotation was a glowing tube of light. It glowed with an illumination more orange than that of Sol, but more yellow than photographs she had seen of the prenova Tau Ceti. The sun tube had to surround the thrust keel they had seen in the hangar bay—but then, Tory realized, there was no reason why an artificial sun couldn't be hollow.

Half a kilometer below the sun tube in every direction lay the artificial terrain that hugged the inner walls of the kilometer-wide cylinder. There were undoubtedly numerous decks below the "farmland," yet the cumulative volume of all such decks must be but a small percentage of the vast cavern that was the ship's habitat. On a planet the human eye sought out the natural bound of the horizon, allowing the brain to put things into perspective. Here there was no horizon, only a gently rising landscape where the details grew smaller with distance until eventually they were lost in the radiance of the sun tube.

Tory raised her eyes to follow the sun tube to where it disappeared into the far end cap some four kilometers distant. Twin rivers gushed from the far end cap just outboard of the sun tube, then fell in matching spiral waterfalls until they disappeared into a cloud of white spray a quarter-kilometer above the habitat floor. Twin rivers emerged from that spray and meandered across the curved surface of the cylinder walls until, having negotiated the full length of the ship, they turned around and headed back. Tory let her gaze follow the course of the nearer river, but the mouth was lost in the distance. Presumably, it entered the far cylinder wall at its base and was then pumped back to the spin axis to begin the long fall again.

From the river, Tory turned her attention to the fields. She found herself looking down on a miniature world of neat hexagonal farms interspersed with villages laid out in six-pointed stars. She remembered the six fingers on each of Faslorn's hands and smiled. The Phelan had learned to count on their fingers just as humans had; as a result, they used a base-twelve numbering system.

The scale of the ship made it difficult to take in everything at once. But by focusing on a single spot, Tory found that she could make out details on an ever decreasing scale. She focused for a moment on a bend in the meandering river where it reflected the yellow fire of the glow tube. She continued her scan, pulling her gaze toward the spot directly beneath her vantage point. She found herself gazing down on a footpath that connected two villages, each composed of several beehive shapes painted in contrasting colors. Midway between the two villages was a stream spanned by a footbridge that would have been at home in a Japanese formal garden.

As she watched, a foreshortened pedestrian strolled onto the bridge and moved rapidly toward the nearer village. In their native gravity, the Phelans' gait was smooth and natural. It reminded her of the knuckle walk of the great apes, or possibly a human being who is especially skilled at moving about on crutches. Yet no human being on crutches moved so quickly while carrying such a load in his extra pair of arms.

Faslorn let them drink in the breathtaking beauty of the view for nearly a minute before booming out, "Ladies and gentlemen of Earth. We welcome you to our home. We hope you will do likewise for us."

12

"SPECTACULAR!" KIT CLARIDGE MARVELED WITHout taking her eyes from the panorama. "Is this what the Phelan home world looked like?"

"It is an idealized rendition. Our ancestors wanted to remind future generations of what had been lost."

"A spectacular reminder," Garth said.

"To those of us born aboard this ship, Phela is but a series of images in our data banks. This . . ." Faslorn moved his oddly jointed arms in an all-inclusive gesture toward the little world beyond the glass, "is all the home we have ever known."

"It's truly beautiful," Tory said.

"Thank you." Faslorn gestured toward the waiting throng of Phelan. "Come, let me present my shipmates . . ."

A Phelan stepped forward at a gesture from Faslorn, moving stiffly. There were wide streaks of gray in its fur, and its eyes lacked the shiny black sheen of the others'. The overall impression was one of great age.

"Captain Van Zandt, I present Rosswin, my chief adviser. He is our acknowledged expert on your race and its works."

The Phelan extended his six-fingered hand to grasp Garth's. The handshake had all of the formality of a treaty being signed. "I look forward to many hours of enjoyable conversation, Captain."

"As do I, Rosswin. May I present my crew?" Garth introduced Tory, Kit, and Eli Guttieriz in turn. The rest of the introductions followed this pattern. First Faslorn would introduce a Phelan, then Garth would return the honor. Tory sensed a formalism behind the ceremony that went beyond mere politeness. It was almost as though she were a performer in an ancient, stylized ballet.

The routine was interrupted several introductions later when a female stepped forward at a gesture from Faslorn. As among humans, Phelan females tended to be smaller than their male counterparts. The other differences were subtle, with few of the outward sexual differences so apparent among humans. Or rather, none of the differences so apparent *to* humans. The differences between Phelan male and female were undoubtedly as noticeable to them as were bulging biceps and bust lines among *Homo sapiens*.

"Miss Bronson. I wish to present Maratel. She will be your personal guide while you are with us."

"Hello, Maratel," Tory said, holding out her hand.

"Miss Bronson," the alien replied in a voice whose timbre matched that of Tory's own.

"Please, call me Tory."

"I am honored, Tory. I hope we will become great friends."

"So do I."

The next Phelan to step from the crowd turned out to be a medical specialist and Kit Claridge's personal guide. Then Garth and Eli Guttieriz were each introduced to their respective guides. Finally, with Phelan ranks and names buzzing in every head, Faslorn signaled an end to the greetings.

"What now?" Garth asked as the crowd began streaming toward an opening to their right.

"We have arranged a welcoming banquet for you, Captain. That is one custom that our two cultures have in common."

The small clump of humans and Phelan followed the crowd. Beyond the bulkhead, a large compartment had been arranged with a table on a raised dais fronting several others that had been arrayed in parallel rows. It was a scene familiar to generations of public speakers and others who frequented the rubber-chicken circuit.

The Phelan conducted the humans to the dais and the head table. Tory found herself seated next to Maratel, with Eli Guttieriz's guide to her left. The chairs in which she and her shipmates sat were human standard designs, but the Phelan balanced on tubular racks that looked decidedly uncomfortable until one noticed how well they intertwined with the Phelan joint structure. As soon as everyone settled down, groups of Phelan entered the hall with pitchers of dark crimson liquid. They moved among the diners, stopping to fill long-stemmed, low gravity goblets before moving on. A waiter reached around Tory's left arm to fill her glass, and the action caused her to drop her attention to the table setting. It was, she realized, a perfect rendition of the place settings found in swank restaurants. At each plate were several forks, two types of knives, and spoons in three sizes. All the flatware appeared to have been carved from crystal. The plates, cups, and saucers had floral designs around the edges, although the flowers were like none Tory had ever seen before. She picked up the small plate normally used for bread. It massed but a few grams and was constructed of a material that seemed neither metal, nor porcelain, nor plastic.

"What's this made of?"

Maratel glanced down at the plate. "I lack the vocabulary to give the proper chemical name. However, it is cast from the same material that is used in our light sails."

Two positions to Tory's right, Garth overheard the comment and began a close examination of his own crockery. Meanwhile, Tory put the plate down and gazed out across the hall. Those at the lower tables were engaged in their own conversations as they ignored the head table. Still, she caught occasional surreptitious glances. She wondered if the Phelan had been taught that it is impolite to stare.

"I am struck by how much this reminds me of home," she told Maratel. "I presume that is no accident."

The female Phelan's chuckle was very human. "You are correct in your presumption. We have copied this from one of your old movies. I can find out which one if you are interested."

"It isn't necessary. Why have you gone to all of this trouble for us?"

"Because this is the most important day in the history of our species since the nova. Also, we thought familiar surroundings would aid in calming your natural apprehension toward us. Have our analysts erred in their reading of the human psyche?"

Tory lifted the smallest of her forks and let the light play across its surface. Every detail was perfect. The three carefully sculpted tines flowed smoothly into the shank, and then down to the lavishly detailed handle.

"No, you haven't erred."

Tory raised the wineglass to her nose and sniffed. The red liquid inside had a definite alcohol smell to it. She lifted it to her lips and sipped. It turned out to be a fairly good imitation of a rosé. As she experimented with her wine, she listened to Eli talking to Faslorn.

"Phela? That was your world orbiting Tau Ceti?"

"As I'm sure you must realize, Professor, most of our names have been chosen for ease of pronunciation in your language. In our own language, Phela is [snort] and we ourselves are the [snort wheeze]."

Guttieriz's trained ears pricked up at the sudden alien phonemes. "Quite a difference."

"We will be glad to teach you if you like, although I'm afraid you will find it a difficult language to learn."

"Of course I want to learn as much as I can," the linguist said. "Ever since you came on the intercom speaking perfect Standard, I've been feeling a bit useless. I'll want to speak to your people in their own language for my studies."

"You may, of course, Professor," Faslorn replied, making a strange gesture. "However, they all speak Standard as well as I do."

"*All* of them?"

Tory made a mental note of Faslorn's gesture. That, she surmised, was what a Phelan affirmative looked like.

"Like humans, we Phelan pass through a stage where we find it especially easy to learn language. We teach both tongues simultaneously."

"But doesn't that cause problems? Socialization, that sort of thing?"

"The result is sometimes interesting until the student reaches the age where he or she can differentiate between the two."

"Surely you don't find Standard as easy to speak as your native tongue!"

"Why not?"

"Because it is axiomatic that speech reflects the thought processes of the speaker. As aliens, you must look at things quite differently from us, and those differences should be reflected in your language."

"You may be surprised at how much alike our two species are, Professor."

"How can that be?"

"Both cultures have their basis in the self-interest of the individual, though you humans tend to be much more individualistic. We even laugh at some of your jokes, although often not for the same reasons that you do."

"What about our tendency toward belligerence?" Guttieriz asked with deceptive composure. "Do you have that human trait as well?"

"We have our quarrels." Faslorn noticed the exchange of looks between Eli and Garth. "Would you believe me if I claimed otherwise?"

"Your honesty is most . . . refreshing."

"My honesty is self-serving, Captain. We seek a home. For

that, we must demonstrate to your people the benefits of helping us. To gain your trust, we must speak plainly. I hope that you will not be offended and that you will return the favor.''

"Far from being offended, we are honored that you respect us enough to be honest. Now then, there are some things my superiors want me to ask as soon as possible."

"Ask."

"How many of you were there on Phela when Tau Ceti exploded?"

"Ten point seven billion."

"And how many aboard *Far Horizons* now?"

"One hundred, twelve thousand, three hundred and sixty-five."

"And the other ships that got away?"

"Approximately the same, I would imagine."

Tory had a sudden flashback to the night she'd first learned Tau Ceti had been inhabited. She remembered the sense of loss at the thought of an entire intelligent species wiped out. Out of nearly eleven billion living, thinking beings, fewer than half a million survived. What a tragedy!

Faslorn noticed the sudden change in mood among his guests. "Grieve not for us, our newfound friends. They died a very long time ago. We, their descendants, must see to it that they did not die in vain."

The silence that followed lasted only a few seconds. Synergist training had taught Tory the art of observation; she noticed that the guides stepped in to engage their charges in conversation before anyone could feel uncomfortable. In so doing, they left the impression that they were part of a well-oiled—or well-practiced—machine.

The waiters returned, some balancing chafing dishes on each of four arms. Tory waited for her own food to be served before picking up a fork. "Are you sure we can eat this?" she asked Maratel as she poked at the green substance on her plate.

"Our biochemistries are similar, but not precisely the same. Humans can eat most of our foods, but they lack essential nutrients. If you did so for too long, you would suffer a vitamin deficiency. The same is true if we eat your foods, of course. Everything you will consume this evening is guaranteed safe and nutritious. I'm afraid that I cannot vouch for the taste. You may want to face this meal in the spirit of a scientific experiment."

Tory smiled. "This won't be the first banquet I've attended in that spirit."

The meal turned out to be one of the most memorable of Tory's life. As Maratel had said, the Phelan understood how human taste buds worked, but not the combinations that people found appealing. Even so, they did remarkably well. Only twice did she feel the sudden urge to retch—once from a dish that had the odor of rotting garbage, and again when she bit into a nondescript square patty and was nearly overcome by the taste of half-cooked liver. To confuse matters, Eli Guttieriz gave the latter dish his highest recommendation.

Generally, however, the first sign of a wrinkled nose or a sour expression was sufficient signal to have a course whisked from sight and replaced with something new. Even the successes proved interesting. While the tastes were generally palatable, the combinations were odd. Who had ever thought of mixing soy sauce with chocolate, for instance? Or flavoring meat loaf with root beer? There was a purple pearlike fruit that possessed a peppery flavor and a citrus tang; a clear broth that might well have been eggnog mixed with tartar sauce; and a meat dish that had overtones of vanilla ice cream. The general impression was of some Phelan chef sprinkling flavorings over food at random, hoping to discover the optimum combination by trial and error.

The Phelan guides made a show of eating their food, but mostly they watched their human charges. Following each course, they quizzed Tory and the others as to their reactions. Tory noticed that mistakes became less noticeable as the meal progressed; whatever the Phelan were doing, they seemed able to make corrections in real time. Tory filed this observation under the category "How well do the Phelan understand us?" So far, she had been forced to conclude they understood human beings too damned well.

After "dessert," which came fairly close to apple pie à la mode, Faslorn rose from his seat and moved to the lectern that had been set up in the middle of the head table. There was none of the slow ebb of dinner conversation that usually greets a human speaker. The Phelan audience ceased talking, dropped their utensils, and turned their attention to Faslorn. It was as though they had rehearsed this whole banquet a thousand times—which, considering the time they had to prepare, was possible.

"Ladies and gentlemen, fellow shipmates, friends," Faslorn began in traditional fashion. "We meet here tonight for a most auspicious occasion. We celebrate the first meeting of two great races—we, the refugee peoples of Phela, and these representatives of *Homo sapiens terra*. It is a Phelan tradition that two strangers who partake of sustenance together are no longer strangers. The breaking of bread with travelers is also a very ancient human custom. I hope this meal is but the first of many in our long journey of mutual understanding.

"To our human friends, I again say welcome. You have come far to meet us and braved dangers on your journey. We appreciate your efforts. Frankly, we had not expected to meet human beings until after we'd finished our swing around your sun. That you were able to come out so far to meet us is most impressive. Let us impress you in return. Sit back, relax, and let us show you the wonders of lost Phela."

The lights in the banquet hall dimmed as the far wall slowly filled with light. The scene was a view from space. A star more orange than Sol glowed in the background, while a blue-white world hovered in the foreground. That world could well have been Earth, save for the strange outlines of the continents and the presence of one large and two small moons.

The world expanded suddenly as the camera swooped. A quick pass over the planet's nightside showed a glittering carpet of city lights that limned the coasts of the major continents. Then the camera ship returned to sunlight just as it entered atmosphere. It continued to swoop until it was racing across an expanse of azure water toward a white city that stretched from horizon to horizon.

Tory found herself eyewitness to cities where spindle-spired buildings breached the clouds and wide swaths of purple-green foliage cut across the landscape. There were domes larger than any ever built in the crater of Olympus Mons, and boxlike buildings larger than small mountains. Villages were arrayed much as she had already seen aboard *Far Horizons*, only far larger in extent. The hexagon and the six-pointed star were recurring themes in Phelan architecture. She suppressed a smile as an errant thought passed through her brain: should someone ask if they were Jewish?

Phela was a world of more than cities. Even with ten billion inhabitants, it had remained a world of pristine beauty. In quick succession, they found themselves looking upon wide bays, snowcapped mountains, and beaches of white sand. They saw the glistening blue-white glow of distant glaciers on a horizon, and the sullen red fire of a volcano illuminating the nighttime sky. There was a giant waterfall that tumbled two kilometers into a cloud of perpetual mist, possibly the progenitor to the twin waterfalls at the opposite end of the cylindrical habitat, and a vast river that wandered like a snake to the sea.

Then came the catalog of Phelan activities and commerce. Massive ships glided silently above steel blue oceans, while small gossamer craft danced before the wind among the islands of some lost archipelago. Long tubes arched across the landscape with swiftly moving shapes dimly visible through their translucent walls. Aircraft flew in long lines across the sky, while spacecraft rose directly toward the heavens.

There were crowds of Phelan hurrying about their business, much as could be seen in any large city on Earth. Then day turned to night and a different crowd dominated the scene. These Phelan reposed on a hillside as lilting music arose from a rainbow of glittering lights. The tone scale wasn't human, but the meter and rhyme were evident even to one unschooled in such things. The next view was of a playground where young beings moved amid the branches of a giant, tangled bush, pursuing some incomprehensible game. There followed a parade of views of daily life among the Phelan.

Then the intimate look into Phelan life was behind them. On the screen, a globular ship rose from a spaceport on a tail of violet-white fire and was soon lost in the flame of its own exhaust plume. The bright star of the exhaust segued into the real thing as the camera zoomed in on the face of Tau Ceti. Even to the untutored, it was apparent that something was amiss. The star's surface layers were roiled by vast plasma storms and stellar prominences that climbed for millions of kilometers into space.

When Tau Ceti exploded, it did so in total silence.

The camera pulled back from the exploding star. When it was again something other than a general whiteness, they could see a tiny black circle and three small dots marring the face of the nova. No one had to tell Tory that the circle was the Phelan world and the dots its three moons. She watched in horrified fascination as the shock wave from the exploding star reached out and engulfed the planet they had just departed.

The scene changed again. This time it showed a cylindrical ship in midspace. The object was *Far Horizons*, or her twin. The ship was attached to a light sail visibly smaller than the one that now slowed them. The sail began to glow red, then white, and finally indigo as it absorbed the energy of the nova shock wave. The sail billowed as though filled by a strong wind and began to accelerate outbound, leaving whatever craft the camera had been mounted on in its wake. The travelogue ended as the starship dwindled into invisibility with surprising rapidity.

The travelogue had lasted a full hour. Throughout, the only sound in the banquet hall had been the background noises that accompanied the many scenes: the crash of waves onto beaches, the twittering of children, and the noises of living, breathing cities. Now the hall was silent. It was the silence of a tomb. The lights came up just as Tory reached up to wipe away the tears moistening her eyes.

Faslorn did not speak for long seconds. "You now know a tiny percentage of what we lost when our star exploded. Over the next several weeks, we hope to show you something of what we were able to save. I think you will agree that it is more than sufficient to repay humanity for a home close to your star."

Dardan Pierce stared at the chronometer readout in the lower left corner of his workscreen and scowled. The timer counted down the days, hours, and seconds to the moment when the expedition ought to have contacted the aliens. An hour earlier the display had ceased counting down and had begun counting up. As the news media were saying, somewhere a zillion kilometers out in space human beings were even now talking to aliens. Unless, of course, they were dead. And here he was in his office, with no way of discovering what had happened for another twenty-four fucking days!

"There ought to be a law!" he growled.

"Eh?" Bernardo Lucci asked. The Italian exchange professor glanced up from where he was squatting on his haunches, pawing through a pile of old journals stacked in the corner of Pierce's office.

"Here they've made contact and I have to wait nearly a month before I find out what happened. There ought to be a law."

"There is, old boy! It's called Einstein's first law of relativity. You're asking for simultaneous knowledge of two events spread widely in a universe where the speed of light is finite. Einstein proved that there is no such thing as 'simultaneous.' It's a fiction, like centrifugal force."

"I know what centrifugal force is every time I climb into the gym centrifuge to prepare for one of my trips to your damned oversize world, my friend."

"Be that as it may, it still doesn't exist. Nor does your desire to know what has happened to your people make any more sense in the real universe. We'll all find out in twenty-five days."

"Twenty-four."

"I stand corrected. Besides, how do you know they will choose to approach the light sail on the timeline that you and the other evaluators put together three months ago? They may have decided to hold back for a month to study the situation."

"If they make me wait another month, I'll strangle them all when they get back."

"Now then, if you had something truly interesting on which to concentrate your intellect, you might not be so jumpy . . . Ah, here it is, I knew I would find it."

Lucci pulled a dog-eared copy of the *System Journal of Astronomy* from the middle of the pile and carried it back to the desk. The library was always complaining that Pierce hadn't returned his faxouts for recycling on schedule, but he didn't care; he enjoyed the feel of the slightly rough plastic under his fingers. It was more real to him than a mere electronic image. The journal that Lucci held bore a date stamp that was nearly eight years in the past.

The short Italian leafed through the pages. "Aha! I knew my memory wouldn't fail me. Here's an item in the 'Two Hundred Years Ago in Science' column. The entry is dated April 12, 2028. Listen to this:

"Despite all efforts, even thirty years after the event the Tau Ceti nova remains the premier scientific mystery of our time. At a recent conference held on Bimini in the Bahamas, noted astronomers converged to take another crack at solving the twin mysteries of this nearest of all novae. The consensus at the conclusion of the meeting was that no real progress had been made at explaining how an outwardly normal, K0 orange dwarf star on the main sequence exploded. The lesser mystery, the initial deficit of 2.5 percent in the expected energy output from the nova, was the subject of much brisk speculation, but no explanation proved convincing. The mystery, it seems, continues."

Lucci's expression was expectant as he looked up from his reading.

"So?" asked Pierce.

"Don't you see? The mystery hasn't been solved to this very day!"

"I'm aware of that. What's your point, Bernie?"

"Isn't it obvious? You have people about to contact beings who actually witnessed the explosion! Perhaps they can shed some light on why their star blew its top. If nothing else, it ought to be good for a paper in this year's *Transactions*."

Pierce thought about it, then nodded. "Might be a good opportunity to get one's curiosity bump scratched at that. How about I work up a question and have it sent off to the ship? They can ask the aliens for any observations they made of the pre- and postnova star. The only problem is that we'll have to wait two months to get a reply."

Lucci laughed. "If you manage to cut out the communications delay, you will let me in on the secret first, won't you? I want to get my investment in before the stampede begins."

"What about this other thing, the light-deficiency question?"

Lucci shrugged. "Can't hurt to ask about that, too."

13

FOLLOWING THE BANQUET, THE PHELAN CON-
ducted their human guests to their quarters. The guest apartments were built at the same level in the end cap as the banquet
hall, with each crew member assigned to an apartment off a
common living area. At the far end of the commons was another
transparent wall that looked out over the ship's habitat volume,
where the scene was considerably changed from what it had
been earlier. The sun tube was no longer a bright orange-white.
It now put out a soft blue glow as a gentle mist floated slowly
from out of the sky. Only the distorted lights of a few villages
were apparent directly below their perch.

"It's raining!" Kit exclaimed as she strode to stand in front
of the window.

"Of course," responded Rolan, Kit's guide.

"But why?"

"The storm is scheduled regularly. It cleans the interior,
freshens the air, and otherwise makes life more interesting.
Don't humans enjoy weather that changes?"

Tory, who had lived her life beneath the artificial domes of
Mars, had never seen rain. To her, weather was a dust storm.
Even at the lowest elevations, the Martian atmosphere was so
diffuse that its winds were little more than gentle puffs. At the
altitude of Olympus Mons, the atmosphere was little thicker
than a poor vacuum. As she watched the tiny rivulets follow
their gently curving Coriolis paths down the window, Tory understood better the terrestrial prejudice in favor of weather.

When no one answered, Rolan continued his explanation.
"We delayed the fall of night and this storm so that you could
see the ship before the banquet. We've now returned to our
normal weather program."

Faslorn suggested that the guides show their charges to their
quarters. Maratel guided Tory to the door nearest the window
on the right side. As they entered the apartment, Tory discov-

ered that she, too, had a transparent wall in what she took to be
the living room. The other three rooms in the small suite were
a bedroom, bathroom, and study. The rooms were decorated in
"modern Renaissance" style, which, while currently popular
on Earth, looked exceedingly ugly to Tory. Maratel guided her
through her new quarters, demonstrating the hidden machinery
that seemed to be everywhere.

The bathroom was the same low-gravity design found on Luna
and Mars. The shower was fully enclosed, with a laminar flow
grid in the floor that sucked the water out as quickly as it could
be injected from the overhead spray ceiling. The toilet, likewise,
was a conventional space design.

In the study, Tory found a desk and a full suite of office machines. The workstation, Maratel informed her, had a direct line
to the computer aboard *Austria*. It would serve Tory's needs
until the Phelan technicians reestablished her link.

"You can interface with *Far Horizons*'s library using this machine, also," Maratel said. She showed Tory how to call up the
data base. The workscreen suddenly divided into two unequal
parts. On the left side of the screen, rows of dots slowly scrolled
upward. On the larger right side, sentences and paragraphs were
formed from glowing letters.

Tory ignored the words and pointed to the moving patterns of
dots. "Is this Phelan script?"

"It is. The translator operates on a direct-substitution algorithm. That is, it takes specific Phelan phrases and converts
them to the closest human equivalent."

"Then this is all we need to study you!"

"I wish it were that simple. The substitution algorithm makes
no attempt to explain the background and the unspoken assumptions underlying the data. Much of what you see will appear to be in complete Standard sentences, but will not make
sense to you."

Tory laughed. "I had the same problem when I first began
studying computers."

"We, too, have difficulties with human broadcasts because
we do not share the audience's conceptions. For instance, most
of us miss the finer points of certain types of humor that are
broadcast late in the night cycle of programming."

Tory considered how she might explain to Maratel that much
of human humor—perhaps most—had its basis in sex. Not that
she thought Maratel ignorant of that fact. The Phelan had shown
far too great an understanding of human beings not to be intel-

lectually aware of it. Still, how much could an alien truly understand? Instead of trying to explain, she pointed to the screen. "How do the dots work?"

"Phelan verbal symbols are represented by a five-by-five matrix of dots. Each word-phrase is a distinct dot pattern, which we then string together into multiple matrices to form complete thoughts."

"Like we use letters to form words?"

"No, more the equivalent of Chinese ideographs. The full matrix gives us two-to-the-twenty-fifth power permutations, more than sufficient. For common expressions, we use a four-by-four subset of the full matrix. In your base-ten numbering system, that gives us a total of sixty-five thousand five hundred and thirty-five separate symbols, not counting the null matrix."

"How do you remember them all?"

Maratel emitted the barking Phelan laugh. "How do you remember the difference between two, to, and too?"

Tory joined in her laughter. "A good point."

They continued the tour. In the living room was a refreshment unit identical to the one in the common area. By placing an order, she could have her choice of nonalcoholic and alcoholic drinks, and also those containing a mild euphoric.

The bedroom was the last stop on the tour. The bed was a giant fluffy thing that looked as though it had come from the set of an orgy holo.

"Where do you sleep?"

"We have living quarters nearby," Maratel replied. "Our understanding of the human need for privacy suggests that you would prefer a room of your own. Or are you mated to Captain Van Zandt or Professor Guttieriz?"

Tory hesitated, wondering how she would explain the living arrangements aboard *Austria*. She decided not to. Since the Phelan would undoubtedly monitor their every action, she was not about to seek Garth's bed while she was onboard the starship. If the Phelan wanted to study human sexuality, they would have to do so from books and recordings like everyone else. "No, we're not mated . . ."

"Then you have someone at home."

"Maybe," Tory replied. She was surprised to realize that she hadn't thought of Ben in weeks. She wondered if he had thought of her.

"If you require my services, you need only say so out loud and I will quickly join you."

The comment confirmed what Tory already suspected, namely that every square centimeter of the apartment was monitored. She wondered idly how many Phelan would be watching her whenever she went to the bathroom, then thrust the thought from her mind, lest dwelling on it give her a serious case of constipation.

"Are the quarters satisfactory?"

"They're downright luxurious!"

"Faslorn thought that you and your friends would wish to sleep now."

Tory checked her sleeve chronometer, something that was unnecessary when her implant was working. She was surprised to find that it was approaching midnight. Not only had it been a busy day, but the long approach had left time for only a series of catnaps. She stretched and yawned widely. "Now that you mention it, I am feeling a bit tired."

"If you need sleeping attire, you will find it in the locker behind you."

Tory turned and discovered a disguised door in the bulkhead. She opened it to find a walk-in closet. On three sides were clothes of all descriptions, and it didn't take long to discover that they were all in her exact size. Now how, she wondered, had they done that?

She quickly undressed and slipped into a sleeping gown that felt like silk. She normally slept in the nude aboard ship—as much a precaution, should it prove necessary to suit up in a hurry, as it was personal preference.

She slipped into bed and was asleep in less than a minute.

Tory woke to soft music emanating from somewhere. She lay there for long minutes, integrating the events of the previous day. Her overall impression of the Phelan was one of a gentle people who were eager to please. Of course, that was precisely the impression they wanted her to have. She remembered Garth's comment about maintaining the eyes of a skeptic. But she had to admit that if Faslorn and his people continued as solicitously as they had begun, it was going to be difficult to maintain the proper objectivity.

Just as she was about to stir, the door opened and Maratel entered, bearing a tray on which several steaming plates were piled.

"Good morning. Did you sleep well?"

Tory stretched to get the blood flowing. "Better than I have in months."

"Good. Here, I've brought you breakfast." Maratel sat the tray across Tory's lap and then straightened the pillow behind her so that she could sit up. Tory picked up a piece of what appeared to be buttered toast and bit in. The taste, she discovered, was very close to the original. She told Maratel to compliment the chef.

"He will be pleased. Of course, we cheated."

"How so?"

"Captain Van Zandt gave us permission to sample your food stocks aboard *Austria*. Our synthesists find it much easier to duplicate your food when we have a sample to work with. Is the bed comfortable?"

"Very. The spin gravity helps, too. I've never been to Earth, but I've had the usual centrifuge training. The full nine-point-eight meters per second squared does pull a person down!"

"In that respect I am more fortunate than you. Phela's gravity is eighty-seven percent of Earth's. I, at least, won't develop fallen arches when we visit humanity's home world." Maratel moved to the closet and began laying out a black and silver jumpsuit in the latest Earthside style.

Tory pointed. "Those clothes. This food. How many people do you have working at providing us with provisions?"

"A few hundred."

"You know, it isn't necessary to wait on us hand and foot. We'll give you a fair hearing even if we have to rough it and eat shipboard rations."

"By providing you with these items, we demonstrate our abilities. You could live aboard your ship and take guided tours of *Far Horizons*, of course, but which makes the greater impression on you: Having Faslorn talk while you watch workers performing tasks you can't possibly understand, or biting into a piece of warm toast you know was synthesized within the past few hours?"

"A good point. Possibly, you people know what you are about."

Maratel gave her "human smile." "We have considered how best to approach humans for more than two centuries. I believe there are specialists aboard this ship who could go into practice as human psychologists if they wished to. Who knows? Perhaps they will."

Tory took a sip of "tea." Here the taste wasn't nearly as close to the original as the toast had been. The liquid, while palatable enough, had a slight oily aftertaste. "Have you considered that it might not be wise to let us know how well you understand us?"

Maratel looked genuinely puzzled, which in turn made Tory wonder how she managed to leave that impression since her brow was obviously not suitable for wrinkling up.

"Why?" the guide asked.

"It makes us feel insecure if we think someone knows us too well."

"Not nearly as insecure as you will feel if you catch us in a lie. As Faslorn explained last night, 'honesty is the best policy.' "

"That's one of those aphorisms that is more honored in its breach than in its observance." There was a long silence while Tory finished breakfast. When she had polished off the tea, she asked, "Is Captain Van Zandt still asleep?"

"He has been awake for several hours. He wished to monitor our technicians when they took your power unit in tow."

"*Starhopper*'s now attached to this ship?"

"To the light sail," Maratel said, her head bobbing up and down on her long neck.

"But how can you do that? The light sail is rotating!"

"The rigging is somewhat complex. Suffice to say, we attached towlines to your power unit and then to various shroud lines from the sail. By actively changing the towline lengths in concert with the sail's rotation, we maintain a constant tension on *Starhopper*."

"I'll have to see it."

"We recorded the entire operation. You can view it at your leisure."

"What do we have planned for today?"

"Faslorn thought you might still be weary. He suggested that we tour the habitat level so that you could see something of our people and our ship. Your formal education begins tomorrow."

"Formal education?"

"We have a full program laid out for you. We hope to teach you something of our culture, history, and science so that you can properly advise your people when you make your reports. You do not have to participate if you don't wish to."

"What do the others say?"

"Professor Guttieriz is off with Corwin and Raal. Dr. Claridge is touring a hospital."

"You mean I'm the only one still in bed?"

Maratel shrugged expansively. It was a gesture that encompassed all four arms. "We thought it best to let you sleep."

Tory set the tray aside and swung her bare feet out onto the carpeted deck. "I can sleep anytime. Come, let's see the ship!"

Garth Van Zandt was strapped into a chair somewhere near the spin axis. The compartment around him had disappeared, giving the illusion that he and Faslorn were floating in the black firmament. How the Phelan managed the illusion was a mystery. That didn't prevent his enjoyment of it.

He moved the joystick control inset in the arm of his chair and caused the view to expand until it centered on *Starhopper*. The lines the Phelan had attached to his ship's booster were too small to be visible against the background of space. Still, their presence meant that the attitude-control jets no longer burped every few minutes to match velocities with the slowly decelerating starship. *Starhopper* now dangled like a fish on a hook at the end of several thousand kilometers of line.

"A marvelous ship you have here, Faslorn," Garth said as he continued his video tour. He panned across the body of *Far Horizons* and zoomed in on the control line's anchor sphere—a porcupine shape with a thousand lines streaming away from it. Each line was encased in a surrealistic violet sheath of glowing plasma.

"Look at them glow!" Garth exclaimed. This was nothing like the episodes of Saint Elmo's fire he had experienced on approach. It was as though the Phelan were concentrating the plasma field intentionally around the control lines. No wonder they stood out so starkly on radar!

"The control lines are superconductors," Faslorn explained. "We are siphoning electrons off the light sail through them. The electrical field naturally attracts the free protons in the plasma wind."

"I would think that you'd eventually run out of electrons."

Faslorn laughed. "You would be wrong, Captain. At this distance from the sun, one hydrogen atom in five is naturally ionized. As we sweep past, free electrons are attracted by the sail's positive charge. They rain down continuously on the reverse side and must be extracted continuously. We use them to operate the ionization laser."

"We wondered about that on our approach. Tell me more . . ."

* * *

The lift was empty except for Tory and Maratel. Maratel had guided her through a maze of corridors to reach a different lift from the one that had delivered them to the banquet. The cylinder end cap was honeycombed with corridors and living space. Tory was just beginning to realize how big a volume the shell of the starship enclosed.

"Are you all right?" Maratel asked when the gravity increased to twice Mars's normal.

Tory's answer was a trifle unsteady. "So far, so good." Coriolis forces were doing strange things to her balance.

The door opened into a real, honest-to-God forest. Tory blinked as Maratel ushered her outside to stand on a stone-paved path that disappeared beneath a canopy of vegetation. The plants were like nothing she had seen on Mars, nor any of the terrestrial flora she had studied in school. Phelan trees were globular in shape, thrusting their limbs out radially from a central point near the ground. At the end of each limb, a single hexagonal leaf fitted in with those around it to produce a hemisphere of unbroken green. The effect was the same as if someone had exploded a bomb in a pile of leaves a few milliseconds earlier.

The path led directly into a tunnel cut through the globe of a tree. It took a moment for Tory's eyes to adjust to the gloom within, and she was surprised to discover more than one pair of eyes looking back at her. The eyes belonged to several small six-legged animals that otherwise resembled spider monkeys.

Tory pointed at one small beast. "The exobiologists on Earth will tear their hair out when they see this. They have proved beyond a doubt that evolution will always reduce the number of legs on an animal to four."

Maratel laughed. "Our own animal specialists can prove just as easily the benefits of having six. It will be interesting to see which rule the next inhabited planet we discover follows."

"They'd probably have five."

"Perhaps all numbers are possible, and chance alone determines the path of evolution on each world."

"You may be right," Tory replied as she watched one little animal who seemed fascinated by her. "Are they intelligent?"

"No more than one of your own monkeys at home. In fact, we have named them *hexamonkeys* in Standard."

"Are all Phelan life-forms hexapods?"

"Many of them are. Some lower animals—the equivalent of terrestrial insects—have eight and twelve legs. We have one genus with no legs at all. They resemble terrestrial snakes, but occupy a different ecological niche.''

"You'll have to point one out to me. I've never seen a snake. The one in the Olympus zoo died before I was old enough to remember trips to the zoo."

Maratel led her slowly along the path, and they came out of the globe tree to find themselves in warm, orange-tinted tube light. Numerous flowers bordered the walk. Some were strange indeed, but others were almost familiar. Tory commented on one flower that could have passed for a rose in poor light.

"The resemblance is coincidental," her guide assured her. "Internally, the *ardt* is quite different from any terrestrial plant."

"An *ardt* by any other name would smell as sweet?"

"William Shakespeare!" Maratel said, laughing. "*Romeo and Juliet*, I believe."

"I'm impressed."

Maratel gestured toward the flower. "Go ahead and smell it."

Tory did so and was nearly overcome with the odor of rancid bacon.

"Whew!"

"The different biochemistry Faslorn mentioned to you."

"I guess so."

They walked slowly for two hundred meters, by which time beads of sweat had begun to pop out on Tory's forehead. Maratel noticed and directed her to a bench beside the pathway. This, too, must be for her benefit, she realized. The proportions were all wrong for the short Phelan legs.

As Tory caught her breath, she tilted her head back and gazed upward at the leading end cap. She gasped as her eyes tried to make sense out of the apparent cliff that towered over them. From this vantage point, the end cap seemed to be solid rock, with thousands of concentric circles of windows rising into the sky until they disappeared in the glare of the sun tube.

There were even plants growing from out of the rocks, and wet rivulets still streaming down the base from last night's rainstorm. Tory spent several minutes trying to find the level where the humans's apartments were located.

"Are you rested?" Maratel finally asked.

Tory nodded. "Let's proceed."

"I thought you might like to see our young at play."

"Very much. How many youngsters are there aboard ship?"

"A few thousand at any given time. Phelan adolescence is

approximately the same length as human. Naturally, we are very careful to match our birth rate to our death rate.''

"Are you taking me to a school?''

"Of sorts. We require our young to spend some period of their lives living in the habitat so that they can know what life on a planet is like.''

"Sort of scout camp?''

"Again, of sorts.''

The two of them walked a hundred meters along the stone path, crossing a Japanese-style bridge over a stream. The path passed through a hedgerow of some yellow-brown plant. On the other side was one of the six-pointed villages filled with beehive buildings that Tory had spied from above.

Like human children, Phelan youths were smaller versions of their parents, and seemed as naturally curious as any other young animal. As soon as Maratel and Tory entered the school village, they found themselves at the center of a chattering circle. Small hands reached out to pluck at Tory's clothes and hair until Maratel said something in Phelan. The tactile investigations ceased, but no one lost interest.

Tory's gaze lit on a very small child standing directly in front of her. He—or she—was barely half a meter tall. Tory sought permission with her eyes from Maratel, then knelt down to pat the baby. She was rewarded by a low humming noise.

"That means that she likes it,'' Maratel reported.

"How old?''

"About three of your years. Standard years, not Martian.''

"Isn't that a little young to be separated from her parents?''

"We raise our children communally. The human nuclear family is alien to us, although we have, of course, experimented with it.''

"With what success?'' Tory asked, getting to her feet.

"Varying. I'm afraid that some of your social forms are not applicable to our species.''

"I'd like to learn more.''

"You shall, beginning tomorrow. Today we are just . . . how do you say it? Sightseeing.''

"Sightseeing is correct,'' Tory agreed. She made note of the first instance she had ever seen of a Phelan grasping for a word.

"Do you wish to continue the tour or go back and lie down?''

"Lead on. I'll have sore muscles tomorrow for sure. Still, that's a small price to pay.''

"Very well. There is a farm just beyond that next stand of trees. I thought you might like to see how we grow our food."

"I'm right behind you."

14

THE NEXT FEW WEEKS WERE BUSY ONES FOR ALL concerned. As they had promised, the Phelan set about educating their human visitors. As befitted an enterprise centuries in the planning, progress was rapid. Indeed, Tory wouldn't have believed it possible to absorb so much information so quickly without the aid of her implant.

The briefings began with an overview of Phelan history. Like humans, the Phelan were descended from a race of hunter-gatherers, but they had discovered agriculture somewhat earlier than had humanity. As on Earth, farming had led to irrigation, cities, and the complex social structure both required. Thus had both species begun their long climbs toward technological civilization.

Yet the similarities between Phelan and human were misleading. A world is a large and wondrous place, and the tapestry of Phela's history had been woven every bit as intricately as had that of Earth. Just as human culture was sufficiently broad to encompass Aztec and Roman, Viking and Sioux, Han and Zulu, so, too, had Phela seen the rise and fall of civilizations. Nor were the Phelan themselves a monolithic people. They, too, had their share of saints, sinners, heroes, villains, yeomen, and rogues over the centuries. Like humans, they were not so much tamed by civilization as taught the necessity of cooperating with one another.

Yet there were general observations that could be made about the Phelan. They appeared somewhat more rational and less emotional than *Homo sapiens*. Their history was less punctuated with wars and strife. As a result, they had progressed somewhat faster up the ladder of civilization. Not that the early Phelan had been pacifists. The few wars they had fought had been ferocious affairs, with victory going to the survivors rather than the winners.

The Phelan had put their wars behind them soon after they

developed spaceflight. The first Phelan spaceship had lifted off in 1625 by human reckoning, and by the time of the American Revolution the Phelan had colonized much of the Tau Ceti system. The future had seemed an unbroken stream of progress, with the Phelan scientists eyeing the vast blackness that lay beyond their own small star.

Then had come several years of anomalous weather. The reason for the change hadn't been difficult to discover: Tau Ceti's output of radiant energy had begun to shift erratically. The swings weren't large—indeed, they were difficult to detect at all. Still, they violated every known theory of how a main-sequence star ought to behave. It had taken several years for the astronomers to realize that the surface oscillations were a symptom of a much deeper problem within the star. For reasons the astronomers could not explain, the core had started to convert greater quantities of helium to carbon than was normal for a star in the hydrogen-burning phase. The excess energy turned the core unstable, and if some way to stabilize it could not be found, the oscillations would slowly build until Tau Ceti novaed.

A small being named Delwin was their instructor in Phelan history. When Delwin reached the moment the astronomers realized that their world was doomed, however, Faslorn took over the recounting. For, as Faslorn explained with sorrow in his voice, what had followed had been an era of shame. The news had caused the rational, peaceful Phelan to go berserk. A culture that had successfully avoided war for half a thousand years had dissolved into uncounted warring factions, each attempting to gain control of the resources needed to build evacuation craft capable of fleeing the destruction of their star.

The war had been fought for nearly twenty years. The Phelan called it the Time of Troubles. When it was over, most of the home planet and the colony worlds lay in ruins, and the victors discovered that much of what they needed to escape had been destroyed in the fighting. In the end, when the surface oscillations of the star had grown so great as to make Phela practically uninhabitable, only four escape ships had been built. Into each of these the Phelan had placed a carefully chosen crew of one hundred thousand. The ships had departed after many solemn ceremonies, to position themselves for the nova that would soon propel them starward.

Four ships had ridden the nova shock wave toward four different stars, leaving billions of dead behind them.

* * *

"They seemed so rational for most of their history," Tory said. "Why do you suppose they fell apart so completely?"

She and the other humans were gathered around the dinner table in the commons. They were alone for once, but this didn't mean they were not being monitored. All of them took it for granted that the Phelan watched them continuously.

The meal had been excellent. The mood was solemn after a full day of watching scenes of chaos.

Eli Guttieriz put down his cup and reached for the last dinner roll. The Phelan cuisine was beginning to show in the linguist's pudgy cheeks and expanding waistline, and Tory had noticed that her own shipsuits were getting tight in various places. Eli looked up from buttering his roll.

"We probably would have done the same if we'd discovered Sol about to nova."

"But it was so senseless! If they'd just cooperated, they might have saved millions."

Guttieriz shrugged. "Which would have still been an insignificant percentage of the total population."

"Aren't you the heartless one, Eli!" Kit chastised.

He grinned and shrugged. "If they saved a large enough gene pool to start over, what difference how many individuals were saved?"

Kit continued. "At least we know the Phelan aren't keeping things from us."

"How do we know that?" Garth asked. He had been looking dour throughout the meal. Tory had put it down to the effect of the day's history lesson.

"Because if they were going to hide something, the Time of Troubles would be a damned good place to start."

"I wonder."

"Care to expand on that comment, Captain?"

"It's nothing I can put my finger on. Still, don't any of you find it strange that the Phelan are so like us? How can two races separated by twelve light-years of vacuum be so similar?"

Eli shrugged again. "Similar environments produce similar solutions."

"Right down to overlapping senses of humor?"

"What do you mean?"

"The other evening, Faslorn and I were telling dirty jokes. I told him the one about the Mother Superior and the Blind Man. He got it!"

"He was, of course, simulating his laughter," Eli said. "The Phelan sense of humor is considerably skewed from ours."

"How do you know that?"

"From their language. I am beginning to get a glimmer of the underlying structure. Faslorn is right—learning it is quite difficult. It is nothing like any Earth tongue I have ever studied."

"What has that to do with their sense of humor?"

"Language is a window into the brain. All human languages have certain characteristics in common because all human brains are constructed along identical lines. If the Phelan brain structure were similar to ours, their language would be similar, at least in its most basic structure."

"Then why do they *seem* so human?" Tory asked.

"Because they go to great lengths to leave that impression. That is the purpose of the human gestures they use and the colloquialisms with which they pepper their speech. They know that we have a strong tendency to anthropomorphize everything, even inanimate objects. They are playing on this defect in our character to make us accept them. Their motives are obvious."

"You've picked this up in only a few days?" Garth asked.

The linguist shrugged. "It's my job. Besides, most of my conclusions are highly preliminary. I may change my mind tomorrow."

"Then keep at it. It might be important when we make a recommendation concerning whether we will allow them colonies."

"How can we *not* allow them?" Tory blurted. "Where else can they go?"

"A point not lost on the politicians back home. They've been peppering me with demands for more information about Phelan military capabilities."

"Does that mean they plan to refuse the Phelan request?" Kit asked.

"No, just that they're being cautious. The more we learn, the better off everyone will be. That includes the Phelan. We need more information, if for no other reason than to put a fair price on our services." Garth turned to Tory. "How is the implant work going?"

"Slowly. They managed to produce a carrier wave I could detect on their last attempt. When I attempted to synchronize, though, I developed a splitting headache."

"It's nice to know there are a few things we're better at. I was beginning to develop an inferiority complex."

"I know what you mean. I thought they'd whip up a link as soon as I provided them with specifications."

"Well, keep trying. It's damned inconvenient to have you go up to the hangar bay every time you want to use the computer."

"Tell me about it."

"Anything more we need to discuss?" When no one spoke, Garth suggested that they all turn in. Between the education and entertainment, the Phelan were running them ragged. One by one, they drifted to their individual apartments. Tomorrow was going to be another busy day.

Over the next several weeks, the education sessions became less formal and more a matter of individual instruction. As Garth had suggested, Eli Guttieriz threw himself into his study of the Phelan tongue. Kit Claridge spent most of her time soaking up Phelan medical knowledge. All four humans submitted to extensive medical examinations, while several Phelan spent hours allowing Kit to prod and poke them.

Garth Van Zandt continued receiving demands from Earth that he provide information on the Phelan request for colonies. They had been aboard the Phelan ship seven weeks, and were just now receiving requests generated shortly after the first contact report had reached Earth. The speed-of-light communications delay was aggravating for parties on both ends of the microwave link. Mostly, the team blindly transmitted everything of interest home, with the preparation of reports often absorbing more than half of each day.

With Kit and Eli absorbed in their respective specialties, and Garth engaged in negotiations with the Phelan, Tory was assigned the job of becoming the expedition's synergist. It was her task to learn all she could, then correlate it with everything in the ship's computer, in the hope of coming to useful conclusions. Mostly she wandered around the ship with Maratel, taking in the sights.

In the long weeks since their arrival, they had sampled all manner of Phelan activities. One of Tory's most memorable visits had been with Maratel to a symphony orchestra practicing for an open-air concert they would be giving in the humans's honor. Tory noticed with some amusement the modifications they had made to the traditional instruments. The entire brass section, for instance, had appended intricate bits of plumbing to their mouthpieces. With their snouts and lack of lips, it was impossible for the Phelan to blow a conventional trumpet. The string adaptations were equally interesting.

As Tory and Maratel lolled on a grassy knoll beneath the sun tube they listened to the orchestra practice Beethoven's Fifth Symphony in short spurts. Between sections, the conductor would call a halt and critique the performance. Tory noted that there were advantages for a conductor to having four arms rather than two.

During a lull in the rehearsal, Tory turned to Maratel. "Why do you do this sort of thing?" she asked.

"What sort of thing?"

"This!" Tory let her hand sweep the orchestra. "We're honored, of course, but why should you try to emulate our music, let alone adapt our instruments so that you can play them?"

"Why do your people hold concerts, Tory?"

"Because they enjoy music."

"So do we."

"But surely you have music of your own. Why not play that instead and honor your own culture?"

"I thought we had explained that," Maratel replied. "If we are to make our homes among humans, we must learn to fit in. Your culture is now our culture."

"It isn't necessary for you to paint yourselves gray. If your ways differ from ours, we'll respect them."

Maratel got the sorrowful look on her face that she adopted whenever she had to disagree with Tory. "I believe you are wrong, my friend. We have studied your race most carefully. You have an inbred instinct for conformity. As one of your wags once put it, 'That which is not illegal shall be compulsory!' "

"He was joking."

"In jokes often lie deeper truths. One of the most constant of all human traits is your intolerance for those who are different. One must therefore conclude that fitting in requires that we be as like you as possible. Since there is nothing we can do to change our physical form, we must strive to be 'more human than human' in other ways."

"I think you underestimate us," Tory objected.

"I don't believe so. Have not those who are different been persecuted throughout your history?"

"We've outgrown such prejudices."

"You have covered them up with a thin veneer of civilization. You have not outgrown them. We once prided ourselves that we had outgrown our passions, too. The Time of Troubles taught us otherwise.''

"But you aren't human and can never be human.''

"Nevertheless, we have freely embraced human culture. We have done so because it is a matter of survival.''

"But you're faking it!''

"Not at all. Are you faking your beliefs?''

"That's silly.''

"Is it? Why do you believe what you do?''

"I don't know,'' Tory replied, suddenly uncomfortable with the way the discussion was going. "I just do.''

"You acquired your beliefs at an early age from your parents. They inculcated you with all their prejudices, preferences, superstitions, and values.''

"I think you're being a little harsh.''

"Not at all. Would you like an example?''

"All right.''

"Like most humans, you are an adherent of what was once called 'Western civilization.' Overlying those basic beliefs are another set that you inherited from the period of Martian Independence. You believe in the rights of the individual, the benefits of democracy, the superiority of science over all other methods of gaining wisdom. Deep down, you truly believe that every problem has a technological solution. Need I comment on how different these attitudes are from those of a Confucian scholar of a thousand years ago?''

"All right. What's your point?''

"Simply that I, too, have been programmed with those same values. Alien though I may be, I am also an adherent of 'Western civilization.' I believe in all these things no less than you do.''

"But you're an alien!''

"So what? Are not canines able to learn human values of right and wrong, at least in a limited sense?''

"I think it's more a matter of learning what will get them rewarded and punished.''

"Does that differ so from the way most human beings go through life? Do people obey laws because they are right, or because to break them will bring punishment?''

"I'll have to get back to you on that. I have some thinking to do. Meantime, how about introducing me to the conductor? I'd like to compliment him on his skill with a baton . . .''

* * *

Rosswin sat across the table from Eli Guttieriz and listened as the linguist practiced his Phelan vocabulary. The human's accent was atrocious, but he was slowly picking it up. Rosswin was impressed. For, despite the cover story that Phelan had little trouble learning human speech, he remembered his own struggles many cycles earlier. It had seemed as though he would never utter an intelligible sentence.

"Very good, Professor," he said when Guttieriz finished the exercise. "We will have you giving the oration before the next meeting of the ship's council if you keep improving this way."

Despite his attempt to appear blasé, Eli was obviously pleased by the compliment.

"I believe that is sufficient for one session," Rosswin said. "Shall we get to the next item of business, the seemingly endless series of questions your people at home have asked you to answer?"

Guttieriz laughed. He was normally cold and stiff with people, but he liked the old Phelan. They were kindred spirits in many ways. "Not *seemingly* endless, Rosswin. Endless in fact! I shudder when I think of how many more questions are in the data stream winging their way toward us."

"Yes, curiosity is the most human of all traits. Well, if we are to keep our snouts above flood tide, we had best eliminate a few."

Eli reached into his belt pouch and pulled out a recorder along with a printout of the numerous questions the specialists at home were asking. Rosswin spent twenty minutes answering queries ranging from how the Phelan economy was organized to the fertility rate among Phelan females of childbearing age.

Finally, their allotted time was nearly up. "Here's one from Professor Pierce," Eli said. "He's the astrophysicist who built *Starhopper*."

"Yes," Rosswin replied, "I am familiar with Professor Pierce's accomplishment. What does he wish to know?"

"He's asking for data on the Tau Ceti nova and wants to know if you understand what caused it."

Rosswin raised his upper hands palms up. "We were hoping that your astronomers might have progressed to the point where they could explain it to us."

"Not much chance of that," Eli said as he checked off the question and scanned the list preparatory to putting it away. It was then that he noticed that Pierce's question had included a second query. "Uh, another thing. Our astronomers recorded a two-point-five-percent deficit in the light curve from the nova during the first several hours. After that, it conformed precisely to theory. Pierce asks if your own observations might throw some light on the discrepancy.''

Rosswin considered the question for nearly five seconds before responding. ''I am not an astronomer, Professor Guttieriz. However, I will make inquiries. Now then, I must attend a conference, while you, I believe, are scheduled at one of our schools that teach Standard.''

Eli gathered up the printouts he used to study Phelan vocabulary and made his farewells. After he left, Rosswin sat where he was. Only another Phelan would have detected his agitation.

''Did you hear?'' he asked thin air.

''I heard,'' Faslorn replied. The ship commander had been summoned by Rosswin's emergency signal via a method the humans did not suspect. He had replayed the recording of Rosswin's discussion with Eli, listening carefully to the incriminating question and Rosswin's noncommittal answer.

''Do you understand the significance?''

''Only too well. Do you think they suspect?''

''I do not. I believe it was just what Professor Guttieriz said it to be: a routine question from Earth that requires an answer. Still, I think it best that we move up our timetable. Do we have sufficient information to make the selection yet?''

''Not yet. We have a candidate, but the psychologists want several more watches to evaluate the observations.''

''Tell Raalwin to expedite his analysis. If they ever realize the significance of what they just asked me, we will be in serious trouble.''

''What answer will you eventually give?''

''That we have no data concerning any luminosity deficit of the nova. Perhaps their instruments malfunctioned.''

15

MARATEL WAS ESPECIALLY CHEERFUL TEN DAYS later as she glided into the commons after breakfast one morning. "How would you like to see the light sail attachment?"

Tory glanced at her guide with as much enthusiasm as she could muster. After two full months of playing tourist, details of her many visits about the ship had begun to blur into one long string of images. Had it been yesterday that she had sat through the interminable ceremony honoring Phela's dead, or the day before? What had been the name of that artisan who showed her his sculptures? He had been especially proud of his rendition of a human male *à la* Michelangelo's *David*. She hadn't had the heart to tell him that he had grossly oversized the sex organs—at least insofar as her own rather limited experience was concerned.

"Would I like to see what?" Tory asked. She had had a headache when she awoke. A tablet had largely solved that problem, but left her feeling out of sorts.

"I thought we'd travel to the opposite end of the ship so you can see where the shroud lines are anchored. It is quite an impressive sight. Also, your captain expressed an interest in the arrangement when he surveyed the ship following our taking your power unit in tow."

"Is Garth going with us?"

"No, he is with Dr. Claridge today. They're discussing the safeguards required before Phelan plants can be introduced into Earth's biosphere."

Tory nodded. Earth would require rigorous testing before they allowed any plant or animal to enter atmosphere. Even then, it would require a vote of the full system council to overcome the usual not-in-my-backyard protests. Since human foodstuffs were as lacking in certain critical proteins for Phelan chemical processes as the aliens's food was for humans, no one saw any other choice if a colony was to be established. It would be a great deal less expensive to grow food than to synthesize the needed additives, as *Far Horizons*'s chefs were doing with their human fare.

"If we're going to the opposite end of the ship, may we stop and see the falls?"

"If you wish."

Having been raised on Mars, Tory was fascinated by the idea of free-running water. She had become used to the gentle streams she had seen during her travels, but was still in awe of the pair of half-kilometer-tall waterfalls at the other end of the ship. She had often gazed across the kilometers to that spectacular double waterfall spilling down from the central axis, trying to imagine what it was like to hear the roar of all that water pounding down in a cloud of white spray. Despite her intention to visit them, something always seemed to come up to short-circuit the visit.

"Then let's go."

Maratel led her through the now familiar maze of corridors to the lift. Instead of dropping toward the outermost deck and the rim of the habitat volume, they rose upward toward the spin axis. Tory felt the pull of gravity diminish with each meter climbed. Her forays to the outer decks had done wonders in developing her muscles, but still, after a day in heavy gravity it was all she could do to hold her eyes open through dinner. Microgravity would feel good again.

The sun tube extended like an axle from one end of the starship to the other, held taut by the tension of the entire ship hanging from the space parachute behind them. Despite the energy radiating from the sun tube's surface, its interior contained both a transport system and vital utility lines. The transports were small capsules not unlike those of Olympus City. Tory and Maratel clambered into one. Both sat hunched forward, their heads a few centimeters apart, their bodies braced against the spherical walls to keep from floating away. The smell of cinnamon and paint thinner was overpowering.

"Mind if I ask you a personal question?" Tory asked as the car accelerated smoothly away from the station.

"Not at all. We are friends, are we not?"

"How do we smell to you?"

Maratel made a display of inhaling deeply. She wrinkled her nose as she did so. "That is difficult to describe."

"I mean, do we stink?"

"Your odor is . . . strange, but not unwholesome. We have a small flower that blooms during the high summer phase of our weather program. Its odor is vaguely reminiscent of your own. What of us? How do we Phelan smell to you humans?''

Tory smiled. ''Your odor reminds us of a highly valued spice mixed with a small amount of a certain chemical solvent.''

''That doesn't sound too bad,'' the Phelan said with an expression so serious that Tory had to laugh.

They were both laughing a few seconds later when the capsule signaled its arrival at the opposite end of the starship. The whole journey had taken less than a minute. Maratel let them out and led the way past the lifts that would take them down into the higher-gravity sections of the ship. As they moved through the spin-axis corridor, Tory realized that the Phelan had an advantage over humans when it came to moving about in micrograv-ity: their extra pair of appendages allowed them to move hand over hand with far more grace than Tory could manage. While Tory plodded along behind, Maratel swarmed forward like a spider in its web.

The corridor ended at the junction of six downward-leading passages. Unlike the lifts she had gotten used to, these small shafts had ladders affixed to their sides.

''These are for maintenance,'' Maratel said, indicating the tubes. ''We'll have to climb down.''

Tory suppressed a groan and told Maratel to lead on. The alien positioned her body to enter the tube feet first, then grasped the rails of the ladder loosely with her intermediate hands and pushed off with the upper set. A moment later, she was drifting downward like a terrestrial diver sinking into a deep well.

Tory followed Maratel's example. She wrapped her feet around the outside of the rails and pushed off with her hands. She then let the rails slip slowly through her lightly clenched fists. Looking down, she could see Maratel a dozen meters below, still falling. The two of them passed several openings in the walls of the maintenance tube. As they fell, spin gravity began to reassert itself. Tory found herself accelerating. She gently gripped the rails to slow her descent so that she wouldn't overtake Maratel.

Finally, when the pull had increased to approximately one-half the gravity Tory was used to at home, Maratel halted her fall and stepped off into a horizontal access tube. Tory followed. She felt clumsy compared to the Phelan's liquid grace. They had gone fifty meters through the too small tunnel when they came to a compartment that was little more than a widening of the corridor—except that half the cylindrical wall had suddenly turned transparent and through it shone the pearly glow of the light sail.

Tory moved to the window and gazed out. The sail was a glowing wall that covered half the universe. In front of it, barely a kilometer distant, hovered the large spherical shape from which sprouted a forest of infinitely long lines. The lines glowed with the violet light of electrons shimmering in vacuum. This, then, was the anchor point from which *Far Horizons* was suspended as it fell toward Sol.

Because of the difference between the starship's rate of rotation and that of the light sail, the whole assemblage seemed to be performing a giant dance. It was like standing near the hub of a great bicycle wheel and watching the spokes turn—except that no bicycle had ever possessed so many spokes as the Phelan starship. The shroud lines crisscrossed one another so thoroughly that they formed an ever changing kaleidoscope, violet and black over pearl white, as they pinwheeled across the sky.

Tory stood hypnotized for long seconds before she shifted her gaze to the attachment itself. A cable as thick as a human torso extended forward from the anchor sphere, disappearing as it dropped behind a lump on the starship's stern. She didn't have to see the end of the thick cable to know that this was the point from which all of *Far Horizons* was suspended.

Above the attachment sphere, the shroud lines fanned out. Each was as thick as the handle on a whip where it exited the black sphere, diminishing in cross-section until it became invisibly thin.

"How do you adjust line length?" Tory asked Maratel. The mystery of how the aliens controlled so unwieldy an object as the light sail had been the subject of several discussions in the commons after dinner.

"See the thick portions?" Maratel pointed to the whip-handle shapes jutting from the sphere. "We vary the line lengths by contracting or extending them. The thick region is where we store the extra material."

"I don't see any slip joints to allow rotation," Tory said, gazing at the sphere. To do its job, the attachment had to take up the difference in rotation between starship and light sail. How it managed that task was not obvious.

"We use a molecular slip system. If you're interested, I'll have someone explain it when we get back."

Tory laughed half heartedly. "Explain it to Garth or Kit. My brain is about to explode from information overload."

They stood for long minutes watching the grand pirouette in the sky. Finally, Maratel asked if Tory was ready to leave.

"Sure. Are we going to the falls now?"

Maratel nodded. "We must work our way around the periphery a bit to reach a power lift. I presume you have no desire to climb the maintenance ladder."

"In your gravity field? Not likely!"

"Do you mind if we make one stop on the way?"

"Where?"

"You'll see."

Tory didn't push. Several times Maratel had been mysterious as to where she was taking Tory, and each time the destination had proved worth the wait. She had sometimes wondered if springing surprises on people was a Phelan trait, or merely something Maratel liked to do as an individual.

The alien led her back the way they had come. They were forced to climb fifty meters to reach the intersection of a main corridor. After that it was a matter of hiking along the circumference. This close to the spin axis, the curvature of the corridor was pronounced. They always seemed to be at the base of a large dip, with the corridors sloping upward in both directions. Yet no matter how far they walked they were never able to reach the incline.

Maratel approached a heavy double door. The entryway swung back at their approach, as though someone inside had been watching their progress. Beyond the door lay a large pie-shaped compartment filled with busy Phelan. The compartment walls were covered with viewscreens displaying scenes from all over the ship. Tory saw passageways, compartments filled with machinery, and panoramic views of the habitat interior. She saw exterior views as well, including one that showed a tiny *Star-hopper* keeping station with the starship.

Tory had no time to gawk. Maratel led her along a raised walkway to another door. It, too, opened at their approach. Within she found a dimly lit room with a single massive console. A floor-to-ceiling holoscreen provided a backdrop for the being who awaited there. Standing before the console was Faslorn.

"Welcome to Command Central," the Phelan commander said.

"To what do I owe this singular honor?" she stuttered. So far as she knew, no one else in their party had ever been allowed inside *Far Horizons*'s command center. Requests to see it had always been met with polite evasions.

"I asked Maratel to arrange this visit because I have a proposition for you."

"Oh?"

Faslorn made the Phelan gesture of assent. "We Phelan know a great deal about your species. I think we have amply proved that point in the last few months."

"You have indeed."

"Yet, as aliens, we can never hope to understand you as well as you understand yourselves. It has been obvious to us for centuries that if we are to be successful in obtaining refuge in your system, we will need to gather talented human beings to our cause. Not hirelings, but true advocates of our position. We would like you to be our principal advocate."

Tory blinked. "Why me?"

"You have much personal empathy for us and are sympathetic to our cause. You are also equipped with a computer implant and know something of human law. Of the four humans we have met, you are the best candidate by far."

"There are probably millions on Earth who would better meet your requirements—people who make their living as lobbyists. Once you reach Earth, you'll have your pick of the very best."

"We will hire such people, of course. But they will be employees. We need an ally. Our extrapolations tell us that you are possibly the best ally we will ever meet. In any event, we cannot wait. Your captain and I have already spoken of your return to Earth."

"You have? He hasn't said anything to us."

"The decision to plan for a return voyage was made less than an hour ago. Perhaps he will tell you tonight. In any event, when you go, several of us will go along in coldsleep. It is important that we select our advocate before departure."

"Why?"

"For good and sufficient reasons that will become clear if you accept our offer. Will you help us convince your people to give us refuge?"

Tory hesitated. The truth was that she had come to like the Phelan. They were like eager little puppies in their mimicry of human culture. Except that there was very little resemblance to an eager puppy in Faslorn's manner. He seemed far more distant than she had ever known him. No, he seemed more *alien*! It was as though the thin veneer of human mannerisms had been stripped away, leaving behind a core that was pure Phelan. She noticed that he had ceased using human gestures altogether.

She stalled with a question. "What if I agree to represent you, then find that your interests run counter to those of humanity? I could never betray my people, Faslorn."

"There will be no question of betrayal," he assured her. "On the contrary, by serving us, you will be serving your own people, too."

"You are referring, of course, to the advanced technology you will give us in exchange for accepting you on our worlds."

"That and more important things."

"That seems a rather extreme statement. Can you back it up?"

"Should you accept our offer, I promise that you will know the truth before you leave this chamber. Do you accept?"

"I'd like some time to think about it."

"I am sorry, but we require your response now. There is much we must teach you, and little enough time."

Tory swallowed hard. She would have liked to talk this over with the others, but something in Faslorn's manner suggested that she wouldn't be allowed to. The truth was that she *did* believe in giving the Phelan sanctuary. With Earth going through its current bout of xenophobia, obtaining sanctuary for *Far Horizons*'s refugees was going to be difficult enough. It might not be possible at all if the aliens were left on their own. Their ability to mimic humanity reminded her of the old tale of the dog who could growl a few phrases: that he spoke badly was of less significance than the fact that he could speak it at all.

If she were to sign on as the Phelan's ambassador to humanity, she just might make the difference they needed. She had no false modesty about her own abilities. She was good, having excelled at everything she had ever attempted. If she became their advocate, she would do a much better than average job for them. Could there be any greater goal in life than helping this shipload of likable aliens come in from the cold and dark of interstellar space?

She considered her options and discovered that they were few indeed. It was as though fate had been steering her toward this for most of her life. She chewed her lower lip, took a deep breath, and finally nodded. "Based on your assurances that I will be helping my own people, I accept your offer. When do we start?"

"Immediately," *Far Horizons*'s commander said. He touched

a control stud and the lights dimmed. The large holoscreen behind him came immediately to light. From out of its pseudo-depth shone a thousand cold, distant stars. Dimly lit by starlight in the foreground were rank upon rank of cylindrical shapes. Tory felt a geyser of puzzlement well up within her. Each cylinder looked just as *Far Horizons* had upon approach, except that there was no evidence of a light sail on any of them.

"What the hell is this?" she asked as she gazed at the perplexing scene.

From somewhere nearby came Faslorn's disembodied voice. "You are looking at the Phelan Third Fleet, some six years behind us."

"What are you talking about? The other three ships of your fleet are all headed for other star systems."

"The story of the four ships is a work of fiction. Nor was there ever any Time of Troubles. It is pure fiction."

"But why lie about it?"

"To keep you from asking some rather obvious questions," Faslorn replied. "For one, how a race with our industrial potential only managed to construct four escape ships with fifty years' warning of the coming nova. Also, we hoped to engender sympathy for our cause."

"Then there aren't three other ships heading for other star systems?"

"That wasn't wholly a lie, Tory. Except the three ships are actually three other fleets. You see before you a small part of the fleet for which *Far Horizons* is a scout vessel."

Tory felt her throat constrict around the next words as she formed them. She barely managed to croak forth the question: "How many?"

Faslorn fixed her with a steady gaze as she in turn stood transfixed by the dimly glowing shapes inside the holoscreen.

"The Third Fleet numbers slightly more than twenty-two thousand vessels."

"And the number of Phelan en route to Sol?"

"During the last census, the fleet population numbered three billion individuals."

16

TORY FELT RAGE BUILDING WITHIN HER. HOW could they have studied humanity for so long, yet be so damned stupid? Hadn't their centuries of eavesdropping told them anything? Earth was deep in the throes of isolationism, and Mars could barely support her current 250 million. Tory had been worried sick for the last few weeks that Earth would reject *Far Horizons*'s paltry one hundred thousand refugees! How did Faslorn think the terrestrials would react when they learned there were twenty-two thousand other ships following right behind?

She retrieved what little self-control remained to her. *"Are you out of your skinking minds?"*

"I hope not," the Phelan commander said. If he noticed the murderous look she gave him, he showed no sign. His outward calm had the desired effect on Tory. With each gulp of air, she became a little less wild-eyed.

"But damn it, Faslorn, be reasonable! Earth can't absorb another three billion mouths, not even if they wanted to. They don't have the resources. Neither can Mars. We'd have trouble resettling the people off even a single ship, let alone the whole damned fleet. We'd all starve together!"

"We recognize the magnitude of the problem, and we wish we didn't have to impose on you, but we must."

"We'll fight if you try to force yourselves on us."

Faslorn fixed her with a steady gaze. "I hope it won't come to that. *Far Horizons* is merely the Third Fleet's advance scout. It is our privilege to reveal ourselves to humanity so those who follow can observe our fate. If peaceful means fail, they are prepared to try others."

"Are you threatening war?"

"War is certainly an option," Faslorn agreed. "You cannot imagine how powerful a weapon even a single light sail can be. We have studied several scenarios. Unfortunately, none of them offer us much hope of conquering an indigenous species on its home territory. We can exterminate humanity, but not conquer it.''

''Damned right!'' Tory said. A moment later, she wondered at the sudden surge of adrenaline in her veins. It wasn't fear so much as the primal call to arms that was affecting her. The hot blood that coursed through her was the legacy of a thousand generations of warrior ancestors.

''Unfortunately, while exterminating humanity, we would also exterminate most life on the worlds we hope to inherit. The Earth would not support our colony afterward. It would be a Pyrrhic victory.'' Faslorn emitted a sound that Tory knew to be the equivalent of a human sigh. ''If your people reject us, we will be forced to do something far worse than war.''

''What can be worse than war?'' Tory asked, her anger suddenly submerged by her curiosity.

''Know this, Victoria Bronson. Our star was not a victim of stellar evolution. The reaction that eventually destroyed Tau Ceti was artificially induced. I'm afraid that we Phelan destroyed our star.''

''You destroyed your own star?''

Faslorn signaled his assent. ''Those who began the nova reaction were from a faction we call the 'usurpers.' I will not attempt to describe their reasons, as no human could possibly understand them. Even we, raised aloof from Phelan custom, have difficulty understanding the nature of the argument that caused Tau Ceti's destruction. Suffice to say that the usurpers's aim was to gain advantage by threatening the rest of our species with a weapon of ultimate destructive power. They planned a small demonstration to convince their opponents the threat was real. Someone miscalculated and so upset our star's equilibrium that the damage could not be repaired. Our scientists were able to retard the reaction, but not to stop it. Fifty-two cycles after the initial mistake, our sun went nova.''

''What happened to the usurpers?''

''They remained behind to observe the culmination of their handiwork at close hand.''

Tory shuddered. ''How awful!''

''We prefer to think of it as justice.''

''You realize, of course, that we'll never accept you once this story becomes public. People who explode their own star are capable of anything.''

''You do not yet understand,'' Faslorn replied. ''If those who command the Third Fleet feel their cause to be hopeless, they will seek another star by initiating a nova reaction within Sol.''

Tory's mouth dropped open. It took her a moment to regain control. ''You'd blow up the Sun?''

''With the greatest reluctance, I assure you.''

''But why?''

''We require the nova to propel our light sails. Without it, the journey between stars is a matter of millennia rather than centuries. None of our ships would remain operable over such a long journey. The Third Fleet would be peopled by corpses by the time it arrived at the new destination. So you see, Victoria, I spoke the literal truth when I said that you will help humanity by helping us. Find us a place to live and we will make your species rich. Deny us and your race is doomed!''

It was nearly a minute before Tory ran out of obscenities to hurl at the two Phelan. Only when she began repeating herself for the third time did she begin to wind down. Through the whole outpouring of vituperation, Faslorn and Maratel stood impassive.

''And this is your plan?'' Tory asked. Her words dripped sarcasm. ''After two centuries, this is all you've been able to come up with?''

''Unfortunate, but true.''

''There has to be a better way.''

''We've spent all our lives looking for a better way. There is none.''

Tory brushed back an errant lock of hair and tried to think. There were times in life when matters were too serious to allow emotions to interfere with one's judgment. When she had been a child, a dome had ruptured at home. Most of those who had kept their wits about them had survived. Those who panicked had died. That incident had been trivial compared to what she now faced. Tory ruthlessly forced her raging emotions into a tightly locked compartment in the back of her mind and began to think furiously.

''Look, I don't buy the crap you're shoveling for a second, but for the sake of argument, let's say you are telling the truth. How can you possibly expect to get away with it? In six years your fleet will begin to unfurl its sails and anyone with a pair of binoculars will see the twenty-two thousand tiny lights blossoming in the sky. There will be riots in the streets!''

''By that time, we must achieve a position in your society that will allow us to ride out the shock just as we once rode the nova's shock.''

"How the hell do you expect to do that?"

"We have observed that human motivation is steeped in self-interest. Therefore, if we are to be accepted, there must be a strong constituency whose self-interest lies with us. With your assistance, we will demonstrate to certain powerful and influential humans how they will benefit from our advanced technology. If properly done, we will have enough allies when the time comes to ride out the storm.''

Tory gave a low whistle. "That's a powerful order.''

"That is why we need your help. Without you, we have no hope of success. With you, there is a slim chance.''

Tory fell silent. Her mind raced wildly as her stomach did nervous flip-flops. The taste of bile was strong in her mouth. Too late she recognized the trap Faslorn had set for her. It was a construct of almost fiendish cleverness, and one that reinforced the idea that the Phelan knew humans better than humanity itself did.

For if a human were to attempt such an outlandish scheme, he would most likely recruit her with fanciful lies. By telling her the awful truth, Faslorn had bound her to him and his cause more tightly than if he had used a chain and a welding torch. She could trumpet the warning to Earth, but to what avail? The news would lead to panic. The Phelan request for sanctuary would be rejected out of hand, and sometime within the next six years, Sol would explode into a twin of the Tau Ceti nova.

No, if she was to avoid the Sun's destruction, she would have to keep Faslorn's secret for him. That, in turn, had other implications. If she kept the secret, then humanity's safety would depend on her alone. She must guard her every word and action for years to come. Even a single slip of the tongue could end everything. The weight of responsibility would be crushing. Could she do it? Did she have the inner strength to stand up under the pressure?

Yet, even if successful, she was doomed. When the truth of the Third Fleet became known, she would appear a traitor to her species, a Mata Hari who had suborned others to treason. She wondered what penalty would be meted out on that inevitable black day. Would she be arrested, or simply torn limb from limb by an enraged mob? The worst of it was the realization that she would be hated for as long as the human race survived. She would go to her grave with the knowledge of the service she had rendered to her people.

She had a sudden wild urge to tell Faslorn to go to hell. She suppressed it. It would be hugely satisfying, but counterproductive. No, there was no choice in the matter. She must ignore the gnawing emptiness within and aid these engaging monsters in their scheme, at least until she could think her way out of the quandary.

"All right, Faslorn. I will keep your secret because I must."

"Thank you, Victoria. With your help, perhaps we will succeed."

Faslorn's apparent sincerity was too much for her. She had reached the point where she could no longer ignore the weakness of the flesh. The frightened little girl locked away deep inside had to be let out. Tory opened the locked door in her mind and let her emotions come gushing forth. She sank to the carpeted deck and succumbed to a storm of racking sobs. Neither alien moved to comfort her. There was nothing they could do.

Hours later, Maratel guided her back to the forward end of the starship. They sat again in the small capsule with nose and snout close together. Again the odor of cinnamon and paint thinner was overpowering. Only this time, Tory felt none of the bonhomie that she had felt on the outward journey. Suddenly, Maratel was no longer an oddly shaped friend. She was as alien as Faslorn had become, an enemy whom Tory was being compelled to help.

"You must not think too badly of us," Maratel said, breaking a silence of many minutes. "You would do the same in our place."

"Sorry, but I can't accept that."

"That isn't your brain speaking, Tory. It's your heart. I can cite you thousands of incidents in which one group of humans did far worse to another group."

"That's our business, not yours."

"True. I merely point out that we wish your race no harm. We must, however, insure our own survival."

Tory thought about it, then nodded. "I suppose I can recognize that intellectually. Still, I can't help hating you for it."

"You must get over your hatred. We do not ask you to love us. If we are to be successful, we must work well together. If you hate us, you will not be an effective advocate."

"You'll at least give me a few days to get used to my servitude, won't you?"

"We owe you that. What will you tell your fellows? They are bound to notice the change in you."

"I'll tell them I don't feel well."

"That you are ill?" Maratel mused. "Will not Dr. Claridge then examine you and discover that you are, in fact, well?"

"Do you have a better solution?"

"Perhaps we can blame your condition on a failed attempt at getting your implant working."

Tory thought about it, then nodded. "That'll work. A loss-of-synchronization accident often leaves the victim feeling a bit suicidal. We'll use that as the excuse for why I'm snapping everyone's head off."

"Would it help if we activate your implant now?"

"Are you saying that you've been faking these troubles in establishing a link?"

"It seemed wise. After all, had you been in touch with your ship when Faslorn told you the news, you would have recorded it in *Austria*'s computer. There might have been a chance that the recording would have been viewed by someone else."

Tory looked at Maratel and thought of all the times she had wished her implant were working. All along they had never had any intention of activating her link with the ship's computer. After what she had just been through, the anger she felt at the news seemed oddly misplaced. "Well—I'll—be—double—damned!"

Two obsidian eyes stared into her own. "If we are successful in the coming venture, Tory Bronson, I think it more likely that you will be declared a human saint!"

When Maratel delivered Tory back to the human living quarters, it was well past the beginning of the sleep period and she found the commons dark and deserted. Tory had lost all track of time during the meeting with Faslorn. Despite not having eaten all day, she was not hungry. She wondered if she would ever be hungry again. What she mostly felt was tired down to the marrow in her bones. All she could think of was to hop into bed and sleep for a week. Maybe when she woke, this nightmare would be over.

As she turned to enter her own apartment, she felt another stirring deep within, on a level so primal as to be below the level of conscious thought. She hesitated for a moment as she wrestled with an impulse that was not only silly under the circumstances, but also potentially dangerous.

Against her better judgment, she made her way to the door. It was not that of her own apartment, but Garth's. Once inside, she quietly slipped out of her clothes as she listened to the soft sound of his steady breathing. She managed to climb into bed and press her body to his before he stirred. He came awake quickly, sputtering, "What the hell?"

"Hold me," she commanded him.

He instinctively reached out and enfolded her in his embrace. After a few moments, gentle hands began to stroke the bare skin of her back.

"What's going on?" he whispered.

"I feel like company tonight."

"Why, what's wrong?" he asked, all the sleep-induced blur suddenly gone from his voice.

"I'll explain in the morning. For now, just hold me."

"All right."

They lay together for what seemed an eternity. Then, at a welcoming gesture from Tory, Garth initiated that most ancient of all means of delivering solace.

Faslorn and Maratel watched the display carefully. The low-light sensors were working perfectly, rendering an image that if viewed by humans would have been considered pornographic.

"Do you suppose she will tell him?"

Maratel did not answer immediately. She had studied Tory more carefully than most beings studied their offspring. The complexity of the human mind awed her, and frightened her a little. Tory was intelligent, possibly even a genius by human standards. When coupled with her implant, her intellect was enhanced far above normal. Still, a human with direct mind access to a computer was still a human, and human actions were ruled by unpredictable emotions. Tory might well charge into the commons in the morning and announce their secret to everyone. Or she might bide her time, pretend to cooperate with them, and then send a message to Earth as soon as *Austria* was away from their ship. Or she just might cooperate.

"Unknown" was Maratel's answer to Faslorn's question.

"Monitor carefully," her commander ordered. "We will take no chances. If you even suspect an attempt to pass the information on through subtle signals, we will go to the backup plan."

"That would be a mistake," Maratel said. "The death of the

explorers in a sudden accident would be viewed with great suspicion on Earth. It is doubtful we could ever overcome the impression that would leave with the human masses.''

"Mistake or no, it would be necessary. The safety of the race is not to be gambled with.''

Maratel made no answer. She didn't have to. Faslorn's statement was more than a command, it was a lesson drilled into every Phelan child almost before it could talk. The species had been threatened with extinction once. It must never face that risk again.

17

TORY AWOKE THE NEXT MORNING TO FIND GARTH asleep on the next pillow. His mouth was open and he was snoring gently. Typical man! she thought. Then the events of the previous day came flooding back to her. She rolled over to face the wall while she came to terms with her raging emotions. So preoccupied was she that she failed to hear the cessation of snores behind her.

She jumped when Garth spoke. "What was last night about?"

Tory composed herself, turned over, and began to lie. "Sorry if I frightened you. I just didn't want to be alone. Maratel and I had a little accident yesterday."

"What sort of accident?"

"I thought the Phelan had solved their problem with the implant link. I wouldn't have tried it otherwise. Honest!"

His complexion blanched and his voice turned gruff as he asked, "What happened?"

"I established contact here in the commons and it worked fine. Maratel suggested a test at the opposite end of the ship. We made a picnic of it. She showed me the sail anchor mechanism and we were on our way to Spiral Falls when I tested the link. I made contact without difficulty, then tried a full sensory transmission."

"And?"

"I lost synchronization. Maratel says that I passed out. Anyway, when I came to, I found her leaning over me. If you want to know what fright looks like in a Phelan, I can tell you."

"Never mind. Are you all right?"

"Except for feeling sick down to my soul, I think so."

Tory carefully studied his expression as she embroidered her lie. His concern had turned to open fear at the mention of loss of synchronization. More than one synergist had been driven permanently insane by such an incident.

Garth reached out and stroked her cheek with gentle fingers. "We'll have Kit look you over."

"Later. Now I need my sleep. I didn't get much rest last night," she said with total honesty.

"I remember," he replied.

This time Tory said it aloud. "Typical man!"

Garth got out of bed and went into the sanitary compartment while Tory pretended to fall back to sleep. She nearly succeeded. After Garth had returned to slumber around midnight, she had tossed and turned for hours as her overheated brain refused to calm down. It had been like some wild animal in a cage, pacing back and forth between the boundaries of her dilemma, always looking for the weak spot that would signal a way out. She didn't remember blessed unconsciousness overtaking her, but she knew that she had slept less than two hours the entire night.

Besides needing her rest, there was another reason for avoiding Kit Claridge. A loss-of-synchronization accident left indelible marks on the victim's reflexes. Tory could not submit to a medical examination because the results would reveal that there was nothing wrong with her reflexes. She would have to avoid the doctor until enough time passed that she could plausibly claim to be throwing off the effects.

Garth came out of the compartment wiping depilatory cream from his chin. "You will make no further attempts to link with the ship's computer. We've lived without that receiver in your skull this long, we can do without a few weeks longer."

Just in time, Tory remembered she was not supposed to know that their departure had been fixed. "What do you mean?"

"I mean we're going home."

"Huh?"

"That's right. We launch three weeks from tomorrow if we can get ready in time. There's a lot to do. Faslorn and three others will be coming with us. We'll have to install their cold-sleep tanks in the hold, along with a supply of Phelan dietary supplements."

"What of our own food?"

"We'll move it into the living quarters. We'll be a little crowded on the trip home."

Three weeks! No wonder Faslorn had been in a hurry to find an advocate. If she was going to think her way out of the dilemma, she had a maximum two months in which to do it. Once *Austria* climbed the mountain of velocity again, the human crew would follow their Phelan passengers into sleep tanks. Their return to Earth would take a year—a year lost to all but cold dreams. A great deal can happen in a year. Earth might see through the Phelan masquerade, or they might discover the Third Fleet, or reject the Phelan petition for sanctuary. Tory had a nightmare vision of waking to find the Sun exploding around her—except, if the Sun exploded, there would be no waking . . . ever.

For just a moment she considered blurting out her problem to Garth. Even if she were being monitored, the Phelan wouldn't be able to react fast enough to stop her. But the impulse died before it was born. At best, the Phelan would take all of them prisoner and cut off communications with Earth. Or possibly they would maintain the charade that everything was normal, stage *Austria*'s departure on schedule, and then explode the engines. It would be easy enough to send their condolences for the brave lives lost.

Perhaps there was some signal she could give Garth that the Phelan would fail to recognize. But to what end? If she alerted him and he was clever enough to get a message off to Earth, then the Sun would shine a million times brighter than normal in six short years. As she had discovered the previous day, Faslorn's bonds upon her were all the stronger for being immaterial.

"Are you sure you're all right?" Garth asked again as he prepared to leave.

She gave him a wan smile that was as much a lie as her recounting of the implant accident had been. "I'm fine. All I need to put my psyche back together is rest."

"I'll explain what happened to the others. Kit can examine you this evening."

With that, Tory found herself alone. It was a feeling she had best get used to, she decided. It would be with her for a very long time to come. She gathered the covers about her with hands that had begun to shake.

Everything continued as before. The Phelan guides showed up each morning to take their charges to various appointments. Kit was excited by the medical techniques the Phelan doctors were demonstrating, and her reports to Earth were filled with superlatives and the impenetrable jargon with which doctors communicate. Eli continued his slow, plodding progress in learning the Phelan language. He could now converse with the younger children if they did not speak too quickly. When Garth wasn't supervising the modifications to *Austria*, he spent his time conferring with Faslorn, Rosswin, and the other high-ranking starship commanders. Tory, too, spent hours in the hangar bay watching over Phelan technicians. Her shifts were usually in the afternoon. Her mornings were spent with Maratel.

For Tory, everything was not as before. She now recognized the whole operation for what it was—a carefully staged ballet in which every muscle twitch and phoneme was as stylized as a performance of Japanese Kabuki theater. Outwardly, the Phelan remained as charming as ever. The only problem was that she could now see the strings holding the puppets erect. That soured the play for her.

Slowly, Tory began to regain her equilibrium and her appetite. She still hated what Faslorn had done to her, but she could at least think about it without flying into a rage. The nightmares came less often, and she could go for days without having visions of the Sun suddenly blazing forth to swallow her world. Kit thought her counseling helped, and it had. But much of Tory's recovery from her "implant accident" was the result of her own inner resilience. "People," a wise man had once said, "can get used to anything except death!" In the days following her recruitment, Tory found reason to believe him.

Her trips with Maratel were ostensibly to show her some part of the ship. Sometimes, they really were tours. One of the first places Maratel took her was Spiral Falls. The two of them sat for an hour where the roaring torrent splashed down on the habitat's outer deck. The noise was so loud that it was difficult to think—and easy to forget. The gray spray quickly soaked Tory to the bone, and she slipped into a shivery trance upon which no external stimulus intruded. Later, she and Maratel warmed their frigid bodies under the distant sun tube. Baking oneself on a hot rock, Tory discovered, was as pleasurable as it was atavistic.

However, most of her tours with Maratel were clandestine training sessions. Before she would allow the Phelan to speak of anything else, Tory demanded to know how Tau Ceti had been destabilized and destroyed. The explanations were concise, and so far as she could tell, complete. They involved the interaction between neutrinos at a particular energy level and the superdense hydrogen plasma that is found at the heart of stars. She lacked the background to understand all that she was told, but what she was able to understand sounded plausible. In any event, she had no desire to put the Phelan explanation to a practical test.

Once the Phelan had convinced her that they could indeed do what they threatened, they immersed her in the details of their master plan to insinuate themselves into human society. She had to admit that they seemed to have thought of everything . . . everything, that is, except the obvious.

In the abstract, the aliens might well win over enough of Earth's influential class that they could ride out the public furor after the Third Fleet's discovery. As the Phelan were forever pointing out to her, it was only logical.

But Tory knew that people followed their own brand of logic. In practice it would matter little how many captains of industry the Phelan bought, politicians they bribed, or scholars they convinced as to the rightness of their cause. The average man or woman could be pushed only so far before rebelling. Once the magnitude of their deception became known, no one would dare speak well of them. Those foolish enough to do so would be swept away by a hurricane of public outrage. Like Tory, the Phelan ambassadors probably would be lynched, as would anyone else who had helped them.

So, while pretending to play tourist, Tory also pretended to play along with the Phelan while she searched for a way out of her dilemma. In this she was aided by her implant, which, unknown to Garth and the others, she used almost continuously.

"When do we tell my shipmates that I'm to be your advocate?" Tory asked Maratel one day while they were touring a food-synthesis plant. Kit had accompanied them, but was being distracted by her guide while Tory and Maratel talked.

"Best not to reveal our arrangement until we reach Earth. To bring it up sooner will pique curiosities and might get the wrong people to thinking."

Tory agreed, but not for Maratel's reasons. The Phelan were concerned about awkward questions while Tory worried that her friends would think her a traitor. She was human enough that she did not want to face ostracism any sooner than she had to.

The farewell banquet was held in the same hall as the welcoming banquet, with the same important functionaries in attendance. Again the four humans shared the raised dais with Faslorn and their Phelan guides. The two Phelan who would accompany Faslorn and Maratel to Earth were also present. Neirton was a specialist in human psychology, while Raalwin, an ortho-sibling of Rosswin's, was a political specialist. They would design the public-relations and lobbying campaign that the Phelan hoped would breach the indifference of human public opinion.

All four Phelan would be placed in coldsleep in *Austria*'s hold in the morning. After that, the four humans would board, check out the ship's systems, and if all went well, depart the hangar bay. They would stop to mate with the *Starhopper* booster and spend several more hours making sure that nothing had gone bad during their long absence. Then they would line up their bow on the bright yellow star in the constellation of Virgo and boost for home.

Though the initial banquet had been stiff and formal, the farewell included a great deal of humor. The Phelan grasp of human humor had improved since the team had first come aboard. Several Phelan, their lower arms strapped to their bodies, put on a comedy sketch for their guests. They presented a parody of each human explorer so perfect that Garth, Eli, and Kit clutched their aching ribs as they laughed. Even Tory laughed as one of the Phelan pranced about in a recognizable version of her own walk. For a while, at least, it was easy to forget what underlay the entertainment.

At the end of the meal, Faslorn rose at his place and regarded the human beings on either side of him. It seemed to Tory that his gaze lingered on her a fraction of a second longer than the others.

"Friends, I stand before you as host one last time. Tomorrow I will become your cargo, and then your guest. During these months we have tried to give you some understanding of who and what we are—" Tory, who had just begun to sip the excellent ersatz wine, sputtered momentarily as liquid went down the wrong way. She felt Faslorn's stare as she quickly moved her napkin to her lips, both to clean herself and to hide her expression. The Phelan leader went on without seeming to miss a beat.

"We who have crossed the great gulf came here to find peace around your beautiful yellow sun. We have found much more. Separately, our two species have overcome much to reach this point in our individual histories. Together, there is no limit to what we will do."

Faslorn lifted his glass, as did everyone in the room. Tory was slow, but managed to retrieve her glass without a noticeable delay. "To the descendants of Mother Earth, from the children of lost Phela. May our association be long and fruitful!"

There were shouts of agreement from around the crowd. As

Tory drank, she had to admit that she shared the sentiment. Of all the humans on the dais, she alone knew the true alternative.

"They're coming home!" Dardan Pierce said to Bernardo Lucci as the Italian astronomer strode into his office.

"When did you hear that?"

"Just this minute. The communications supervisor switched off as you came through the door. Garth's message announcing the departure arrived about twenty minutes ago. They're coming home and bringing four Phelan with them. They'll be here this time next year."

"When do they leave?"

Pierce glanced up at the chronometer on the wall. "If they kept to their timetable, they've already left. We should see their drive flare in a couple of weeks."

Lucci rubbed his hands together. "Any news as to the data they will be bringing back?"

"Unknown," Pierce said. "I imagine they will have a great deal of science with them as samples to convince us to allow their colony."

"Any close-up views of the exploding nova?"

"How the hell should I know? Besides, didn't they already send us that travelogue? It shows the nova exploding."

"That travelogue isn't much better than a home holo of some stranger's little darlings at play," Lucci sneered. "Where are the calibration curves, the time marks, and all the other data we need to do real science?"

"Seems to me that Tycho Brahe did pretty fair astronomy with just his naked eye and a sextant."

"It was a quadrant, not a sextant," Lucci replied. "No, we need real data to work with. About all we can get out of that travelogue is that their star exploded, something we can see with our own eyes."

"Don't be so glum. They've solved one mystery for us."

"You mean the light deficiency? I hardly call putting it down to experimental error a solution. If the instruments were bad, why did they track the theoretical curve so precisely for several weeks afterward?"

"I have no idea. Instead of grousing about it, why don't you see for yourself? The Union undoubtedly has the original data locked away in their archives somewhere. Get a copy and see if you can't find out where our predecessors went wrong."

Lucci struck Pierce's desk with his fist. "By damn, I'll do just that! If our modern techniques can't resolve the discrepancy, we don't deserve to be called astronomers."

18

GARTH VAN ZANDT LAY IN HIS CONTROL COUCH aboard *Austria* and stared pensively at the main viewscreen. The small telescope that had once scanned the skies for a first sight of *Far Horizons* was now focused on two tiny crescent disks. At full magnification, Earth and Luna were twin marbles three-quarters in shadow. Earth's night hemisphere was ablaze with tiny diamond sparkles, the lights of vast megalopolises. Even three centuries after the race had first won free of its home world, fully ninety-five percent of humanity lived beneath blue skies and fleecy white clouds. Most had never been higher than the peak of a suborbital transport's trajectory. Most never would.

The sight of home triggered a flood of emotions. It was common for travelers long absent to feel acute longing at their first sight of home. Garth felt that and more. Mixed with the longing was exhilaration, and a certain sadness. The exhilaration was natural: they were alive and the mission successful. More than once he'd had his doubts on both counts.

The sadness was natural, too. The small family they had become these past several months would soon be sundered. Each expedition member would go his or her separate way. Tory, Kit, and Eli would undoubtedly be assigned to the alien-assessment teams, while he would return to the fleet. With this voyage on his record, there was a good chance he would be assigned command of a cruiser.

The emotion he felt was that of an ending. A part of his life was over, never to be regained. It was natural to feel a little bit of a letdown at the end of a long patrol, but this was more than that. This wasn't just the end of a mission, but of an era. Never again would humankind look to the night sky and think the lights there sterile. Henceforth, everyone who tilted a head back to gaze at the stars would wonder if other eyes were gazing back. There were more stars in the sky than all the grains of sand and motes of dust on Earth and Mars combined. No matter how wildly improbable life was in the universe, a billion-trillion stars must have thousands of spacefaring cultures sprinkled among them. The Phelan were the first; they would certainly not be the last.

His sense of melancholy had a more personal cause as well. The end of the voyage also meant separation from Tory. He had had more than a few shipboard romances in his career, and they had always ended amicably enough. Come home orbit, the partners packed their bags, kissed each other passionately one last time, then moved on to the next assignment. But lately Garth had found himself thinking about making his arrangement with Tory permanent. He had been serious enough to suggest a limited marriage contract. To his surprise and hurt, she'd turned him down. Her reasons for rejecting him had become increasingly evasive as he pressed her.

Of all of them, Tory seemed the most changed by contact with the aliens. She had been pensive, withdrawn, and preoccupied ever since leaving the starship. He had tried to cajole her out of her mood, with only limited success. Even on those few nights when she made her way to his cabin, she had seemed a stranger.

Nor had Garth been the only one to notice. Kit ascribed the personality change to the lasting effects of the synchronization accident. Eli had no cause to offer, but had tried to be a sympathetic listener, a role for which he lacked talent. Nothing seemed to help. Whatever was wrong, Garth hoped a return to human society would snap her out of it.

As he stared vacantly at the blue-white world on the viewscreen, he heard a quiet sound behind him. They were under boost with half a standard gravity of deceleration on the ship. He recognized the quiet thud of bare feet mounting the rungs of the ladder leading up from the deck below. Tory's head and shoulders appeared out of the access tunnel a moment later.

She was clad in her usual costume of singlet and shorts, which showed off her long legs to good advantage. Her hair had been trimmed short just prior to departure, and hadn't grown much during their year in coldsleep.

"Won't be long now, will it?"

"Not long," he agreed. "We take up parking orbit in another seventy-two hours. Where's Eli?"

"Oh, he was grousing about getting behind in his studies. I told him I'd take his watch for him."

"What about your own watch?"

She shrugged. "So I'll do two in a row. I can do my correlations here as well as anywhere."

"All right, but don't overdo it."

"Yes, sir."

She lounged against an instrument console and stared at the viewscreen while he made some end-of-watch notations in the log. A long sigh brought his attention back to her.

"What's the matter?"

"Nothing. I never really expected to get to Earth."

He smiled. "Just a hick from the sticks, eh?"

"A what?"

"Sorry. Antique slang. Just a digger from the darly, I should have said."

"That's me." She flexed her arms in a way that hiked her bosom up in the low gravity. "I wonder if I still have my high-gravity muscles?"

"From where I'm sitting, you do."

"Lecher!"

"Can I help it if I appreciate the human form?"

"Well, on that note, I relieve you, sir."

"I stand relieved," he replied formally. In a more conversational tone, he asked, "Who was that showering about half an hour ago?"

"Kit."

"Did she leave me any water?"

"Don't know."

"She better have! I feel like I haven't washed in a week."

Tory made a show of sniffing the air and screwed up her face. In truth, the smells aboard a spaceship were such that it was often difficult to tell where the ship's odor left off and that of the crew began.

Garth turned to leave. Out of the corner of his eye he caught Tory's expression. The impish look was already beginning to fade, to be replaced by the long face she had worn habitually since leaving the starship. Whatever her private demon, he thought, it seemed to be getting the best of her.

Tory gazed for long minutes at the Earth and Moon. As more than one poet had noted, there are few sights more beautiful than the Earth from space. To a Martian, one raised amid the driest desert in the Solar system, the watery home planet held a certain intellectual beauty. Still, Tory would have preferred to be back in Dome Three on Phobos, gazing up at the ocher plains and walking walls of red dust. The little girl within her wanted to slink back to the womb, to return to the familiar sights of childhood where she could forget her terrible secret.

She had to admit that there was something restful about watching the home world grow slowly larger day by day. She drew peace from the evidence that humankind still lived beneath a well-behaved star. Or maybe her newfound tranquillity was the result of fatalism. Like the heroine in a Greek tragedy, she was resolved to play her part in the Phelan drama though she knew it to be hopeless. Any other action on her part would only accelerate the inevitable.

Having resigned herself to her fate, Tory had turned her intellect to the problem of pushing the inevitable as far into the future as it would go. To do that required her to take some actions she did not want to take. Still, she faced her choices squarely. Her synergist training helped her in that respect. As a professor had once said, "A synergist faces facts. To do otherwise is dishonest. Besides, it doesn't work."

To play her part in the drama, she would have to hurt people she cared for. She had already claimed the first of her victims: Garth had asked her to sign a limited marriage contract. She remembered the hurt look in his eyes when she had refused and the even greater hurt he had shown when she wouldn't tell him why. Despite the ache she felt within, she had remained steadfast. How could she let him know that she could not be his wife because she was bound body and soul to a gaggle of alien monsters? What if he had wanted children? What kind of woman would bring children into a world that had fewer than six years to live?

Garth had been the first victim. He would not be the last. After she came out of coldsleep, she found a string of messages from Ben Tallen. He had been promoted again, and was now the principal aide to his old boss, former Underminister for Science Sadibayan, now humanity's ambassador to the Phelan. He had spoken in glowing terms about resuming their relationship.

Funny, but she had trouble remembering what Ben looked like. Could coldsleep damage a person's memories, or was it the time-heals-all-wounds principle at work? His letters had also spoken of a position waiting for her on the ambassador's staff. Ben had gushed on about how good it would be to work together. She fretted over how she was going to break the news that she was joining the opposition.

How many others would she hurt before this was done? Hundreds? Thousands? In a sense, she would be hurting all the billions who lived throughout the Solar system. For the short time they had left to live, the name Victoria Bronson would be synonymous with that of Judas Escariot.

Even the longest journey must eventually end, Tory thought as she listened to the silent countdown in her brain. Their voyage had been the longest in human history, and was likely to remain so for quite some time. On the aft viewscreen, Earth had grown from a tiny spark amid infinite blackness to a great blue-white ball that overflowed the camera's field of view. The only part of the home world still visible was the curving arc of the planet's limb with its impossibly thin atmosphere line. The scene was softened by the iridescent fog that spewed from their exhaust and spread outward in a gently glowing cone of light.

Then, without fanfare, the countdown ended. The fires of matter/antimatter annihilation were extinguished. Thrust waned and Tory rebounded in the straps that lightly held her in place. Her body had not stopped oscillating when Garth ordered her to prepare for booster separation.

Tory issued the command sequence while Garth took the necessary precautions for separating *Austria* from its booster. This time there was no tedious effort to unplug the fiber-optic assemblies from their interface boxes. This time their links with the booster were severed by a pyrotechnic charge. The giant power unit had dwindled in size until it was barely larger than the corvette. All the gleaming white fuel tanks but one had been jettisoned, and all but a few milligrams of antimatter consumed. They were home and would have no further need for the module.

Garth handled the separation with practiced deftness. At the sight of the truncated pyramid receding into the black, Tory felt a sudden flash of nostalgia. This would be the last time she laid eyes on the machine she had helped build. The booster would be towed into Solar orbit where it would be parked amid the other space junk. When the neutron-induced radioactivity of its power section had cooled for a few decades, it would be broken up and its components reclaimed. Nothing in space was ever thrown away forever.

They watched the booster until it had dwindled to invisibility before Garth switched to forward view. There, slightly off center on the viewscreen, lay a rotating cylinder. It wasn't until one noticed the small ships hovering around one end that the scale of the thing became apparent.

Elysium Station was one of the oldest of humanity's space habitats. It had been built as a proof-of-concept design for the first Lagrange colony, and the station had seen its share of history. It had been the site where the treaty that ended the Martian rebellion had been signed, and the launching point for a dozen voyages of exploration to the outer planets. One of these had been the ill-fated Brandenburg-Cheng expedition to the moons of Saturn. The station was about to make history again—today it was to be the greeting place for humanity's first alien visitors.

The station had been added to and modified extensively over the years. Originally a solid cylinder, its latest incarnation had converted it to a hollow tube. A dozen circumferential decks surrounded an axis passage two hundred meters in diameter. Clusters of communications antennas sprouted from both ends of the station, while the interior was kept clear of clutter. It was in the long tunnel that the ships of deep space were moored during loading operations. Smaller vessels, such as *Austria*, and the hyperjets of Earth, were winched inside the hangar bays that dotted the inner cylinder walls. Larger ships were spun about their long axes until synchronized with the station, then moored at the axis of rotation.

Garth kept the controls in manual as they made their approach. Every few minutes, he fired attitude-control jets to correct adverse drift. Slowly they glided toward the station's open maw. Tory noted that there were stars in the bottom of the deep well toward which they were falling.

The light around the ship changed as they passed out of sunlight and into shadow. There were lights all around the cylinder's interior. Some of the lights were large floodlamps focused on them to give the station controllers a clear view. A line of colored lasers on the opposite rim of the station kept them aligned with the station axis. In front and below, an open hatchway blazed forth with interior lights. There were other, smaller lighted squares around them—windows through which they could see several small figures craning their necks upward to catch a glimpse of *Austria*.

Garth pushed on his control one last time, and was answered by a burp of the jets. A quick twist followed and *Austria* began to slowly rotate about its own axis. The stars at the bottom of the well began a stately dance around their prow, while the moving wall overhead began to slow. A minute later it was only the stars that rotated, and the surrounding station seemed rock steady. Tory felt a moment of discomfort as the fluid in her semicircular canals tried to come to terms with the new forces exerted upon it. Garth released his control stick and watched the alignment lasers for long seconds. Satisfied, he reported their arrival to the station controllers.

A second later, three lines snaked upward from around the station's interior wall. They attached themselves to different points on *Austria*'s hull with a dull clang, then grew taut as three computer-controlled winches took up the slack. After a few seconds, the ship began to drift out of position toward the open hatchway.

The light outside changed again as they entered the docking bay. The ship lurched a last time as the landing jacks touched deck. Two of the winch cables released and quickly disappeared upward through the open hatch, which then closed. There followed a silence of long seconds before a minor hurricane of wind sounds buffeted *Austria* as air was returned to the bay. In half a minute, the wind sounds died as well.

Garth let out a huge sigh, then switched on the general intercom. "All hands! Secure the ship. We're home!"

19

GARTH, TORY, KIT, AND ELI GATHERED AT THE midships airlock. They were each in newly cleaned and pressed shipsuits. The small suiting chamber just inside the airlock was crowded; besides *Austria*'s human crew, it also held Faslorn, Maratel, Neirton, and Raalwin. The four Phelan had been revived three days earlier to give them time to recuperate from the effects of coldsleep. The mixed scent of human and Phelan was strong in the enclosed space as the eight of them crowded together, waiting for the debarkation bridge to be moved into place.

Garth had exercised the privilege of rank to be the first to disembark. Faslorn would be next, with Tory, Maratel, Kit, Neirton, Eli, and Raalwin following close behind. They would be welcomed by dignitaries, newspeople, and a large crowd of the merely curious. Despite the general anticipation with which everyone viewed the end of the journey, Tory was nervous at the prospect of so much attention. The Phelan, too, were exhibiting signs of stress.

"Ready?" Garth asked Faslorn after the loading bridge was secured.

"Very much so, Captain."

Garth opened the airlock door and stepped out onto the spidery framework of the bridge. Tory watched as he disappeared through the opening in the station bulkhead. Faslorn followed somewhat more slowly, using the Phelan knuckle walk. She noticed several people pointing from behind the thick glass window that overlooked the landing bay. She could almost hear their gasps of amazement as Faslorn came into sight.

Then it was Tory's turn. She hesitated in the airlock chamber as she looked over the narrow footpath strung two meters above the landing-bay deck. Local spin gravity was approximately half a standard g. It would increase as they moved to the outer decks. As she stepped onto the bridge, she was paralyzed with a momentary spasm of fear. She drew a deep breath of frigid air, then willed her legs to move. She moved as though in a trance across the slowly oscillating bridge. As she reached the station airlock, the crowd noise enveloped her. There was an excited buzzing and then a cheer as Faslorn raised his upper pair of arms to wave at the crowd.

Tory stepped over the inner airlock coaming and into the station proper. She found the compartment jammed with people, some literally hanging from overhead. Many held small holocameras. The professional news media and private citizens seeking their own record of this historic event were mixed indiscriminately.

She moved to where Garth and Faslorn had stopped in front of a small clump of dignitaries. She recognized the familiar face of Ambassador Sadibayan. Scanning the crowd, she spotted Ben Tallen at the rear. He was difficult to miss—his face was split into a wide grin and both arms were flailing over his head to draw her attention. She smiled at him, then returned the wave self-consciously. She was acutely aware that she was the focus of dozens of cameras.

The rest of *Austria*'s passengers and crew followed. Each time a Phelan entered the reception hall, a cheer went up from the crowd. For their part, the Phelan looked a little bewildered by the attention. Pandemonium continued for several minutes before Ambassador Sadibayan stepped onto the small dais that had been set up for the occasion.

Sadibayan gestured for silence several times before the crowd subsided. He smiled into the cameras focused on his broad brown features, then gestured for Faslorn to join him. There was a sudden hush as the Phelan climbed onto the small platform and Sadibayan began to speak.

"Faslorn, on behalf of myself, the first minister of the system council, and the people of the whole Solar system, let me welcome you to Earth. We have awaited your arrival these long months with growing anticipation. The first minister asked me to convey his good wishes and to tell you that he looks forward to working with you and your people. I am sure that together we can work out a mutually beneficial arrangement."

The crowd erupted in cheers and whistles. When the commotion again died away, Faslorn took his place as the focus of a dozen directional sound pickups. "Ambassador Sadibayan, people of Earth and Mars, and of the great spaces between. I thank you for your welcoming words and the honor you show us here today. I would like to publicly commend those you sent so far to meet us. Captain Van Zandt and his crew were most diligent in representing all humanity among us. We learned much from them, and I daresay they learned a great deal from us. We have made a good beginning toward the goal of interspecies understanding and cooperation. Our task is now to build on that beginning. Our two races stand today on the threshold of a new era. Let us link arms and step together into the future!''

There were several more speeches, including one from Garth in which he told everyone how good it was to be home again. Tory found herself thrust before the microphones. She suffered a spasm of stage fright, but managed to get out a few words. Afterward, she could remember nothing of what she said. Then they all posed for pictures before being led by security people to the lifts that would deliver them to the outer decks.

Once in the plush corridors of the Elysium Station Hotel, they were ushered to individual suites where they could rest before the evening's festivities. They would stay a few days aboard the station while the doctors examined everyone. Though no one believed there was any danger, doctrine demanded a quarantine check.

Some twenty minutes after leaving the ship, Tory found herself alone. Her head was awhirl with the excitement of homecoming. Suddenly, her misgivings and weeks of worry seemed very distant indeed. She was among her own kind and determined to enjoy it while she could.

The suite had a carpet of bioengineered grass. On Mars such a display would have been considered ostentatious, and Tory suspected that the same was true of Elysium Station. She felt deliciously decadent as she removed her shoes and ran her toes through the short green blades. Moving into the bedroom, she noticed that someone had delivered her kit bag, so she busied herself unpacking. She was interrupted by the suite's annunciator and hummed as she padded barefoot to the entrance.

The door retracted into its recess to reveal Ben Tallen in the corridor beyond. He had a large bundle of flowers tucked into the crook of his arm and a broad smile on his face.

"Welcome home, darling." He stepped forward, enfolded her in his arms, and then stooped to kiss her. After a moment of surprise, she concentrated on cooperating. After long seconds, he released her. "I've been waiting three years to do that.''

"I'd say it was worth it," she replied as she tried to catch her breath. "Please, come in."

He stepped across the threshold, causing a sensor in the wall to note that the door was no longer obstructed. It slid silently back into place. Ben presented the flowers with a flourish. "For the loveliest lady between here and Tau Ceti."

She took the flowers and buried her nose amid the blossoms. The scent was a welcome change after breathing recycled air. It was reminiscent of the smell of the bushes lining the stone walkway Maratel had guided her down that first day aboard *Far Horizons*. "I'll call room service for a vase to put these in."

"Later. We've a lot of catching up to do."

"So we have," she agreed, leading him toward the couch.

His left eyebrow lifted as he managed to leave the impression that he had been thinking more in terms of the bedroom.

"It's been a long trip, Ben," she answered the unspoken question.

"And you're tired. I understand." He sat facing her. She, in turn, tucked one foot beneath her and gazed at him. He had changed. He was heavier than she remembered, his expression was haughtier, and he was older. She remembered that he had lived through those long months when she had been in suspended animation. Effectively, Ben was now two years older than she was. It was an insignificant difference that seemed significant somehow.

The silence stretched uncomfortably as they gazed at one another. She finally broke it. "You've made quite a name for yourself while I've been gone."

"Not nearly as great a name as you've made for yourself. All of you are heroes, you know. Still, those of us who stayed behind have done our bit for the cause. For instance, I was in charge of the politicking that got Underminister Sadibayan his current job. As you can imagine, the competition was rather keen."

"Really?"

"Indeed. We had to fight off several council members. In fact, some of them are still disgruntled."

"I would have thought they would leave dealing with the aliens to specialists."

"Are you kidding? Can you imagine how much exposure the ambassador to the Phelan is going to receive over the next several months? A politico can't buy that kind of publicity. If we play our cards right, Ambassador Sadibayan just might end up the next system comptroller."

"Do you really think so?"

"Absolutely! Guess who his right-hand man will be as he sits at the right hand of the first councilor?"

She laughed. "I can't imagine!"

"Yep, none other than Mrs. Tallen's fair-haired little boy. Enough about me. Tell me about your trip."

She shrugged. "Nothing much to say beyond what we sent back in a few million words of reports."

"Come now, Tory. This is old Ben. Remember me? We'll leave that dry technical stuff to the boys with crinkled foreheads. I'm interested in what these aliens *really* want."

"They want sanctuary. They want us to give them a small plot of land somewhere where they can grow food for their people," she lied. "They want to be accepted into human society so they can at last live without fear that their environmental systems are going to wear out and smother them all. In other words, they want the same things we would want in their place."

"Sanctuary can certainly be had—for a price. Just tell me how far you think we can push them. No reason we have to help them for nothing, is there?"

"Frankly, Ben, I don't see any advantage in haggling. They have a treasure trove aboard that ship."

"Eh?"

"Knowledge. Everything they learned in several thousand years of civilization. If we help them, they'll give it all to us."

Tallen laughed the high-pitched laugh that had always gotten on Tory's nerves a little. "My poor naive darling! Some are going to obtain political advantage out of this situation, others aren't. How can we wring the most advantage from the predicament these Phelan are in? Come now, you must have thought about it a lot on the trip home."

"Actually, I did do a lot of thinking."

"Good. So how does one go about parlaying negotiations with these aliens into the comptrollership? You've lived with them. You must have some insight into how they think."

Tory's laugh carried no mirth with it. "You'd be surprised, Ben."

"So surprise me. How do we turn this thing to our own advantage . . . while serving good old *Homo sap* at the same time, of course."

"Sorry, but I can't advise you on that."

"Sure you can."

"No, I can't. In fact, I can't give you any advice at all."

"Huh? Why not?"

"Because I don't work for you."

She could see the preconceptions melting away as his gaze became suddenly calculating. "I don't understand."

"We're not on the same side, Ben."

"Has some other councilor offered you a position?"

She laughed. "It isn't that. I've accepted Falsorn's offer to be advocate for the Phelan in the coming negotiations."

"Impossible! Why would you do such a thing?"

She looked into his familiar eyes and saw a stranger there. It was a sight she knew she would see often in the months to come, and it frightened her to her core. When she spoke, it was in a voice so soft that he had to strain to hear her.

"I had my reasons."

If Praesert Sadibayan had been angry when he heard the news, Boerk Hoffenzoller was livid.

"What the hell's going on here, Sadibayan?" he demanded from the phone screen. "I sent you up there to run a simple welcoming ceremony, and you tell me one of our 'heroes' has gone over to the enemy?"

"I'm afraid it's true, First Minister." Sadibayan didn't particularly like the leader of the council, but had to admit that he knew his job. Also, he had the votes, which in the world of politics was the only recommendation that mattered.

"Did this assistant of yours . . . ?"

"Tallen, sir. Benjamin Tallen."

"Did he tell you why Victoria Bronson has gone over to the aliens?"

"She wouldn't say. He pressed her on it for an hour. Things became pretty heated toward the end, so he backed off. He thinks he's in love with the girl, you know."

"Any chance this is just a lover's spat? Maybe she told him that because she was mad at him."

"Not a chance, Minister. The head alien issued a press release two hours ago. He announced that he is retaining the Bronson woman as his aide-de-camp. The release speaks of her dedication to building peaceful bonds between our two great races."

"What do we do now? Arrest her?"

"On what charge?"

The irritation was evident on Hoffenzoller's face. "How should I know? Charge her with smuggling in rare alien gems, or treason, or endangerment of a space habitat by leaving the window open. For God's sake, be creative!''

"I don't think that wise, sir. The press seems to have taken Miss Bronson to its heart. She is the better-looking of the two women who went on this expedition, and seems quite personable when she is tongue-tied in front of the cameras.''

"What are you suggesting? That we do nothing?''

"For the time being. We may yet turn this to our advantage. She may work for them, but she's still a human being. Perhaps we can prevail on her to act as a conduit of information from inside the alien camp.''

"You mean she would spy for us?''

"Possibly.''

"Do you have any leverage on her?''

"Tallen.''

"I thought they had an argument.''

"As you suggested, sir, a spat. I'm sure Tallen can convince her to forgive him.''

Hoffenzoller's pained look suddenly disappeared. He had not really enjoyed life since the light sail had been discovered. These aliens presented him with an entire range of problems, most of them major. Yet every problem is also an opportunity. If they could convert Victoria Bronson into a spy in the alien camp, then her recent conversion might work to his advantage.

"Very well, Pert! I leave it in your hands. I'll expect weekly reports, and more often if things get interesting.''

"Yes, sir.''

"Good-bye and good luck.'' With that the phone screen went dark as the first minister cut the connection.

Praesert Sadibayan sat and stared at the blank phone screen for long minutes. What he had just received was his hunting license. Now, how best to use it?

3 EARTH

20

TORY BRONSON STOOD AT THE EDGE OF THE ROOF garden and stared pensively out across the lighted city. Spread before her was a carpet of diamonds that overflowed the nearby shore and swept out into the pier communities beyond. A cool evening breeze drowned out what little traffic noise survived the kilometer-long climb out of the man-made canyons below. Despite the city lights, the sky was an obsidian dome, with conditions perfect for stargazing. The lack of sky glow was due to the polarizing effect of the city's weather field.

Tory craned her neck until she fastened on a red star halfway to the zenith. Mira was a long-period variable that was normally too dim to be seen with the naked eye, but which occasionally flared into one of the brightest stars in the sky. Mira was flaring now, making it the perfect guide star for Tory's search. From Mira she let her gaze drop down and to the east, tracing the invisible path to Tau Ceti. The nova remnant lay low on the horizon, near the lights of several distant aircraft. By squinting, Tory could just make out a second star that almost touched the nova. The second star was the color of an electric arc and so dim that it kept fading from view. Tory found that if she looked away every few seconds, then back again, she could reacquire it.

She realized that she had been holding her breath. She let out a long sigh and breathed deeply of the cool evening air. Twice before she had made this search and had come away disappointed. Tonight *Far Horizons* was close enough for its light sail to be visible in the terrestrial sky. The tiny star would grow steadily brighter for months until it disappeared behind the sun. As it grew brighter, it would spark a surge of interest in the Phelan and their works. This was the goal toward which Tory and her employers had worked ever since their arrival on Earth. The Phelan master plan was about to enter its final—and most dangerous—phase.

It had been five years since the telescopes of Farside Observatory had first detected the alien light sail at the edge of the Solar system. For all that time *Far Horizons* had been falling sunward as it shed its velocity to the surrounding interstellar medium. The light sail had crossed the orbit of Pluto months ago, and would soon cross that of Mars. It was a shame, Tory thought, that her home world was on the wrong side of the sun just now. The sight of it sliding across the indigo sky of home would have been spectacular.

As she watched the tiny point, Tory thought of all that had transpired in the nearly two years she had been on Earth. They had been busy years, with little time to brood. Still, she was bothered by her fellow humans' low opinion of her. She still winced at the memory of that last fight with Ben Tallen aboard Elysium Station.

Ben had taken her announcement that she was going to work for the Phelan badly. They had argued until she had asked him to leave. Afterward, she had cried herself to sleep, and then spent the whole next day rerunning the incident in her mind. When Ben called to invite her to lunch, she had resolved to patch things up with him.

She should have suspected something was wrong when he acted uncharacteristically humble during the meal. It had not been until after dessert was served that he broached the idea of her spying for Ambassador Sadibayan while working for the Phelan. Tory had been so surprised by the suggestion that she had spilled hot coffee down her front. After a minute spent dabbing at the stain, she had asked Ben in a level voice to repeat his offer. To her amazement, he had.

Rather than say another word, she had gathered her things and left. Except on matters of business, that had been the last time she had spoken to Ben. Even two years later, she was still angry that he could think so little of her as to even suggest such a thing. What the hell did he think she was? It was true that she had prostituted herself to the Phelan, but God damn it, at least she was a high-priced whore!

Nor had Ben been the only one who had tried to talk her out of working for the Phelan. She had seen Garth off on his way to his new command, and he, too, had quizzed her about why she was throwing in with the aliens. Since she could not tell him the real reason, she had stuck to her cover story—that she truly believed the Phelan deserved a home and that she wanted to work for that goal. Later, when she was interviewed by several

government officials, Tory had discovered that the most effective
tactic was to swear that her motives were altruistic, yet leave the
impression that she was doing it for the money.

Eventually the doctors gave everyone a clean bill of health
and there was no longer reason to hold the Phelan aboard Elysium Station. Tory and the four aliens had taken the first ferry
down to Mohave Spaceport, where they had transferred to a
suborbital flight to New York. It had taken less than a month for
the Phelan to auction several of their technologies to industry
for more money than *Starhopper*'s entire budget.

Having solved the problem of finances, they leased the penthouse and the upper two floors of a Manhattan residence tower
for use as an embassy. They hired talented people and set about
casting their net of power and influence around the globe and out
into space. The initial phases of the master plan had gone very
well. Partly that was due to centuries of careful planning, but also
because Tory discovered that she had a talent for lobbying.

The old Tory Bronson had avoided cocktail parties and university teas whenever possible. Her idea of a good time was a
few friends, soft music, and Martian beer to keep the vocal
cords lubricated. Yet, in the space of twenty months, aided by
an unlimited line of credit, she had transformed herself into a
high-society hostess. The weekly parties at the Phelan embassy
had become the talk of three continents.

Tory had discovered other skills within herself as well. Running the Phelan conspiracy was not all that different from building *Starhopper*. Instead of watching over the interstellar probe's
development, she now organized publicity, arranged junkets,
and entertained the rich and powerful Where her implant had
once informed her of the progress of construction, it now kept
her current on a hundred different schemes to gain influence.
Her daily cajoling of programmers, construction workers, and
engineers had given way to similar activities with politicians,
industrialists, and influence peddlers. As for the gifts, bribes,
and political contributions, they were merely the obverse of the
Starhopper fund-raisers. She now knew what Dard Pierce had
suffered for the twenty years that had preceded the interstellar
probe's construction.

She felt a rosy glow at the thought of her old mentor. She had
learned that Dard was on Earth, and had invited him to this
evening's party. He had been hesitant at first, but had finally
agreed. The festivities were ostensibly to honor a scientist who
had been awarded one-fifth of a Nobel Prize. The real purpose,

of course, was to collect a few more IOUs against the day when the Third Fleet began unfurling its light sails at the edge of the Solar system.

Tory felt rather than heard the quiet sound behind her. She glanced over her shoulder to see a six-limbed figure silhouetted against the light, making its way in her direction.

"I thought I would find you out here," Maratel said. "What are you doing?"

"Stargazing."

Maratel's eyes also sought out Mira and the small yellow dot on the horizon that was Tau Ceti. Phelan vision was not quite as sharp as human, making it impossible for Maratel to spot the light sail. "The stars are beautiful tonight. It must have been like this at home before the nova."

"Phela *was* very like Earth," Tory mused. She had seen many views of the destroyed world aboard *Far Horizons*, but had not realized how alike the two worlds had been until she came to Earth.

Maratel let her eyes scan the city lights and the dark sea beyond. "I wasn't sure about this place when we first arrived, but now I think we're going to like it here."

The two of them lapsed into silence. In the two years they had worked together, Tory had lost all resentment toward Maratel. Their relationship had grown into true friendship. After all, Tory often reminded herself, the Phelan was merely doing the best she could for her people. Besides, Maratel worked at being likable.

Each Phelan ambassador had a specialty. Faslorn was in charge of policy, while Raalwin concentrated on the day-to-day details of human politics. It was his job to convince the system council that their interests lay in granting the refugees' request for a home on Earth. Negotiations had progressed to talk of ceding a tract in the Australian outback to the aliens. Neirton specialized in psychology and sociology. He guided the public-relations campaign aimed at convincing the average human that the Phelan were harmless. The holomovies and other entertainments in which Neirton invested did not mention the aliens, but all of them preached tolerance and understanding.

As for Maratel, her primary job was looking after Tory. Not that the aliens doubted her loyalty to the task—not with the survival of the human race at stake. Still, Maratel was always around to jolly Tory out of her periodic bouts of depression, or to give her a sympathetic shoulder—actually four of them—to cry on. Tory could have done much worse for a jailer.

"It's about time for the first guests to begin arriving," Maratel reminded her after a few seconds spent gazing at the stars.

"Right."

The two of them turned and made their way inside. The penthouse that served as the Phelan living quarters was filled with last-minute preparations. White-coated waiters hurried about, stocking the refreshment stations. One floor down, other waiters were laying out the china and silver service for dinner. A few discordant musical notes announced that the string ensemble in the main salon was also getting ready.

Tory moved to a full-length mirror and checked for wind damage. Her hair was piled high tonight, with jewels sprinkled through the black tresses. Her complexion, which had been unmarked by the sun upon arrival, was now several shades darker. Tory found the change distasteful, but most terrestrials complimented her on her tan. Her gown was a translucent fabric that revealed as much as it concealed. She carefully rearranged the few wisps that had been blown out of place, then adjusted the simple chain of gold around her waist. Pendant earrings and a small gold bracelet made up the remainder of the ensemble, along with mirrored high-heeled shoes that peeked out from under the hem of her gown.

"You are very beautiful tonight," a voice said from behind her.

She glanced in the mirror to discover Faslorn standing behind her, and sighed. "If only those weren't just words."

"Nonsense. I have studied the human parameters of beauty most carefully. By nearly all of them, you are beautiful."

"Thank you."

Faslorn was dressed in an expensive copy of a human gentleman's evening tunic and formal kilt. Like Tory's, his jewelry was understated and very expensive.

"Is everything ready for this evening?"

Tory consulted her implant. "Just about. The hostesses are doing their final primping and the kitchen reports that dinner will be served at twenty-one hundred sharp."

Faslorn used the Phelan gesture that corresponded to a nod. "Let's get someone down to the tube station to receive our guests. Make sure they can recognize the guest of honor."

"All taken care of. Two greeters are standing by. Both have several holograms of Professor Garrity."

Faslorn "smiled." "You are not only beautiful, Tory, but efficient."

"Thank you again."

He reached out, took her arm in his upper right hand, and squeezed reassuringly. "I understand *Far Horizons* is visible to humans tonight."

She nodded. "I was just outside to see for myself."

"Then we are entering our final phase. If we all do our jobs properly, both of our species will benefit from our efforts."

Tory looked at him sharply. Over the past year, she had learned to read Phelan gestures fairly well. It would not have been apparent to another human being, but she thought Faslorn betrayed more anxiety than usual. Could it be that he was as frightened as she was?

It was something she would have to think about.

"Dard, you look marvelous!" Tory enthused. The party had been in progress for an hour, and it was getting along toward dinner. Tory, who had been circulating among the guests, finally spotted the balding figure of her old boss. She crossed the salon to where he stood with a man and a woman. All three had the look of new arrivals.

"Hello, Tory. You look positively ravishing tonight!"

Tory found herself blushing at the compliment—or was it the presence of a friend? Her official position as advocate for the Phelan required that she look upon virtually every other member of her species as an adversary. It felt good to let the old emotions flow again, if only for a few minutes.

"Thank you. Who are your friends?"

"Victoria Bronson, may I present professors Bernardo Lucci and Pauline Francovich? Pauline works out of Farside Observatory. She's the discoverer of your alien friends' ship. Bernie is from the University of Lyons, where he occupies the Galileo chair of astronomy. His recent enthusiasm is paleoastronomy."

"Huh?"

"The study of old astronomical records, Miss Bronson," Lucci replied.

"Please, call me Tory. Everyone does."

"Tory, then."

She turned back to Pierce. "Well, Dard, what do you think of our little party?"

Pierce sipped from the drink he had snagged off a passing tray and gazed about the salon. "I'm envious. Look, there's

Angus MacCrory and Raphaella Higgens! If I'd been able to attract them to *my* fund-raisers, we could have launched *Star-hopper* a decade early.''

"Then we wouldn't have had it available to send out to meet *Far Horizons*.''

Pierce scratched at one ear and gave her a quizzical look. "As I remember, you were opposed to using the probe in that manner, and quite vocal about it!''

"So I was. It just goes to prove that we all make mistakes.''

"Hmmm . . .''

She remembered him at times in the past when he had been avoiding painful subjects. "Out with it, Dard.''

"I don't know what you mean.''

"I want to hear whatever it is you aren't saying.''

He shrugged. "I had a conversation with your ex-beau the other day. He seems to think that you are making a mistake right now.''

She sighed. "Yes, I know. Ben and I had a long discussion about my helping the Phelan the night I came home, and again at lunch the next day. We haven't spoken socially since.''

He grinned. "Well, if the truth be known, I never really liked Tallen that much. He was always too damned smug for my taste.''

"Why, Dard! You never told me that.''

"Do I look like someone who is dumb enough to catalog a man's defects to his beloved?''

Tory laughed. "What is important enough to bring you to Earth?''

"I'm attending a scientific conference Bernie arranged. We're trying to clean up some mysteries that have hung on far too long.''

"Actually," Pauline Francovich said, "it's just an excuse for a lot of academics to gather, sit around the pool, and lap up alcohol. We justify our expense vouchers by talking about astronomy while working on our tans.''

"I love old mysteries. What's this one about?''

Pierce hooked his thumb in the direction of Neirton, who was talking to another group a few meters distant. "Indirectly, it relates to your friends.''

"The Phelan?''

"We're studying the Tau Ceti nova," Lucci explained. "It was a rather anomalous event, you know. Not only are single stars not supposed to nova, but when it did, it got the light curve completely wrong.''

"Oh?" Alarm bells began to ring inside Tory's head.

"We asked the Phelan about it and they suggested that our instruments were fouled up. Well, I can tell you that I've studied the old data for the last three years and there's nothing at all wrong with it. Tau Ceti was putting out two-point-five percent less light than it should have for the first several hours after it exploded. We have no idea why.''

Tory tried to keep her voice under control. "None at all?"

"Nary a one," Pierce replied. "That's what makes it interesting. If one main-sequence star can explode . . .''

". . . then why not another?" Pauline Francovich said, finishing his sentence for him. "The sun is a main-sequence star, you know.''

"Do you need any help?" Tory asked as she thought furiously about how to change the subject. Unlike her guests, she had a good idea what had caused the nova's light deficiency.

"What sort of help?"

"Funds, facilities, computer time?"

"What are you suggesting?" Pierce asked. At the mention of possible support, the old fund-raiser's reflexes took over.

"Since your studies concern Tau Ceti, the embassy might be willing to underwrite your conference, and possibly even some original research. The Phelan are as baffled as we are about why their sun blew up.''

"I find that hard to believe," Pauline replied.

"Remember, their civilization fell apart as soon as the astronomers announced what was to happen. The observatories were hit especially hard by rampaging mobs. Many records were destroyed.''

"I didn't know that.''

"We can send you information on the Time of Troubles if you like.''

"Never mind that," Pierce said. "The Phelan would be willing to underwrite a line of inquiry into why their star blew up?"

"Sure, if they thought it would be productive." Tory left unsaid the fact that Phelan funding would give the Phelan some measure of control over the research. They could make sure that inquiries into natural causes for the Tau Ceti nova were well supported while any suggestion that the cause had been unnatural was quickly snuffed out.

"What about their space observations of the buildup and aftermath of the nova?'' Lucci asked. ''I know they have such recordings. They sent one with that travelogue they beamed to Earth.''

''There are probably hundreds of hours of observations aboard *Far Horizons.*''

''Can we get those?''

''Not until after the ship reaches parking orbit, I'm afraid. With close encounter only ninety-four days away, they're going to be much too busy to fill orders for historical data. But I'm sure the Phelan will have no objection to you rummaging around in the records once they make orbit.''

''Excellent!''

''In fact, why don't I get you an appointment with Faslorn to discuss it?''

''You would do that?'' Pauline asked.

''Certainly. Is Wednesday at ten all right with you?''

''Bernie and Pauline can attend,'' Pierce said. ''I have another engagement then.''

''Wednesday at ten is fine,'' Lucci said.

''Very well. The appointment is confirmed. I notice Dard has finished his martini. May I interest each of you in some Martian Scotch instead?''

21

THE PHELAN EMBASSY OCCUPIED THE TOP TWO
floors of one of Manhattan's most luxurious towers. Except for
the holographic views of lost Phela scattered about the public
areas, there was little to distinguish the alien mission from hundreds of similar establishments. Nor were the embassy's routine
operations much different from those of any other large political
or commercial lobbying operation. Each day the receptionist
received a steady stream of favor seekers, politicians, peddlers,
job seekers, and the merely curious. The visitors were directed
to low-ranking functionaries whose task was to route them to
the proper departments. Job seekers were given applications,
peddlers were directed to the procurement office, politicians
were given over to protocol officers. The rest—those with no
place in the Phelan master plan—were given refreshments and
a few minutes with a sympathetic ear and then sent on their way.

Some visitors were schoolchildren, who were given a quick
tour, shown a holo program about Phela, and allowed to circu-
late around a large cutaway model of *Far Horizons*. They, too,
were given refreshments before being sent away with a packet
of literature that contained a commemorative medallion.

Some visitors were VIPs. These bypassed the screening process. They were met at the embassy's private tube station by
high-ranking protocol officers, then escorted directly to the
penthouse living quarters.

The embassy employed more than a hundred human beings
directly, and several thousand others through various contrac-
tors that included caterers, public-relations firms, hoteliers, sur-
veyors, geologists, and a hundred other specialties. No human
but Tory knew the real reason behind the aliens's frenetic attempts to gain public acceptance. Nor did the embassy staffers
feel they were being disloyal to humankind. Most of the lower-
ranking employees viewed their employment as just another job,
and the more motivated perceived that the aliens's interests par-

alleled their own. In this they were absolutely correct, although not for the reasons they imagined.

Despite the studied ordinariness of the embassy, one installation set it apart from its surroundings. The Phelan had built a large spherical structure on the roof of their tower, where it loomed over the penthouse that served as their living quarters. Known colloquially as "the Egg," the sphere was the one place on Earth where they could speak freely with a reasonable assurance of not being overheard.

Once each week the five conspirators shut themselves inside the Egg, activated six concentric layers of electromagnetic shielding, and discussed their progress toward completing the master plan.

"How go your lobbying efforts?" Faslorn asked Raalwin midway through one weekly conference.

The Phelan political scientist made a gesture Tory had yet to learn. "I believe we have been successful. Councilor Norris has confided to me that the council will probably offer us the Australian district for our colony."

"Is that the wisest choice?" Neirton asked. "Would not the Antarctic site be more suitable to our needs?"

"Your advice, Tory?"

"I recommend against it. The climate is far more severe."

"Climates can be modified. A suitably positioned light sail could provide Antarctica with an optimum environment within a few decades."

"Not without melting the ice caps and raising sea level all over the world!" Tory objected.

"There would be disruptions, certainly. But the overall result would be a net gain for both our species. In exchange for a relatively narrow strip of marginal farmland on the edges of the continents, we would make the south pole the breadbasket of this world."

"You forget that most Earth cities are located in those coastal strips."

"I agree," Faslorn said. "Even a hint that we plan to modify the Earth's climate would wreck our cause. There will be no more such talk."

"But the Third Fleet will need that land," Raalwin persisted. "The southern continent is icebound and largely sterile. Introducing our crops into such soil is far easier than competing with the terrestrial organisms that infest the rest of the planet."

"For the same reason, there will be no talk of introducing our crops into the bare soil. We will rely on sealed domes to grow our food. The humans must be given plenty of time to get used to the idea of Phelan organisms loose in their biosphere.''

Raalwin was obviously not convinced, but deferred to Faslorn's authority.

''Are there any other objections to the Australian colony site? If not, let us move on. Tory, you have the last item on the agenda.''

She nodded and went on to recount what she had learned about the scientific conference looking into the mystery of the Tau Ceti nova.

''Do they suspect the nova was not a natural event, then?''

''How can they?'' Maratel asked. ''No, our arrival has merely caused renewed interest in the nova. It's just another case of monkey curiosity.''

''Do you agree, Tory?''

''Sounds right.''

''Then we can safely ignore this conference.''

Faslorn's gesture was sharply negative. ''I think not. Remember, these scientists have a datum their predecessors lacked. They know Tau Ceti to have been inhabited. If they can find no other explanation for our star's destruction, might they not wonder if we are the cause?''

''So what do we do?''

''We follow Tory's suggestion and sponsor this conference. We provide research grants to anyone who shows an interest in investigating the nova. That way we gain some control over events. If nothing else, an investigator is less likely to be suspicious of his benefactor than of a stranger.'' Faslorn turned to Tory. ''You know these people. Will you set it up?''

''Gladly.''

''Very well. Is there anything else? If not, I declare this session adjourned. Raalwin, open the shields and transfer us back to external power.''

Boerk Hoffenzoller, first among equals, chief terrestrial delegate to the system council, and, by a narrow plurality, the first councilor, stood with his hands clasped behind his back as he gazed out his office window. The window faced the man-made cliffs of Manhattan across a strip of green, a park that fronted council headquarters and was a gathering place for lunchtime strollers. From Hoffenzoller's vantage point the people sprawled on the grass or walking among the colorful beds of flowers all seemed diminutive dolls. Yet as powerless as they might appear individually, collectively they held the power of life and death.

They called it "the will of the people." He knew it for what it really was, a fickle, ravening beast. A politician might bask in the soft, purring embrace of public approval one moment, then find himself devoured in a carnivorous feeding frenzy of public outrage the next. Hoffenzoller had seen too many promising careers torn apart because of some trifling misstep. Yet, despite a lifetime spent studying the beast from which all real power flowed, he was no closer to understanding it than when he had been a young legislator from the Zunderdorp district of Amsterdam.

What, for instance, was the will of the people with regard to the aliens? At the moment there seemed to be three basic opinions on the subject. A vocal minority strongly opposed allowing them to settle anywhere in the Solar system, let alone on Earth. The most extreme of these demanded that the navy drive off the starship. A second group, equally passionate, lobbied strongly in favor of the alien request for sanctuary. Some of these came close to wetting themselves in their eagerness to gain access to Phelan technology.

Neither group particularly worried Boerk Hoffenzoller. After all, committed, passionate activists were a breed with which he had successfully dealt for decades. He understood them, and even more important, they were predictable. Their strengths were well matched, for a net sum of zero in the political equation.

The group he worried about was the largest by far. These were the people who professed no knowledge of, nor interest in, the aliens. The latest opinion polls showed fully sixty percent of the public unable to identify the word "Phelan" when asked, while another twenty-five percent knew who they were, but had no opinion regarding them. As usual, the masses were preoccupied with day-to-day living and too busy to worry about things that did not directly affect their lives.

The moment of danger would come when they decided that the Phelan had begun to affect them personally. The masses would stir themselves at the eleventh hour and fifty-ninth minute to demand why they hadn't been consulted. Posturing politicians would make thundering speeches demanding to know how things had gotten so far out of control, and a council investigation would be launched. This, too, was SOP—standard operating procedure. All that was required for political survival was to be on the side doing the investigating.

The danger lay in not knowing which side that was. Those who asked the questions and those who answered them would be determined solely by where the man and woman on the street came down with regard to the Phelan question. Would they buy the idealistic propaganda being pumped out by the Phelan embassy and demand sanctuary for the noble refugees from the stars? Or would the raging monster of xenophobia be let loose in the land, devouring all who had ever said a kind word about the six-limbed aliens?

Hoffenzoller noted that the political question had little to do with the facts. The fact was that the aliens were here to stay. The astronomers who tracked *Far Horizons* had been warning him for months that they had lost too much velocity to seek another star. At its current speed, the starship would take ten thousand years to cross the blackness to its next destination, and those who studied the reports sent back by the Starhopper Expedition estimated the starship would not support its passengers much more than another century. If they sought another star, the Phelan would be dead ninety-nine centuries before they arrived.

So, whatever the outcome of the council vote to cede a tract of land to the aliens, the light sail would grow large in the night sky come late summer. The question was really *where* to settle them, not *whether*. How to tell that to the masses?

The terrestrial media had lately been touting Mars and Luna as settlement sites. Not surprisingly, neither the Martian nor Lunarian governments were keen on the idea. Neither was Hoffenzoller. Not only would the cost of establishing a Phelan colony on either world be terrible, but having the aliens settle somewhere other than Earth would give nonterrestrials the advantage in access to their technology. Boerk Hoffenzoller was the first councilor, but he was also the chief terrestrial delegate. He had learned forty years earlier which side his bread was buttered on.

No, for a variety of reasons, the Phelan must be given a home beneath the blue skies and fleecy clouds of Earth—but where? They themselves had provided a list of three possible sites. One was a tract midway between Alice Springs and Brisbane in Australia. Another was located in the Wilkes Basin of Antarctica, and the third was the al-Quatrun district in the southern Sahara Desert.

Hoffenzoller wondered how the aliens had chosen their colony sites. The Australian outback was the only one that was even marginally habitable; the other two would require nearly as great an effort as Mars or Luna. The only common denominator was the total isolation of the three. Each was surrounded by millions of hectares of sparsely inhabited—or uninhabited—desert. Did one hundred thousand refugees require such vast tracts, or was there some factor at work of which he was unaware?

His reverie was cut off by the sudden sound of a chime. He turned away from the window in time to see his office door opened by Jesus de Pasqual, his minister for science.

"You're late, Jess!"

"Sorry, First Councilor. I was delayed in data integration. The report was still coming off the printer."

"Let's have the recommendation."

"Australia."

Hoffenzoller sighed. "That's just great. How am I going to explain to three hundred million stiff-necked Aussies that they have to share their continent with aliens?"

"That, sir," de Pasqual said without any sign of regret, "is not my problem."

"No, it's mine. Why not another site?"

The science minister shook his head. "Too environmentally sensitive. If you give them the Wilkes Basin, half the councilors will be screaming about damage to the last true frontier on Earth. As for al-Quatrun, the Sahara reclamation project plans to turn that into farmland in another fifty years or so. The North Africans are counting on it."

Hoffenzoller nodded. "And we need the North Africans to keep our coalition intact."

"Whereas the Aussies are already in opposition."

"You always were one to keep the important points in mind, Jess. Very well, Australia it is. When do we make the offer?"

"I propose to dangle it in front of them at next week's regular negotiation session. We can raise our price at the same time."

"What do you plan to ask for?"

"Some free samples as a token of good faith. Dr. Claridge says she witnessed some amazing medical procedures. Perhaps we can ask for those."

The first councilor looked sourly at his science minister as he rubbed his stomach. "Do you think they have a cure for ulcers?"

De Pasqual grinned. "It won't hurt to ask."

* * *

Praesert Sadibayan gazed at his aide and scowled. "I am un-happy with the quality of intelligence that has been coming out of the Phelan Embassy, Ben."

Ben Tallen scowled back. One good thing about being a syn-ergist was that you didn't have to take any crap from anyone. The worst Sadibayan could do was fire him, which meant that he would have another job—probably better paying—within twenty-four hours. Still, the boss had a point.

"I agree, but what the hell do you want me to do? Nobody in that damned place seems to know anything."

"Someone does, but you handled her recruitment poorly."

Tallen swallowed his anger, though his complexion reddened in response. The knowledge that Sadibayan was correct did nothing to soften his ire. He remembered the night he and Tory had spent in the environment tent on the side of a mountain. He had commented on the fact that she had matured since college. Yet, when she had returned from the starship, she had not looked a day older than when she had left. Subconsciously, he had thought of her as a kid, and had assumed she would do what he told her. As a result, he had lost the best opportunity to penetrate the Phelan ranks they would ever have.

"So what do you want me to do about it? She's barely spoken to me these past two years."

"Perhaps the time has come to try again."

"How?"

"You might try apologizing for your behavior."

"I did that last time. It didn't help."

"Perhaps if you mean it this time, it will. I know such things come hard to you, Ben, but sometimes in this life they are nec-essary."

Tallen sighed. "I'll apologize, but she'll probably spit in my face."

"Having observed her across the table for nearly two years now, I daresay that she will be civil. Besides, perhaps we can give you some bait for your hook."

"Yes, sir. When should I make my approach?"

"The regularly scheduled meeting is tomorrow. Why not then?"

Tallen grew pensive, as though he was deep in thought or accessing his implant. After a few seconds, he smiled. "It's worth a try!"

"It is worth far more than that," Sadibayan warned. "We are

getting down to the end of the negotiations. If we are to succeed, we need a better source of information. Unless you care to romance one of the Phelan, Victoria Bronson is our only hope.''

22

THE HEADQUARTERS BUILDING OF THE SYSTEM council was a large, airy pile of glass and steel constructed in the architectural style of the early twenty-second century. Tory found it to be more than a little ugly. She was especially put off by its stark use of angles and overhanging upper tiers. Standing close to the building and looking up, one had the impression of a pyramid balanced on its point. It was easy for the mind to stray into thoughts of how well such a precarious structure would withstand an earthquake. In this one aspect, the building mirrored the organization that it housed: how well the council would withstand the discovery of the Phelan Third Fleet was also open to question.

Though the system council's publicists had recently taken to referring to it as "The Parliament of Humanity," its roots were far more humble. The council had originally been established by the newly independent space colonies to present Earth with a united front on matters of mutual interest. The first terrestrial nation to join had been France in 2120. The French had petitioned for membership to argue in favor of a voluntary limit on the export of vacuum-distilled spirits to Earth.

The unofficial bar to terrestrial nations broken, several others had petitioned over the next few decades. They had been admitted as observers, and later as full-fledged voting members. It had not been long after that that the council headquarters had been moved to New York from Luna City.

It had been twelve weeks since the Phelan petition for a colony site had been formally presented to the council. As Tory, Faslorn, and Maratel arrived for their usual Wednesday session, Tory wondered if today's meeting would be different from the previous eleven. If their informants were right, they would be offered the Australian site.

The three of them made their way toward the public lifts. Despite the presence of a sound-deadening field, Tory's footsteps echoed hollowly in the vast open space, while the Phelan knuckle walk was silent. Rising above them was a tall atrium roofed over by translucent panels. Surrounding the atrium was a dizzying collection of office balconies from which several heads watched the two aliens.

"Tory, may I speak with you a second?"

The call to her implant startled her for a moment, almost making her lose stride. Not only had such direct messages been few since she had taken up service with the Phelan, but the source was unexpected. The voice that echoed in her brain was that of Ben Tallen.

"Where are you?" she asked to cover her surprise.

"Look to your left."

She did so and discovered Tallen standing next to an island of potted plants that broke up the glimmering expanse of marble floor. He waved to her.

"What is it?" Faslorn asked.

"Ben Tallen. He wants to speak to me."

Faslorn consulted the human watch he wore on his upper left wrist. "Make it quick. We're due in the committee room in five minutes."

Tory strode to where Tallen was standing. The two Phelan watched her go. She had long since gotten used to their silent gazes following her everywhere. Despite the terrible secret that bound her to them, Tory knew, they worried about her loyalty. She could not blame them—she often worried about it herself.

"What do you want, Ben?"

He smiled. "First, I want to apologize for the way I acted aboard Elysium Station. I was a fool for blowing up the way I did, and an even bigger one for trying to get you to go against your employers."

"It's been almost two years. Why apologize now?"

He shrugged. "I guess it's taken me this long to realize what a jackass I was. You have your reasons for going over to the Phelan, and I should have respected them."

"I didn't 'go over' to them, Ben," she replied with a hint of frost in her voice. "I'm aiding them because they need my help, and because I think it benefits both of our species."

He held up his hands as though to ward off her attack. "Peace! I never meant to imply anything else. Like I said, I should never have yelled at you the way I did."

"Then why did you?"

"I suppose I was hurt. I had plans for us, and they didn't include yonder beasties."

"So what do you want?"

"How about having dinner with me this evening?"

"Why?"

"I'd hoped you might want to. If you need another reason, I have something to discuss that your bosses might like to hear."

"What is it?"

"Unh-unh. I'll only tell you over dinner."

She chewed her lower lip and weighed the possibility that this was a ruse to get her drunk and take her to bed. In truth, she wouldn't mind all that much. She had been celibate since that night she and Garth had said good-bye aboard *Austria*, and she missed having a warm body to cuddle with. She was also tired of being on duty every second of every day. She wanted to let her hair down, if only for a while.

"Very well, I'll go out with you."

"Excellent. Where should I pick you up?"

"It isn't necessary. I can meet you."

"I wouldn't hear of it. Shall we say the penthouse, about twenty hundred?"

"Twenty hundred is fine."

"I'll see you then." Ben turned and walked toward a side entrance leading down to the tube station. Tory hurried back to where Faslorn and Maratel waited.

"What was that about?" Faslorn asked.

She recounted the conversation, finishing with, "As to what he really wanted, I guess I'll find out this evening."

Ben arrived precisely on time. He was wearing a formal dinner outfit consisting of cerise coat, shorts, and calf-length boots. For her part, Tory was outfitted in a conservative sleeveless jumpsuit.

"I forgot to ask you what sort of dinner it was to be," she said. "Shall I change into something more formal?"

"No need," he replied with a smile as he presented her with a small bouquet of flowers. "You look beautiful just the way you are."

She made a show of smelling the flowers. "Thank you, Ben, but you really shouldn't have."

"Why not? As I remember, you always liked flowers."

"I still do, but they aren't really appropriate at a business dinner."

He grinned at her. "Then we'll just have to talk about something else, won't we? Ready to go?"

"Sure. Where are we going?"

"I know a little Italian restaurant out on the island."

"Sounds wonderful. I haven't had Italian food since I left Mars."

Half an hour later they were wending their way along a country road. The only sign of civilization was the distant row of lights marking the residence towers that stood three deep along the Long Island shore.

The restaurant was housed in a small building that had once been a private home. Groundcars were parked haphazardly in front, forcing Ben to park on the narrow street. Ben folded her arm in his and guided her to the entrance under a small sign that read EMILIO'S. He halted on the front step and suggested that she run her hand across the building's facade. She did so, then peered closely at the ancient surface. "Is that real wood?"

"The same."

Mentally, she let out a low whistle. Trees were precious in the domed cities of Mars, and the idea of cutting one down for building materials was close to sacrilegious. Yet here before her was proof of the outlandish notion that people had indeed once felled trees to build homes.

The maître d' was an ebullient man with a waxed mustache and a belly that hung over his belt. Their table was covered with a white and red checked tablecloth and had the required candle atop a wine bottle. They were handed a wine list, from which Ben ordered a Chianti. She noticed as she looked it over that there were no prices.

"Nor on the menu," he replied to her question. "You know the old saying. 'If you have to ask . . .' "

" 'You can't afford it,' " she finished. "Can you afford a place like this?"

He grinned. "I'm not quite as impoverished as when we met."

"Neither of us are."

He reached out across the table and laid a hand atop hers. "Do you miss those days?"

"More than is good for me sometimes. The universe was such a simple place then. All we really had to worry about was finals week."

"And getting our research papers done."

She laughed. Early in their relationship, they had often been in bed before 2200 hours, but had seldom gotten to sleep until well after midnight. She had accused him of trying to keep her from completing her senior thesis. It had become a private joke between them.

"I miss you, Tory," Ben said as he squeezed both her hands. "It's a damned shame we have to be on opposite sides of this Phelan thing."

"As I tell everyone who will listen, Ben, we aren't on opposite sides. We're on the same side. You haven't seen *Far Horizons*."

"I've seen the pictures of it."

"Not the same at all. You have to stand at the base of the end cap and stare out across the habitat volume toward Spiral Falls before you can get an idea of the size of the thing. It would be a damned shame for them to come so far and fail. They deserve better than that."

He grinned. "You never could resist taking in strays, could you?"

She felt a moment of irritation at his comment, then wondered if he wasn't right . . . just a little. After all, she had been in the Phelan camp even before they had revealed the horrible truth to her. That was the main reason they had approached her. How much of that sympathy remained? She probed gently at her conscience and concluded that she could not answer the question. Which proved that old adage about people's motives being mysterious, even to themselves. "What would you have us do?" she asked after a long silence. "Turn them away?"

He shrugged. "That's up to the council. I certainly didn't ask them to come here."

"Neither did they. People forget that the Phelan who launched *Far Horizons* are long dead. Faslorn and the others had no say in the matter. Now that they're here, they have no choice but to stop. There are no other stars within reach."

"We on the advisory committee are well aware of the situation."

"If you know that, then why all this foot dragging? Why not pass the resolution welcoming them and cease these endless Wednesday interrogations?"

"You know how the bureaucracy works. We've got to at least pretend we're earning our pay. Besides, who's foot dragging? Didn't we offer them a site at today's meeting?"

"I thought that was supposed to be secret," she said. At the meeting, Science Minister de Pasqual had emphasized that there was to be no public announcement until the council cleared it.

He was clearly concerned about upsetting Australian sensibilities.

"You forget who I work for. My boss had to sign off on the selection. One thing bothers me, though."

"What's that?"

"The three sites your bosses asked for. Why did they choose such godforsaken places to settle?"

"I don't understand the question," Tory replied. In truth, she understood it all too well. The Phelan had asked for the three sites because they were surrounded by vast tracts of sparsely populated land that would be needed by the Third Fleet. She could not very well tell Ben that, of course.

"What do they find so attractive about the hinterlands?" he asked.

She forced a laugh and hoped it would not sound too phony. "Actually, Antarctica and the Sahara were my ideas."

"I thought you liked the Phelan."

"I figured that the assimilation would go better if they were isolated from the major centers of population. Not all the Phelan are like Faslorn and the others, you know. On average, they're about as diplomatic as the ordinary human."

"That bad, huh?"

"Perhaps I exaggerate just a bit. Still, it would be better if the two populations don't mix until the Phelan get used to us. Then there's the need for land to grow crops on. You have no idea how difficult it will be for them to compete with the Earth's natural biosphere."

"Just so they don't release any plagues or anything."

"Impossible."

"That's what the biologists tell me. I hope they're right."

Tory emptied her glass. Ben refilled it for her. He studied her for a long moment, then cleared his throat. "Have your people given any thought to when we should hold the vote?"

"Is that why you invited me to dinner this evening?"

"My boss thought we could discuss a few dates in private and see if we could come up with one that is mutually agreeable."

"How about scheduling the vote for next week?"

He shook his head. "Too soon. The population has to be psychologically prepared for it, otherwise the anti-Phelan factions will monopolize the agenda and the news."

"You have a better idea?"

"We thought two weeks after the starship's close encounter with Sol."

"Why so late?"

"Easy. You people are planning an extravaganza when the light sail dips down into the corona, aren't you?"

"How did you know that?"

"The council's intelligence agents would be a sorry bunch of spies if we didn't. How about briefing me on your plans?"

Tory quickly sketched the embassy's arrangements to publicize the starship's brush with Sol. The event was sufficiently newsworthy that the major news organs would cover it, drawn by the drama of the encounter and the very real possibility that *Far Horizons* might not survive its plunge into the thick soup that surrounded Sol. The embassy's contribution would be to make available sympathetic experts who would emphasize the aliens's courage. Besides straight news reports, the Phelan planned a live telecast of the several-hours-long encounter. The program would be loaded with pro-Phelan propaganda and every trick of the advertisers's art.

When Tory finished, Tallen nodded. "As soon as the starship rounds the sun, we will officially schedule the vote. If your embassy has done its job, the vote will be overwhelmingly in favor."

"Besides, if *Far Horizons* doesn't make it, the council will be off the hook," Tory observed.

"There is that factor to consider, of course. But let's be optimistic. Assuming the resolution passes, when does Faslorn propose to turn the Phelan library over to us?"

"First disclosure will coincide with the first shipload to land on the colony site. We'll make further disclosures as the colony is constructed, and the final one at the end of the tenth successful year."

"Agreed," Ben said. "It will take us a good decade to absorb the new technology anyway. The first councilor has asked for a demonstration of good faith by the Phelan."

"What sort of demonstration?"

"Nothing major. Perhaps a few medical tricks we can display to the populace. You will make points with Hoffenzoller if the Phelan can do something about stomach ulcers."

"I'll have to ask Faslorn."

"Of course."

"Anything else?"

"There are a few more points we should discuss . . ."

* * *

Tory returned to the penthouse shortly after midnight. She had expected Ben to invite her to his place to spend the night, but he had surprised her by acting the gentleman. Only when they shared a good-night kiss had even a shadow of the old ardor returned. She found Faslorn waiting for her as she let herself into the living quarters.

"Just like the old days," she said.

"I beg your pardon."

"My father used to wait up for me when I returned late from a date. I think he did it to intimidate the boys."

Faslorn laughed. He had the best laugh of any of the Phelan. "Despite all of my years of study, I have to admit that human sexual mores are still a mystery to me."

"They are still a mystery to most humans."

"What did Tallen want?"

She recounted her discussion with Ben concerning the vote and the establishment of the Phelan colony afterward.

Faslorn "frowned." "Who do you suppose he was representing in this overture?"

"Praesert Sadibayan, possibly First Minister Hoffenzoller."

"Why do you suppose they asked for this back-channel discussion? Why not discuss all these things at the meeting this morning?"

"Maybe they thought they could learn more if I was alone with Ben in a social setting. He plied me with wine all evening. Maybe he was trying to get me drunk."

"Did he?"

"No, worse luck! That's what I hate most about this job. I don't dare let myself get out of control."

"It will only be a few more months. After that, *Far Horizons* will be safe and we can begin building our colony." His words were for the benefit of anyone who might be eavesdropping. The truth was that they had another six years of hard work to prepare for the arrival of the Third Fleet. "Did he say anything else?"

"He wanted to know why we picked the colony sites we did. I explained our concern about getting your people acclimated before they mixed with large numbers of humans." This too was for the benefit of unseen listeners.

"Did the two of you patch up your quarrel?"

She smiled. "A little, I suppose."

"Are you going to see him again?"

"He asked me out next week. I haven't decided whether I'll go or not. Depends on my schedule."

"I think you should," the Phelan replied. "It will be good for you to spend more time with your own kind."

"Oh?"

"I think you've been working too hard."

"What did you have in mind?"

"Perhaps you can show Maratel something of Earth. She's expressed a desire to meet people in a purely social setting."

"I'll have the embassy travel desk arrange something."

Later, in her apartment, she found that she had difficulty drifting off to sleep. She kept thinking about Ben. Was it possible to rekindle an old flame? She was still asking herself the question as she drifted into a fitful sleep.

23

THE ARCH OF THE SOLAR PROMINENCE REACHED out toward the tiny black dot of the Phelan light sail like the tentacle of some glowing monster. The scene was a striking one, emphasizing how small the planet-sized light sail was when silhouetted against the most diminutive of stellar features. It was one of those defining images that stick in the public consciousness for decades, and no less impressive for being an illusion.

In truth, *Far Horizons* was still some three million kilometers from Sol, and would not reach perihelion for another three hours. As for the "tentacle," it was a fountain of charged particles that had erupted from somewhere behind the Sun's limb, wrenched into the arch by the Solar magnetic field. The starship would not pass within a million kilometers of the glowing arch. Only the fact that both were in the same line of sight made them appear to be on a collision course.

The scene originated in Earth's largest Solar telescope, perched high in the Andes Mountains at the Cerro Tololo Observatory. To make the corona visible, the astronomers had electronically blanked out the Sun's disk, transforming it into a dark hole encircled by a ghostly halo. The halo was the Sun's corona, normally visible only during a total Solar eclipse.

Despite being three million kilometers out, those aboard the starship were already feeling their coming encounter with the Sun. The light sail was now a giant parachute stretched taut by the thick soup of gasses through which it flew. The gasses would grow steadily thicker. Just before *Far Horizons* reached its closest point of approach, the ship's deceleration rate would peak at over three gravities. That is, if nothing went wrong.

If the sail ripped or any significant number of shroud lines parted under the stress, the alien craft would be hardly slowed at all. It would continue around the Sun in a hyperbolic orbit and head back into the infinite black with no way to return.

The opposite would occur if *Far Horizons* passed too close to the Sun. If it did not burn up from a combination of Solar and frictional heating, it would climb back into space in a high lob, then plummet back into the Great Hydrogen Bomb in the Sky.

Tory, Faslorn, and Maratel were acutely aware of the things that could go wrong as they sat in front of the entertainment holoscreen in their penthouse living quarters. As the three watched, the view moved in until the tiny black dot became a small circle. A moment later, a brilliant violet spark appeared next to the light sail.

"We have acquisition of signal," announced the narrator, one of Earth's most popular actors. Tory had worked long and hard to obtain his services for this telecast. "Stand by for pictures from inboard the Phelan starship!"

The laser that had once swept the interstellar medium to harvest ions now carried information on its modulated beam. The view from Cerro Tololo faded from the screen, to be replaced by a blinding white light. It took a moment for Tory to recognize *Far Horizons*'s anchor sphere with its thousands of converging shroud lines. The sphere was ablaze with light. Behind it, the light sail was a sheet of fire that blanked out the sky with a distorted reflection of the sun. The scene was straight out of Dante's *Inferno*.

The view changed again. When Tory's eyes readjusted to the dimmer scene, she recognized the panorama of *Far Horizons*'s habitat volume. The camera mounted high up in the forward end cap looked straight aft along the lighted sun tube. She had a moment of disorientation as she realized that Spiral Falls was gone. So too were the farms, villages, forests, lakes, and streams that had graced the outer walls of the great cylinder. What had once been a patchwork of greens, yellows, and blues was now a monotonous gray, broken only by a new forest of beams, columns, and braces.

For most of the past year, *Far Horizons*'s crew had been preparing for the coming encounter with the Sun. The transformation of the habitat volume was merely the most obvious of their preparations. For more than two centuries, spin gravity had been the major force aboard the starship. "Out" had always been "down" and the spin axis the zenith. Even the light sail's deployment had meant little to the starship's inhabitants. The deceleration that came from plowing the interstellar medium had produced too small a force to notice.

That was about to change. Soon the "floor" of the habitat volume would become its "walls," and the solid ground underfoot would turn into a sheer cliff. Three gravities along the spin axis would cause any of the volume's loose contents—plants, animals, Phelan, water, soil, houses—to slide forward until they lodged against the forward end cap. To prevent this, *Far Horizons*'s crew had dismantled the small artificial world of the habitat volume. Villages were taken down and packed into storerooms, crops harvested and seeds collected, the great waterfalls turned off and all free water pumped into tanks. Even the soil that covered the decks had been scraped up, replaced with beams and braces to stiffen the starship's spine.

The narrator droned on, describing the scene for the billions watching. Then the screen changed again, this time to a compartment where thousands of Phelan lay strapped down in regimented rows. Already the temperature in most of the ship was near the boiling point of water. Soon the outer decks would begin to glow from the heat. Only in a few hundred shielded and refrigerated sanctuaries were conditions suitable for living things, and it was in these that *Far Horizons*'s thousands awaited their fate with a stoicism few human crowds could have managed.

"It looks as though they've prepared well enough," Tory said, more to relieve the tension than to inform her two companions of anything they didn't already know.

She got no response. Both Phelan were totally absorbed in the holo scenes. Their expressions were alien, reminding Tory of the day they had revealed their terrible secret to her. She had gained some facility at reading Phelan body language since then, and knew that Faslorn and Maratel were as frightened as she had ever seen them.

Logically, they had little reason to fear. After all, any craft capable of surviving inside the heart of a nova should be able to dip close to Sol without difficulty. But those who had ridden the ship outward from their exploding star were long dead. Faslorn's generation had no experience with stars, except as distant points of cold light. To see one close up was more daunting than anyone born on a planet could possibly imagine.

On impulse, Tory reached out and laid a comforting hand on Faslorn's shoulder. Black eyes turned to lock with green.

"Take heart. It will all be over in another six hours."

"That is what worries me," he said. He reached up to pat her arm, showing that her attempt at comfort was appreciated.

On the screen, *Far Horizons* continued its long fall toward the sun that would soon capture it.

* * *

Two hours and twenty-seven minutes later, the violet spark of the comm laser winked out as *Far Horizons* slipped from view behind the Sun. Though Mars was on that side just then, there was no Solarscope or other equipment on the red planet able to read the laser. There would be no communication with the starship until it reappeared above the eastern limb of the Sun 124 minutes hence. Only then would they learn its fate.

Maratel shivered in the Phelan gesture that equated to a human sigh. "Now we wait. How long to perihelion?"

"Sixteen minutes," Tory replied.

"We should have arranged some method for maintaining contact throughout the encounter."

"We've been over this argument a hundred times," Faslorn said, his voice empty of human inflection. "There just wasn't time to build the necessary equipment, nor to get it into position. We will just have to wait."

"It will be hard," Maratel murmured. She, too, made no effort to maintain her human personality. "Someone should make an appearance in the pressroom."

"I'll go," Tory said.

"Perhaps I should," Faslorn replied.

"You have too much on your mind. Let me."

"Very well."

The pressroom was equipped with a large holoscreen, two dozen folding chairs, and a coffeepot kept full at all times. Those assigned to the embassy during the close encounter were not media stars, but working journalists. Mostly they watched the same video as everyone else. Their assignment involved background stories for the afternoon faxes with which their services would fill out the major news of the encounter. The only holo reporter present hovered near a pocket-sized stereo camera that looked like a pair of binoculars mounted on a spindly tripod.

Only about one-quarter of the chairs were occupied as Tory stepped into the room. Four newspeople clustered around the refreshment table. There was a sudden reaching for recorders as she moved to stand behind the lectern flanked by terrestrial and Phelan flags—the latter designed by a public-relations firm.

Tory scanned the faces of the assembled reporters as she waited for the rattling of chairs to die away. "I have a brief statement to make before taking your questions.

" 'At eleven-twenty hours, 27 June 2245, Standard Calendar,

the Phelan starship *Far Horizons* passed behind the Sun. Ambassador Faslorn has asked me to pass on his overall satisfaction with the way things are going. He requests all people of goodwill to pray for the safety of the starship and those who sail aboard her. The ship is now approaching perihelion and maximum dynamic stress on the light sail and its shroud lines. Analysis indicates that the sail has sufficient strength to withstand the stresses, but the degree of turbulence during the encounter is unknown. If all goes well, ship and light sail will reappear at thirteen-twenty-three hours.' " Tory looked up from her notes. "I will now take your questions."

"How are the Phelan ambassadors taking this?" a reporter in the third row asked.

"How would you take it if your family, neighbors, and everyone you ever knew was in imminent danger of being broiled alive?"

"That doesn't exactly answer my question."

"Sorry. Faslorn and Maratel are naturally anxious about the fate of their shipmates."

"What about the other two?"

"They are traveling, so I can't tell you their moods from personal observation. However, I imagine they are equally anxious about the safety of their people."

Another reporter held up his hand. "Tad Matthews, Interplanetary Newsfax. How long after the ship reappears will you know whether this worked?"

"Immediately. The very fact that it reappears when we predict will tell us the capture maneuver has been successful. If the ship slows too little while behind the Sun, it will reappear early; if it slows too much, then it will reappear late."

Another hand went up, this time from a reporter Tory had met at a few embassy parties. "Yes, Joyanne?"

"How long after this encounter can we expect *Far Horizons* to reach Earth?"

"Latest projections are for a sixty-day transit time. That can vary depending on how they adjust their orbit with the light sail, of course."

"How does that work exactly?"

"Just like a sailboat tacking in front of the wind, or so they tell me. You have to understand that we don't sail that much on Mars . . ." That drew a polite laugh. Tory waited for the noise to die down before she continued. "Essentially, a light sail derives its propulsive force from light pressure, or, to be technical about it, from the change in momentum of the reflected photons. That force acts normal to the sail's surface no matter its orientation. In other words, by tilting the sail, they can steer the starship. That is not a Phelan invention, by the way. Our own light sails move cargo between the planets in the same fashion.''

"I suppose they'll be coming straight out from the Sun," the reporter said.

"Left unmodified, their postencounter orbit would take them to where Earth was three months ago. As soon as they leave the vicinity of the Sun, they will orient the sail to modify the orbit to a sweeping curve. They will pass inboard of us, then take up a Solar parking orbit a million kilometers foreorbit of Earth.''

"Why not a regular parking orbit?''

"The size of the sail makes maneuvering difficult in the vicinity of a planet. Remember, as small as it may look on the screen, the light sail is nearly twice as wide as Earth!''

"Now that the starship appears to have arrived, can you tell us what plans there are for bringing the Phelan Resolution to a vote?''

"I can tell you that we hope to see the bill reported out of committee fairly soon, and then acted upon by the full council. We expect that it will pass long before *Far Horizons* actually reaches Earth.''

"How will the opposition respond to today's events?''

"I hope they will recognize that their demand for the Phelan to find another star is unrealistic, and that they will join the rest of us in welcoming our cousins to the Solar system. They have made some excellent points that the council will surely factor into their deliberations. There comes a time, however, when constructive criticism turns to obstructionism. The Phelan are here to stay. It is to everyone's benefit that they be absorbed into our society with a minimum of friction.''

"May we quote you?''

"The truth should always be quoted!'' Tory made a show of glancing at her wrist chronometer, although her implant kept her constantly aware of the time. "I have time for another question.''

"What are the Phelan ambassadors's plans for the rest of the day?'' Matthews asked.

"They will remain in their quarters until we have reacquired communications with *Far Horizons* and they have talked to their people on board. After that, Ambassador Faslorn will have a statement to make.''

The light sail reappeared from behind the eastern limb of the sun at precisely 1323:18 hours. Two minutes later, the violet spark of the laser beam sought out the giant Solarscope to announce that all had gone well. An hour after that, *Far Horizons* set sail for Earth.

24

THE RESTAURANT WAS TWO HUNDRED STORIES UP and occupied one entire quadrant of an office tower. The prices reflected the altitude and the panoramic view. Tory paused with her knife halfway through a real beefsteak smothered in grilled onions as she glared at Ben Tallen. He stared back with that insufferably superior look she knew so well.

"What the hell is taking so long with the council?"

"Now, now!" he chided. "We had an agreement, remember? There is to be no shop talk after the food arrives."

"I'm serious, damn it! Your people promised us they would bring the Phelan Resolution to a vote within two weeks of *Far Horizons* rounding Sol. Six weeks later, the damned resolution is still bottled up in the Interior Affairs Committee."

"These things take time," he said as he raised a crystal glass to his lips and sipped his wine.

"Space dust, Ben! Hoffenzoller is stalling."

Tallen sighed and put down the glass. He stared at her with serious eyes. "If we discuss this now, can we then drop the subject for the rest of the evening?"

Her smile was the barest lifting of the corners of her lips. "Maybe."

"Not good enough."

"All right, I promise. You tell me what is going on and I won't bring it up again tonight."

"Good."

Tory smiled broadly this time. She and Ben had turned their first dinner date into something of a tradition. Each Friday since then, he had shown up at the embassy at 2000 hours with an armful of flowers, ready to escort her to dinner. Afterward, they went to a show, or museum, or a city night spot. Twice she had succumbed to his advances and accompanied him to his apartment at evening's end. Most often, however, after the obligatory pass, Ben would deliver her back to the embassy and accept his good-night kiss without complaint. Though the spark of their college days had not been rekindled, they still enjoyed one another's company. Their dates had also become an informal channel of communication between the Phelan embassy and the system council, and a friendly contest to see who could gather the most information while giving up the least.

In the six weeks since the alien starship had survived its brush with the sun, there had been no visible progress toward acquiring the tract of land the Phelan sought. Each week seemed to bring a new excuse. Now, with *Far Horizons* only two weeks out, the Phelan were beginning to suspect bad faith by the council leadership. As a result, Faslorn had given Tory very specific instructions concerning the subjects to be covered during her weekly tryst with Tallen.

"What do you want to know?" Ben asked.

"I want to know the real reason for this delay. Has the first minister gone back on his word?"

"Absolutely not."

"Is that the truth, Ben, or what they told you to say?"

He grinned. "Are you asking whether I would lie to you if it were in the best interests of my principals? The answer is yes. Wouldn't you?"

Despite herself, Tory blushed. The question reminded her of the many lies she had told in the service of the Phelan. No amount of rationalization about the greater good would totally salve her conscience.

Seeing her reaction, Tallen pressed the point. "I've been watching you, Tory. Something's bothering you, something big. What is it? What sort of hold do they have on you?"

She felt her face grow even more crimson. "Let's get back to the subject, shall we? What the hell's going on with the council?"

He studied her for a moment, then decided not to push it. "Unfortunately, we can't condemn the outback site without a funding authorization, and that has to go through the Interior Affairs Committee. As you know, Joshua Kravatz, the committee chairman, is violently opposed to allowing the Phelan to settle on Earth, or anywhere else in the Solar system. We haven't been able to determine his motivation. Ambassador Sadibayan thinks he may have religious objections."

Tory shook her head. "No, he's merely peeved with us."

"Oh?"

"I first met Joshua Kravatz at an embassy party about a year ago. He came in his capacity as representative of the university faculties rather than as interior affairs chairman. He wanted the Phelan to license their information-retrieval technology to his group free of charge. Faslorn refused because he was already negotiating to license the same technology for a hefty fee. Kravatz stomped off and we didn't hear from him again until the bill entered his committee.''

''And I thought the Phelan understood human politics,'' Ben said, laughing. ''Tell Faslorn that he should never, never, *never* refuse the request of a councilor for a bribe.''

Tory shrugged. ''It seemed a good call at the time. Anyway, what's done is done. The question before us is how we spring the resolution out from under Kravatz's hobnailed boot!'' Tory had never actually seen a hobnailed boot, of course, but the expression lived on two centuries after the item it described had ceased to exist.

''It won't be easy. Besides Kravatz, we've got the Aussies against us, also a manure pile of industrial interests who are betting they will do better under the status quo.''

''So we are supposed to accept this impasse?''

''It won't be an impasse for long,'' Tallen assured her.

''How's that?''

''The first minister thinks he can get Kravatz to cave in, at least enough to allow the resolution to go to the full council. If Kravatz continues to obstruct things, Hoffenzoller is ready to declare it a matter of vital interest and invoke an order of first-councilor privilege. That will bring it to the floor for immediate debate.''

''Then he should have done that four weeks ago!''

''Invoking privilege isn't something you do lightly. For one thing, it triggers an automatic vote of confidence. If Hoffenzoller risks such a vote and loses, your precious Phelan would find themselves stuck in orbit for the next century or two. Which, by the way, may not be all that bad.''

''Are you joining the opposition, Ben?''

''I only meant that we're rushing things because of an artificial deadline. So what if they have to stay in parking orbit for a few weeks or months until we get things settled here on the ground?''

''You know as well as I do,'' she replied acidly. ''We've orchestrated our whole campaign around *Far Horizons*'s encounter with Sol. The plan was to hold the vote just as public interest peaked. Well, that happened five weeks ago. The longer we wait, the smaller the constituency the Phelan will have here on Earth. You've seen how easy it is to inflame public emotions, Ben. What do you think the political climate will be like a year from now if we give the demagogues free rein?''

"The only outright propaganda I've seen to date appears to have come from you and the embassy," Tallen responded.

"We've made no secret of the fact that we're funding a public-relations campaign," Tory said defensively. "Can you blame us? We're trying to overcome fifty thousand years of inbred distrust of strangers."

"I wasn't 'blaming' you, merely making an observation. Anyway, Hoffenzoller is scheduled to talk to Kravatz this evening. If he relents, fine. If not, we'll hit him with a writ demanding that he report the resolution to the council. In either event, debate begins Wednesday morning. Satisfied?''

She thought for a moment, then nodded. "I suppose."

"Good. Then let's get back to discussing the important things in life, namely how beautiful you are this evening."

The Great Chamber of the Solar System Council was a bowl-shaped auditorium surmounted by a polarized geodesic dome. The chamber reminded Tory of a sports arena with its sloped sides and multiple tiers for spectators. In the council chamber the spectators were the councilors themselves. Each delegation was assigned an enclosed observation box connected via a short hallway to the offices clustered around the chamber periphery. The observation boxes were fronted by glass walls that could be retracted to allow those inside to follow the floor debate directly, or they could observe via screen. The arrangement was intended to promote efficiency. Despite this, council deliberations often flowed with the speed of lubricating oil exposed to the cold Martian night.

However, even the slowest snail must eventually reach its destination. Monday evening the Phelan embassy was notified that debate on their bill would begin promptly at 1000 hours Wednesday, August 21, 2245—precisely the time predicted by Ben Tallen. Raalwin left shortly after the announcement was received to poll his many contacts within council headquarters. He found a disturbing lack of consensus concerning how the Interior Affairs Committee had disgorged. Some maintained that they had done so voluntarily, hinting that the opposition expected to defeat the bill. Others reported mysterious meetings among opponents and supporters. The only thing on which everyone agreed was that there had been no need for the first councilor to invoke his privilege.

Along with word of the impending debate had come passes to the gallery where interested VIPs could watch the action. Despite invitations to the four Phelan, Faslorn decreed that only Tory would attend in person. Otherwise, he reasoned, the sight of aliens in the gallery might awaken primitive impulses among some councilors. Once the resolution passed, there would be plenty of time for the Phelan to express their gratitude in person.

Tory was in her place when the foreshortened figure of Boerk Hoffenzoller strode to the presiding officer's box and called the session to order. A small screen inset in a console before her showed the first councilor's features in close-up. There followed a general stirring up and down the tiers. For once, every glass wall was retracted and each councilor's seat filled. Tory's gaze was drawn to where the small Martian delegation sat on the third tier opposite. Next to them were the Lunarians, and down a tier, the Lagrangians. The representative of the tiny Europa colony sat on the topmost tier, one-third of the way around the circumference from her. These four delegations had once been the whole council. Now they were but a few islands of space dwellers adrift in a sea of terrestrial humanity.

"Ladies and gentlemen of the council," Hoffenzoller announced without preamble. "We will waive the reading of the minutes. I draw your attention to Docket Number 184394, 'A Resolution to Cede Certain Territories on the Continent of Australia to the Tau Ceti Refugees for the Purpose of Establishing a Phelan Colony.' Know you that this is to be a full debate of the pros and cons of this resolution, followed by a vote. Pursuant to Special Chamber Order Number Ten, there will be no amendments, clarifications, or riders. Know also that it is the intent of the leadership to support this measure. Now, then, Councilor Kravatz of the Alliance of University Professors has requested the honor of speaking first. Councilor Kravatz will speak in opposition."

Tory watched as a portly man ascended the steps to the speaker's box. She remembered Kravatz primarily for his habit of jutting his chin out when he wasn't speaking. On the one occasion she had met him, she had thought the mannerism faintly ridiculous. There was nothing ridiculous about him now as he stared out across the chamber with angry eyes. Nor did he have the manner of someone recently mauled in a political fight. As she watched him, Tory's stomach began to knot into a hard ball.

"Ladies and gentlemen of the council," the councilor began in a clipped British accent. "I stand before you an ogre and a monster, a molester of children, a robber of graves, and a denigrator of dreams. You must believe that of me, and more, for have you not listened to the deluge of propaganda flowing from that nest of aliens a few blocks from here?

"Or is it mere coincidence that I and others who have spoken against this abomination we debate today have been pilloried ever since the alien ship rounded the Sun? I leave it to you to decide, my colleagues, and to consider what right these aliens have to meddle in our affairs."

Kravatz stared directly into the camera with flaring nostrils. "These aliens charge that I am an insensitive brute who would cast their poor brethren into the infinite black from where they came. To this charge alone I plead guilty. How can anyone be so heartless, you may ask? There is but a single answer to that question. Despite what the Phelan Embassy's propaganda would have you believe, these interlopers from the stars have no claim to this, our world. Nor do they have a right to any of the planets of Sol, nor to its golden sunshine or life-giving warmth. These are things that belong to humanity. It is humanity, and humanity alone, who will decide whether they are to be shared.

"Please do not misunderstand me, colleagues. Like you, I feel for their plight. I, too, am saddened by their loss. Like you, I thrill at the epic story of their two-century-long voyage to find another star. Yet, their plight is not of our doing, their voyage made necessary by no act of humankind. We have heard enough sentimental mush about the sanctity of all living things. The time has come for clear vision and a strong understanding of our own self-interest. The time has come for us to determine what is best for humanity!"

Kravatz paused to let his words sink in. After a few seconds, he glanced down at his prepared speech, then continued. "We are met here, my colleagues, to decide whether we will award the survivors of the Tau Ceti nova a few thousand hectares of largely uninhabitable scrub land. Some of you argue that the land is largely worthless, and that the Phelan technology we receive in return will pay us for our troubles many times over. I respect your right to that opinion. As for me, I would no more lend these aliens my world than I would lend them my wife. To do so would be to sell our human heritage for a few shiny baubles. Our history is replete with such bargains. I hope we have learned to recognize their folly."

Kravatz turned to the first councilor. "Sir, I have additional remarks that I wish to make later. I am prepared to yield to the next speaker."

"Very well," Boerk Hoffenzoller replied formally. He turned to the cameras. "I now call on Minister for Science de Pasqual, who will speak for the leadership."

Jesus de Pasqual was cool and reasoned where Kravatz had been emotional and demagogic. He pointed out all of the reasons why it was impossible for the Phelan to seek a new star. He then listed the benefits to be gained from Phelan technology. It was a long list. Tory and Maratel had worked on it most of the previous night.

When the science minister completed his speech, an opposition councilor took his place at the podium. The debate continued that way throughout the morning. The two sides took turns. Opponents maintained that the Phelan starship could be refurbished and sent on its way by a bank of lasers that would substitute for the power of the nova. Supporters called such claims fantasy, and did their best to explain the technical difficulty of interstellar flight. Just before noon, the councilor representing Mars made his way to the podium. He followed an opponent of the resolution, and thus, was to speak in support.

The Martian began by lauding the far-reaching vision of the scientists who had constructed the *Starhopper* probe. Without it, he reminded them, there would be no debate this day. Rather, they would be awaiting the arrival of the alien starship with no knowledge of who or what was aboard. He spoke of the genius of Dardan Pierce, the skill of Garth Van Zandt, the courage of Katherine Claridge, and the knowledge of Eli Guttieriz. After long minutes, it became clear that he had no intention of mentioning the daughter of Mars who sat in the gallery. So far as his words were concerned, Tory Bronson had never existed.

Tears welled up in Tory's eyes as she sat wooden-faced, staring straight ahead, lest some questing camera see her react. The snub, coming from an unexpected quarter, had breached the carefully constructed wall within her subconscious. Every doubt, fear, and worry she had faced in the past two years came boiling to the fore, and it took all her willpower to sit and listen as her planet's representative droned on. Her inner turmoil was so great that she missed much of what he was saying. Only after he relinquished the podium did she realize that he had said not a single word in support of the resolution.

Before the next speaker could rise, Boerk Hoffenzoller ordered the debate suspended for two hours for lunch. He, too, seemed shaken by the Martian councilor's nonendorsement. Tory waited for a long minute to compose herself before she left the gallery to face the reporters who would be clustered outside.

25

AS SOON AS THE LIFT DOORS OPENED TORY FOUND herself awash in reporters. They swarmed forward to stick their pickups in her face as she pushed through the jostling crowd to freedom. "Miss Bronson! How would you score the debate so far? . . . What about the Martian councilor's speech? . . . What will the Phelan do now?"

"I don't know what you're talking about," she muttered.

"Are you saying your home planet hasn't defected to the opposition, then?"

"All I heard was Councilor Mannheim extolling the virtues of the Starhopper Project. He said not a word against the resolution."

"Nor in favor of it. Any comment?"

"Only that you should ask Councilor Mannheim what he meant by his speech. He speaks for Mars, not me."

"How do you feel about his snub of you personally?"

"I didn't notice any snub."

She ignored the rest of their shouted questions until her security entourage extricated her. A flying wedge of uniformed guards cleared her way to the tube station, where they all rode back to the embassy.

"What the hell happened?" Tory demanded as she slammed her attaché case down in the living quarters.

Maratel was standing in front of the holoscreen, watching a replay of her encounter with the newspeople. Tory winced at the wild look in her eyes and the grim expression on her face as she snarled her answers.

"We're not sure what is going on," Maratel replied without taking her eyes from the screen. "Raalwin is checking his sources. Things are definitely not going as planned."

"Do you suppose Hoffenzoller has double-crossed us?"

"It is too early to say. Wait for Raalwin's report."

Five minutes later, the political specialist entered the living

222

quarters and signaled for them to join him in the Egg. Faslorn was waiting for them. Neirton was absent, on the west coast of the continent arranging a special public-opinion poll. The wait for the electromagnetic seals to activate seemed an eternity.

"Something is up," Raalwin announced as soon as the light board showed it was safe to speak. "I spoke with Ben Tallen. He told me about the first minister's session with Joshua Kravatz."

"And?" Faslorn asked.

"Apparently, Kravatz volunteered to release the resolution to the full council even before Hoffenzoller could bring it up. The first minister's people assumed Kravatz had counted the votes and was trying to lose gracefully. This morning's session would appear to explode that theory."

"Maybe he'd counted the votes and figured he could win," Maratel said.

"What happened to Mars?" Faslorn asked Tory. "Your people have been the strongest advocates of gaining access to our technology."

"That is what makes it so strange. Your light sail material will revolutionize dome building. I've seen half a dozen other things aboard *Far Horizons* that will transform how we live at home. It would take one hell of a shock to make Mars throw all of that away."

"Yet they seem to have done just that. Use your implant to scan our informants's reports for the last few weeks. See if we have anything unusual on Councilor Mannheim or his people."

"I can't without dropping the spy shields."

"Right," Faslorn said, remembering that they were in the Egg. The oversight was an indication of how distracted he was. "Then use the hand terminal."

Tory set about manually coding the command. Since their arrival, the Phelan had engaged the services of several political operatives. They had also gained a reputation for paying well for useful information developed by free-lance informants. Their network generally kept them well apprised of events at council headquarters.

While Tory worked, Faslorn turned to Raalwin. "When did you last poll the Martian delegation?"

"I spoke personally with Mannheim's political assistant sixty hours ago. He gave me assurances of Mars's support."

"Could he have been lying?"

"I monitored the call with the usual instruments. They say he was telling the truth."

"Perhaps Mannheim didn't confide in him."

"The profile we have on the Martian councilor says that he is not an independent actor. It is unlikely that he would change sides without confiding in his assistant."

"Then we must conclude that something has happened within the last three days to change the equation. What?"

"I know," Tory announced.

She felt three sets of black eyes fix on her as she fidgeted before the workscreen. Like the rest of the Egg, the secure facility's computer was cut off from the outside world at the moment. However, it was connected to the embassy computer whenever the spy shields were down. That gave Tory access to everything in the embassy computer until the moment they had sealed themselves in. In fact, much of the delay in that process was caused by the final computer update that preceded raising the shields.

"Dardan Pierce is back on Earth. He was seen having dinner with Councilor Mannheim last evening. Our informant filed his report at seven-thirty this morning."

"What is the significance?" Faslorn asked.

"The last time Dard was on Earth was the night he came to our party. I asked him to call me next trip so we could go out to dinner. He didn't call."

"Perhaps he was too busy," Maratel interjected.

"Then he would have contacted me to express his regrets. That sort of thing takes about a second via implant. I know Dard—he believes in keeping his word. No, if I haven't heard from him, it's because he has something to hide."

"What?"

"It might be connected with the Tau Ceti research project. Wait a second." Tory typed another command into the computer, cursing the clumsiness of fingers as input devices. Because the Tau Ceti research project was partially funded by the Phelan, the embassy had a direct link to the project files in Paris. Updates of all project data were made every six hours, including the guest log. In seconds, the file she had been searching for began to flow up the screen in glowing letters. "Here it is. Professor Dardan Pierce, appointment for ten-hundred-hours last Thursday."

Faslorn snapped something in the Phelan tongue to Maratel. She replied in Standard. "There have been no reports of useful findings from the research project, especially none questioning the origin of the nova. So far as everyone there believes, our star exploded of its own accord."

"What else could they have discovered from two-hundred-and-fifty-year-old data?"

"Nothing," Raalwin hissed. "We transmitted their data to our own astronomers. They claim there is no way to tell that the explosion was not natural."

"I can think of one way," Tory said.

"How?"

"What if they penetrated the Egg's security and heard us talking about it?"

Faslorn considered the idea, then signaled his disbelief with a sharp Phelan negative. "If true, then the spies would report to the first councilor. He seems as much in the dark as we are."

"That may be a trick," Maratel said.

"To what purpose?" Raalwin asked. "The Martian councilor made him look like a fool this morning. Surely Hoffenzoller would not allow that with everyone in the system watching."

Tory nodded. "I agree. I saw his expression. He was shocked by what Mannheim did."

"Then we will trust your human instincts. What can we conclude from this? Apparently the astronomers studying the old data have uncovered something that hurts our cause. We are agreed that it is unlikely they know the nova was artificially induced, so what else can it be?"

When no one spoke, he went on. "We have but an hour to solve this puzzle and find a way to counter it. Any suggestions?"

It was a very worried Tory Bronson who found herself seated in the gallery for the start of the afternoon council session. During the morning she had been virtually alone. Now every seat was taken. Word that something was up had spread through council headquarters at the speed of light. Suddenly, everyone who had the power had a pass to one of the visitors's galleries. Adding to Tory's discomfort was the hurriedly gulped sandwich that lay in her stomach like a rust red rock from home.

Again, Boerk Hoffenzoller strode to the presiding officer's box and took his place behind the large ceremonial desk. He reached out and pressed a control, and the amplified sound of a gavel echoed through the great hall.

"The council will come to order."

He waited until the banks of glass walls were retracted and

the delegations had returned to their seats. The tiers, like the visitors's galleries, were now packed.

"Ladies and gentlemen of the council. I ask unanimous consent to interrupt the scheduled roll of the debate so that we may hear again from Councilor Kravatz. Those opposed, please signify." The hall was silent for half a minute as the electronic tally board remained blank. There had been no objections.

Kravatz emerged from a side tunnel and made his way to the podium. He was no longer alone. A familiar figure strode beside him: Dardan Pierce.

"Colleagues," the committee chairman began, "I have shocking news that I do not feel competent to express. For that purpose, I ask that Professor Pierce of the University of Olympus, Mars, be given the courtesy of the hall. If there are no objections, Professor Pierce."

It seemed to Tory that Dard looked directly at her as he stepped to the podium. She decided that she was imagining things. After all, from the speaker's position, she was a dimly perceived figure behind a glass wall. She leaned forward to closely study her ex-boss on the screen. His expression reminded her of the time when she had been invited to attend the faculty Friday-night poker game. That had been the night he'd been dealt a straight flush and strove mightily to conceal the fact.

"Ladies and gentlemen of the council," he began. "I am here today to report on a rather startling discovery made by my colleagues at the Sorbonne. Before I do so, it will be necessary to give you some background. Please bear with me. It will all become clear in a few minutes.

"Throughout human history Tau Ceti was a nondescript fifth-magnitude star of spectral class K0. Slightly cooler than Sol, it had very little to distinguish it until it lit up the sky on the night of August 25, 2001. Many people took it as an omen to mark the beginning of the new millennium. Astronomers were mystified. You see, Tau Ceti, like Sol, was a main-sequence star. That is, it was in the hydrogen-burning phase of its life, with more than five billion years remaining before it should have swelled into a red giant, and then eventually ended life as a white dwarf. It was believed at the time that main-sequence stars did not nova. Our ancestors were very mystified by this nova and never truly explained how it happened.

"Because of the public interest in Tau Ceti caused by the appearance of the Phelan starship, several colleagues and I decided to look again at the old data. We thought that, with two hundred and fifty additional years of science on which to draw, we might be able to solve the mystery that had stumped our predecessors. In this effort we have been unsuccessful. We have developed several theories to explain how a main-sequence star might nova, but none of these is particularly compelling. Nor are any of our theories supported by the data, which have several peculiarities that I will now address.''

Dard Pierce reached down and pressed a control on the podium. His face disappeared from Tory's screen, to be replaced by a jagged curve. ''What you are looking at is the spectrum of the Tau Ceti nova in the first moments after telescopes were brought to bear on it. Yet, in studying the spectrum, our ancestors found a deficit of some two-point-five percent in the star's light output in the initial phases of the explosion. In nonscientific terms, some light that should have been produced when the star exploded is missing.''

The graph disappeared and was replaced by an image of the exploding star. ''Here we have a photograph from an orbiting observatory taken within hours of the nova's first appearance in the sky. It is one of a series of observations made at different wavelengths. Here, ladies and gentlemen, is a modern composite image using data from the entire observational series . . .'' The screen changed to show a different image of the exploding star. The bright starburst now showed a subtle texture. Where before Tau Ceti had been an intense blue-white spark, now it was mottled, its texture faintly resembling that of an orange peel.

''What we discovered,'' Pierce continued, ''was that two point-five percent of the star's visible surface was obscured by multiple small objects during the initial stages of the explosion. This phenomenon lasted for approximately sixteen hours. Afterward, the light output of the exploding star was precisely what theory predicts it should have been. We have postulated that the objects, whatever they were, became submerged in the expanding shell of superheated gas and thus became invisible. Why our ancestors did not detect this mottling is something of a mystery. Perhaps they never thought to combine the multiple wavelength images, or lacked our computer routines for doing so. Maybe they did detect the phenomenon and failed to note its significance. In any event, our people in Paris have analyzed this image extensively. The obscuring objects are approximately twenty thousand kilometers in diameter—precisely the size of a

Phelan light sail. What we have here, ladies and gentlemen, is a picture of *Far Horizons* and her sister ships as they launched!

"You can imagine our excitement when we realized what we were looking at. However, a quick calculation proved that four light sails could not possibly have obscured two-point-five percent of the nova's light. To cover up that much of the expanding fireball would have required many more light sails."

Pierce took a deep breath and glanced up from his prepared text. There was no mistaking the look of triumph in his eyes. "Ladies and gentlemen, if we assume that the Phelan craft were arrayed twenty degrees to either side of their system's ecliptic when Tau Ceti exploded, *the number of light sails required to produce the observed obscuration is more than one hundred thousand!*"

26

TORY STOOD ON THE BALCONY OUTSIDE THE EMbassy's living quarters and scanned the sky for aircraft. There were a surprising damned lot of them. Immediately above and beyond the railing were three police hover cruisers, each balanced on underjets as though pinned to that particular patch of sky. Their normally quiet hissing was amplified to a shout in the sounding-box canyons below. The warm wind induced by their hot jets washed across the roof, tugging at her clothes and ruffling her hair.

Much higher up and farther away, several bright sparks orbited in the clear blue sky. These were military craft. Unseen in the canyons below were the squads of uniformed police that had blocked off eight full city blocks. The police had taken over the whole of the office tower below the embassy, evicting the thousands who normally worked in the building. Guards were everywhere. The lower two floors of the embassy were also deserted. None of the human staff had shown up for work in the past three days.

Tory grimaced as she watched the patrolling aircraft. She had fully expected to reach this point, but not for another six years. Now they would never know whether the Phelan grand plan could have worked. Like the carefully woven tapestry of fiction that it was, the plan had been unraveled by a single dangling thread of truth.

The reaction to Dard Pierce's revelation had been both instantaneous and devastating. Even normally unflappable councilors had risen to their feet to shout defiance at the Phelan. Ringing denunciations had followed as various politicians rushed to place themselves on record as opposing the Phelan Resolution. The denunciations were still going strong three days later. It seemed as though every public official on the planet wanted to make known his or her loathing for the aliens.

The story had flashed around the world and out into space at the speed of light. With it had gone a shock wave of disbelief and anger. As that first shock subsided, news organizations turned to embellishment to retain public interest. A gold rush had begun to find scientists willing to make increasingly lurid estimates of the size of the Third Fleet. The highest Tory had heard so far was 250,000 starships carrying more than thirty billion refugees. The embassy had made no attempt to correct these gross exaggerations. The truth, after all, was bad enough.

For two years Tory had suffered through sweaty, sleepless nights worrying about what people would think of her part in the deception. She need wonder no longer. Within minutes of Dard Pierce's revelation, she had found herself a pariah among her own people. She had barely made her way to the exit of the visitors's gallery when she was intercepted by a squad of fleet marines decked out in riot-control gear. A lieutenant whose courteous manner had not extended to his eyes informed her that he had been assigned to escort her back to the embassy. Of Tory's own security detachment, there had been no sign.

At least they were still respecting the sanctity of the deserted embassy. She had warned Faslorn and the others that this probably would not last. The Phelan had no method for protecting their representatives. Any courtesies rendered were just that— courtesies.

A flash of light from a nearby office tower told Tory that her watchers were not only in the sky. She wondered how many telephoto lenses were currently focused on her, and how many telescopic sights? She found the idea disturbing. It robbed the open air of its usual freedom. Frowning, she turned and made her way back to the living quarters through the rooftop garden.

What would happen next did not bear thinking about.

All five of them were sealed into the Egg to discuss strategy. Except for a single warning message flashed to *Far Horizons*, there had been no communication with either the starship or the system council. The commlink to the starship was still operative, however, as was Tory's link with the city computer. How long before the authorities decided to cut even these tenuous lines of communication was anyone's guess.

It was a somber group that gathered around the small conference table at the center of the spherical enclosure. The air was thick with the smell of human sweat, paint thinner, and cinnamon. The overhead lights had been dimmed, with the primary illumination provided by the glowing holoscreen on which was displayed *Far Horizons*'s orbital track.

"What are they waiting for?" Maratel asked. "Why don't they arrest us?"

"It's *Far Horizons*," Tory said, gesturing toward the screen. "The authorities don't know whether to board now or wait until your people make parking orbit."

"They mustn't!" Faslorn warned. "That will convince the fleet that all is lost. Those who command will begin preparations for another interstellar voyage."

"They'd blow up the Sun if your ship were captured? Just like that? No warning?"

"Preparations at this stage would involve repositioning the fleet to pass well clear of Sol. They wouldn't want to be caught too close to the nova. The actual seeding of your sun would not begin for three or four years."

"Then there is still time to change minds."

Raalwin's gesture was a Phelan negative. "The capture of the scout ship at this time would almost certainly trigger a redeployment of the fleet. Once that is completed, the decision to continue on to another star is irreversible."

"What do you mean, 'at this time'?" Tory asked.

Faslorn signaled permission before Raalwin responded. "There have been developments we thought best to keep from you, Tory. *Far Horizons*'s primary communications array, the one we use to communicate with the fleet, was damaged during the transit through your star's corona."

"Damaged how?"

"The array is embedded in the light sail. Several vital junctions were eroded by whipping gas."

"You must have a backup."

"The alternate array is on the trailing end cap near where Maratel showed you the anchor sphere. It is currently masked by the sail. We cannot use it until the sail is discarded after *Far Horizons* achieves parking orbit."

"I still don't see the problem."

"For three long months, those who command will have only human news sources and their own imaginations to judge our progress. You have experienced the vitriol of the past three days. How do you expect those who command to respond when the speeches of denunciation reach them in a few months?"

"Badly," Tory said glumly.

"Correct. Now imagine their reaction when they receive reports of *Far Horizons*'s capture or destruction."

"But they've come so far! Surely they won't throw everything away on a whim."

"It isn't a whim," Raalwin said. "The fate of our species is at stake. We must know absolutely that humans can be trusted or we must seek another star."

"Damn it! Most of your ships can't take another interstellar voyage. You've told me that yourself a dozen times or more."

"True," the Phelan political scientist replied. "Projections call for a seventy-five-percent failure rate on the second leg of the voyage. Hundreds of millions will die slowly as their life-support systems degrade to uselessness."

"And you consider that better than making peace with us?"

Maratel reached across the table and placed a hand on top of Tory's. "You don't understand. Many will die, but not all. The race will survive. That is why we chose to build so many small ships rather than a few large ones. We can make up to three voyages like the last one before the last ship wears out."

"If your people blow up the Sun, they will kill you and everyone aboard *Far Horizons*." Even as she said it, Tory realized that her objection was too obvious not to have occurred to them.

Faslorn's lower hands fluttered in a gesture that Maratel had once demonstrated for her. It was an acknowledgment that some things are beyond one's control, a gesture of absolute resignation.

"That is our function, Victoria Bronson," he said, using her full name for the first time in months. "We were sent here to determine if human beings can be made to accept us. Our studies of your people tell us that the risk has always been very great. Perhaps we would have succeeded if we'd been given time to prepare humanity for the shock, perhaps not. We have always known that our own lives would be forfeit if we failed. After all, a ship of specialists on *Homo sapiens* is of little use once your race no longer exists."

"Damn it, you can't just give up!" Tory yelled. "We need to buy time while we think of some way out of this mess."

"Things have progressed too far. Your people have decided to reject us. There is no chance that we can change their minds."

"Nonsense. There's *always* a chance." Tory noticed the glances the four aliens exchanged. She wasn't sufficiently skilled at interpreting Phelan emotions to recognize the nuances, but it didn't take a genius to know what they were thinking. They were wondering if their poor human servant was suffering a breakdown.

"What do you suggest, Victoria?"

She frowned. In truth, she had no idea what they should do next. "You'll have to tell the full council that you will destroy the Sun if they reject you," she said in desperation. "Let them know the consequences of their actions."

Faslorn shook his head slowly from side to side in a very human gesture. "That is something that we must never do."

"But why?"

"What was your first reaction when we revealed our secret to you?"

"I wanted to tell you to go to hell!"

"Why didn't you?"

"Because it wouldn't have done any good, except possibly to make me feel better."

"And having concluded that, you reasoned that it was better to assist us in our deception than it was for you to tell your people the truth."

"Of course."

"And how have you slept these past two years, knowing that you were doing the right thing for humanity?"

"You know damned well how I've slept."

"Precisely," Faslorn said. "Yet you are a highly intelligent individual, able to rationalize a decision with which you are not comfortable. Too bad the psychology of individual humans does not hold for humans en masse. If it did, we might be able to reason with your people."

"You can't know their reaction in advance."

"But we *do* know. We've run the simulation millions of times, always with the same result. Your people are in a highly emotional state just now. They have, in effect, ceased thinking and have gone on automatic control. They are resolved to punish us because we concealed the existence of the Third Fleet. By telling them that we also have the power to destroy your sun, we only reinforce their opinion that we are evil incarnate. Also, revealing the truth will give your people reason to fear us, and you humans try to destroy that which you fear. You cannot help it. The 'fight or flight' response is buried too deeply in your genes.

"Besides, no one will believe us. Most will refuse to face the unpleasant truth. They will claim we are lying. Others will be defiant and dare us to do our worst. Any leader who counsels conciliation will be shouted down by those who demand war. And in the end, there will be war, and those who command our fleet will order the sun destroyed.''

Tory's frown turned into a scowl. He was right, of course. Since there was no possibility of fleeing the menace, the natural reaction would be to fight. The drums of war would sound, a fleet would be raised, defenses seen to. Probably, hundreds or thousands of alien starships would be intercepted or destroyed as they swept in from deep space. Yet whatever score the space navy ran up, it would not be enough. A single surviving Phelan ship could still destroy Sol and ride the shock wave outbound. Indeed, neutrinos of a precisely regulated energy would penetrate the Sun long before the Third Fleet came within range of the navy. Once the instability was started, there would be no stopping it. Had it been otherwise, one-quarter of the Phelan species would not now be transiting the outlands of Sol. Besides, with their light sails as weapons, Tory doubted that more than a small fraction of the twenty-two thousand inbound starships could be killed by the navy.

Light sails as weapons . . .

Tory treated the errant thought gently, lest it escape her. There was something about it that sparked a resonance in her mind. Perhaps the Phelan had not considered the problem properly. Revealing their power would indeed frighten the people of the Solar system. But would it frighten them enough? She chewed her lower lip as she considered what she was about to suggest. It was a truly harebrained idea, with a million things that might go wrong. And even if everything went right, there was no guarantee of success.

She glanced at the screen that marked the progress of *Far Horizons* toward its parking place in Solar orbit. The ship was only a few days away from the end of its journey. There were the problems of communications and timing, of course. Would they be allowed to communicate at all? Would the navy give *Far Horizons* the time needed to make the plan work, or would they board it and seal humanity's doom with pictures of marines marauding through the starship's corridors?

She thought of Garth Van Zandt somewhere out in space. Was he even now closing in on the light sail? What about the other craft the navy must have shadowing the starship? How close were they? Would they figure out what *Far Horizons* was up to in time to prevent it?

Lastly, she considered her own responsibility in all of this.

She was already judged a traitor by practically everyone. What would they think when they learned this had been her idea? Would they ever understand, or would the name of Victoria Bronson be added to those of Judas, Quisling, and Daman on the blacklist of human history?

She found that she had no answers to any of her questions. To one used to the instantaneous information flow of a computer implant, not knowing was a hard thing to endure. Still, she did not see that she had a choice in the matter. To do nothing would lead to the sun's destruction.

She took a deep breath and looked at Faslorn. "I may have an idea on how to retrieve the situation. It carries some risk. They may just decide to kill us outright . . ."

It was a beautiful day when next Tory found herself in the great hall of the system council. Shafts of late-summer sunlight shone down through the transparent dome overhead, pierced the air, and lit up the floating dust motes that had somehow evaded the air scrubbers. Again the hall was filled. It seemed as though everyone on the planet wanted to be present at this critical moment. Those who hadn't been able to obtain passes were planted in front of their viewscreens at home.

The timing had been the hardest to arrange. When Faslorn had first requested permission to address the council, Boerk Hoffenzoller suggested an emergency session that same evening. He had been mystified when the Phelan had refused the opportunity and had insisted on a delay of four full days. Hoffenzoller's initial impulse had been to deny the request as unreasonable. He had not done so because the matter was too important to play the usual dominance games. Besides, he was curious to hear what the aliens had to say.

Tory and the four Phelan arrived at the appointed hour and were immediately ushered to their seats on the floor of the great hall. The Phelan had dropped their human personas for the occasion and were again alien creatures doing the bidding of their species. Tory felt herself at the focus of a thousand hostile glares as she took her seat next to the four white-furred aliens.

At the agreed-upon minute, Boerk Hoffenzoller stepped to the podium and called everyone to order. A hush fell over the delegates as the first councilor shuffled papers on the lectern. When he began to speak, it was in the heavy, sonorous voice politicians used for funerals and the most grave announcements.

"Ladies and gentlemen. One week ago, we learned that we

are about to be descended upon by thousands of alien starships bearing God knows how many new mouths to feed. The Phelan leader has asked to address this council to clarify the situation. I ask that you hear him out, and I leave it to the conscience of each of you to determine how much stock to place in his words. I give you Faslorn, leader of the Phelan.''

At the mention of his name, Faslorn rose and knuckle-walked to the podium. He and Hoffenzoller passed one another, pausing long enough to exchange a few words. The contrast between the furred alien and the graying elderly human was stark.

Faslorn reached the podium and began to speak. ''Ladies and gentlemen of the council. People of Sol. I bring you greetings from the people of Tau Ceti, who are sorely in need of your help. Many of you feel betrayed because we did not tell you of the numerous ships that are now inbound for your star. I do not blame you for that. I do ask, however, that you try to put aside that emotion to consider the very serious situation in which both our species find themselves. I think you will find what I have to say worth listening to.

''There have been many speculations about the number of ships now en route to Sol. The Third Fleet consists of twenty-two thousand, three hundred and eighteen starships, each the same size as the scout vessel you know as *Far Horizons*. The total Phelan population aboard these ships is two-point-eight billion.''

Faslorn waited for the angry buzzing noise that followed his announcement to die away. ''This, then, is what we have been protecting. We had hoped to convince you of our worthiness before the fleet made its presence known, but that is now impossible. So be it.''

Faslorn told of the terrible day when the Phelan realized that their star was doomed, leaving out only the fact that it had been the Phelan themselves who were the cause. He told of the massive effort to construct the ships necessary to save the Phelan race. He described the nova and the violence with which the four fleets had been flung starward on their long voyages. He described what it had been like to grow up watching the tiny yellow spark of the Sun grow steadily brighter, and to wonder what humankind's reaction would be once they learned of the Phelan.

Those in the hall listened in complete silence as Faslorn reminded them of the wonders that would flow if only they would give his people refuge. For more than twenty minutes he painted a glowing picture of the bright future that awaited human and Phelan alike. Finally, he stopped and scanned the sea of human faces around him.

"If you accept us into your lives, ladies and gentlemen, we will provide you all of the benefits that flow from superior knowledge. However, I would be remiss if I did not remind you that we have another option. For the past hundred hours, many of your leaders have urged that your ships of war be used to drive us back into interstellar space. Since retreat is impossible, we will resist all such efforts with all of the means at our disposal. Any attempt to interfere with the Third Fleet will be considered an act of war.

"Many of you are undoubtedly wondering whether we have the power to fight the human race on its home territory. That is only natural. After all, some in this body have accused us of being liars and braggarts. A healthy skepticism is a useful thing in any thinking being, but too great a mistrust can be dangerous. So that you know that we can do what I say, we will now provide a small demonstration of our power."

Faslorn turned and walked back to his seat. The hall was filled with expectation as Tory scanned the bewildered looks that followed him. It was a few minutes before anyone noticed that the light streaming in through the windows had begun to fade.

27

GARTH VAN ZANDT SAT ON THE BRIDGE OF THE cruiser *Aurora* and watched the light sail climb the black sky as Luna's Orientale Basin slid silently astern below him. The jagged peaks and jumbled floor of the giant impact crater were crossed by long shadows as both the alien starship and the glowing orb of the sun climbed into view above the tan line of the horizon. At a range of only two hundred thousand kilometers, *Far Horizons*'s light sail was the largest object in the black sky, dwarfing even the full Earth that hovered directly astern.

"Target in sight," Terence Bremer, Van Zandt's second-in-command, commented over the intercom. "That's one big mother!"

"Big, but fragile," Van Zandt replied. "The light sail is only a few angstroms thick most places."

Following the revelation in the system council that a huge number of Phelan light sails and starships were inbound toward Sol, fleet headquarters had ordered *Aurora* and four other warcraft to Luna to await the passage of *Far Horizons* en route to its final parking orbit. Headquarters's orders were to shadow the alien craft and await further instructions. Since Van Zandt was the only officer in the navy who had been aboard the starship, he had been given overall command of the small fleet. It was a command he would have as soon forgone.

"Gawd, Captain! Look at that!"

"I see it."

A bright spark had formed at one edge of the sail's surface and was slowly gliding toward the center. Garth was perplexed by the phenomenon until the spot revealed itself to be a distorted image of the Earth. The angle of incidence between *Aurora* and the light sail was just right so that the mirrored surface was reflecting the light from the full Earth directly at them.

"What's going on?" Bremer asked.

"They must be reorienting the sail for a course change. Comm officer, notify fleet command. Eyes, get me a reading on the sail attitude and a projection of their new tack.''

"Right, Captain.''

If the Phelan commanding *Far Horizons* had detected the fleet orbiting Luna and was attempting to flee, he was wasting his time. It would be hours before they would build up any significant change in their velocity. Even this close to Sol, the starship's acceleration rate was only a few hundredths of a standard gravity. The ships under Garth's command could make three g's of sustained acceleration. They would overtake the light sail before it could possibly move out of range.

Ten minutes passed. The tilt of the sail was such that Earth's reflection was no longer being diverted precisely in their direction. The sail's surface was now undulating slowly. Whoever was controlling it was taking a risk. If the flapping became severe, the sail could be ripped asunder. Wherever the starship commander was going, he was in a hurry.

"It looks like they're tacking hard to reflect light back along their line of flight, Captain," the radar operator reported.

"They're slowing?''

"Looks like it. No measurable velocity change yet, but tilting the sail in that direction will have the effect of robbing them of orbital velocity.''

"Course projection?''

"None yet.''

"Keep me informed" was Garth's only response. Something had apparently spooked the aliens. He wondered what it had been.

Ten minutes later, the sail was tilted even more radically to reflect sunlight forward along the ship's line of flight. The undulations were becoming much more pronounced as whoever was controlling the shroud lines fought for control.

"Any suggestions what he's doing, Mr. Bremer?''

"Don't know, Captain. It almost looks like he's trying a panic stop. He's very nearly matched velocity with Earth.''

"Captain," the sensor operator reported. "They are definitely altering their course track to the north and slowing. They're approaching the ecliptic. It looks like they're planning to head back in-system.''

"Comm!''

"Yes, Captain.''

"General order to the fleet. It looks like they're trying to run away. All ships stand by. We'll pick up the chase on the next orbit.''

"Aye, sir.''

"Captain!'' Bremer shouted.

Van Zandt felt irritation at his first officer for interrupting him while he was issuing orders to his command. "What is it, Mr. Bremer?''

"Captain, look at the Earth!''

Van Zandt glanced at the aft viewscreen. The Earth was a round, glowing ball hanging low over the lunar limb. It would set in another few minutes as *Aurora*'s orbital velocity carried it across Luna Farside and out of sight of the home world. At first Garth did not understand what his first officer was talking about. When he finally understood, he realized the starship had no intention of running away. He swore under his breath and issued orders for an immediate departure from Lunar orbit. Unfortunately, he and his command were out of position. There wasn't a damned thing he could do to counter the alien maneuver.

The light streaming through the transparent dome of the great hall weakened minute by minute. As darkness fell in the world outside, panic ensued within. Tory had never seen a Solar eclipse; the moons of Mars were too small. Only the inner one was capable of casting a shadow on the surface, and then only fleetingly.

She had heard about eclipses, of course, and was surprised at the psychological effect the eclipse was having on her. It was as though the superstitious dread of a thousand generations of ancestors who had feared the dark had suddenly come boiling to the surface. Her reaction was especially surprising since this eclipse had been her idea. She wondered what thoughts must be running through the minds of those who had no idea what had happened to the Sun.

In a natural eclipse, the shadow of Luna sweeps across the Earth in a band of totality less than five hundred kilometers wide, while people a few hundred kilometers to either side barely noticed any change at all. Tory had read of nineteenth- and twentieth-century scientists who had traveled halfway around the Earth to be present for the few minutes that an eclipse lasted.

This eclipse would not be normal in any fashion. The Earth was a sphere 12,800 kilometers in diameter. *Far Horizons*'s light sail was more than twenty thousand kilometers across. At Faslorn's instruction, the commander of the Phelan starship had altered his course slightly to interpose his light sail directly between Earth and the Sun. Since the starship was only six hundred thousand kilometers distant—one-and-a-half times the distance between Earth and Luna—Earth fit completely within the light sail's cone of shadow. Nor was the Solar corona visible, as it was during natural eclipses. *Far Horizons* had plucked the Sun totally from the sky, causing night to fall across all the planet's lighted hemisphere.

As the light sail's shadow first touched the Earth, *Far Horizons's* commander reoriented the sail to match his ship's orbital velocity with that of Earth. The sun would remain blocked for more than an hour before orbital mechanics forced the sail out of position. To the frightened billions of terrestrials, that hour would seem an eternity.

To judge by the reaction of those in the hall, the eclipse was having all the effect Tory and the Phelan had hoped. Not a hundred meters from her, a grizzled veteran councilor cried like a baby as he stared upward with mouth agape. Everywhere couples were holding on to one another for comfort. A chill had fallen in the chamber. Whether that was psychological or real, Tory wasn't immediately sure.

She activated her implant and tuned in to the news channels. They, too, were in pandemonium. Correspondents were crying freely as they announced that darkness had fallen across the planet. Only those reporting from the hemisphere that had already been in night seemed calm. Yet, the panic of the daysiders seemed contagious as more of those for whom night had fallen began to question what was going on.

Tory called up the views from various traffic-control cameras throughout the city. Everywhere people were pouring into the streets to congregate under the lamps that had come on automatically as darkness fell. As she scanned randomly across the city, she discovered a park where the lamps were few and far apart. It, too, was filled with surging humanity, and a vast crowd heaped fuel onto a newly lit bonfire.

Tory glanced upward through the dome. Someone had dialed for full transparency, giving those in the hall a clear view of the stars overhead. She estimated where the Sun should be and squinted at that particular patch of blackness. No, the darkness wasn't total. She could see a faint grouping of stars that looked like the Pleiades seen from Mars. These were caused by sunlight shining through small rips in the surface of the light sail, the same rips that had disabled the Phelan ship's ability to communicate with the fleet.

She slowly became aware of frantic activity to her left. There, in the well of the chamber, dozens of councilors were crowded around information screens. Some of these were tuned to news channels, while others communicated directly with the councilors's homes around the globe. Curses and prayers could be heard as the Solar system's mighty realized the full extent of the darkness.

By the time the eclipse had lasted twenty minutes, Tory was no longer in doubt about the temperature in the chamber. It was definitely getting colder. She thought of the quintillions of ergs that normally shone down on the Earth each minute—ergs that were now being intercepted by the light sail far out in space. She shivered as heaters turned on to glow cherry red around the walls. The temperature continued to drop. What had been a balmy late summer day was now frigid. And it would get colder. A lot colder!

Forty-two minutes into the eclipse, snowflakes began to fall. Tory had made a point of looking at the sky before entering the building. There had been a few fleecy white clouds, but nothing to indicate a midday storm. "Warm air is able to carry more moisture than cold," her sixth-grade teacher's voice said inside her brain. At the time, the concept had been an alien one for a twelve-year-old on a planet where atmospheric moisture was unknown. The concept was alien no longer. She watched the tiny flakes pelt against the dome transparency, then melt as they contacted the still-warm glass.

She wasn't the only one. A thousand ashen faces were upturned in astonishment at the midsummer snowstorm. Much of the pandemonium had subsided. News channels carried reports from ships out in space that described the cause of the eclipse. Officials were pleading with the populace to stay calm. The smell of smoke coming in through the air-conditioning ducts told Tory that not everyone was taking that advice.

Reporters at naval headquarters cited unconfirmed reports that the entire fleet had sortied toward the alien starship. Still, the closest ship was reported to be more than a hundred thousand kilometers from the light sail, still too far away to do any good.

Throughout it all, the four Phelan sat impassive and observed the frightened humans around them. Only Neirton showed any emotion. He was in a vast laboratory practicing his speciality, and had to be fascinated. Tory found herself watching various people around her. The most interesting were the fleet marines who had surrounded the central dais within minutes of the onset of totality. They, too, shot worried glances at the sky every few seconds, but that did not stop them from doing their duty. They formed a cordon around the aliens who had caused this calamity, both to make sure they did not leave and to protect them.

Precisely one hour into the eclipse, Faslorn stood and mounted the podium. It took a minute before anyone noticed him, then several more before sufficient order had been restored that a speaker could be heard above the din. Order might never have been restored, but for the wan light that was beginning to show through the snow flurries. Faslorn waited until twilight returned to the world outside before he continued his interrupted speech.

"Know you, people of Sol, that this is the least of our powers. Our ship's light sail could just as easily have concentrated the sunlight onto this planet and vaporized great regions of its surface. Twenty thousand such ships can plunge you into darkness for years on end, leaving this orb a frozen ball of ice; or else sterilize it completely with enough heat to boil your oceans.

"But let us speak no more of horrors. We Phelan are not monsters, merely desperate. Work with us, humanity! Help us! We ask for nothing more than what you have given yourselves— a place to live, sufficient food to eat, and a modicum of safety. I beseech you, humanity! Make room for us close to the welcoming fires of your star, so that we, too, may be warmed by its golden rays."

Faslorn paused to allow his words to sink in. It was difficult to tell what effect his entreaties were having. Tory detected an angry undercurrent in the susurration of voices around her. Besides, the outcome would depend greatly on how the news media chose to play the story over the next several days. The terror that people felt would fade in memory, to be replaced by a deep, dark anger. As the Phelan had told her, a frightened human is a dangerous human. She only hoped they had frightened people enough that they would contemplate the consequences of their actions. It was vital that they begin reasoning again, and stop reacting as though they were on autopilot.

The light overhead had very nearly returned to normal. "Ladies and gentlemen of Sol," Faslorn concluded. "We of the starship *Far Horizons* place our fate into your hands. You may do with us as you will. What will it be? Life for all, or war to the death?"

Faslorn moved away from the podium and made his way toward the steps that would take him down to the main floor. Maratel, Raalwin, and Neirton rose to follow. So, too, did Tory. The Phelan eschewed their knuckle gait, choosing instead to walk erect like humans. Tory held her head high as she descended the steps side by side with Maratel. They reached the bottom to find their way blocked by an officer of fleet marines.

"Faslorn, Maratel, Neirton, and Raalwin. I arrest you in the name of the council, and of all humanity. The charge is threatening to make war upon the human race. Victoria Bronson, I arrest you on the same charge, and on the charge of treason. Will you come peacefully, or must I order my men to use force?"

28

TORY'S CELL MIGHT EASILY HAVE BEEN MISTAKEN for a suite in a hotel. In addition to bedroom and bathroom, it held a small living room with an entertainment screen. Only the lack of a phone revealed the true nature of the facility—and, of course, the fact that her implant steadfastly refused commands to synchronize with the city computer. No doubt there were hidden cameras overhead to follow her every move as a precaution against suicide. Twice biological necessity had forced her into the bathroom, and both times she had answered nature's call with clenched jaw and a self-consciousness she hadn't suffered since the second grade.

The plush furniture was more an obstacle than a comfort as she paced a lopsided triangle around the living room. It had been hours since she had been locked up, hours in which she had been cut off from the Phelan. They might be in the adjacent cells, across town, or on the other side of the planet, for all she knew. It was the not knowing that wore on her nerves.

Earlier she had made the mistake of turning on the screen. The airwaves had been filled with news of the eclipse and its aftermath. She had turned it off after the third time she'd watched herself and the Phelan being arrested by the tall marine officer. It sickened her to think of those same images winging their way toward the alien fleet. She could imagine the reaction a few months hence when the Phelan commanders saw how their emissaries had been treated. In Tory's imagination, six-fingered hands were already powering up neutrino generators and swinging them into line with the Sun.

For the thousandth time, Tory had visions of the Sun's fires reaching out to engulf terror-stricken humanity as the light filled the sails of the Phelan. The vision had a new, terrifying solidity about it. Always before she had been able to tell herself that things would never go that far. No longer. The last few days had made Sol's destruction seem almost preordained.

And it was all so damned stupid!

A mind-numbing, consciousness-defiling rage descended on Tory as she contemplated the full import of the disaster. The emotional storm was like a physical blow as she slowly sank to the carpeted floor and curled into a tight fetal ball.

The rage was unfocused and all-consuming. Damn Boerk Hoffenzoller and the system council for the fools they were! Couldn't they see that the Phelan had no choice but to seek sanctuary around Sol? And damn the Phelan for thinking they could lie their way into favor with humanity! What fool had thought up that idea in the first place? Damn the Phelan usurpers, without whom none of this would have happened! But most of all, damn Tory Bronson for being too dimwitted to think her way out of this mess!

The realization that the human race was going to die because of her ate at Tory's insides. Her parents, her sister, her friends, her relatives, even that pimple-faced boy she had had a crush on all through high school—all were doomed. It was hard to grasp the idea that everyone she had ever loved, hated, or been indifferent to; everyone she had yet to meet and would never meet; all would be dead within a few years. Hard? No, impossible. Even the babes in arms would die.

It just was not fair!

With that most useless of all complaints, Tory began to gain a grip on her emotions. Slowly she concentrated on slowing her breathing and quelling her racing heart. When she could no longer feel her heartbeat in her temples, she unwound and got unsteadily to her feet. The aftermath of the storm was a lethargy that was palpable, and it required all of her concentration to make her way to the bathroom, where she dashed cold water on her face. Glancing into the mirror, she noted red-rimmed, puffy eyes and wished she could repair her makeup.

Her self-inspection was interrupted by a quiet chime from the living room. It took a moment to get over the incongruity of placing an annunciator in a jail cell. It was with a bitter smile that she moved to the door and voiced aloud permission to accept the visitor.

"Hello, Ben," she greeted as Tallen stepped across the threshold. The door hissed quietly closed behind him. She did not need to hear the click to know that it was locked to her.

"Tory," Tallen responded with a nod.

"What can I do for you?"

"I thought we could talk. Isn't it about time you told me what the hell has been going on?"

"I don't know what you're talking about."

"The hell you don't! You've been bothered about something for months. I want to know what it is. What hold have the aliens on you that you would betray your own people?"

"I haven't betrayed them."

"Have it your own way. What did the aliens think they were doing with that fool stunt with the light sail?"

Tory shrugged. "As Faslorn said, demonstrating their power if it is to be a choice between peace and war."

"If they expected to win converts, they went about it the wrong way. There have been hundreds of death threats against all five of you in the past several hours. We've had to put extra security on alert to discourage lynch mobs. People seem especially upset about your part in all of this, by the way. They are calling you traitor."

The information came as a blow, despite the fact that it was what she had expected. She said nothing in reply.

Ben continued as though he had not noticed the sudden quiver in her lower lip. "We're still tallying the casualties, you know."

"There were casualties?"

He nodded. "At least fifteen hundred heart attacks, a like number of suicides, countless traffic accidents, more than one hundred thousand arson fires, and God knows what other damage. Why the hell didn't you warn us? Don't you think you owed us that much as a fellow human being?"

Tory's sudden burst of laughter sounded unhealthy, even to her.

"What's so funny?"

"If I had warned you, Ben, you would have stopped it."

"Damned right we would have."

"Then our point would never have been made. I couldn't warn you, Ben, because the eclipse was my idea."

"What?"

"We had to do something. Everyone had turned their minds off. The council was determined to punish the Phelan for lying, the individual members were stumbling over one another making bellicose speeches, the public was demanding blood. I hoped the eclipse would scare everyone into thinking again. Apparently, I was too optimistic."

"You scared us, all right. You demonstrated just how dangerous a weapon a light sail can be. As a result, people are screaming for the navy to destroy *Far Horizons* before they use their light sail to vaporize our oceans.''

Her heart stuttered at the news. ''They wouldn't!''

Tallen shook his head ruefully. ''Calmer heads are prevailing at the moment. The first councilor has ordered the starship boarded, however. If the Phelan resist, no telling what the navy will do.''

''You've got to stop them, Ben. Tell the first councilor to rescind the order.''

''Why should I?''

Tory fought down a renewed wave of panic. She opened her mouth to respond, then closed it so hard that her teeth rattled. An icy calm descended over her as the analytical part of her brain took over. The conundrum she now faced was the same one that had deviled her since that terrible day in *Far Horizons*'s control room. All the work, the lies, the political maneuvers had been for naught. The question of whether to blurt out the danger or hold her tongue was still with her. Either way, disaster seemed inevitable. If the eclipse had driven people even deeper into frenzy, what of news that the Phelan could blow up the Sun? Perhaps compromise might still be possible if the news was limited to the dark confines of the council's inner workings. But what could be done if the man and woman in the street learned they were in danger? Once the news became public, the only thing more powerful than the demands for *Far Horizons*'s destruction would be the nova that followed.

On the other hand, perhaps she had been on the right track with the eclipse, but too timid. Surely news of the Sun's pending destruction would drive some sense into people. Were the Phelan so bad that humankind would rather die than accept them? All that was really required was for the great mass of people to believe the Phelan would do what they threatened.

But what if they did not believe it? That was the most chilling prospect of all. What if she revealed the Phelan threat and no one believed her? What then? Being honest might accomplish nothing more than trading her current cell for one in a mental hospital.

Tory's intestines knotted and the taste of bile was strong in her mouth as she considered the most important decision of her life. She became aware of Ben's steady gaze and wondered how many other pairs of eyes were watching her just now. The thought was like an icy knife shoved into her bowels. It was the shock she needed. If she was going to reveal what she knew, at least she would know to whom she was speaking!

Tory set her jaw and looked directly into Ben's eyes. "I'll talk, but only to Boerk Hoffenzoller and only with the Phelan present."

"You're in no position to make demands, Tory."

"That is my price, Ben."

Tallen spent a long minute apparently deep in thought, but more likely accessing his implant. Finally, he nodded. "Very well. I'll make the arrangements."

"Tell the first councilor that the fewer who hear what I have to say, the easier his job will be afterward."

"I'll tell him."

"Also, he must call off the boarding party. He can order *Far Horizons* captured later."

"Sorry, but things have gone too far. For all I know, the navy is already boarding the starship."

Tory blinked. Events were moving too swiftly to control. She felt as though she had fallen into a river and was being swept along by the current. It was a chilling thought, especially for a daughter of Mars, but one that crystallized her resolve. After three long years of searching for an answer, she knew what she must do.

"Then make the arrangements quickly. You have no idea of the danger!"

Garth Van Zandt gazed at the tactical display on his screen and cursed silently from within the confines of his pressure suit. The corvettes *Xenia* and *Haver* were closing on *Far Horizons* at high speed, while *Aurora* and two destroyers, *Battle* and *Evanston*, followed at a more leisurely pace. The target of the two corvettes was the sphere containing the ionization laser a kilometer in front of the main habitat cylinder. Out beyond Pluto, Van Zandt had worried about running into the laser by accident. Here, with Earth and Luna looming large in his rear viewscreen, he was more worried about being shot down.

The ionization laser was a weapon of immense power. The same energy that had once stripped the electrons from hydrogen atoms would work just as well against ships and men. At any moment the violet beam of light might reach out to vaporize the five space navy warcraft. Garth did not doubt that the Phelan had the power to destroy his entire command. The only unknown was whether the humans would have time to launch their weapons before being converted into a cloud of glowing gas.

He breathed in the stink of his own fear as the two corvettes continued to close on converging orbits. If all went well, they would use their own lasers to cut loose the ionization laser from its mother ship and clear the way for *Aurora* and her sisters.

"Captain Perlman announces that he is in range, sir," the communicator said over the intercom. "Captain Savimbe also reports ready."

"Give them weapons free."

"Aye, aye, sir."

Van Zandt listened as the order went out and the corvettes powered up their batteries of X-ray lasers. Two interminable minutes followed as the attackers closed to optimum range. Then, with no more visible sign than a small flash, the cable was cut and the laser cast adrift.

"Both captains report mission successful, sir. No collateral damage to the alien ship. They have passed their closest point of approach and are now receding."

"Send them 'Good job!' and 'Return to Luna.' "

Battles in space were nothing like the stylized ballets of atmospheric craft. Orbital mechanics were a matter of momentum, acceleration, and vectors. *Xenia* and *Haver* had spent hours getting into position for their attack. Their single pass completed, they lacked the fuel to reverse course. In terms of velocity, Luna, three hundred thousand kilometers distant, was closer to them than the ship they had just attacked.

Garth's mouth was dry as he gave his next command. "Order *Battle* and *Evanston* to begin their attacks. First Officer, take us in."

He watched on the screen as the two other ships's drives flared and they accelerated toward the quarry. Van Zandt sank into his acceleration couch as the muted roar of *Aurora*'s engines carried through the hull. Ten minutes later, the three ships turned end for end in preparation for slowing.

"Marines are ready, sir," the commander of the boarding party announced over the battle circuits.

"Stand by, Major."

"Aye, aye, sir."

As it had once before, *Far Horizons* loomed large in the viewscreen. The cruiser was aimed for a point amidships and just beyond the starship's hull, her velocity precisely matched to the starship's rotation rate. In her launch bays, four powerful armed pods were filled with men ready to do battle. The two destroyers were closing on other portions of the starship's outer hull.

When the giant rotating cylinder had become a wall in the black sky, the battle pods leaped across the hundred-meter gap.

"All pods report contact, Captain," the communicator announced. "*Battle* reports all pods launched and attached. *Evanston* was forced to break off their approach due to debris in their path."

"What sort of debris?"

"Shreds of the cable *Xenia* and *Haver* cut."

"Very well. Tell *Evanston* to proceed to the aft end cap. Order the marines in."

The order was sent to the two corvettes, now functioning as communications relays to men and machines out of sight around the curve of the starship's hull. When *Far Horizons*'s rotation brought his boarding party into view, Garth could see men dangling from cables anchored to the starship's hull as they worked to set explosive charges. The points of entry had been carefully chosen to minimize damage to the starship. Within seconds, the starship's rotation carried them once more from view.

Garth found the wait for their reappearance nerve-racking. When the pods came again over the cylindrical horizon, the marines had disappeared into a small dark hole punched through the starship's hull.

Half an hour later, the marines reported *Far Horizons* had been secured. There had been no casualties on either side.

A guard escorted Tory down a wide hall to a conference room. It had been four hours since her interview with Ben Tallen—and it felt like four centuries. Inside the conference room, Faslorn, Maratel, Neirton, and Raalwin were all seated in human-style chairs at the far end of a long table. Separated from the aliens by half a dozen empty seats were Boerk Hoffenzoller, Jesus de Pasqual, Praesert Sadibayan, and Joshua Kravatz. Ben Tallen was hovering over Sadibayan, whispering something in his boss's ear, but he straightened and strode to greet Tory as the guard removed the wrist restraints she had worn for the fifty-meter trip down the hall. Ben made a sweeping gesture that encompassed the whole of the conference room.

"Arrangements are as you requested."

"May I speak with Faslorn before we begin?"

"Certainly."

Tory moved to the Phelan end of the table and took the place immediately to Faslorn's right. She huddled with the four aliens and quickly outlined the reason for the meeting in a breathless whisper.

"I thought we settled this three days ago in the embassy, Victoria," Faslorn said when she had finished. "To reveal our secret will only end in disaster."

"Things are already headed for disaster. The navy has orders to board *Far Horizons*."

Faslorn's ears drooped at the news. "Then it matters little what we tell them. The fleet will begin preparations for another voyage as soon as the news reaches them."

"Not if we can convince the first councilor to call off the boarding party. To do that, he has to understand the true stakes of this game. He'll believe it more if you tell him."

Faslorn hesitated, then "nodded." "Very well. It will make no difference, but perhaps I will have the pleasure of seeing their faces when they learn what they have done."

Tory nodded and turned to face Boerk Hoffenzoller while the four Phelan straightened in their seats. "Sir, I asked you here so that Faslorn can explain some things to you."

"You have the floor, Miss Bronson," the first councilor said. "I must warn you that none of us are likely to believe what any Phelan has to say."

"There will be no more lying, Mr. First Councilor," Faslorn replied. "Because Tory has served us well, I will honor her request. It will make no difference to humanity's fate, but at least you will understand the service she attempted to render your species."

Faslorn began by explaining how neutrinos, normally the most elusive of all subatomic particles, could be made to interact with the stellar fires that burned in the heart of every star. His audience wore perplexed expressions as he recounted the tale of the usurpers and how their miscalculation had eventually grown into the Tau Ceti nova.

"Does any of this make sense?" Hoffenzoller demanded of his minister for science.

De Pasqual chewed his lower lip and shrugged. "We've known that supernovas produce neutrinos since the late twentieth century, but this is the first I've heard of them creating a nova."

"The process relies on certain quantum mechanical resonances in stellar reactions of which your scientists are still unaware, Mr. Minister," Faslorn explained. "Have you another explanation for how a main-sequence star may nova?"

"None that we buy."

Hoffenzoller signaled his impatience. "This is all very fascinating, Faslorn, but what has it to do with us?"

"Everything, Mr. First Minister. To reach another star we require a new nova. This time it will be your sun that provides the impetus to our light sails."

For several minutes it appeared to Tory that Boerk Hoffenzoller was going to have a stroke. She didn't recognize the language he was cursing in, but there was no mistaking the emotional content of the words. Faslorn waited impassively for him and the others to run down before continuing.

"Gentlemen, let me be perfectly clear. My species has the power to destroy your star. It is a power we are loath to use, for we already have our own star on our consciences. Do not take false hope from our reluctance, however. We *will* blow up the sun if you force us to do so. If we cannot settle here, we must find another system. We have come much too far to meekly die without a fight!"

"Why the hell didn't you tell us this before?" Hoffenzoller demanded.

Faslorn explained the Phelan reluctance to tell the whole truth, even when it seemed as though everything was lost.

"Sadibayan?" the first councilor asked when Faslorn finished.

The ambassador to the Phelan shrugged. "He's right about there being hell to pay when this gets out."

Tory interrupted. "That is why it must never get out. It has to remain a secret among those of us in this room."

Hoffenzoller cast a glare in her direction. "This news is too damned important to be kept from the people."

"I repeat, Mr. First Councilor. Their lives depend on it being kept secret."

"What would you have us do?" the first councilor asked.

"Accept the Phelan, of course."

"I doubt it possible to accept them, Miss Bronson. They can't be trusted."

"That is the same reason the commanders of the Third Fleet will give when they blow up the sun. Surely you prefer talking to dying!"

"There would appear to be very little to talk about," he said.

"We can't very well absorb two-point-eight billion new mouths on this planet. We'd all starve."

"It's a problem, but possibly not as intractable a one as you think." She strained to sound as reasonable as she could. She had no idea how successful she was.

Joshua Kravatz spoke for the first time. "How do we know they can do what they claim?"

"There is the Tau Ceti nova," Tory reminded him. "Care to bet the lives of your constituents that they are bluffing?"

"We've the navy to protect us, you know."

"The starships will start beaming well beyond the orbit of Pluto. By the time even a single light sail comes into range of the navy, it will be too late."

"It is already too late," Faslorn said from beside her. "If marines have boarded *Far Horizons*, the fleet commanders will order immediate redeployment."

"Have they boarded, Mr. First Minister?"

He avoided her gaze. "The navy gained control of *Far Horizons* two hours ago."

There was a quiet wail from the Phelan end of the table. It was Maratel. "All is lost! Capture or destruction of the scout ship is the one thing that will convince the fleet that humans can't be trusted."

Tory's head snapped around so quickly that she felt the strain in her vertebrae. *"Then don't tell them!"*

For the first time in a long time, Tory thought she had truly surprised Faslorn. His blink of astonishment was almost human. "What?"

"If news of the boarding will set them off, then don't tell them," she repeated, once again straining to be the voice of reason. "Your ship's communications are inoperative, so they couldn't have gotten off a warning message. Nor has the operation been announced in our media. How will they find out?"

"There will be such reports."

"Not if the first councilor acts quickly to clamp a lid of secrecy on it. There are still some secrets we can keep when we have to."

"You are asking me to lie to my commanders."

"You've had me lying to my people for three long years. Now it's your turn. With the fate of both our species at stake, don't you think a few little white lies are in order?"

Tory felt despair seeping forth as Faslorn did not answer. But the emotion was overtaken by a bubbling sense of hope as the senior Phelan turned to the others and began speaking in rapid-fire alien speech. It went on for several minutes, with all four of the Phelan taking part. When it was over, Faslorn turned to his human audience.

"Mr. First Councilor. Do you think you can keep the attack from being leaked to your media?"

"I can try."

"Do you believe there is something to negotiate?"

"I dislike very much talking under a cloud of threats, Faslorn, but considering the stakes, I'm willing to try if you are."

"Then we will try. It will likely be fruitless in the long run, but we owe both of our species the attempt. Please, let us resume our negotiations."

"When and where?" Tory demanded.

This time it was the humans's turn to huddle. When they had finished their impassioned whispers, the first councilor spoke. "Since there are preparations to be made to insure that the situation stabilizes, I suggest a twenty-four-hour delay."

"And the marines aboard my ship?" Faslorn asked.

"I won't order them to withdraw, but I will order them to treat your people correctly. So long as no attempt is made to use your light sail as a weapon, no hostile act will result. I will also provide you with a secure channel of communications to your ship so that you can give your own orders."

Faslorn turned to Tory. "Do the arrangements satisfy you, Victoria?"

She let out a huge sigh of relief. "They're not perfect, but they beat blowing up the Sun."

No one answered, but from their postures and expressions, it was obvious that for once Phelan and humans agreed on something.

29

TORY BRONSON STOOD AT THE EDGE OF THE ROOF garden and gazed out across the lights of the city toward the first glow of impending dawn. The spot of gray on the horizon matched her mood precisely. The tension of the past two years, followed by the agony of the last two weeks, had left her feeling drained and empty. It was as though nothing really mattered any longer. To hell with the fate of stars, planets, or entire species! All she really wanted was to be left alone, to submerge herself in the sensual caress of the wind, and to forget the marathon bargaining session in the living quarters behind her.

Faslorn, Boerk Hoffenzoller, and their respective staffs had been at it ever since their return to the embassy. Negotiations had continued nonstop for six days, with halts called for hurried meals and a few hours grudgingly devoted to sleep. Progress had been slow. Yet, after several false starts, the two sides finally seemed to be making progress. What had seemed utterly unattainable as she had paced her prison cell had now become merely improbable. Intellectually, Tory could cheer the progress, but she was too emotionally drained to feel enthusiasm.

Nor had they made home orbit yet. One concern was whether the secret of marines aboard *Far Horizons* would hold. So far there had been no report in the press, but the situation was still precarious.

If the negotiators ever agreed on a draft treaty between human and Phelan, Faslorn would use human facilities to transmit it to the Third Fleet. With speed-of-light delay, plus time for the fleet commanders to make a decision, it would be a year before Earth received its answer. A year was a long time to wait to learn whether the human race would live or die.

The tentative language of the treaty called for humanity to cede the Phelan all the large tracts that had originally been considered for their use. Phelan colonies would be established in Australia, Antarctica, and the Sahara Desert, but limited to a total population of one hundred million individuals. Mars would accept half that number, while the other space colonies would open their doors to token numbers of refugees.

As for ninety percent of the almost three billion Phelan en route to Sol, they would remain aboard their ships, orbiting between Venus and Earth. Having already survived two and a half centuries in space, they could survive a few more decades while they constructed large space colonies in which to live. Once in orbit about Sol, the fear that their ships would slowly break down was no longer valid. With the resources of a star system at their disposal, they could overhaul all their ships and, if need be, live in them for another century or two. With so many humans already dwelling above atmosphere, it was likely that neither species would ever again be totally planetbound.

The Phelan would be given long-term, low-interest loans to finance initial construction of their colonies. As each colony was occupied, it would be expected to become economically independent. The Phelan would sell their technology to the highest bidder, while paying fair market prices for the resources they consumed.

To aid in the assimilation, humans would be encouraged to emigrate to all the alien colonies. There they would live, learning Phelan ways, and, it was hoped, helping both species learn the hard lessons of living together.

In return for the colonies, the Phelan ships would disarm immediately upon arrival. As soon as each ship achieved its permanent orbit, it would jettison its light sail. From the human viewpoint, the loss of the light sails would produce two highly beneficial conditions. It would deprive the Phelan craft of their most fearsome weapon, while irretrievably committing their passengers to the assimilation process. Without the means to ride a nova shock wave to the stars, it was unlikely that the Phelan would trigger an explosion in the Sun. Yet, by retaining their ability to do so, the aliens protected themselves against human treachery. Any serious attempt to exterminate them in the future would become an exercise in mutual suicide.

The solution was far from perfect, but it was the best that could be worked out. For the past forty-eight hours negotiations had centered on the details of the treaty. As often as not, the human factions had turned to arguing with one another, while the Phelan maneuvered for as much advantage as they could wrest from the chaos. And more times than she could count,

Tory had found herself the target of evil looks as she advised Faslorn that he was walking into a trap.

That had been what had finally sapped her will. The hatred toward her had been palpable. After one particularly violent clash with Praesert Sadibayan, she had stalked away from the table and disappeared into the predawn darkness. It had been her intention to calm her raging thoughts, then return to the task. But calming her emotions had proven more difficult than expected. Nearly two hours later, she stood alone under the stars and watched the impending sunrise.

Dawn was only minutes away when a momentary increase in illumination behind her announced that someone else had come out into the garden. Irritated, she turned to see Katherine Claridge walking toward her. Though Kit had been working with the alien-assessment teams since they had reached Earth, their paths had rarely crossed. Because of their experience with the Phelan, Kit and Eli Guttieriz had both been called in to support the first councilor during negotiations.

"Hello," Kit said as she reached Tory's side. The crunching sound her shoes made in the gravel pathway seemed supernaturally loud in the predawn quiet. "Aren't you freezing in that light outfit?"

Tory shook her head even as she ran her hands over the goose bumps that dotted her upper arms. "It helps to clear my mind."

Kit tilted her head back to look straight upward. "I see you've found a good vantage point for the show."

"Something like that," Tory muttered. "Is that why you've come out here?"

"I feel bad about the way Ambassador Sadibayan treated you in there. When you didn't come back, I decided to find you. You look like someone who needs a friend to talk to."

"Are we? Friends, that is?"

"Of course! Why wouldn't we be?"

"I'm surprised anyone would want to be my friend after . . ."

"After what?" Kit asked in a mild voice.

As Tory turned to Kit, she felt a dam burst somewhere deep within. For two years she had guarded her every word. Suddenly, all the things she had wanted to say came gushing forth in a torrent. She sobbed as she recounted what it had been like being the sole human to know that the Sun could explode at any time. She told of the constant fear of discovery, and the uncertainty that came from living a lie twenty-four hours a day. By the time she finished, tears were flooding freely down her cheeks.

Through it all, Kit listened without comment. Tory finally turned away to wipe her eyes in the near darkness. "Feel better now?" Kit asked.

Kit sensed rather than saw the tiny upturnings at the corners of Tory's mouth. Her voice was less anguished as well. "A little."

"No wonder. You've had a great deal bottled up inside for a long time. I'm surprised you were able to handle it as long as you did."

Tory turned back to the doctor. "Tell me the truth, Kit," she pleaded. "Did I do the right thing?"

There was a long pause. When Kit finally spoke, it was with more hesitation than Tory had expected. "I think I understand why you did what you did, Tory. I'm not qualified to answer whether it was the right thing or not. Neither, I might add, are any of those loudmouths inside. If all this works out, then you did the right thing. If not, I guess it really doesn't matter."

"You should hear what they're saying about me on the talk shows."

"I have. Saying something loudly doesn't make it so, you know."

"But damn it, I did it for them!" The anguish had crept back into Tory's voice.

"Unfortunately, gratitude is not one of our species's strong points. It will be a long time before people understand what you've been through."

"Do you think they'll ever forgive me?"

Kit shrugged. "Some will, some won't. That's the price you pay sometimes. Besides, it isn't really important whether the public understands your motives or not. You know why you did it, and all that really counts is whether you can live with yourself afterward."

Tory took a deep breath, then exhaled heavily. It was not what she had wanted to hear, but it was probably right. Whatever others might say, her own opinion was the only one that really counted. Others had not been there. She had. She alone had faced the terrible knowledge; she alone had made the decision to help the Phelan with their deceit; and when the time came, she alone had decided that the secret must be revealed. Only the future would tell if she had done the right thing. Meanwhile, she would try not to let the opinions of the small-minded bother

her. A nice Olympian attitude, she thought, but how successful would she be in actually maintaining it? That, too, was something she would have to wait to see.

Behind her, the broad doors leading from the living quarters moved silently into their recesses, and a crowd of humans and Phelan ambled out into the rooftop garden. Tory and Kit turned at the sudden commotion to see Boerk Hoffenzoller and Faslorn striding toward them, side by side.

"That's it," the first councilor boomed. He was rumpled and sported a two-day growth of beard. Faslorn, too, looked as though he was near the end of his endurance. His four-limbed gait was not its usual seamless motion, and his sleek fur was ruffled. "We shook hands ten minutes ago and Faslorn recorded his message for the Third Fleet. It will be transmitted within the hour."

"Just in time," Kit said, pointing.

Directly overhead was a disk twice the size of the full moon, but lacking Luna's distinctive features. The disk glowed softly with reflected sunlight. When Tory had first come out into the garden, the apparition had been halfway up the eastern sky. Now it was approaching zenith.

The crowd of humans and aliens stood with their heads tilted back. As the first golden light illuminated the rooftop, the strange moon overhead began to change shape. *Far Horizons* had matched velocities and, with no further need of the light sail, had jettisoned it. No longer tethered to the heavy ship, the sail crumpled as light pressure pushed it back toward open space. In the coming months the loose sail would accelerate to Solar-system escape velocity and return to the interstellar void from whence it came. The watchers hoped it was the first of many.

Humans and Phelan alike watched in openmouthed wonder as the sail grew perceptibly smaller by the minute. No one spoke, lest they puncture the mood. Finally, when the sun had risen completely out of the sea to paint the sky blue and nearly blank out the image of the sail, Boerk Hoffenzoller cleared his throat. "All right, everyone back to work. We've a future to plan!"

Tory found herself trailing after the small crowd of diplomats, scientists, and the four aliens. She was struck by the symbolism of the grouping. Never again would human or Phelan be alone in the universe. Wherever they went, they would go together. And the start of the new era would forever be measured from the moment when *Far Horizons* released its sail. With hard work and goodwill—and a little luck all around—the collaboration could benefit both species beyond the dreams of either.

Then there were the other three Phelan fleets to consider. Would they, too, find intelligent beings in orbit about their star sanctuaries? If so, the fleet headed for Epsilon Eridani only 5.4 light-years from Tau Ceti, had already done so. That fleet had arrived a full century earlier. Those headed for Alpha Centauri and Epsilon Indi, 13.5 and 15.8 light-years from Tau Ceti, would not make starfall for decades to come. Whatever alliances they might make were for the future.

Who knew? Perhaps it would one day be possible to contact the other Phelan fleets. It would not be difficult to send Starhoppers to those other systems to learn the fate of the Phelan First, Second, and Fourth fleets. Once contact was made, communications could be established via radio telescope or comm laser.

Tory halted a moment and prodded her own psyche. An hour ago she could not bring herself to be interested in whether her own race lived or died. Now she was scheming to contact the other Phelan fleets. Sometime while watching *Far Horizons*'s arrival, she had come to a decision. The turmoil that had dogged her and interrupted her sleep for months was gone. Deep within herself, she had found a wellspring of peace. Tory felt her step grow lighter as she reentered the hot, crowded living quarters.

Whatever else might happen, she had done the best she could. Whether people understood or not really did not matter. Besides, Boerk Hoffenzoller was right.

There *was* a future to plan!

About the Author

Michael McCollum was born in Phoenix, Arizona, in 1946 and is a graduate of Arizona State University, where he majored in aerospace propulsion and minored in nuclear engineering. He has been employed as an aerospace engineer since graduation and has worked on nearly every military and civilian aircraft in production today. At various times in his career Mr. McCollum has also worked on the precursor to the Space Shuttle Main Engine, a nuclear valve to replace the one that failed at Three Mile Island, and a variety of guided missiles. He is currently engaged in the effort to build Space Station Freedom.

He began writing in 1974 and has been a regular contributor to *Analog Science Fiction*. He has also appeared in *Isaac Asimov's Science Fiction Magazine* and *Amazing*. *The Sails of Tau Ceti* is his eighth novel for Del Rey.

He is married to a lovely lady by the name of Catherine and is the father of three children: Robert, Michael, and Elizabeth.